NIGHTVINE

FELICIA DAVIN

To my brother

CONTENTS

1

GLORIFYING AND TRUTHFUL

EV AND ALIZHAN HAD BEEN in Nalitzva half a shift before things went wrong.

They'd set out to find Prince Ilyr with volume eleven of *A Natural History of the World* in hand. They'd left Ifeleh and her crew in the harbor with a promise to report back before the ship's scheduled departure. Things might have gone smoothly if they'd taken Djal or Mala or even Gad, anyone from *Vines* who knew the city, but the crew had work to do. Perhaps if Alizhan could speak a word of Nalitzvan, or if Ev's schoolroom grasp of the language had been more sophisticated, they could have explained things better. But instead, after the uncomfortable experience of having their papers scrutinized at the docks, Ev and Alizhan had struck out on their own, heading directly for the palace gates.

The harbor reminded Ev of home—the salt air, the colorful square sails and painted ships, the people in all shapes and sizes chattering in every language—but the rest of Nalitzva was alien. Wide straight streets cut through the imposing white stone buildings in a grid, and at every square intersection, larger-than-life human statues loomed over the citizens. They raised swords and scepters and their staring white eyes followed her. Everyone in the streets felt their presence, otherwise why would they all be so quick and quiet in their walking? The grand square leading to the palace gates was nearly silent, populated by statues instead of people.

And guards. Statues and armed guards.

Ev wasn't sure if it was a sin against God's Balance to carve images of people out of stone, as Laalvuri priests of the Balance said. She wasn't inclined to trust priests after the discoveries of the past month, but the statues still made her uneasy. Ev preferred to let God's Balance alone in the hopes that it would do the same for her—a plan that wasn't working out at this moment, as Ev got five sentences into her request and two guards seized Alizhan by the arms. She cried out in pain.

"Let her go!" Ev shouted, but two more guards grabbed her by the arms. She struggled. She could elbow them in the stomach and break free. But Alizhan was still captive, and Ev didn't want to be separated from her. They couldn't win this fight—even if they managed to take down four armed men, there were more guards in the square and the palace, and they'd get caught eventually.

One of the guards grabbed *A Natural History of the World* from Alizhan and rifled through it, pausing when he saw a stamp on the flyleaf that identified the book as part of Iriyat ha-Varensi's library. He conferred with the other guard, who still held Alizhan.

"What did I say?" Ev whispered to Alizhan. She'd only tried to express that they'd heard of the prince's talents with language, that they'd brought him a book no one could read, and that they'd be very grateful for his help if he could decipher it for them. She'd been as polite as possible, given how little of their language she spoke. Maybe she'd pronounced something wrong.

Alizhan grimaced as the guards bound her hands behind her back. Their hands were gloved, but Alizhan was wary of any contact. "It doesn't matter, Ev," she said. "They're on high alert, suspicious of everything. The mention of a book set them off. They won't let us anywhere near the prince now."

Alizhan hadn't understood a word of the conversation. But she knew what the guards were feeling.

"They can't arrest us," Ev said. "We haven't done anything."

The guards ignored this as they'd ignored everything else Ev had said. They were marched out of the wide, clean streets into a shaded alley and through a wooden door that clanked shut behind them. The building they'd entered had low ceilings and poor lighting, and Ev saw almost nothing before the guards began to strip her.

"Smoke and—" Ev swore, and she rounded on her captors. She got a punch in before she heard Alizhan yelp, and when she turned to make sure Alizhan wasn't dead, her guards pinned her arms behind her back and forced her to her knees.

"It's okay, Ev," Alizhan was saying, her breathing labored. "Not now. Later."

They were hurting her. Alizhan had learned to cope with crowds since Mala had given her some rudimentary training aboard *Vines*, but enduring the grim manhandling of a strip search by two strangers was too much for her. The guards confiscated the book. Alizhan held herself together long enough to pull on the new clothes she was given. Then she passed out.

Ev barely managed to catch Alizhan, slumped into unconsciousness, before both of them were pushed into the cell. The heavy door slammed shut behind them. Ev sat down, carefully adjusting Alizhan's slight weight until Alizhan's head was cradled in her lap and none of their skin was touching.

Ev shivered. When she'd first stepped into the cell, her bare feet had curled involuntarily at the touch of the cold stone beneath them. It was so much colder here than in Laalvur. The loose, rough-spun fabric of her prison clothes offered no warmth. There was a single, barred window high in one cell wall, open to the outside air. The rest of the cell was unremarkable—there was straw scattered on the floor, and a bucket in one corner. It was only on her second look that Ev noticed there was a pile of straw in the darkest part of the room, and that pile of straw contained a human being.

Ev opted not to speak to the other person. Prison wasn't a good place to make friends.

She wanted to touch Alizhan. To feel her pulse. To check for bruises. It was an instinct, nothing more. Ev wanted to reassure herself. But Alizhan still couldn't bring herself to touch Ev's skin even when she was awake and in control of herself, so touching her while she was unconscious and vulnerable was out of the question. Alizhan wouldn't like being in Ev's lap when she woke up, but Ev couldn't bring herself to dump Alizhan's prone body on the floor.

Instead of touching Alizhan, Ev whispered her name. "Wake up, Alizhan."

The other prisoner didn't stir. Ev was speaking Laalvuri, so he probably couldn't understand her. She kept her hands at her sides, not touching Alizhan, and continued speaking softly.

"They took the book, but it's okay," Ev said. "We'll get it back from Ilyr. After we break out of prison. I guess we'll have to steal some normal clothes before we get near the prince. We'll figure it out. Or you will, once you wake up. I know you will. You'll be okay."

It was easier to say it than to believe it. Ev had never felt so far from home. "You'll wake up just fine. We'll get out of here, and we'll get your book back, and we'll go home and we'll fix things. And then we can go back to the farm, where it's warm and the light is just right, and we'll see my parents and Kasrik and Eliyan and Zilal and Tez and the cats and you can stay—"

Alizhan's eyelids fluttered.

A moment later, she vaulted out of Ev's lap and landed clumsily a short distance away. Trembling and wild-eyed, she rubbed her hands up and down her arms furiously.

"I know," Ev said, but it did nothing to calm Alizhan. She was still hugging herself, either trying to warm herself or trying to rid herself of the feeling of other hands on her skin. "Breathe."

Alizhan took a ragged deep breath. And then another. Another. Even through her sack-like prison tunic, Ev could see her chest rise and fall.

"Too many people," Alizhan said. She was still working to get her breathing under control.

Their cell was quiet, but Ev could hear the din of prisoners shouting, sobbing, and striking the walls of the other cells. That wasn't the reason Ev wanted out—*being in prison* was enough of a reason for her—but she had no intention of quibbling with Alizhan. "If I lift you up, maybe we could get to that window. Do you think we could work those bars free?"

The window was too high for Ev to reach all by herself. It was also so small that it was hard to imagine even Alizhan squeezing through it, and the metal bars were solidly embedded in the wall, but Ev didn't have a better idea.

"It's rude to plan an escape and not invite me," the other prisoner said, startling Ev.

He spoke Laalvuri. *Smoke.*

"It's rude to eavesdrop," Ev snapped.

She'd thought he was asleep or unconscious, and even if he'd been awake, he hadn't seemed interested in either of them. But he must have been listening. He lifted his head from his prone position, then sat up. With one hand, he brushed off some of the straw and dirt clinging to his clothes. He somehow managed to make the action look graceful, even regal.

"What's rude is you being so unbearably dull," he informed Ev.

Ev started to stand, but Alizhan said, "Wait."

"Ooh, the little one's in charge," said the prisoner. "I was picturing it all wrong."

What had he been picturing? How could he make Ev so angry and uncomfortable with just his tone of voice? Ev wouldn't have hit him. She might have loomed over him in a silent, threatening way, though. She missed her stick fiercely.

"Don't worry, Ev," Alizhan said. She wasn't even looking at Ev. Her eyes were still locked on the prisoner. It was fiery unsettling sometimes, having a conversation with Alizhan. She pulled things out of the silence with eerie accuracy. "He smells good."

Alizhan crawled across the cell and sat down cross-legged in front of the prisoner.

He laughed, a single flat sound with no humor in it, and directed his gaze at Ev. "There is something *tragically* wrong with your friend's nose."

Ev might have laughed and explained it to him if he'd been a little nicer. As it was, she was mystified by what Alizhan saw—or smelled—in him.

"He's sad. And hurt," Alizhan continued, addressing Ev as if the man in front of her couldn't hear her. "He's trying to hide it."

So he was hissing at Ev to distract her, like a wounded tomcat hiding in a dark corner of the barn? She would've had patience for the cat. Unfortunately for her cellmate, Ev's sympathies didn't extend to sharp-tongued strangers.

"He is not," the prisoner said. "He is in perfect health and would make a useful accomplice for any escapes you might be planning. In fact, out of an astonishing generosity of spirit, he will mastermind said escape plans for you, since your previous attempts have been so lackluster."

It was dim in the prison, but he didn't look or sound Nalitzvan. Despite speaking flawless Laalvuri, he didn't look like anyone Ev had ever met in Laalvur. His skin was a golden shade of tan, lighter in color than Ev's or Alizhan's, but not the milky shade of most Nalitzvans, either. He was wearing the same loose beige tunic and trousers as all the other prisoners, so his clothes gave no clue as to where he was from. He sat with his legs crossed. And since Alizhan had mentioned it, Ev noticed he was cradling his right hand in his lap. His black curls were matted with dust. A sparse scattering of stubble dotted his cheeks.

"You're an islander," Alizhan said. Ev wouldn't have blurted it out so casually, even if she had put it together. "How did you end up here?"

"An excellent question. Also rather rude."

Alizhan wasn't deterred. Good manners were not among her skills. She stopped trembling and focused all her attention on the prisoner. "If you're an islander in prison in Nalitzva, then how and why do you speak Laalvuri?"

"There isn't a good Laalvuri word for it," he said, which wasn't the answer Ev expected, although it was hard to say what she'd expected. Was he some kind of international criminal? Or was he like them, unjustly imprisoned?

"You know, we're not all the same. I don't go around calling you *mainlanders*. I know you're Laalvuri."

"Well, which island are you from, then?" Alizhan said, as if she were being very patient. "Tell me and I'll call you that instead."

"I'm from Hoi," the prisoner said. There was a note of amusement in his voice, which was usually a good sign in people's dealings with Alizhan, but Ev didn't want to think well of him just yet. "And I'd very much like to get the watery hell out of Nalitzva and go back there, but first I want to know what you think I smell like."

"It's not always a smell," Alizhan said, unfazed by the Hoi's priorities. She waved a hand in the air, drawing a series of vague circles, in a gesture Ev guessed was supposed to be helpful and explanatory. "Sometimes it's a feeling. Or a color. A sound. An image. Words, maybe, if someone's really loud. Anyway, I can't tell much about you, which might be because you're in so much pain, or—"

Ev wanted to hear the end of that sentence, but the prisoner interrupted. "Well, prison is terribly hard on my complexion, you understand. I shudder to appear before you in this state, but I suppose it is a lesson in what life is like for those who haven't been graced with dazzling good looks."

Ev didn't have time for this. For him. She supposed under all the filth and bruises he might have been handsome, but she couldn't imagine a less important subject. She crossed her arms over her chest and tried not to tap her fingers with impatience.

"So I haven't been able to attend to my toilette as usual. And the beds in this place! Let's not even mention the food. Or lack thereof. A little ennui is to be expected. Anyway, clearly you're a mind-reader. I'd say 'why didn't you just say so,' but I suppose the answer is obvious, given where we find ourselves."

Alizhan nodded.

In a different tone, rougher around the edges, the prisoner said, "You're lucky these barbarians just threw you in prison instead of killing you on the spot."

"Lucky," Ev repeated. He knew about magic, this man. He wasn't suspicious or even surprised. He thought magic-hating Nalitzvans were barbarians. Maybe he could help them after all, even if he was glib and snide. Was he really in pain, like Alizhan said? Ev squinted at his hand.

"Yes, lucky," he said seriously. "In the same way I'm lucky

that it was only one hand, and the wrong one, at that." With his left hand, he gestured at the hand in his lap. Now that Ev was invited to examine it more closely, she could see it was swollen. Bruises darkened his skin. Some of his fingers were bent at unnatural angles. "We're all marvelously lucky, aren't we?"

"They broke your hand," Ev said, outraged. She felt guilty for all her uncharitable thoughts toward him. She didn't like him, but he didn't deserve to be maimed. And what could he possibly have done to incur such an inhumane punishment? What would the guards do to Alizhan and Ev if they couldn't escape? A frisson of fear ran down her spine.

"Beauty *and* brains," the prisoner drawled.

He was really testing the limits of her sympathy, this stranger.

"Why?" Alizhan said. "What did you do?"

"What did *you* do?" he shot back. Alizhan probably couldn't tell that he was glaring at her when he said it, since she rarely looked at anyone's face, but Ev could.

"Nothing," Alizhan said, unmoved by his tone.

There was a long silence, and finally the prisoner relented.

"Well, I wrote something," he said. "The guards are possessed of strong literary opinions and they took it upon themselves to end my career."

"What did you write? Was it libel? Did you criticize the royal family?" Ev said.

"Neither. It was both glorifying and truthful." A joyless smile. "But really, why talk about how we ended up here—a dull, trivial subject—when instead, we could talk about how to get out?"

"It's not right," Ev said. "We didn't do anything wrong. We don't deserve to be here, and whatever you wrote, you didn't deserve that. It's not like you killed someone."

"Yes, yes," he said. "I'm so glad to know your sense of justice is offended. Now, about that escape plan. I hear you need to get to Ilyr. To get to him, you need someone who can speak Nalitzvan and someone who knows the palace. Coincidentally, this shift Mother Mah Yee and all your gods have rained blessings down upon you," here he paused, and with his good hand, the prisoner made a graceful, sweeping gesture, indicating himself, "granting you the good fortune of meeting me. Get me out and I will get you in."

"More of a trickle than a rain," Alizhan said, laughing.

"More of a drought," Ev muttered. Then she mentally pushed aside all the nonsense he'd said, and responded to the important part. "You know the palace?"

"And you speak Nalitzvan as well as Laalvuri?" Alizhan said.

"Naturally."

His words gave Ev pause. She hated his little reminder that he'd eavesdropped on her private conversation with Alizhan earlier. But it was more than that. What could he possibly mean by "naturally"? His Laalvuri was perfect. Nothing about him made sense. Islanders rarely left their home. Ev had never met one in Laalvur, but she knew there was a trader who sold medusa venom and products made from it. She'd assumed Nalitzva would be similar. What was someone from Hoi doing in prison here?

"Also, the window will never work. Alizhan, can you tell me about the guards?"

Alizhan shook her head. "They're too far. There's too many people." And then she added, "How do you know my name?"

"Ev and I had a chat," he said. "If the guards come closer, could you read them?"

"Probably." Alizhan shrugged. Then she said, caught between curiosity and suspicion, "Ev doesn't like to talk."

"She does," he replied. Ev didn't appreciate being spoken about as if she weren't there, but the prisoner was already continuing. "We have to distract the guards somehow. Get them to open the door. There are almost always two of them, and we'll only have a second. Ev can take one and you and I will take the other."

"Ev could take both if she had her stick," Alizhan said. As always, she had far more confidence in Ev than Ev did.

"Could she," the prisoner said, and for the first time, he really smiled. It flashed across his face and was gone. Alizhan smiled in return, a quick mirror. Ev felt very far away. How had they already come to like each other?

"That's good to know," the prisoner continued. "But as Ev does not have her stick, I won't assign her the task of taking out two very large men by herself. Once we get out of here, I'll direct you to Ilyr. You can probably even get your book back, whatever you want it for."

"Why are you helping us?" Ev asked.

"I should think it obvious. I want to get out of prison."

"Why are you helping us *with Ilyr*," Ev said flatly. The prisoner always slipped out of the way of questions. He hadn't said his name yet, he'd barely explained what landed him in prison in the first place, and he hadn't explained how he could possibly know his way around the palace. Alizhan's instinct wasn't enough for Ev to trust him.

"Oh, that," he said. "It's a long story."

"We're very busy, as you can see," Alizhan said, gesturing at the cell.

"I do like a captive audience."

Alizhan laughed. Ev stared at the prisoner until he began to talk.

"THE FIRST THING you should know is that Ilyr is a fraud and a liar," the prisoner began.

"I've met him," Alizhan said. "I liked him."

"How wonderful for you," the prisoner said, his voice dripping with poison. "If I am going to tell this story, I must insist that you not interrupt me. It's delicate."

"Because it's the story of why you're so sad," Alizhan said.

"What did I *just say*."

Alizhan shrugged, unrepentant.

"But perhaps that isn't the first thing you should know. It's difficult to know where to start. Ilyr is indeed a prince of Nalitzva. He was born to wealth and power. He grew up knowing he would inherit the throne. He's had every privilege you can imagine, and some you probably can't. In the unfair way of these things, he's also intelligent and beautiful and kind."

"I know," Alizhan said. "I told you, we met. At a party in Laalvur. I served him a glass of wine and read his mind."

Ev hadn't known silence could be haughty, but the prisoner was very expressive.

"Perhaps you'd like to tell the story," he said, after a suitably icy interval of time had passed.

"No," Alizhan said, unaffected.

The prisoner huffed, then took a fortifying breath and picked up where he'd left off. "Ilyr's education sparked his curiosity about the world, and when he was twenty, he embarked on a long voyage. He went to places as far Nightward as Estva and as far Dayward as Adappyr—and he traveled to Li, Kae, and Hoi.

"The islands don't allow foreigners to visit. But Ilyr had studied our languages and our ways, and he knew just what to say. It was a personal journey, not a royal visit or a diplomatic mission. He admired our arts—what little he knew of them, since no mainlanders have been to the islands in centuries, and our people rarely leave. He wanted to know more. He wanted to live among us.

"In Nalitzva, they say when Ilyr went traveling, even the coldest star-watching monks of Estva were in awe of him. I've never been there, but I understand it. It's hard not to love him. He's tall and broad-shouldered. Eyes like gems. Hair like gold. He listens so carefully that you feel like the only person in the world.

"So we granted him permission, of a sort. He would come alone, with no retinue of servants or guards. He would take nothing from the islands but himself and his writings. He would spend three triads on each island. Ilyr did exactly that in Li and Kae.

"And then he came to Hoi, and he met my sister.

"I've already told you how beautiful Ilyr is. My sister looks nothing like him, and yet she is his equal. Not just in beauty, although she's very beautiful—slender, graceful, dark-eyed—but in wit and charm as well. She has a gift for languages, and while Ilyr had studied enough Hoi to have a simple conversation, he still needed an interpreter. My sister spent every minute of those three triads with him. I've never seen two people fall in love so fast.

"She begged the elders to allow Ilyr to stay longer. I think they wouldn't have granted it, had the two of them not made such a beautiful pair. The way they could talk for hours, caught between languages, their hands fluttering and landing like birds. The way they danced. You wouldn't have thought a man as big and broad as Ilyr could move with such precision. It would have been a crime to break them apart. My people value beauty."

The prisoner said this as though no other people valued beauty. Ev thought of the first time she'd met Alizhan back in Laalvur, and Iriyat ha-Varensi's grand entrance into Arishdenan market in her embroidered silks, and privately disagreed. Even the Nalitzvans valued beauty, although theirs was a stark, cold kind.

"The elders said yes. Ilyr stayed for a year. He lived among us as he'd wanted to from the beginning—he spoke our language and ate our food. He even put aside his prudish insistence on Nalitzvan clothing. He loved my sister so much I thought my heart would burst from it. It was a happy year.

"And then Ilyr was called home for his wedding.

"He'd been betrothed to a Nalitzvan girl for years. His parents knew nothing of his life in Hoi. There was nothing for him to do but go home and wed this girl. He had to leave. He would not be coming back.

"The whole island heard my sister shout at him. She screamed. She wept. Nalitzvans would tell you my sister is 'dramatic,' in a very disapproving tone, but they think expressing emotion is a weakness. It isn't. It's a strength. My sister was so heartbroken and angry that she nearly attacked Ilyr, but he caught her by the wrists and they kissed instead. They made love ferociously—oh, I see that Laalvuri don't like to talk about that any more than Nalitzvans do. I've never understood why. It's the best part of the story."

"She's your sister," Ev said, with quiet horror.

"What did I say about interruptions?" he said.

Alizhan and Ev shared an incredulous look.

"Anyway, as they were lying in the bed that was still warm from their lovemaking," the prisoner continued, and Ev was certain he invented that detail just to needle them. "Ilyr proposed to my sister that she come home with him. She could live among his people as he had lived among hers. He'd still have to wed his betrothed, but he wouldn't be separated from my sister. They could be together, and she could help him write his book about the Hoi. Perhaps they could build some kind of trust between their peoples.

"My sister agreed. She could speak Nalitzvan, but their culture was a mystery to her, and she wanted to see the city. She didn't know Nalitzvans believe it is a crime—no, a sin—to make love outside of marriage. Nalitzvans marry in pairs, one man and one woman, and it lasts until death. Ilyr didn't tell her this, or many other things.

"I went with them. It was a long journey, and Nalitzva was white and cold and strange when we arrived. But my sister loved it, because she loved Ilyr. Those first few months were the adventure of her life. She even loved his betrothed, a girl as blond and beautiful as he was. Her name was Aniyat. She didn't know that Ilyr loved my sister—Aniyat was too innocent to have suspected him of such a thing—and so she and my sister became fast friends.

"But after those first few months, the thrill began to fade. Keeping their love a secret took its toll on Ilyr and my sister, and Ilyr became distant. He only ever came to my sister when he wanted to use her gift for languages. They were working on a book together, about Hoi culture, and Ilyr was publishing essays about his travels. He was publishing translations of Hoi poetry, too, but they were my sister's. Her name appeared nowhere in his publications. Ilyr had suddenly become ashamed of her—or perhaps he wanted to claim her talents for himself. He now had a reputation as a genius polyglot. Rumor has it that he can speak any language, or decipher any text, even if he has never encountered it before." The prisoner huffed.

Beside Ev, Alizhan shifted. So this was why the prisoner had called Ilyr a fraud. Had they come all this way for nothing?

"Ilyr stayed away from my sister unless he wanted something from her. He kept her sequestered at the palace because he didn't want anyone to discover his secrets—that he'd loved my sister, and that she was the source of his miraculous ability. My sister grew bored. There is only so much homesick exile poetry one can write. But Aniyat was always there, and Aniyat was sweet and kind and beautiful.

"My sister falls in love quickly, as you may have guessed. She's impulsive. Foolish, perhaps. But she was desperately lonely. At first there was no more to it than that. Aniyat was the product of a sheltered Nalitzvan upbringing, and my sister's attentions were a revelation to her. But when Aniyat understood what was being offered, she did not say no.

"There. You see? I can describe sex in the dull, oblique way you approve of. You do understand that they had sex, I hope. I know Laalvuri don't approve of women lying with women—" the prisoner seemed to linger over these words, his eyes on Alizhan and Ev, searching for a reaction, "—or men lying with men, but it happens. It even happens here in Nalitzva, where they kill you for it.

"In light of all that, my sister looks like a fool, I know. But knowing her as I do, I understand that there was a kind of love-addled logic to her actions. If Ilyr had loved her, and he now loved Aniyat, and my sister loved Aniyat as well, perhaps there was no problem at all. She was naive. She didn't understand anything about this place or its customs. Most of all, she didn't understand Ilyr. How could he could love her in Hoi and feel ashamed of her in Nalitzva?

"You can guess the rest. Ilyr caught my sister and Aniyat, and instead of being delighted and politely asking to join like a civilized human being, he reacted with outrage and betrayal. My sister couldn't have predicted that. She truly thought the three of them could work things out. It happens all the time at home.

"My sister didn't intend to hurt anyone, least of all two people she loved dearly. But Ilyr couldn't see things the way she did. For him, what my sister had done was the worst kind of treachery. He felt deceived. He felt abandoned—even though my sister felt that he'd abandoned her. They fought. He hurled wild accusations at my sister—she was a jealous bitch who'd been plotting his ruin the whole time, she'd seduced Aniyat out of spite, she'd tell the world his secrets to humiliate him. My sister tried to explain that she'd been lonely, but Ilyr wouldn't hear her.

"Worst of all, my sister had misjudged Aniyat. Aniyat wasn't sweet and innocent. She wanted to do exactly what Ilyr accused my sister of doing—she wanted to use the prince's secrets against him. But she didn't want to reveal them to the world. She wanted to control him. My sister tried to stop her, but Aniyat made sure Ilyr would never listen to my sister again. She preserved her own reputation in the most vile and conniving way possible. She told him she'd been my sister's unwilling victim.

"My sister was furious at this lie—sex is sacred to us, and rape is a sin. She would never, ever have forced Aniyat. To save Ilyr from Aniyat's control, my sister wanted to tell the truth. It was the simplest solution. But Ilyr thought she was threatening to expose him as a fraud—no better than Aniyat. Ilyr could not afford to have any aspect of this story exposed. My sister had unknowingly become his dirty little secret. Nalitzvans would be scandalized by this story, as I can see that you are. Ilyr did everything in his power to hide the evidence. The strangest thing is that even after everything, my sister still loved him, and I think—I think Ilyr loved her, at least a little bit, right up until the end.

"I don't know why I believe that. It doesn't change what happened," he said with a sigh. "I don't know if Ilyr and Aniyat have forgiven each other fully, but they're still going to be married. I have, as you can see, been uninvited."

The prisoner spread his arms wide to encompass the cell.

"You didn't answer the question," Ev said. She'd asked why he'd help them find Ilyr, and instead he'd told a story about how

Ilyr couldn't help them at all. "Do you want to help us find Ilyr so you can find your sister?"

Alizhan hadn't moved since the prisoner stopped speaking. Instead she fixed him with her eerie, unfocused stare.

"I see I've thoroughly shocked you both," the prisoner said lightly. It sounded to Ev like he was trying to slip out from under Alizhan's gaze, as if he could distract her with a joke.

"No," Alizhan said, still staring. Ev had the impression that Alizhan was working on something, but it was hard to tell what.

Ev put aside her thoughts about Alizhan and returned to the conversation at hand. It was an awful story, and a sad one, but she wasn't shocked for the reasons the prisoner thought. Her father's people, in distant, sunny Adappyr, also saw nothing wrong with two men lying together, or two women. The subject had come up twice in his frequent grumblings about Laalvuri society and its moral failings. Ev had always listened especially attentively when he brought it up.

"Just because I don't want a stranger in a prison cell to tell me a story in lurid detail," Ev started, intending to defend herself.

"What's your sister's name?" Alizhan interrupted.

"Lan."

"Hm," Alizhan said, and Ev didn't have a chance to ask her what that meant, because the guards arrived.

2

LYREBIRD SHIFT, 2ND TRIAD OF SIMOSHA, 761

I LOST MY MOTHER'S TRAIL for years. After she and my father tried to force me to have an abortion, and I attacked both of them, she fled. She must have thought—as I did—that I had killed my father.

In our confrontation, I flung a cup of hot tea at her face. I thought she might have burns after the encounter, and so my spies were always watching Laalvur and the neighboring towns for white women with blond hair and facial burns. But I also thought I might have wounded her mind with my touch. I thought she, like my father, might not remember anything.

Why else would she have fled her own home?

Unless she feared me.

It took me no time to come up with this possible answer, and a great deal of time to accept it. Was I really more powerful than the parents I had spent my life obeying? Had my mother run from me?

I had incapacitated my father, but the damage I did to my mother turned out to be much less serious. Neither her physical nor her mental wounds were lasting. When she surfaced at last —not in Laalvur, but across the sea in Nalitzva, six years after her disappearance—the skin of her face was unmarked. She did not appear to suffer from memory loss. Prideful creature that she was, my mother continued to go by her first name, Merat, and had returned to using her maiden name of Orzh, rather than Varenx. As a gifted Lacemaker, she had no trouble threading herself back into Nalitzvan high society and weaving around any questions that threatened to unravel her little knot of lies. To explain her sudden reappearance in Nalitzva, Merat told people that a long illness had kept her away for years. The only sign of any infirmity was a slight tremor in her hands—possibly a trace of my attack?—which she had trained herself to keep from view.

My spies were very observant of such details.

I employed several people in Nalitzva for purposes of information gathering. The only one who remains in contact with me at the moment is a wet sop of a man named Mihel Pelatzva, a minor noble whose only useful quality is how much he longs to please me.

As careful as they were, my spies were unable to answer the questions about my mother that obsessed me. Where had she been in the six years since I had announced to Laalvur that she died tragically in the wave that hit the city in 745? Did she think I had forgotten her? Was she biding her time? Was she plotting to come back to Laalvur and take Varenx House from me?

Was I powerful enough to kill her, if she tried?

Perhaps you will think less of me, for giving voice to such thoughts in these pages, and that saddens me, but nevertheless I strive to be truthful with you. My mother was a murderer just as surely as if she had killed Arav with her own hands. He would never have been aboard that ship if she hadn't altered his memory.

And Arav's death was not her only crime: my mother would

have killed you, had I not attacked her. I could never forgive her for that.

And now, when she came back to Laalvur, my mother would kill me, too.

Alive but across the ocean, she haunted me. I would sleep better if she were dead. Fear stopped me, but not fear of my mother. The thought of killing her brought me nothing but relief. But I could not bring myself to set foot aboard a ship.

I had seen the ocean crush the life out of too many people.

I could have sent someone to kill her in my stead. I considered it. But given that my mother was a powerful Lacemaker, and anyone who got close enough to kill her would be in danger of having their memory altered, how could I ever trust anyone else to do the job? Even if they sent me some gruesome evidence back across the ocean, how could I believe it? How could I rest until I knew for certain?

It had to be me. Eventually, she would come back for what I had taken from her. To Laalvur. To Varenx House. And when that happened, I would strike.

Until then, I would watch.

3

A RAIN OF BLESSINGS

"WE DON'T HAVE A PLAN," Ev hissed. Then she regretted the words. She'd already assumed someone didn't speak Laalvuri and been proven wrong. The guards were right outside the door. What if they'd heard?

"We don't need a plan," Alizhan replied. Why was she so calm? Didn't she ever panic? "We have me."

The prisoner made quite the face at those words, but whatever he intended to say was cut off by the sound of Alizhan screaming.

Ev and the prisoner flinched, then cautiously exchanged glances. Alizhan was still sitting cross-legged on the floor facing the prisoner. The only difference was that she had thrown her head back to emit an unholy wail.

She's fine. She's not in pain. Ev took a breath.

The key clanged against the lock and the door swung inward by a few inches. Ev had to scramble out of the way. Alizhan, on the other hand, leapt up and threw herself at the guard who had peeked in the opening. She only got a hand around his wrist, but it was enough. He grunted in pain and fell forward, throwing the partially open door wide. Alizhan danced out of the way.

There was another guard standing behind him, but Ev was ready by then. She knocked the door into his face as he tried to enter the cell after his partner. He fell backward into the corridor beyond the cell.

Ev pulled the door back open, looking over her shoulder to see Alizhan leaning against a wall for support. The prisoner was standing now.

He didn't look nearly astonished enough. Most people, if they saw a tiny woman take out a man twice her size with a touch on the wrist, would at least let their eyes go wide. A gasp or two would be perfectly expected. The prisoner shrugged, sauntered out the open door, and didn't pause to wait for Ev and Alizhan.

"Need help?" Ev asked.

Alizhan shook her head, pushed herself upright, and walked out of the cell under her own power. The tremor in her limbs was counterbalanced by the determined set of her jaw.

Once Ev was in the hallway, she noticed that the guard at her feet had a ring of keys. "There are probably lots of people in this prison who don't deserve—"

"Don't you dare," their new friend—Ev couldn't very well call him *the prisoner* now—snapped. "This is not part of the plan. You still need my help and I did not sign up to right wrongs or fight for justice or save kittens or whatever the depths-drowned *fuck* you think you're doing. Swoop in and play hero on your own damn time."

"You're awful," Ev told him. She picked up the first guard's ring of keys and tossed it to Alizhan. Then she stepped back into the cell to retrieve the other guard's keys.

Alizhan caught the keys and offered the ex-prisoner a delightfully sunny smile. "What plan was that, again?"

"There are other guards," he insisted.

"I'm sure they need a distraction from torturing people," Ev said, unlocking the cell next to theirs. There was a group of women inside, huddled together so it was hard to tell how many, and as soon as they saw Ev, they all started speaking. The cascade of foreign words was too much for her to understand, so she just smiled and gestured to the open door. She moved to the next cell.

Alizhan made her way down the corridor in the opposite direction, unlocking doors and pushing them open, not waiting to see if anyone came out.

The ex-prisoner blew out an annoyed breath. When Ev turned around next, he was gone.

Smoke. They really did need his help. She shouldn't have pissed him off. Still, she hadn't been looking forward to spending more time in his presence, and she wasn't entirely sorry to lose him.

She finished unlocking the last few cells and hurried to collect Alizhan. The halls were filling with people now, so there was no need to be stealthy on their way out. They had to be fast, though. Their former cellmate was right about other guards.

The halls of the prison formed a grid with intersections at right angles. Their cell had been dug into the ground, so Ev kept an eye out for stairs leading up. She kept an eye out for anything staff-shaped, too, but she was disappointed on that count. The stairs, at least, were easy to find.

And waiting at the top was their former cellmate, wearing a pair of slippers with pointed toes and gold embroidery under his rough-spun prison trousers. In his uninjured arm, he was clutching two other pairs of shoes, one small and one large, and a pile of clothes in familiar colors.

"What?" he said, when Ev looked at him in surprise. She'd thought he was long gone. She certainly hadn't expected him to do anything useful. "You can't escape barefoot. It will slow us down more than you already have."

Alizhan accepted the clothes and the pair of slippers from his hands readily.

Ev hesitated. "You didn't happen to find…"

"A ring?" He opened his left hand and offered it to her. "You arrived recently enough that none of your things had time to go home with the guards. Sadly, the same cannot be said for what I was wearing when I arrived."

Ev slipped the ring over her thumb and took the rest of the clothes from him.

"I wanted to know if you saw a book," Ev corrected, although she'd wanted the ring back more. The ring was a gift. The book was a burden.

He shook his head. "I didn't see any books."

"Smoke."

"You swear like an Adpri. Charming," he said, and his smile was just slight enough to be confusing. Was that an insult or a compliment? "We'll have to go straight to my tailor," the prisoner continued.

Now *that* had to be a joke. Ev laughed.

The prisoner looked at her in silence until she stopped. "Change," he said.

Alizhan wasted no time, stripping out of her prison uniform in the stairwell. It happened so fast that Ev nearly got whiplash trying to look away. Alizhan deserved some privacy, after all.

The prisoner rolled his eyes at Ev. "If you don't put these clothes on, then I will. The fewer of us who are obviously escapees from a prison, the better."

Alizhan was already dressed, wearing a red and yellow printed tunic and trousers that Ev had bought for her. Alizhan was the only woman Ev had ever met with even less interest in clothes than herself. Still, she seemed to like the things Ev bought her, and she'd developed an attachment to this particular outfit. In traditional Laalvuri style, its intricate, geometric pattern suggested flowering vines and fruits without representing them. The colors suited Alizhan.

The sound of slamming cell doors and shouting brought Ev back to herself. "Turn around," she snapped at the prisoner. He followed her instructions as disdainfully as possible, but he did follow them.

While Ev was changing, he said, "You didn't ask Alizhan to turn around."

"She's a woman." And Ev didn't mind if Alizhan looked. Alizhan knew that, but she didn't seem to have taken Ev up on the invitation. She was staring off into space.

"Are you worried that I might be shocked senseless by the sight of a pair of breasts?" he said. "I'm touched by your concern, but I assure you, I have seen them before. Yours can't be *that* extraordinary."

As long as they had to work together, Ev planned to ignore as much of what he said as possible. It was the only way for both of them to get out unharmed. She pulled her shoes on and said nothing.

"Can you lead us out of here before we get trapped again?" Alizhan asked.

"Gladly, if your friend is done being a prude."

Ev responded with a stony stare, and the prisoner turned down the hall at the top of the stairs.

Alizhan's expression betrayed confusion. She looked like she wanted to say something, but with one more glance between Ev and the prisoner, she shook her head.

"Can we trust him?" Ev said quietly.

"He's hard to read, and *very* confusing, but... I think so. I know you don't like him, and he is talking a lot of shit, but he feels like a good person to me. He hasn't had any really loud, awful thoughts, at least. Besides, who else is going to help us?"

"When you say he's hard to read," Ev said.

"I think he might be like me," Alizhan said. "Or like Mala, or..."

"Iriyat," Ev finished. Because that would be great. She hoped he didn't have mysterious abilities of any kind, and she especially hoped he wasn't like Iriyat. Ev wanted to keep her memory intact. It was disconcerting enough that Alizhan, who could see right through everyone, found their new friend difficult to read. "Well, don't let him touch you, just in case."

Alizhan blinked. It was a wasted warning: she never let anyone touch her.

"Right," Ev said. Alizhan wasn't going around hugging or shaking hands. "Was his story true?"

Alizhan frowned. "Yes," she said. "But not all of it."

"Which part was a lie?"

"Something was wrong the whole time he was talking. I'm just not sure what." Alizhan shrugged, and turned to follow the prisoner, who was halfway down the hall already. Ev had only just started after her when they saw the prisoner get stopped by a guard. The guard grabbed him by his left arm. A rapid exchange of incomprehensible Nalitzvan ensued. The guard was loud and angry. The prisoner spoke Nalitzvan with unruffled calm and absolute authority, as if he was accustomed to being obeyed.

For a fraction of an instant, it occurred to Ev that she and Alizhan could sneak back down the stairs and abandon the prisoner. In the chaos they'd created, they could probably find a way out of the prison on their own.

He might do it to them, if the positions were reversed.

"We don't have to get involved," Alizhan said, watching the scene in front of them, and likely listening to Ev's thoughts as well.

Ev sighed. "We do, though."

Alizhan grinned. "This is why I like you."

They approached the prisoner and the guard together, and just as the guard finally noticed them, the prisoner began speaking Laalvuri again, slowly, grandly. "Yes, please do come closer, my esteemed Laalvuri colleagues, and tell this guard how profoundly disappointed you are in Nalitzvan hospitality."

Ev and Alizhan stopped just out of the guard's reach. The prisoner looked at them, and said in Laalvuri, "Well?"

"I do not speak much Nalitzvan," Ev said in that language, halting over the difficult sounds and addressing the guard. This was a terrible plan.

The prisoner smiled as if he were having a fantastic time, rather than being gripped around the bicep by a guard who could easily throw him back into a cell to be tortured. "Yes, of course, it is so polite of you to try to speak Nalitzvan," he said in Nalitzvan, slowly and clearly enough that Ev could follow. "But that is not *necessary* since I am here as your *interpreter* so you should let *me talk*."

Still smiling, the prisoner stressed "me" and "talk" with so much emphasis that he probably pulled a muscle. Ev nodded.

"As I was saying," the prisoner said in Nalitzvan, addressing the guard, and then he became so formal that Ev could no longer follow what he was saying. But when he turned back to them, Alizhan took a decisive step forward.

"Of course," Alizhan said in Laalvuri. She couldn't possibly have understood any of what he'd said in Nalitzvan. She was even more useless than Ev when it came to languages. But she spoke Laalvuri perfectly, and as she addressed the guard, her words came out in a slow, even cadence that she never used in real conversation. "It doesn't matter what we say because you're going to translate it however you want. Also, Ev, if this doesn't work, his last-ditch desperate plan is for one of us to knock the guard out and run. I vote you."

The prisoner didn't give any indication that Alizhan had said anything funny. Instead, he launched into a lengthy, lecturing interpretation of what Alizhan had just said. The guard's eyes widened. Ev could only catch a word here and there: *Laalvur, important, Ilyr, mistake.*

Her teacher had said that last word all the time in class.

The prisoner was still talking. The guard's grip on his arm had gone slack. The prisoner's broken hand, Ev noted, was concealed behind his back. Best not to draw attention to the fact that he'd been tortured, if he was spinning a story about how they were important visitors from Laalvur and this whole thing was a terrible mistake.

That was Ev's best guess at what he was saying, anyway. She tried to look serious and important. Meanwhile, she subtly shifted her stance, since she was definitely going to have to punch out this poor guard when the prisoner's stupid plan failed.

And then the guard let go of the prisoner.

Ev had to stop her mouth from dropping open.

The guard was bowing, and showing them the way to the door, and suddenly they were standing in the cool shade of a narrow alley. The prisoner—now Ev really had to start thinking of him as the ex-prisoner—smirked at both of them.

"Like I said, a *rain* of blessings."

The light, quick patter of Alizhan's laughter followed them all the way down the street.

4

AN UNMARKED LETTER

M Y CHERISHED FRIEND,
THE ROYAL Temple bells are ringing the hour of
Holy Honor on this, the second quartet of the Archer's month, of
the year 1144 of the Crown—in your charming foreign calendar
of birds and forgotten gods, I believe that translates to the shift
of the Lyrebird, the 28th triad of Alaksha, and the year 764—and
I have just learned some very interesting news.

Those two you warned me about—your pet thief and her
stray—did indeed arrive in our city. They tried to present a
foreign book to the Prince, and were immediately thrown in jail.
The book was confiscated by the guards and delivered to Ilyr.

I will, of course, do my best to retrieve it.

Our two young friends were undoubtedly unaware that the
city is currently consumed by suspicion of all books, foreign and
domestic, and that we keep ourselves warm in the cool Nightward air by piling these paper outrages to good decency in our
grandest public squares and setting them alight.

If this letter arrives smelling faintly of smoke, you will
know why.

The rash of book burnings was sparked by a single volume,

an incendiary little collection of poems called *Loves*. Rumor has it these *Loves* are dedicated to—inspired by—our Prince, and the ink certainly did not flow from our future Princess's quill.

I mean you no offense, my dear, and you know I treasure your correspondence, but I am obliged to point out that my fellow countrymen consider it vulgar for ladies to hold writing instruments in their delicate hands. Any shape longer than it is wide can be suggestive, especially one with a tip that drips.

And we are all quite certain that no lady wrote this volume of poetry.

Indeed, the question of *instruments* comes up rather frequently in the poems, as you will see; a copy is enclosed.

Book peddlers caught with this stack of kindling are imprisoned and interrogated. Only the incompetent ones get caught with copies. The competent peddlers can hardly keep it in stock. It is the talk of every party.

I am still watching M, as instructed. I suspect her involvement in recent events at court—not only the sudden publication of the obscene *Loves*, but also the disappearance of Lady Lan, as detailed in my previous letter. I have yet to uncover the full workings of the matter. Lady Lan muddied the waters by making a great many enemies at court. Her mysterious absence is a relief to all but our poor, defamed Prince.

PLEASE ACCEPT, my friend, my most sacred and sincere vows,
  MP

5

NAMES

A FRECKLED, BLACK-HAIRED GIRL answered the door at Erinsk's shop. She didn't look taken aback by the three bedraggled strangers in front of her, but she didn't look ready to let them in, either. Then Erinsk himself, still as portly and dapper as ever, bustled up behind her, his bushy, grey eyebrows raised high at the sight of them. He tapped the black-haired girl on the shoulder and she stepped aside to let them pass.

"*Darling.* Your *clothes.* Your *hair.* You look *terrible.*"

Sweet, reliable Dyevyer Erinsk always had his priorities in order. Or perhaps he simply hadn't noticed the broken hand yet. Thiyo himself had been able to push the thought of his hand aside during the rush of slipping out of prison. The pain had never gone away, but it underscored everything he said and did with sharp urgency, painting the world aching bright. Escaping had kept him focused. Then their trip through the city had been quick and uneventful, and his focus had started to fade. But every time Thiyo thought the pain might fade along with it, he accidentally jostled his hand and brought everything roaring back.

He desperately wanted medicine, but couldn't risk it. There was still too much to do.

"You must forgive Liyet—the girl—her hesitation," Erinsk was saying. "She's new here and doesn't know all my clients yet. But she's an excellent assistant, brilliant with numbers, and perfectly discreet. Madam Zhenev found her for me and you know her standards. You can trust Liyet as you trust me."

Liyet took her leave with a nod and walked to the back of the shop. There was something funny about how she looked at him, but through the haze of pain, Thiyo had difficulty placing it. Perhaps it was that she *didn't* stare at him like he was a curiosity in a cage, the way everyone else in Nalitzva did. But she couldn't possibly have recognized him. There were only two full-blooded islanders in Nalitzva—Lady Lan and an elderly *wai* trader—and he didn't look like either of them. Not with his face bruised and his hair shorn.

Thiyo swayed on his feet. It was a wonder he hadn't passed out in front of his new companions yet. They were standing behind him, hovering in the threshold of the tailor shop. The big one, Ev, was still and looming like a statue of some ancient warrior goddess. Even knowing that she cared about justice or kindness or nobility of spirit or whatever other boring selfless traits, and that she'd never hurt him unless she had cause, Thiyo felt a little chill.

He shouldn't have provoked her as much. But she made it so easy. Her reactions were a tiny pleasure, and he'd been starved of pleasure for a long time. Thiyo had, perhaps, been meaner than he should have. Suffering cruelty had made him cruel. He regretted that.

The little *uheko* one—Alizhan—was practically bouncing behind him. She'd looked ragged after taking out the prison guard with a touch, but she seemed to have recovered. Her gaze jumped from the bolts of cloth to the unfinished outfits to old

Erinsk himself. The short, rotund tailor produced the city's finest gowns and he always dressed to showcase his own talents. He'd appreciate the attention to his gold-embroidered scarlet coat, even if Alizhan was sure to offend him soon enough.

Erinsk was still talking. He wasn't the only brilliant tailor in Nalitzva, but he was the only brilliant tailor who had no qualms about fulfilling Thiyo's unusual requests. As far as Thiyo knew, Erinsk had been both loyal and discreet, which was something of a miracle, considering how chatty he was. Thiyo forced himself to listen. What if Erinsk knew something useful? The man loved gossip. It was why they got along so well.

"What *happened*, darling? We thought you had run off, you know, no one—and I mean no one—knew where you went. I kept working on all your orders, of course! I don't give up so easily. And you entrusted me with so much—well, anyway, I don't mean anything by this, so please don't get offended, but I thought you might have gone off in a huff to sulk somewhere. I know how you get, with your feelings. You're a delight, of course, I wouldn't change a hair—well, I would change that mess you've got on your head now, but you know what I'm talking about.

"But then Zhenev's girls happened to mention to me that all the book peddlers were selling something really spicy, something forbidden, and I went out to have a look for myself. Don't look so horrified, I might be old but I'm not *dead* yet. And I would know you anywhere, darling—oh all the gods above and below, your *hand*!"

Erinsk reached for Thiyo's broken right hand. Thiyo recoiled.

"You need a doctor."

"I can't go to a doctor." Erinsk knew that.

Then Alizhan interrupted in Laalvuri, "We know someone who would help you. She's a healer on a smuggling ship, so she'll keep your secrets."

Thiyo liked Alizhan. She fascinated him. The brutality of his life in prison had been so simple. Monotonous. Either they were beating him or he was waiting to die. Despair was boring. Thiyo hated being bored. But now he was free—and free to entertain himself—and Alizhan could cure what ailed him. She was such a puzzle. All the *uheko* at home were trained from an early age to cope with their own powers. They often remained eccentric even after their education, depending on the nature of their gifts. But they were never allowed to go untrained. That was a disaster waiting to happen.

She couldn't have been in Nalitzva very long before someone had noticed her. That was probably why she'd been thrown in prison, although it didn't explain the presence of her ungifted friend. The Nalitzvans feared magic too much to let an *uheko* with no control—and with such obvious and overflowing power —wander among them. They were wrong in their violent solutions, but their fear was justified. Thiyo had seen what Alizhan could do with her hands.

The young woman herself was direct. After a year of courtly euphemisms, Thiyo found her refreshing. She was a singular creature, rough around the edges and all the more charming for it. But it was a shame, the way her gift had been allowed to grow wild and overrun her life. Even in the scant hours they'd spent together, it was clear how she yearned for and feared touch.

They'd part ways soon enough, but perhaps Thiyo could teach her something before then. Solving that puzzle might distract him from the wreckage of his own life.

"And *who* are your *friends*," Erinsk was saying, but Thiyo was having trouble concentrating on the words. He needed that healer, or medicine, or maybe just to lie down. He could close his eyes. Erinsk wouldn't let him die. Think of all the revenue he'd lose if Thiyo died.

Alizhan and Ev introduced themselves in the briefest possible way. There was a buzzing in his ears.

"Alizhan, watch out, he's going to—"

"Darling, sit down." Erinsk switched from Nalitzvan to accented Laalvuri. "Yes, good, help—help my client to a chair."

Someone's hands closed around his shoulders. He was slow to react. The touch was unexpectedly gentle. Were they going to hurt him again? No, no, he wasn't in prison anymore. He was in Erinsk's shop, being guided toward a chair. It couldn't be the funny little untrained *uheko* touching him, so it had to be the other one. Not gifted, but no less unusual.

Thiyo himself wasn't eccentric, despite the way Nalitzvans gaped when they encountered him. He was very simple: interested in pretty things, pretty words, and pretty people, and utterly lacking in ambition or direction outside those three categories. His mother had always told him he'd never go far in life.

Alone in a cell an ocean away from home, Thiyo'd had ample time to contemplate those words. Technically, she'd been wrong.

Someone was wrapping his good hand around a glass of water and guiding his arm upward until he drank. The water splashed clean and cool against his throat, a momentary distraction from the angry blur of sensation somewhere at the end of his other arm.

Perhaps Thiyo would eventually have the chance to tell his mother how wrong she'd been, now that his death by torture or starvation or execution—secret or public, which would be worse?—was no longer imminent. Thiyo blinked, realized three people were staring at him with concern, and focused on their faces for an instant. Who were they, again? Oh, yes: Dyevyer Erinsk, Ev, Alizhan.

Names. Names were important. He couldn't remember why.

They were still staring, and he wanted to tell them it was

fine, he was fine, he was going to stand up and explain everything in just a second. He had a plan. It was an excellent plan. He couldn't think of the words to describe his plan right then—or any words—but it was going to make everything better.

Instead, he managed half a smile. He was grateful to them. For the water. For the chair. For postponing his death. He was especially grateful that Alizhan had enough ability to consider him trustworthy, but not enough training to find him totally transparent. But he was floundering now, so maybe she could see through him after all. Was this how it felt to be floating in dark waters, hovering just above the faint glow of a giant medusa? To be in the presence of something beautiful, feral, and deadly? Thiyo had never wanted to sail out into the ocean and find one of the monsters, but that was how he imagined it. Awe and admiration at the same time.

Alizhan was much cuter than a giant medusa. So little. And funny. Thiyo would keep her if Ev wouldn't kill him for it.

That was cute, too, the way they cared for each other. There was no one in the world who cared about Thiyo like that. Not anymore.

The pain was making him maudlin. He wanted to close his eyes, but there was something he needed to remember. Little by little, it floated up from the depths and came into the light. *Darling. My client.* Erinsk hadn't said a name yet. He hadn't said any pronouns, either. Mother Mah Yee bless Dyevyer Erinsk with smooth seas and good hunting. Thiyo was going to pay him double for everything. Triple.

Thiyo was safe. Right now, that meant only one thing. "I want to lie down."

THE PRISONER HAD LIED to them. Not the kind of lie evil people told to cover up their wrongdoing, but the kind of lie that terrified, hunted people told to protect themselves. Alizhan could treat that kind of lie gently. She watched the old tailor and Ev—mostly Ev—help the prisoner out of his chair. He stood unsteadily. Ev waited behind him, her arms ready in case he fell.

She didn't even like him. But Ev was Ev, and she wasn't going to let a wounded man drop unconscious on the floor in front of her. When Erinsk pointed toward a set of stairs at the back of the shop, Ev took one look at the prisoner and scooped him up. They made a funny picture, since the prisoner was almost as tall as Ev and his long, slender legs hung over her arms.

Having nothing better to do, Alizhan followed them up the stairs. Long falls of drapery in every texture and hue—Alizhan could reach out and touch one in pale, gauzy pink and another in flowing, satiny blue—were spread over all the tables and dress models she passed. They looked like things Iriyat might wear, if she dressed in the Nalitzvan style. Erinsk's clientele must be rich.

The prisoner had left himself out of his own story, but he'd obviously lived at court with all the people he described. He'd have to possess that level of wealth to frequent a tailor like this. And Erinsk was obviously a trusted friend. He'd been very concerned with the prisoner's secret.

People said "deepest secret." Sometimes that was the case, and forbidden thoughts were buried under layers. But often enough, people caressed their secrets. They brought them out of the dark, like a rich man opening his safe every triad to make sure his gold was still there. Erinsk was worried about the prisoner—and unaware that he'd been in prison—and extremely concerned about the two strangers he'd brought to the shop. Erinsk didn't yet trust Alizhan and Ev. That was why he couldn't say the name *Lan*.

He couldn't say it, but it flew high in his mind like a flag in the wind. Erinsk was wringing his hands as he labored up the stairs after Ev, thinking to himself: *what happened to Lan?*

Lan. The woman in the prisoner's story. That was the lie.

Alizhan ought to have put it together herself. She'd met Prince Ilyr once, three years ago. He'd been an anxious mess at Iriyat's party and she'd found him outside in a hallway, trying to slow his breathing. They'd talked just long enough for her to offer him a drink in secret. But she'd learned something about him in that moment: another secret so important that its holder kept it in his thoughts at all times. Ilyr had been upset at the party because he didn't want to marry Ezatur's daughters. He didn't desire any of the women there, not Sideran or Iriyat, no matter how beautiful or charming they were, and no one would leave him alone about it. His whole life was a series of invented excuses and polite refusals and he was tired. He'd never wanted a woman like that and he never would. It would mean his death and shame for his family if he said so, but he was firm in his thoughts.

Ilyr didn't like women. He'd never bring home a *Lady* Lan from the islands for a secret affair. And he wouldn't be jealous if *she* slept with Princess Aniyat.

But the prisoner, under that explosion of purple and green bruises and that layer of grime, was a well-made man. Alizhan couldn't tell what his face looked like, but with a little work— clever tailoring—that long, slender body of his could pass for feminine.

And Dyevyer Erinsk had lamented the loss of the prisoner's hair.

Ev laid the prisoner on a downy white bed while Erinsk thanked her in Laalvuri. Alizhan walked right up to the bed. She should kneel or take the prisoner's hand or do something sweet and reassuring like Ev would, but she couldn't touch him and it would be better just to get things over with.

"You're Lan."

His eyes flew open and he jerked up, fully awake now and reeling from the pain of moving. He reached out, not to touch her but to gesture expansively. "No, no, you don't understand—"

"You're your 'sister.' You're Ilyr's lover."

She hadn't touched him, and yet he winced. "Former lover."

"So I do understand," Alizhan said, breezing past that painful admission. When she'd first spoken, Erinsk had moved closer to her as if he could protect the man in the bed, even though Alizhan was just standing with her hands at her sides. But now he took a step back. "And it's okay. We're not going to tell anyone else. Ilyr doesn't like women. I feel silly that it took me so long to remember, really, but we've been busy escaping from prison and I passed out and all that, so it wasn't that long when you think about it. Anyway, I don't care and neither does Ev. You helped us and we're going to keep helping each other and I just thought you should know."

"Maybe you can tell us the real story after you rest," Ev said.

"It was real enough," he said, his voice quieter now that he was lying back against the pillow.

That shocked Ev and she was about to have some kind of outburst, but Alizhan raised a hand and shook her head, and Ev choked back her surprise.

"Lan's not your name," Alizhan said. Erinsk, who hadn't said much, but who was following the Laalvuri conversation, was taken aback by this. Alizhan tilted her head toward him. "But that's how your tailor thinks of you."

The prisoner said something genuinely apologetic and grateful to him in Nalitzvan, offering his good hand to Erinsk, who leaned forward to take it. Erinsk inclined his head in acceptance of the apology and let go of the prisoner's hand.

The prisoner switched back to Laalvuri and said, "Erinsk knows me as Lan because I always came here as her. He accepted me and kept my secret and I'm grateful to him. I didn't give him another name to call me. He already knew enough for you to discover me."

The prisoner offered his good hand to Alizhan. What did that mean? He was friends with Erinsk, but he'd only just met Alizhan. Was it a gesture of apology? A confirmation of her suspicions? An offering? His hand might as well have been a venomous snake. She stared at it and didn't move until he let it drop back to the bed.

Alizhan was relieved. "It was noble of you to try to protect him, I guess, although maybe you were only protecting yourself. But anyway, I was going to ask what your real name is."

She still couldn't understand much of what he was thinking or feeling, but underneath the raging storm cloud of his physical pain, there was a funny tinge of amusement and sadness. "As I said, I've been Lan for a year and it was real enough. But the rest of the time, I'm Thiyo."

THIYO WOKE UP IN A SOFT, unfamiliar bed, with a soft, unfamiliar woman sitting next to the bed and touching his broken hand. Nothing hurt. He felt happy and peaceful. A lightness. An indescribable bliss.

The woman was dark-skinned, wearing a long orange dress and a matching scarf around her hair. Probably Adpri. Older than him. Average height. Plump. She was making him feel better than anyone else, family or friend or lover, ever had. She should touch him some more.

He smiled at her in invitation. "Come here, beautiful."

The woman smiled back at him with a little shake of her head and didn't move. That was okay. He was comfortable. He closed his eyes again.

Next time he woke up, after a while, he remembered he was in Erinsk's apartment above the shop. Erinsk had been there with him at one point, along with the two women from the prison. They knew he was Lan. No one had killed him yet and that was good. He asked the Adpri woman who she was. Even to his own ears, he sounded dreamy and distant.

She smiled at him again. Using a very soothing tone, she said several sentences he didn't understand at all.

That wasn't right. Thiyo shot up in bed. Once his hand was out of her grip, pain flooded his senses and he gasped. He pulled his injured hand toward his body, as if he could protect himself from further pain. Some of his fingers were splinted. There was a linen bandage wrapped around his palm. His hand, though still bruised, looked cleaner than it had in a long time.

"Shh, it's okay," the woman was saying in warmly accented Laalvuri. "I'm trying to fix your hand, but I'm not done yet."

"You gave me venom," Thiyo accused in that same language.

"So you do speak Laalvuri," she said, surprised.

"I do when people don't drug me out of my mind."

"I didn't, I promise," she said. "My name is Mala. Our mutual friends Ev and Alizhan brought me here half a shift ago. 'Here' meaning the apartment above your tailor's shop. You've been unconscious almost the whole time I've been here. If you let me touch you, the pain will get better. I can't make you heal any faster, unfortunately, but I'll do what I can."

So she was *uheko*, too. He didn't immediately return his hand to her, even though he wanted to. He needed his wits.

Thiyo couldn't recall dreaming, but he'd woken up happy and relaxed, and that was cause for concern. He had nothing to feel happy or relaxed about. Thiyo vaguely remembered flirting with the woman. He wasn't troubled by that so much as all the other things he might have said. "Did I say anything while I was unconscious?"

"Not in any language I know," she said. And then added, smirking: "I got the gist, though."

"My apologies."

"Not necessary. I get that a lot," she said, and shrugged.

He hadn't offended her or accidentally revealed anything. That would have to be good enough. His hand was throbbing. He touched it carefully and then hissed out a breath of agony. Did it feel worse than before? Was that even possible? "What did they tell you about me?"

Mala's eyebrows went up. "My friends say you're a friend of theirs. They didn't want to tell me more, and I know better than to ask questions."

From his studies of Adappyr, Thiyo knew it was a freer place than Nalitzva. Mala might not flinch at the idea of two men lying together. Still, he judged it safer to wait.

Erinsk came up with a bowl of broth, followed by the two women. They stood at the foot of his bed, brimming with unspoken questions. Erinsk tried to hand the bowl to Thiyo, but Thiyo had only one good hand, so holding the bowl and feeding himself at the same time was out of the question. He forced himself up so he could hold the bowl in his lap and the spoon in his good hand. He was starving, but he wasn't going to have this conversation while being hand-fed.

They let him eat a few spoonfuls in silence. None of them moved or made any attempt at conversation. He sighed. "Just ask your depths-drowned questions already."

It was Ev who broke the silence. "You lived as a woman the whole time you were here?"

"You don't think of yourself as a woman," Alizhan said. "At least not all the time."

"Yes," Thiyo said, in answer to both of them. If Mala was surprised by any of this, it didn't show. She sat perfectly still next to his bed. "Although I did rather enjoy being one. Some parts of it, anyway. The clothes." Thiyo smiled at Erinsk.

"I'm sorry," Ev said. "I just want some clarification. That whole story was true, and it was about you? You slept with the prince, and then when that wasn't working out, you slept with his fiancée? Because you thought that would fix things? And you think *I'm* dumb?"

"I never said that, but thank you, I cherish the judgment you've passed on my recent, painful heartbreak—please tell me more."

Ev closed her mouth, abashed.

Thiyo thrust his bad hand at Mala, and bless her, she held it. He was flooded with warmth. His whole body relaxed. He almost said *you're right, I made a lot of mistakes.* But no magic was that good. Still, Mala's touch made him generous with his forgiveness, so he dropped the subject and said, "Anyway, I was going to explain all of this, because it's our way into the palace."

"They threw you in prison!"

"They threw Thiyo in prison. They drugged me and beat me so badly that I can't remember any of it. Not even where or how I was caught. But I know it was all done in secret. For all anyone knows, Lan has been sulking in her bed for two weeks."

"That's absurd. Who could possibly sulk in bed for two whole weeks?"

Thiyo decided to consider Ev's response harmless and naive. Practical. Sweet, even. Viewed from a certain angle—a certain magical, medicinally induced angle—her whole selfless, stoic, set-my-jaw-and-ignore-my-feelings attitude was kind of attractive. Thiyo graced her with a smile and she looked absolutely baffled.

Next to him, Mala shifted her hold on his hand and sighed.

Erinsk shook his head, smiling a little. "She's known for her moods, our darling Lan."

"And her sense of style," Thiyo said. Erinsk beamed.

"Okay, I figured out the story, but I don't understand how this part helps us," Alizhan said to Thiyo. "You were hard to read earlier, but now your whole head's a mess. Ilyr knows about you, right? So if he's the one who threw you in prison in the first place, and you show up at his palace as Lan, he'll still know it's you."

Mala was giving Alizhan an approving look. Well. If Mala didn't hold Thiyo in high esteem, that wasn't his fault. He'd met her in unfortunate circumstances. He regretted flirting with her, whatever he'd said. Thiyo removed his hand from hers. Alizhan was right: his head was a mess.

"He didn't," Thiyo began, and found himself unable to say *throw me in prison*. The sentence was too painful to finish. Thiyo could accept the simple heartbreak—*he doesn't love me anymore*—but the betrayal was too much to comprehend. Ilyr had loved him. They'd fought, of course. Ilyr had fallen out of love. Those things hurt. That didn't mean Ilyr was the one who had sent anonymous men to abduct Thiyo and bash his head so hard he couldn't remember it.

Ilyr was an asshole, not a monster.

The trouble was, even with a gut-deep certainty that Ilyr would never, ever have shared those poems with anyone, Thiyo didn't know who else could have. He'd never shown them to Aniyat. They'd been so careful. Who knew the truth about him? Who knew the truth about Ilyr? Who wanted him in prison—or dead?

Or perhaps someone had wanted to hurt Ilyr, and Thiyo had been collateral. But that would mean that Ilyr still cared for Thiyo, and that was too much to hope for. Or perhaps the architect of Thiyo's imprisonment had erred. Perhaps the shadowy figure behind this plot had gone to Ilyr with threats against

Thiyo, or proof of Thiyo's incarceration, and Ilyr had let it happen.

No. There were the poems to consider. Ilyr wouldn't have let anyone see those. Thiyo'd had so much time to think on this in prison, and still the answer eluded him.

He realized everyone in the room was staring at him, and it had been a long time since he'd said anything. "It doesn't matter," Thiyo concluded. "It's true that Ilyr and Aniyat know, but no one else does. And Ilyr and Aniyat can't reveal my secret without coming dangerously close to revealing their parts in it. There are five hundred guests attending the wedding anyway—"

"The wedding," Ev said.

"You mean your ex-lover's wedding to your other ex-lover," Alizhan clarified helpfully. Thiyo glared. She took no notice.

"It's our best shot at entering the palace," Thiyo said. "There will be so many people. A perfect distraction."

Mala interrupted. "Am I done here? I have a ship to get back to. And so do you two, if you want to get out of this city safely. *Vines* departs on the second triad of Yahad at the shift of the Rosefinch. Don't miss us. Also, I'm not your mother, but please don't get yourselves imprisoned again. Or tortured or killed. Ifeleh wouldn't like that and she shouts when she's angry. And Djal will cry."

She blinked and swallowed and said nothing of her own feelings.

"We won't," Alizhan said, and she crossed the room to take Mala by both hands. It was the first time Thiyo had seen Alizhan touch someone without hurting them. Mala clasped Alizhan's hands as if she were any other person. Alizhan didn't react to Mala's touch as if she were being drugged. That suggested excellent control on someone's part—Mala's, he assumed. "Thank you. For everything."

"Thank me by staying alive, little sister. Be there when we

leave." Mala turned toward Thiyo. "You, keep those splints on. Don't do anything with that hand until it's healed. And I swear by all the smoke and fire in Adap, if you get these girls hurt with your crazy plan, we will find you."

Thiyo really regretted flirting with her now. "Um. Thank you?"

"You know how to thank me," Mala said. She hugged Ev, nodded at Erinsk, and left the room.

"I don't like crowds," Alizhan said to Thiyo, picking up where they'd left off.

Ev, for her part, looked pointedly down at herself, at Alizhan, and then at Thiyo. They were all three different colors, none of which was pale enough. "You want *us* to blend into a crowd of wealthy Nalitzvans."

Thiyo grinned at Erinsk. "Blend? I prefer to stand out."

6

IRIYAT TO ILYR, LYREBIRD SHIFT, THE 11TH TRIAD OF ALAKSHA, 764

LYREBIRD SHIFT, THE 11TH TRIAD of Alaksha, 764

My dearest Ilyr,

I hope it does not trouble you to be addressed with such familiarity, even from a delinquent friend who does not write you as often as she ought to.

Warmest congratulations on your marriage! My heart yearned to be there to witness your union, but as you know, the ocean disagrees with me, and it is not possible for me to travel to Nalitzva.

Six cases of wine from my vineyards accompany this letter. It is a sweet yellow wine. You will recall the vintage, I hope, from our time together in Laalvur three years ago, when we shared a bottle with Mar ha-Solora on my balcony—the moment that preceded your historic voyage to the islands! It is an honor to know you, my friend, and to have witnessed history in the making, and I hope you drink this wine in good health.

I wish you and your future bride a happy and fruitful marriage.

. . .

ACCEPT, dear Ilyr, my most respectful and sincere friendship, and may God's Balance keep you,

    Iriyat

"THIS IS STUPID," ALIZHAN INFORMED Thiyo. He'd dragged himself out of bed and made Alizhan and Ev sit with him in a little room at the back of Erinsk's shop where clients would try on their new clothes. The bare, white-walled space wasn't meant to hold three people and Alizhan was already feeling hemmed in. She and Thiyo were cross-legged on the floor, facing each other, and Ev was standing, leaning up against a wall. She'd left as much distance between herself and Alizhan as possible. "You're going to get hurt."

"You said Mala taught you some control," he said, skeptical. "Show me. I need to know what you're capable of before we go anywhere together."

"You saw what I'm capable of in the prison."

"I saw that you have lots of power and very little control. If someone bumps into you at Ilyr's wedding, are they going to drop to the floor? Because if so, we might as well walk back into that cell. So right now, I'm going to brush your hand and you're going to make sure nothing happens."

Alizhan took a breath. She could do this. She'd touched Mala and Djal plenty of times, but they both had magical abilities, so their shields were strong. Like them, Thiyo was mostly unreadable, which might mean he had a gift. Most people at Ilyr's wedding wouldn't be like him. They'd be like Ev, unprepared to protect themselves from Alizhan's painful, invasive touch.

Alizhan had hurt Ev the first time they'd touched. Since then, they'd managed once—and only once—to hold hands without any ill effects. Alizhan had cleared her mind and focused and kept herself in check. She still couldn't believe it had worked. She hadn't had the courage to try again. It meant too much. Before, it had been hard enough to clear all of Ev's desire out of her head, and now Alizhan had to contend with her own. She lay in bed during her sleep shift and thought of Ev's warm, smooth skin. With that much *want* inside her, how could she ever hope to concentrate?

Thiyo's hand brushed the top of hers and the shock of it slammed through her. His whole arm went slack. He fainted, slumping forward, and Alizhan caught his head before his face landed on her crossed ankles. Her hands made contact with his skin and sensation poured through her until her eyes rolled back.

From the corner of the tiny room, Ev said, "Smoke and fucking fire," and that was the last thing Alizhan heard.

He clung to his mother's hand as they looked out over the strip of sand and the vast water beyond it. No sails interrupted the horizon yet, but Mama swore Papa was coming home. "You'll grow up to be just like him," she'd said as they'd walked down to the beach.

"But I failed the test." They'd stuck his hand in the water—and his feet, and his head—over and over, but he'd never been able to answer their questions. He'd barely understood the questions to begin with,

even though he liked words. How could he know where a medusa was, just by sticking his hand in the water? And why would he want to? Medusas were terrifying. Every time Papa left with the other hunters, there was a chance it was the last time. Thiyo hated waiting on the beach.

"Sometimes gifts take time to manifest," Mama said. Hunters like Papa were rare and special. They protected the islands from monsters and waves and mainlanders. And they brought back medusas to harvest their venom. "You're young. It might still come." Thiyo knew she was saying it because she wanted it to be true. But he'd done the test dozens of times. He wasn't a hunter. He didn't have that gift. "And even if it doesn't, you can still sail. Papa needs help, doesn't he?"

Mama had a gift, too. She could talk to anyone in Shadeside or Deep Forest or Summit or High Lagoon or Cove. Even people who lived in far away Li and Kae, where there were even more languages. Mama could speak them all. Any time there were visitors, she went to the council meeting to speak with them. Currents of sound rushed all around her and she channeled them through herself. It was beautiful. Better than hunting. When Thiyo had gone with her to the All-Island Council and listened to her manage all the arguments about the number of medusas each tribe could hunt, he'd felt the pull of those flowing sounds, with their meanings shimmering underneath. He'd wanted to dive in and catch them. Words had swarmed and swirled like a school of fish in the shallows, and every now and then, he could snatch one from the rest. Mama never looked happy when he talked about that. She said he'd do better to practice catching real fish.

A sail appeared, cutting across the water. "Here he comes," Mama said. "When the time arrives, you'll be the one sailing, and we'll wait for you on the beach."

If Thiyo ever sailed, he'd go back to the All-Island Council, or he'd listen to people in Li and Kae with their unusual, musical words. He'd cross the whole ocean and listen to all the mainlanders. He'd let their words wash over him until he could breathe them in and out. What *good would he be, chasing after medusas? They were ugly and dangerous and they never made a sound.*

"WATERY FUCKING HELL," Thiyo groaned. He squeezed his eyes shut but an image burned behind his eyelids. A city built at the water's edge on high red cliffs. He'd never been there, but somehow he knew it was Laalvur. He remembered—but how could he possibly remember a place he'd never been?—darting through the narrow streets, keeping to the shadows, scrabbling up a wall, pushing himself up and wriggling through a tiny window. His body felt foreign. There was so much of it. When he opened his eyes, the sight of his legs crossed in front of him unnerved him. Had they always been that long? His feet were gigantic. A wave of dizziness rolled through him. "You could've just cracked my head into the wall and spared me this."

Alizhan's face was startlingly clear in its squinting, accusing expression. He felt as though he'd never seen anyone's features in such detail, although he had. And despite how huge he felt, the dressing room seemed bigger and airier—and so quiet. He couldn't feel what anyone was thinking.

That's what it's like to be her.

"It hurts me too, you know. And I did try to warn you," Alizhan said, closing her eyes and pressing her hand to her head.

Thiyo reconstructed the last few minutes—the immediate past, in his own body, and not whatever he'd just experienced. He'd touched Alizhan. It had felt exactly like cracking his head into a wall. He'd underestimated her badly. He must have lost consciousness. They'd been facing one another at the time, but Ev must have moved them to opposite sides of the dressing room since then.

This house was so much smaller than the ones Iriyat usually sent her to. And it was down close to the harbor, not near one of the fancier neighborhoods. There wasn't a library inside, only a single shelf of books in the dark bedroom. Iriyat hadn't said which one to take, exactly, just that the writing wouldn't be any script she knew. She checked all twenty-two, opening each one and flipping through it. One book was like that. She'd never seen such spiral writing. The whole book seemed backwards. But Iriyat hadn't asked her to read it, only to steal it. Thin and bound in tan leather, it was easy to slip off the shelf and into her clothes.

Thiyo pinched the bridge of his nose. The writing was indistinct in Alizhan's memory because she hadn't been able to read the script. But it was the first one he'd ever learned. Hoi.

There shouldn't be any Hoi books on the mainland. That was forbidden.

"You're a thief," Thiyo said. He'd learned a lot about Alizhan from that little fragment of memory. "You stole a book for Iriyat."

"*For* Iriyat?" Alizhan said. "No, I stole a book *from* Iriyat and that's what started this whole mess."

"Not that book. One from a long time ago, I think. You were —" Thiyo assessed her height, trying to measure her against what he'd felt "—even smaller in the memory. It was about this big, not too thick, and bound in tan leather. I remember thinking—or *you* were thinking, in the memory, that you didn't usually go to small houses in town for her. Iriyat. I'd like to know more about her, before I get any more involved in this."

Alizhan pursed her lips and ignored his last sentence. "You saw a memory. Damn. I was hoping it was only me this time."

That alarmed him, and then he remembered she already knew the secret. It was easier to draw breath after that, but to cover his concern, he favored her with a suggestive smile. "I hope you enjoyed it."

In the corner of the room, for just an instant, Ev scrunched up her face. Alizhan, either oblivious or indifferent, said, "I don't know if I did. It was kind of sad, I think. But your home is beautiful. The ocean always looks so dark in Laalvur, and we don't have white sand like that. And your mother—wow. No wonder you wanted to be like her. She just seemed so tall and powerful and gorgeous. I guess that's how you thought of her as a kid. Did your father come home?"

Depths drown it, why had she seen *that* of all things? Thiyo didn't want to think about his mother, let alone be like her. It was easier to answer the question about his father. "He did until the one time he didn't."

"I'm sorry," Ev said.

"Tell me about that book," Thiyo said, changing the subject.

"I don't remember much," Alizhan said. "I'd never seen that language before and I've never seen it again. I don't know what Iriyat wanted with a book she couldn't read."

"Didn't you come all the way across the ocean with a book you couldn't read?" Thiyo asked. "She must have thought there was something important inside." He closed his eyes and tried to focus on the dissipating memory. Only one character was clear enough to decipher. "That book was about *wai*. Liquor made from medusa venom."

For some reason, Ev froze and Alizhan went sickly grey.

"Is there a *wai* trader in Laalvur? Was that the trader's home?" An islander far from home might have brought a book with him. It was still forbidden, but at least it explained the book's provenance.

"People... drink that stuff?" Ev asked. What did these two know about medusa venom? What was horrifying them?

"It's a rare delicacy," Thiyo said. "And this gives me an idea for how we can get you through the wedding feast. *Wai* will dampen your gift."

"So my choices are to drink poison or keep hurting us both?"

"What choice?" Thiyo said. "Just because I thought of another option doesn't mean you can stop practicing. And it's not poison. It has a pleasant burn, that's all. Now tell me what happened when we touched so we can make it stop."

"I don't know! I was just sitting there!"

"You weren't expecting me. You weren't prepared. Good. What else? What were you thinking about?"

Alizhan had hardly looked at him the whole time they'd been in the dressing room. Her gaze wandered aimlessly and it was easier to ignore it. But even when she was staring into space, her features still jumped and stretched and moved with her emotions, and Thiyo saw an instant of recognition pass through her eyes, followed by horror.

"Ev. I was thinking about Ev before you touched me. I was thinking about—" Alizhan closed her mouth and her eyes at the same time. Thiyo guessed the end of the sentence without any further help: *touching Ev.* Was Alizhan embarrassed? She didn't seem the type. Ev, on the other hand, was shifting behind Thiyo, crossing her arms over her chest and looking down at the floor.

"Well," he said, all too aware of the three people crammed into this tiny room. "Don't do that this time."

"This time? How many times are we going to do this?"

"We do it again until we don't need to." But touching her again meant exposing random snatches of his life. She'd already seen—lived—something that made him heartsick and vulnerable. And what he'd experienced of her life didn't leave him eager for more. Thiyo knew how to protect himself, but that would defeat the point of the exercise. Alizhan had to touch someone who wasn't guarding their thoughts. "And this time, you practice with Ev."

8

LIQUOR WILL FIX THAT

ALIZHAN ARGUED LONG AND HARD against Thiyo's plan. "I don't get *announced*," she said. She always overemphasized words in moments of strong feeling, as though she couldn't understand why everyone around her hadn't instantly intuited all her thoughts, and had concluded they must all be simple. Alizhan gestured sharply at the bright bolts of cloth stacked in Erinsk's shop and the incomplete dresses draped over tables. "I don't get *looked at*. I sneak in."

"You'll do plenty of sneaking," Thiyo promised.

"A map," Alizhan scoffed, responding to something unspoken in Thiyo's thoughts. "I don't *need* a *map*. I can *see* into people's *minds*, in case you forgot what we just spent *hours* doing. This whole plan is unnecessarily complicated. Just let me find a servant's entrance and slip in. I'll get the book and get out."

"You forget this plan isn't only for your benefit," Thiyo said. "I have goals of my own."

"Yes, yes, you want to find out who betrayed you," Alizhan said, as though everyone had known this information for ages. Thiyo must have been thinking about potential suspects. It was taxing, following a conversation that was half unsaid, but Ev was getting a lot of practice. "I still don't see why *I* have to go. Take Ev with you and let me do what I do best."

"Close but not quite. A rare miss for you, Alizhan," Thiyo said. It didn't seem to bother him that Alizhan was eavesdropping on his thoughts. He was no longer hiding from her. Ev supposed they'd already discovered his most pressing secret. What could be left to find?

"Oh," Alizhan said.

Ev made the connection a moment later. "You want Alizhan to find out who betrayed you."

Thiyo smiled. Alizhan looked considerably less happy about this development. "You want me to stay in a huge crowd of people for hours, reading hundreds of minds. Do you have any idea how hard that will be? Mala taught me a little, but crowds will never be easy for me."

Alizhan had sat on a ledge above Temple Street for hours, waiting to find someone—a priest named Eliyan Matrishal—who could help them smuggle nineteen orphans out of Laalvur. But that had been life and death. This was Thiyo's personal vendetta.

"You practiced for the last half-shift," Thiyo said.

Ev's head still ached from it. Alizhan hadn't knocked her unconscious the way she had with Thiyo, but each touch, no matter how light and darting, had raked through her thoughts. Alizhan had hated hurting her, despite Ev's assurances that it was worth it. And while it had hurt, and a ribbon of dread had twined through Ev's gut every time she waited for the next strike, Ev would offer up her bare skin again right now if Alizhan asked. Practice, even painful practice, was the first step to something better. She wanted that something better enough to suffer for it.

"And when we're at the wedding, you'll have *wai* to take the edge off," Thiyo said. "And I don't need you to read hundreds of

minds. Just a few select minds. I'll give you their descriptions."
Alizhan and Ev shared a laugh, and Thiyo's brows drew together.
"Shit," he said, remembering. "You can't tell people apart."

"It doesn't stop me from getting things done," Alizhan said.
"We'll figure it out."

Thiyo was still working through his revelation. "That little
memory was so brief—Mah Yee, I didn't think about the impli-
cations. So you don't know what I look like?"

Of course that was his first question. Ev rolled her eyes.

"I don't even know what *I* look like."

"We're both gorgeous," he said. His grin had a rakish slant to
it, which only Ev could perceive.

"Well, I know *that*," Alizhan said. "But if I'm not looking at
you, I can't remember how far apart your eyes are, or how long
your nose is, or what shape your lips are, or any of eight thousand other little tiny details that everyone else seems to notice
immediately and retain forever."

"So how do you know we're gorgeous, then?"

"Same reason I don't need a map," Alizhan quipped.

Ev, uncomfortable with the topic at hand, said, "Can we
please get back to the plan? What are the two of us going to do, if
Alizhan is doing all the work?"

"Oh, don't worry, it will be very diverting."

———

"Perfect," Thiyo murmured, his lips brushing the shell of Ev's
ear. He'd practically draped himself over her body, and *draped*
was the right word, given the lavish gown he was wearing.
Erinsk had several gowns waiting for Thiyo—or Lan, was she
supposed to think of him as Lan now?—and this one was a
shimmering golden green with luxuriantly long, ruffled sleeves
and skirts that whispered over the smooth stone floor. The color

of the silk suited Thiyo's tan complexion, and if Ev hadn't watched him rub creams and powders into his face for an hour, she might think he had a natural, healthy glow about him. He made an astonishingly beautiful woman.

"Just like that," Thiyo said. "Look stiff and unhappy and like you don't want to talk to anyone."

Woman or not, beautiful or not, Ev didn't trust their new companion any more than she had in the prison. She hated everything about this plan, from Thiyo's ostentatious touches to the echoing stone antechamber where they were standing in line to be announced before they entered the main hall.

While Thiyo was still close enough that no one else could hear, she hissed, "I thought you said Nalitzvans considered men and women touching in public an affront to decency."

"They do," he said, with relish. "And I have a reputation to maintain." Then he kissed the side of her neck just below her ear. His teeth grazed her skin.

Ev's mind went blank for an instant. Then she came back to herself with a flurry of half-formed thoughts. That was so—he was so—her *neck*—no one had ever—smoke and fucking fire, they were in *public*. Her cheeks heated. Why was her heart beating so hard? Had she... enjoyed that? No. Absolutely not. She hadn't. She couldn't have. Thiyo was unbearable. He just wanted to embarrass her. She clenched her thighs together.

Breathe, she told herself. She held her arms at her side and resolutely did not rub her fingers over the spot where he had kissed her. Bitten her. The skin was still tender. Why was he like this? Why was *she* like this?

"You're irresistible," Thiyo murmured.

Now he was mocking her. What an awful smirk. Ev might not be a great beauty—certainly not right now—but he didn't have to tease her about it. And Thiyo could easily have warned her that Lan was famous not only for her moods but also for her scandalous public displays of affection. But of course he hadn't. Did he have to be an asshole in every possible way?

Thiyo's green silk headscarf brushed her cheek as he extricated himself from her, after lingering in the embrace a moment longer than necessary. He seemed to be taking great pleasure in her discomfort. But as he pulled away, their eyes met, and his expression changed. He stopped smiling.

"Oh," he said.

"Oh what?" Ev snapped, still whispering.

"I didn't think—I didn't intend—" he started. "I won't do it again."

"Good."

"But if I behave too properly, people will be suspicious."

"Fine." At least he wasn't asking her to smile. That would have stretched her acting ability to its limit. But she could look stoic and taciturn for a few hours while Thiyo pretended to flirt with her. Then she and Alizhan would get out with the book and never see Thiyo or Nalitzva again.

They had to keep their conversation to a whisper because he'd demanded that she play this stupid role in *Adpri*, of all things. Ev's grasp of her father's native language was childlike at best. If she wanted to say anything to Thiyo in Laalvuri, she'd either have to whisper it in his ear like a lover murmuring sweet nothings, as Thiyo had, or adopt a foreign accent. She planned to use the second option from now on.

In line behind them, Alizhan shifted from one foot to the other, impatient and even more uncomfortable than Ev. Ev resisted the urge to turn around and check on her. There was nothing she could do for Alizhan now.

Thiyo reached up with his good hand and adjusted the silk scarf that disguised his short hair. A little fringe of lustrous black hair at the edges and an artful curl or two at the ears were all that could be seen. Apparently, Lady Lan used to keep her shiny black hair in beautiful waist-length waves and was known for her elaborate, trend-setting styles. But the prison guards had hacked off Thiyo's hair so that only an inch or two remained. There hadn't been time to secure a convincing wig, so the scarf served as a solution. Erinsk had loudly lamented this loss in Laalvuri for Ev and Alizhan. He'd discussed at length how much better all his designs would have looked if Thiyo still possessed long hair, until Thiyo snapped at him.

"I'll tell them it's an islander custom to cut off one's hair in a period of mourning," Thiyo had said. "They'll love that."

"Won't they ask about what you're mourning?" Alizhan said.

"Mourning what could have been." Thiyo softened his voice and put his good hand to his heart, staring wistfully into the distance. The gesture and the words were theatrical, but the change in his voice was subtle and convincing. Little differences in pitch, volume, intonation and accent combined into a transformation. Thiyo never sounded foreign, but Lan did. That was when Ev had begun to understand how he'd fooled all of Nalitzva for a year.

The most complicated part of Lan's ensemble was not, to Ev's surprise, the corseted undergarment with false breasts. One was ready in the shop, and Erinsk had laced Thiyo into it with efficiency. Thiyo's sides were covered in dark, ugly bruises, but he didn't complain. He grimaced once as Erinsk was tightening the last of the lacings, and that was all. Nor was the most complicated part the hip pad meant to emphasize his artificially tiny waist, or the mountain of petticoats required to achieve the desired silhouette.

The real pain and difficulty had come later, when Thiyo had insisted that they remove Mala's splints and bandages so that he could fit his hands into gloves.

"I can't very well tell anyone that Lady Lan of Hoi just spent weeks getting tortured in prison," Thiyo had said, when she'd expressed reservations about his plan. "How else do you propose we explain this horror?"

Then he'd shoved his broken hand toward Ev's face. It had taken an effort to remain still, faced with his injuries, but Ev hadn't wanted to prove his point.

Erinsk had looked at Ev with sympathy. "Is stubborn," he'd said in Laalvuri.

The white gloves the tailor had found didn't match the gown or each other. The right one had to be a larger size to accommodate the swelling, and so it was in a different style with no lace trim at the edges. The long sleeves of the gown mostly covered this imperfection, and with some care, no one would notice.

Currently, Thiyo's right hand was resting lightly in the crook of Ev's elbow while they waited. She wanted to fidget, but she didn't want to jostle his injury.

She might, if he tried to kiss her again.

Behind her, Alizhan sighed in frustration. It brought Ev no comfort that Alizhan was even more miserable than she was. Thiyo had insisted that he could get them both into the wedding feast this way, with fancy clothes and fake names, as long as they would let him do the talking.

Ev snapped to attention as they stepped over the threshold into the great hall with its high white vaulted ceiling, easily the most massive room she'd ever seen. Chandeliers hung with glass globes of lamp fluid and decorative crystal lit the room with a soft glow, reflected in the gleam of the smooth white stone. Hundreds of other, smaller lamps festooned the edges of the room. Ev had never seen such a display of wealth, and she hadn't even begun to catalog the array of dishes on the tables, or the gowns of the guests, or the fleet of servants dressed in discreet grey uniforms.

She was so distracted that she almost missed the herald calling out, "The Lady Lan of Hoi, Ambassador of the Islands and esteemed guest of His Highness Prince Ilyr, and her companion, the physician Djal Udborum of Adappyr, and her dear friend, the honorable Lady Yiran Selevi of Laalvur."

The exact cultural significance of these names—their positions in various social hierarchies and their resemblances to any real people—had been the subject of fierce bickering in Erinsk's shop.

"I don't see why I have to go as a man," Ev had said. "Why can't *you* go as a man, since you are—"

"The plan relies on me being Lan," Thiyo had said, his patience obviously wearing thin. "I haven't been seen in court for weeks. Rumors are flying. Everyone knows that the prince and I were close, but we haven't been seen together recently. I absolutely cannot show up at the prince's wedding alone."

"You won't be alone! There are two of us!"

"People don't care about friendship here," Thiyo had said, with finality. "Not when there's sex to gossip about. I would, of course, be thrilled to take you as you are, but that's not how Nalitzva works. We can't both be women. And Alizhan will eventually be needed elsewhere."

Then Alizhan had turned to Ev and said, in her utterly matter-of-fact, Alizhan way, "You were never bothered by pretending to be a man with me."

The expression of delight on Thiyo's face at those words had made Ev want to dissolve into a puddle and seep into the cracks in the floor.

"You have *experience*," he'd crowed. "Wait, with that figure?" The look he gave her was analytical, rather than leering. After a moment, he'd said, "What did you do about your hips? I have the hip pads and the petticoats, and I changed the way I walked, and even now, I still don't feel I've perfected it. But you'd have an entirely different problem."

He'd given every impression of being truly interested in her answer, and Ev had found she didn't know how to respond when Thiyo was being sincere. "Nothing, really. Just a change of clothes. People see what they want to see."

"That they do," he'd said and smiled. "Excellent. This won't be difficult at all. I'm also going to need you to pretend to be Adpri."

"What?"

Unfortunately for Ev, he hadn't been joking. At least she didn't have to wear stays. Dressing as a man from Adappyr allowed Ev to wear loose trousers and a tunic in a bold red geometric print. The cut was only slightly different from what she wore every triad. She was also wearing a long red overcoat in a thick fabric—Thiyo's suggestion to hide her hips, although "hips" wasn't the word he'd used—and a matching cap. She'd bound her breasts flat, but that was a familiar kind of discomfort, and only a mild one. Ev had reluctantly permitted Thiyo to rub all sorts of mysterious powders onto her face, and she had to admit that in the end, the effect was fairly convincing. There was even a faint suggestion of facial hair. She still looked like herself, but... different, somehow. Heavier brows. A more angular jaw.

Alizhan hadn't been so lucky. Nalitzvan fashion for women looked hellish. All those heavy petticoats and skirts, no room to breathe, and you practically had to put your tits on a shelf for display. They weren't much for embellishments or embroidery, Nalitzvans. It was all soft hues and softer textures, perhaps to make up for the dramatic, wasp-waisted silhouettes that were in style. Alizhan's pale blue silk gown had a fashionably low neckline that revealed the shallow dip between her small breasts, which Ev hadn't noticed and wasn't thinking about at all.

Thiyo and Erinsk had wanted to put Alizhan's long hair in some kind of complicated updo, but Alizhan had balked at being touched. She'd shown no interest at all in their instructions, complete with many gestures, until Erinsk had presented her with an array of small metal pins. Then she'd transformed into a model student. She'd listened attentively and stared into the mirror with great concentration, chewing her lip and stabbing pins into the thick twist of hair at the crown of her head. They were all invisible now, as black as her hair, but there must be forty of them at least.

They'd done well with their disguises, given their limited preparation time. Thiyo must be paying Erinsk a lot.

The three of them were ushered into the room and seated at long tables parallel to the walls. There were a few musicians in the center of the room, surrounded by empty space that would be filled with dancers after the feast. Thiyo was disgruntled about their placement, far from the dais where the wedding party would sit. Ilyr and his new wife hadn't entered yet. More powerful and favored courtiers—Thiyo's potential betrayers— sat at tables closer to the dais. Lady Lan's social status had fallen, and their dinner companions were either minor nobility or extremely wealthy merchants, two classes that didn't mix well. The atmosphere was both tense and tedious.

Still, Thiyo cleared his expression and made introductions. Ev nodded politely at the men and women surrounding them, but retained none of their names or titles. If Thiyo didn't want her to talk, then he was on his own for this part. Alizhan didn't make much of an effort, either.

He didn't seem to mind being on his own. He chatted with everyone around them, at a pace far too rapid for Ev to follow. There were a lot of names, so Ev assumed he was asking after people's health. At one point, he laughed sweetly and laid a hand over hers, then dropped a kiss on her cheek. Thiyo was on her right, so he was touching her with his injured hand. The gesture must be worth the pain to him. Ev tried to look like she enjoyed it.

The musicians began to play something ceremonial, and the

prince and his new bride entered. Ilyr was as beautiful as Thiyo had described him, broad-shouldered and golden-haired. Aniyat was also beautiful, but not in the way Ev had expected. Since finding out that Thiyo slept with men, Ev had assumed any woman who attracted his interest would be possessed of a slender, youthful androgyny—flat-chested and straight-hipped —but Aniyat was neither. The neckline of her silvery white gown was cut to draw attention to the plump roundness of her barely contained breasts, and her skirts flowed over the flare of her hips. She was almost as tall as Ilyr and their hair matched shades of gold, so they made a stunning pair. The two of them looked so radiant with happiness that for a moment, Ev forgot their mission and its charade entirely.

Beside her, Thiyo sat rigid. His jaw tightened.

Before the meal, they were served tiny glasses of translucent green liqueur. From Thiyo's earlier descriptions, Ev recognized it as *wai*. She tried to push away thoughts of sea monsters and torture chambers and focus only on the delicate glassware. It was a small amount of liquid. How much could it hurt?

All the guests lifted them into the air at the same time, looking at the prince and his new wife and wishing them long life, good health, and many children. Ev's small vocabulary was good enough to understand that. After studying the other men at the table, she drank hers in a single gulp. The liquid was obviously alcohol, sweet to the first touch of the tongue and burning at the back of the throat. Ev was prepared for that sensation, but its sting had a curiously long-lasting effect. Luckily one mouthful wasn't enough to get her drunk.

The other guests said something to Thiyo about his glass, raised in a toast but otherwise untouched, and he politely demurred, gesturing delicately at his stomach. Then he turned to Alizhan and said in heavily accented Laalvuri, "*Wai*. Special drink of my people. From the, how you say? Sense fish? Light fish?" He wiggled the fingers of his good hand in imitation of tentacles.

"Medusa," Alizhan supplied.

If the thought of drinking liquor laced with medusa venom horrified Alizhan as much as it did Ev, she didn't let it show. It had only been twenty-two triads—not even a full month—since the catastrophe in Laalvur, where they'd rescued Kasrik from torture with raw venom. He'd once been a mind-reader like Alizhan, but the torture had destroyed his ability and left him with black scars lining his arms. The venom in *wai* was tempered, and there was only a small amount in the alcohol, but it was venom all the same.

"Yes, medusa," Thiyo said, pronouncing the new word atrociously. "Hoi gift to prince."

"You're not drinking it?" Alizhan said.

"Too sick," he said. "But you. *You* will like."

This was part of the plan. Thiyo had claimed it would make the crowd more bearable for Alizhan. Still, she eyed her glass dubiously, and the other guests chuckled at her expression. A few of them encouraged her to try it. Thiyo stared pointedly at Alizhan, which she was unlikely to notice. After a moment she picked up her glass and downed it. There were cheers from the other guests.

Then Thiyo turned to Ev, and said, in grammatically and phonetically perfect but extremely halting Adpri, "Lots of these people speak your language, but it's rare to find anyone who speaks this one. You can say whatever you want."

So this was why he'd insisted she pretend to be Adpri.

His long pauses were clearly for show, just like his fake accent in Laalvuri. Ev noticed he'd carefully avoided any recognizable words when speaking to her: *Nalitzvans, Laalvuri, Adpri*. How had he acquired such accentless Adpri? Adpri speakers had to be rarer on the island of Hoi than they were in Nalitzva, but she decided against mentioning that. Thiyo gestured demonstratively at her empty glass, as if they were still talking about the liquor.

Of all of this shift's little embarrassments, this one was the worst. Ev didn't speak Adpri half as well as Thiyo. His plan was all for nothing. And now she had to make it sound like she could say whatever she wanted. "I can't," she said, hoping it sounded to the others like a gruff pronouncement on the drink.

"He doesn't like to talk," Alizhan remarked in Laalvuri, from the other side of Thiyo. This earned a few titters from the guests who understood Laalvuri, and it saved Ev the trouble of saying anything more, for which she was grateful. Ev almost smiled at the remark. Would Djal Udborum smile? Thiyo had told Ev not to bother with pretending she didn't understand Laalvuri. He had very low expectations of her acting skills.

A Nalitzvan guest said something short enough and simple enough that Ev understood, at last. "Liquor will fix that."

She nodded, in keeping with her taciturn persona, and raised her empty glass in agreement.

Their little multilingual exchange prompted some conversation in Nalitzvan, addressed to Thiyo, and the word *Ilyr* surfaced in the conversation, one clear landmark emerging from the fog, over and over again. Thiyo laughed softly at whatever was being said, but his smile was tight and cold.

Dinner was served. It was a long, rectangular pastry in a pool of thick white sauce. When Ev cut into the pastry, she found an oblong shape of glistening white flesh. Ev poked at it with the metal utensil she'd been given and then said to Thiyo in Adpri, "What is this?"

"Some kind of fish. Why does it matter? Stop poking it and just eat it."

"Fish," Ev said with quiet horror. She glanced at Alizhan, seated on the other side of Thiyo, and saw that she was also hesitant to eat. Ev couldn't remember the Adpri word for what she wanted to say, so instead she said, "We don't eat."

"Now you do."

Ev forced herself to take a bite and almost gagged. She'd always hated the smell of fish at the market. The food was as slimy as it looked. A woman across the table noticed Ev's reaction, then looked at Alizhan, who was regarding Ev with wide eyes, and said in Laalvuri, "I knew some Laalvuri were vegetarians, but I had no idea Adpri were."

A man with sandy brown hair, probably the woman's husband, laughed and said in Nalitzvan, "I thought Adpri ate everything."

It took Ev a moment to comprehend the words, but no time after that to grasp the mean-spirited joke. The underground city, just on the scorching edge of Day, had suffered several collapses in recent years, some of them in the food-growing sectors. Famines had ravaged Adappyr as a result, and reports had emerged that residents were eating sun-baked mud rather than starving to death.

These pale people in their cold-air white stone palace would have no forks to eat with or swords to fight with, if not for Adpri miners and smiths.

Ev could still taste the fish. She wished she had more liquor to burn it out of her mouth. Instead, she gulped some wine, which proved a passable substitute.

"I live in Laalvur long time," Ev said, sending a silent apology to her father. Obin had told her how hard life was as an exile with an accent. Adpri accents were the butt of jokes in Laalvuri novels and plays. It had taken Obin many years to erase his. It was a shame he'd felt the need to. When Ev had been aboard *Vines*, she'd thought the Adpri sailors all sounded rather musical when they spoke Laalvuri. How strange that people treated foreign accents as a mark of inferiority, when really they were a mark of someone else's superior grasp of your language.

The woman beamed as if Ev were a dog that had just performed a trick. Then she said, in loud, slow Nalitzvan, "So your new beau does talk, Lady Lan!"

"Of course he talks," Thiyo said lightly. For one, brief instant, Ev felt the relief of being defended. Then, with lowered lashes and a knowing tilt of the head, Thiyo added, "He speaks all the right tongues."

Time spent in these people's company had improved her comprehension of their language, which Ev regretted. In Adpri, under her breath, she said, "I hate this. I hate you."

"I don't care," Thiyo said sweetly, speaking Adpri so that only Ev could understand. "Eat your fish."

Meanwhile, on Thiyo's other side, Alizhan speared a piece of fish with her fork and put it in her mouth with grim determination. She grimaced, swallowed, and then grabbed for Thiyo's untouched glass of liquor—Ev should have thought of that!— and threw back its contents. The other guests were silent for a moment.

"You could have just asked," Thiyo said mildly. This remark was in Nalitzvan for everyone's enjoyment.

Alizhan's face lit up with a wild smile, and the other guests laughed. Their conversation in Nalitzvan resumed, and Ev could follow parts of it if she concentrated, but she decided to save her energy for later. Thiyo had told them that dinner would be long, and that they should wait until the crowd was as drunk as possible before acting. She let her gaze wander the room, wondering which of these glittering, smiling people had thrown Thiyo in prison. Her attention returned to the table not because of any movement, but instead because of the absence of motion.

Thiyo's food was untouched.

Of course. He couldn't hold a knife in his right hand.

Ev regarded his plate with unveiled revulsion. He'd made her eat flesh, so it would be a fitting and utterly justified punishment to let him go hungry all shift. But she only considered that course of action for an instant. Then she picked up her own utensils, leaned over, and cut his pastry and fish into small pieces.

"Oh, thank you," Thiyo effused in Nalitzvan for the benefit of their audience. "How sweet." In Adpri, he murmured something that Ev guessed meant, "You finally fucking noticed."

"How many dinners?" Ev replied. She wanted to say *courses*, not *dinners*, but Adpri probably didn't even have a word for *courses*. If it did, her father would never have said it, out of protest. Ev almost smiled to herself. She could hear Obin saying *rich people* in a tone of disgust as clearly as if he were right there, looking around the room with her. She missed him. He'd have even less patience for this multi-course feast than she did. Ev looked directly at Thiyo and said, as she withdrew her knife and fork from his plate, "If you are mean, I stop helping."

To her surprise, he ducked his head and said, "Sorry." After eating a bite of fish—thank the Balance he still had one good hand and Ev didn't have to feed him herself—he swallowed and added, "I'm really hungry."

Because he'd been in prison for weeks. Tortured. Starved. Ev didn't want to feel sorry for him, but she couldn't help it. When servers came to take their dishes away and replace them with new ones, Ev cut up his next course without being asked. Thiyo ate with a relish she couldn't hope to match. There was hardly a vegetable or a spice in sight. It was all meat and fish in sauces made of more meat and fish, and the thought of eating any of it turned Ev's stomach. Even the bread with its golden-brown crust and airy white crumb, the only part of the meal Ev genuinely liked, lost its appeal after a couple of slices. Every course was longer and more excruciating than the last, and Ev grew tenser and tenser. They were all going to get exposed as frauds and dumped right back into a cell—or worse.

Alizhan, on the other hand, was handling everything calmly. She'd even talked a little with their companions, smiling and nodding as if she were thrilled to be there. Alizhan didn't need language skills to follow a conversation, and rehearsing their story beforehand meant Ev also knew what Thiyo had said about them. According to the story Thiyo had been telling everyone, Ev—that is to say, Djal Udborum—was an Adpri exile who'd made his career in Laalvur as a physician and an herbalist. Years ago, he'd met Lady Yiran Selevi, head of one of the minor houses in Laalvur, because she suffered from terrible headaches that only he could cure. Lady Selevi had longed to travel Nightward, but feared that her health might prevent her. Udborum, upon discovering her desire to travel, had offered to accompany her and they had arrived in the city two weeks ago.

At this moment of Thiyo's retelling, their interlocutors all made little "oh" sounds of realization. *Two weeks!* That was how long it had been since anyone had seen Lan. "Yes," Thiyo would say, with a dreamy smile that confirmed all their suspicions. Ev knew this part not from the conversations Thiyo had held in front of her at the feast, but from his recitation hours earlier, when they'd put the finishing touches on the story in Erinsk's shop. "I was out for a walk in the Upper City Gardens, and I saw two such people as I had never seen before..."

Alizhan and Ev had argued against this line, since Laalvuri were common enough even across the ocean, but Thiyo had insisted. "I am an islander. They think I am provincial. No. Not provincial. Primitive. They will believe that I walked up to the first Laalvuri and Adpri I saw and asked to touch their face."

When Ev had made a skeptical grimace, Thiyo had continued blithely, "They will believe it because that is what they do to me. You should see the way they gape. And they never appreciate it when I stare back, the hypocrites."

Alizhan had scrunched up her face in disgust at that, but the lines had stayed in the final draft of the story. Thiyo had claimed the whole thing had just enough of a whiff of the taboo— foreigners and sex and suspect medicines—that everyone would be too titillated or scandalized to ask real questions. Even with limited language skills, Ev could see now that he'd been right.

Ev sighed with relief when the meal concluded and the musicians began to play something louder and more lively, but then Thiyo nudged her. A nudge wasn't one of their previously agreed-upon signals, so Ev did nothing. Then Thiyo said to their companions, "He may not be much for talking, but he's an excellent dancer."

Ev blinked. They hadn't discussed that at all. But if Thiyo was deliberately trying to embarrass her, he was out of luck. She *was* an excellent dancer, or at least a good one. And this way, if Thiyo did something inappropriate, she could stomp on his delicate slipper-clad toes. Dancing would definitely be better than dinner.

9

DANCES AND DUNCES

THE DANCE THAT ALL THE wedding guests, including the bride and groom, lined up to do was simple enough: people danced in pairs of one man and one woman, facing each other, and then gliding through a few steps together. Ev took the lead as they went for a turn around the room, gingerly holding Thiyo's injured right hand in her left, and keeping her right hand on his back. Thiyo, of course, closed the space between their bodies until they were almost pressed together. Ev gave up on trying to keep her distance once she realized he was trying to talk privately. He wasn't provoking her on purpose. He'd more or less behaved himself since that strange moment after the kiss.

With his lips close to her ear, Thiyo said, "We're going to pass some people that I need you to take note of. Then later, you can pass by them with Alizhan."

"We can't ask her to dance."

"She'll be fine." He had such confidence and authority, even whispering in her ear. "Look left, that's Kiryet Altvyezh. She hates me because I'm prettier than her, and Ilyr likes me better. Liked me better. She complains constantly about every aspect of life, large or small. Once while she was droning on, I politely inquired if ten gold *tyek* would make her feel better, and Ilyr laughed into his hand. He tried to pretend it was a cough, but she's hated me ever since."

The brown-haired woman dancing near them did have a rather sour expression. Ev hardly had time to memorize the woman's appearance—long, thin face, hair piled on her head in an enormously complicated architectural style, pink dress with frothy lace cuffs—before Thiyo was pointing out someone else.

"That short blond woman over there, that's Orlat Linsk. I flirted with her husband once and he was *very* responsive. I didn't mean anything by it. Now he always finds some excuse to get close to me at social engagements. As if he has a chance! Anyway. She hates me. Either Kiryet or Orlat might have spied on me, I suppose, although I still can't figure out how they would have discovered—oh look over there, that's Torir Tyrenx, he was a little too persistent in his advances and I had to reject him rather publicly, I don't think he likes me much."

"Tyrenx," Ev said.

"You know the family?"

She shook her head. "It just sounds familiar. Kind of like Varenx."

"Lots of Nalitzvan surnames end in -enx or -insk. An absolute rockslide of consonants, this language." Thiyo shook his head minutely, and the shimmering fabric of his scarf caught the lamplight. "Sometimes they end in -ezh, though. I like that one."

Then he picked up his list as if he'd never been distracted from it. "That man in the corner glowering at me, that's Rin Olvyel. He called me a *filthy foreign bitch* after I refused him at a party, so I dumped a pitcher of wine on him. And I suppose if we're making a list of men I've rejected, we have to include Mihel Pelatzva, too. He sent me an absurd number of letters. He's a terrible writer. I sent one back with suggestions to improve his style, but he never took my advice. Oh, and Loryesk Gorbezh grabbed my ass once and I turned around and punched him in the nose. That's not my fault. He surprised me. I reacted. He should have known better than to approach me from behind, the rat. I told him that if I ever saw him treat another woman like that, I'd happily break my hand against his face again. And there's Barold Hyersk over there, wearing a blue coat and an insipid smile on his horrible face. He tried his best to drug me, but unfortunately for him and fortunately for me, I have a high tolerance for venom. I vomited on his shoes and called him a vile fucking rapist, but Ilyr told me afterward that I said it—well, *shrieked* it, it was a moment of high emotion—in Hoi, so we'll just have to hope the vomit conveyed my sentiments. On a different note, I see Merat Orzh across the room. She wanted to make a deal with me to import venom and I declined. I didn't mean to offend her but Nalitzvans are so touchy and they have so many inscrutable rules."

"Lan," Ev interrupted. The list had flowed as smoothly as their dancing, as though every time they turned, Thiyo saw someone to add. The amount of spilled wine, shrieking, and punching in Thiyo's list made Ev wonder what kind of "scene" he planned to enact later. "This would go faster if you gave me a list of the people in this room you *haven't* insulted."

Thiyo paused, looked around, and considered the matter in silence. Ev took the opportunity to turn the two of them around so they stayed in the swirl of other dancers, who were all moving in a grand circle around the room. Thiyo followed her lead fluidly.

Since he was still quiet, Ev said, "Can I ask you something? Why all the languages?"

This was met with an elegant raise of his brow. "You don't think I'm just showing off?"

"That's just it. You're not. You're much better at Laalvuri than you let those people think."

"Oh no," he said, with wide eyes and a shocked gasp. He pitched his voice higher and breathier. "You have it all wrong. Before I met Ilyr, I was a poor, stupid savage. I wouldn't know any Laalvuri at all if His Highness hadn't carried me from my primitive homeland and brought me here to be educated. He's a miracle worker—why, he's almost managed to make me seem human!"

"Ugh," Ev said. It was depressingly easy to imagine the Nalitzvan elite saying those things to Thiyo's face.

"It gets easier if I think about how simple it is to trick them," Thiyo said. He was still speaking like Lan, but not in such an exaggerated way. "They see exactly what they want to see, and nothing more. There's some satisfaction to be found in that."

"I hate it. Don't you feel like you're hurting other islanders, acting like this? Don't you want these people to know how smart you really are?"

"There are no other islanders here."

He didn't answer the other question. They danced in silence for a moment.

Then Thiyo said, "*I* know how smart I am. Sometimes, that's enough."

"And the rest of the time?"

"Oh, I construct elaborate fantasy scenarios in my head where I verbally eviscerate everyone who's ever condescended to me. It happens in some grand public arena. They all realize how wrong they were, and then bow their heads in shame. Afterward, I am inundated with useless apologies from people who now long to be returned to my good graces. I reject them. Everyone is very impressed. They also all come to the realization that it was me, that strange dark-eyed polyglot foreigner, who wrote everything Ilyr ever published. They remember how often I spoke other languages in front of them, and they're all terribly embarrassed not to have put it together sooner. Odes are written to my wit and intellect. I am showered with praises and flower petals." Thiyo lifted his face upward as if to receive these blessings.

"Does that help?"

"Not really," Thiyo said. "But you know what does help?"

He obviously had an answer prepared, so Ev waited.

"*You* know," he said, and favored her with a smile. "I like that about you."

"Oh," Ev said flatly. She should have known he'd ruin things sooner or later. "So that's what I'm good for. Bearing witness to your brilliance."

"That's not what I said."

If he weren't so indignant, she wouldn't find it necessary to correct him. But she did. Ev gave him a level look and explained, "The thing you like about me is actually a thing you like about yourself."

"That's not what I said *or* what I meant."

"Aren't you supposed to be fantastically good at talking?" Ev said. She should have paid more attention at the table, where Thiyo had appeared to be charming strangers left and right. Because if this conversation was the best he had to offer, they were definitely going to get arrested. Possibly executed. "And writing? You wrote some kind of... poetry."

From the way Erinsk had talked about it, and the way the prison guards had crushed Thiyo's fingers, Ev suspected "poetry" was a generous description of what was most likely pornography with rhymes. Did Nalitzvan poetry even rhyme? Ev didn't know.

"I take it back," Thiyo said, testy. "I don't like anything about you at all."

"Back to business, then. Who had the means to hurt you? Who would have known?"

"That's just it," he said. "None of these dunces could possibly have outsmarted me."

"And yet someone did."

"Thank you for reminding me," Thiyo said, sounding significantly colder than he had a moment ago.

"Did you say something about breaking your hand against someone's face?" Ev said. "The man you punched. Lores Gorsomething."

"Loryesk Gorbezh," Thiyo answered. "I did say that to him. He's a brute, though. I'd be surprised if he were capable of any kind of plan. You think he remembered what I said and then had his revenge?"

"Maybe," Ev said. "And the prince and princess, you're really sure it couldn't possibly have been them? Aniyat already betrayed you once, if that story you told was true."

"She cast me aside to please Ilyr, that's true," Thiyo said. "But if Aniyat really wanted me gone, she could have just asked Ilyr to send me home. Or kill me. She had the power. And she never knew about those poems, but if she found them, I don't think she would have published them. Even anonymously. It would have reduced her power over Ilyr. Damaging to her, too. Besides, she wasn't surprised to see me here. If she were behind all this, wouldn't she expect me to be rotting in that cell?"

"She didn't *look* surprised," Ev corrected. "She might have been acting."

"This is why we need Alizhan," Thiyo said, and withdrew from Ev's arms as the dance ended.

"There you are," Alizhan said cheerfully when they returned to the table. "It was so peaceful without the two of you here, but I missed you anyway. Well, it wasn't really peaceful, but all the conflict was boring because I don't care about these people. Did you know everyone here hates everyone else?"

Alizhan was treading perilously close to exposing herself, but Ev couldn't say anything about that, so she said, "I'm beginning to understand that." The Laalvuri speakers at the table, the woman and her sandy-haired husband who'd spoken to Ev earlier, were gaping at Alizhan. Next to Ev, Thiyo was vibrating with so much silent laughter that he was having trouble breathing. That damn corset. If he fainted again, Ev would have to carry him out of here like she carried him upstairs in Erinsk's shop earlier. "You're in good spirits."

"I like being drunk," Alizhan said.

At this, the man who had told Ev earlier that liquor would fix her silence raised his glass, and Alizhan beamed at him.

"Take me dancing," Alizhan ordered. She grabbed Ev's hand and stood up. Ev stared at their interlocking hands and the contrast of Alizhan's white glove against her skin. Was Alizhan's hand too warm, or was it Ev who suddenly felt feverish? Alizhan had never touched her so freely before. A shift ago, they'd been sitting in Erinsk's dressing room, holding their breath before every brush of their hands. What did this moment mean?

Ev blinked. She was being ridiculous. Her face was hot and she had to clear her head. Had she been expecting ceremony with every touch? Something like Thiyo's fantasy triumph with poetry and rose petals? Of course it would happen like this, sudden and unremarkable, as if they'd always done it this way.

"I had to bite your neck in public to get that kind of a reaction. All she has to do is touch your hand," Thiyo said in Adpri, sighing. "Terribly unfair."

"I don't know what that means and I don't care," Alizhan replied in Laalvuri, and then she pulled at Ev's arm until Ev escorted her to the dance floor. "I've never been able to stop listening before," she said to Ev, as they took up their positions.

"Before, everything washed over me all the time and I had no choice about it. Now, I don't hear anything unless I focus really hard. Mala spent all her time trying to teach me to shut it all out, but all I really needed was some liquor."

"*Wai*," Ev corrected. "I don't think plain alcohol will help you."

"Yes, but I drank a lot of it anyway. Dinner was boring."

As a dancer, Alizhan wasn't as good at following as Thiyo was, but Ev felt far more at ease in her company. Still, she couldn't help but worry. "And that won't be a problem later? Or now?"

Alizhan blew a dismissive "pbbbbt" sound through her lips, which highborn Laalvuri ladies were probably not supposed to do, and Ev laughed. Let people stare. The two of them already looked different enough, and people were going to be staring at Ev later if they weren't now.

"So we're passing by one of our new friends now," Ev said in a low voice. "Brown hair, pink dress, behind you."

Alizhan glanced over her shoulder, then quickly turned back. "She doesn't know anything good," she said, dismissing Kiryet Altvyezh even faster than Thiyo had. Alizhan didn't bother to lower her voice, and she didn't lean in like Thiyo had, either. "She hates Lan for stupid reasons. She's been talking to people about it all shift—Lan will like that. Altvyezh didn't plan anything."

"Lan will like that?"

"Of course she'll like that," Alizhan said. "She loves attention. It's her fondest hope that both the prince and the princess are obsessing over her right now."

Ev nodded, feeling foolish. She should have known. She didn't bother to ask if Alizhan was speculating about Thiyo's hopes or giving a straightforward report. "And the people Altvyezh talked to? Who were they?"

Alizhan groaned. "I can't tell. She didn't really notice or care, except that they would listen to her talk shit about Lan."

"How many people were willing to listen to Altvyezh complain?"

"A *lot*," Alizhan said. "I don't think Lan was very good at making friends."

"I can't imagine why," Ev murmured.

"Me either," Alizhan said, with apparent sincerity. "She likes words and pretty things and she doesn't think I'm creepy and weird! She's the only person—except for you—who likes me without going all drippy with pity."

Ev recalled that not long ago, she'd also thought Thiyo's warmth toward Alizhan was a mark of good character. It was still one of Thiyo's few redeeming qualities. It wasn't enough. "You're being too hard on other people. My parents like you. Mala and Djal like you. Eliyan, too." Ev didn't bring up Kasrik or Mar, although she believed they'd come around to liking Alizhan eventually.

"You're not listening," Alizhan said. "Don't be jealous that I found another friend."

"I'm not jealous," Ev said. But Alizhan had instilled the tiniest of doubts: was she jealous? That would be absurd. Alizhan could be friends with whoever she wanted. Ev's concerns were legitimate. "I'm worried. She's selfish and mean, Alizhan. We shouldn't trust her."

"I know your opinion," Alizhan said, rather archly. "All of your opinion, not just the parts you say out loud. But I'm not allowed to talk to you about that stuff, by your own dumb rule, so don't get mad at me later for not explaining things to you. You don't have to like Lan, but you can't stop me from liking her. I don't want to talk about this anymore."

Ev sighed. She was dancing with Alizhan. They'd never touched each other this much or been so close to each other.

What if they never got the chance again? She should enjoy this. Alizhan recovered quickly from their little spat, looking around the room with bright eyes and a slightly drunken grin. The high ceiling, the hundreds of lamps, and the dancers in swishing skirts made a dreamlike scene.

"I never thought I'd see anything like this," Ev admitted. A gleaming royal ballroom all the way across the sea where people ate strange food and chattered in strange tongues and moved their feet to strange dances, with strains of music drifting through the air.

"Me either. I'm glad I don't have to listen to how much they all hate each other. It ruins the mood."

Ev laughed. "Surely some of them like each other."

"Some of them," Alizhan agreed. "And some of them like each other *too* much. Can I try something?"

Without waiting for an answer, Alizhan removed her hands from Ev so she could peel off her right glove. She crumpled it in her left hand, which she quickly put back on Ev's shoulder so they could resume dancing. Then she lifted her bare hand up as if she were going to place it back in Ev's grip. Ev offered her own hand up without a word, her heart reckless and rapid and ready.

Instead of slipping her hand into the traditional grip, Alizhan placed her palm parallel to Ev's, pressing their hands flat together and matching all their fingertips. Ev stiffened for an instant, waiting for pain or unconsciousness, but there was nothing. And there was everything: the feel of Alizhan's naked skin against her own, the warmth of it, the smoothness, a kind of magic neither of them had ever experienced.

Alizhan's grey eyes went wide, staring at their hands. Then she said, her tone somewhere between astonishment and glee, "I don't know what you're thinking."

That Alizhan was beautiful. That Ev would like to touch her more. That this moment ought to last forever. That the world would be a better place if they could do this all the time. That life must have been very, very lonely for Alizhan. That Ev's heart was going to break.

It was too much, so Ev only said, "Well, I never know what you're thinking."

Alizhan laughed, a little exhalation of joy and relief, and Ev saw that there were tears in her eyes. "It's nice."

Alizhan had talked for paragraphs in Erinsk's shop, quick and emphatic and passionate. She'd blurted out inappropriate, candid comments only moments ago at the dinner table. And yet of all the things she'd said recently, the most significant was *it's nice*. A tiny platitude brimming with meaning. A puff of smoke over the peak of a volcano.

Ev pressed her lips together in the tiniest of smiles. Then she asked, "It's nice that we're touching or it's nice not knowing what anyone is thinking?"

This time, when Alizhan laughed, a tear or two spilled, and she mopped them up with the back of her gloved hand, unwilling to stop touching Ev. "Both," she said with certainty. Her gaze wandered from their hands to Ev's face. "Ev, I want—"

Ev knew the end of that sentence, no matter what it was. She wanted, too. But it wasn't time to cause a scene yet, and they were passing another of Thiyo's suspects. Alizhan shook her head as they passed Mihel Pelatzva, the writer of terrible letters.

"I can't get much from him. He's thinking about women," Alizhan said. "No women in particular, though, which is kind of strange. People are usually more specific."

"You think it's suspicious?"

Alizhan shrugged. "Thiyo said he was a bad writer. Maybe he's bland on the inside, too."

Ev wasn't surprised to learn that Orlat Linsk, the jealous wife, was innocent of everything except bad feeling toward Lan. Lan's other rejected admirers, ranging from clingy to dangerous, were also not involved. Ev was disappointed to learn that the men who'd grabbed Thiyo and tried to slip things into his drink weren't their targets. She would have liked to see those men suffer.

"He's disgusting," Alizhan said of Loryesk Gorbezh, the erstwhile ass-grabber, "but he didn't betray Lan."

"And Barold Hyersk, the attempted rapist? He's over there in the blue coat. Talking to a man in grey. Looking far too happy."

Alizhan considered him for a moment. "There's something wrong with him."

"Obviously."

"No, not that. His mind is... most people are full, thinking and feeling too many things at once. He's not."

"You mean he's coldhearted and calculating?"

"Think of the inside of a person like the inside of a house. Most are stuffed with memories and thoughts and feelings in different states of disarray. A few are orderly. That's the result of serious mental discipline. And some people lock me out entirely —they feel blank, even if they're not. But Hyersk has all the doors and windows wide open, and there's barely anything inside. It's not orderly, it's just empty. No memories. No beliefs. He has a thought occasionally, but it's always about the immediate present, and then it disappears. He has no plans, no intentions. I'm not sure he could form any. It's sort of amazing that he's still walking and talking, with a mind like this." Alizhan paused. Since touching Ev's hand, she'd pressed closer and lowered her voice. Ev was glad to see her exercise a little caution, even if the language of their conversation protected them from the majority of potential eavesdroppers. "That man next to him pities him. He's thinking about how different Hyersk is. He's wondering if Hyersk hit his head, and if he'll ever be the same again."

"You think he hit his head?" Ev said. She tried not to stare in

Hyersk's direction. Thiyo had called his smile *insipid*. Maybe that blandness was an outward sign of some internal emptiness. "In the house metaphor, that would be... moving out? Or having the whole house collapse?"

"People with head injuries are common enough. This doesn't feel like that. I don't think it was an accident," Alizhan said. "I think somebody robbed him. And they torched the place afterward."

"It's awful, but I can't say I feel sorry for him," Ev said, and then the full importance of what Alizhan had just said dawned on her. She shivered. "Someone altered his memory. You don't think it was Iriyat, do you?"

"No. Iriyat *hates* the ocean. She hasn't sailed anywhere since her parents died in the wave. She couldn't come here. But it was someone like her."

"Revenge, maybe?"

"Not just revenge, but somebody making sure that whatever Hyersk did, he couldn't do it again."

"Wow," Ev said. They danced in silence for a moment, and then she said, "So I think that's all of Lan's rejected suitors. Plus the two jealous women. We're done."

"We didn't figure it out, though."

"I think she should be grateful to be here and that we should move on."

Alizhan frowned, but all she said was, "Let's pass by the prince, then."

Ilyr was dancing with his new bride. Everyone wanted to gawk at them, so it was difficult to get close. Ev and Alizhan had to weave through other pairs of dancers, and they attracted a few glares. Approaching the royal couple revealed no flaws in their beauty and symmetry. If anything, their smiles and finery were more dazzling. Ilyr didn't look like a man who was worried about the sudden appearance of a confiscated Laalvuri book among his many possessions.

Alizhan giggled just loud enough to remind Ev that despite the serious conversation they'd been having, she was still very tipsy. "All of Lan's dreams are coming true."

Ev thought it was probably small consolation for Thiyo to remain in Ilyr's thoughts, after being betrayed, imprisoned, and maimed. But Ev would also be the first to admit she didn't understand Thiyo. She could hardly get a word out before Alizhan whispered, "He's upset that Lan is here, but even more upset that she's been gone for two weeks. He missed her. Ooh, he's really mad at you, specifically. He doesn't know who you are or where Th—Lan found you but he's sure you're using her and you're going to break her heart."

"Ironic," Ev said dryly.

"He wants to know what she sees in you. Are you better at sex? Are you better-looking than him? Ugh. This is boring. Of course you are."

Ev ignored the first question. "You don't know what either of us looks like."

"You're cuter on the inside," Alizhan insisted. "Why is Lan in love with this guy? It's like you and Ajee. You and Lan should get along better, since both of you have terrible taste in men."

"Could we get back on topic?"

"He doesn't like the look of me, either. I guess he doesn't remember meeting me at Iriyat's party. Maybe he doesn't recognize me because of the dress," Alizhan said. "Anyway, he's very suspicious. Where did Lan find all these foreigners? Where has she been? I guess he's innocent, at least on that count. Guilty of lots of other stuff, though." Alizhan's face lit up with excitement. "Hey, he knows about the book! He's worried it has something to do with us, and that maybe Lan is trying to humiliate him some-how. And he's worried that people will keep bringing him mysterious texts to read and he won't be able to do it. And if that secret gets revealed, all the rest will come crashing down."

"Is that why the guards threw us in jail?"

"Ilyr had the city guard start a clandestine campaign to arrest book peddlers and destroy any obscene or foreign material they might be carrying," Alizhan said. "Books are causing him a lot of trouble lately. He's worried about his reputation as a scholar. Anyway, our book's in his rooms. That's that, at least."

Now all that remained was for Ev and Thiyo to cause a scene so Alizhan could slip out of the room. There would be shrieking and punching, no doubt. Ev wouldn't be able to bring herself to hit a recent torture victim with a broken heart, no matter how much of a prick he was, so she couldn't even look forward to a good round of sparring.

"Ev," Alizhan said abruptly, and Ev didn't have time to remind her not to use their real names before Alizhan hissed, "Aniyat should know about Lan, right?"

Thiyo had said they slept together, so presumably the princess knew Lan's little secret. As soon as she had the thought, Ev had to close her eyes to avoid rolling them—it was too easy to hear Thiyo's voice in her head saying *you're mistaken, it's a* big *secret. Enormous, really.* But that was the least of their concerns. "You're saying Aniyat doesn't know?"

Alizhan shook her head. "She thinks Lan's a woman and has almost no memories of her. She feels a kind of friendly indifference toward her."

If there was one thing Ev had learned at this party, it was that Lan could inspire just about any feeling *except* friendly indifference. "That's bizarre."

"She's noticed that Ilyr keeps looking over at Lan. She can't figure out why, and it's beginning to upset her."

"So there's something she doesn't know about Ilyr, then." Ev felt sorry for the princess, even knowing what she'd done to

Thiyo. "It must be strange for both of them, having this history between them and being unable to discuss it."

"Very strange," Alizhan said slowly. Then she said, "When Iriyat altered Vatik's memory, she was precise. Almost undetectable. The whole point was that no one would ever notice, not even him. I spent my whole life around him and I didn't notice anything until I saw it happen."

"But the person who hurt Barold Hyersk left a mark."

"So that person isn't as good at covering their tracks," Alizhan said, finishing the thought. "Maybe they went a little too far with Aniyat."

"You described Hyersk as being *robbed*," Ev said. "Do you think the magic works like that? It's not just an erasure of memory, but a transfer of some kind?"

Alizhan shrugged helplessly. "You know as much as I do. But nobody needs magic to get information out of a person."

"So somebody found out what Aniyat knew, somehow, and then removed all her memories relating to it."

"Neither Aniyat nor Barold remembers that person, if it even is the same person. So not only do we have no clue who it is, but I also won't be able to feel their mind," Alizhan said, frustrated.

"Lan might know something," Ev said. "You should get out of here."

The prospect of burglary—or the prospect of leaving the party—made Alizhan smile. They walked back to the table, where Alizhan sat down heavily, putting a hand to her forehead. "I think I drank too much."

"Like a hole in the ground," muttered the same woman who'd spoken Laalvuri to Ev.

Her husband, slightly more sympathetic, said, "Drink some water."

Ev gallantly offered Alizhan a glass of water, which she accepted. Then Alizhan sighed and said, "I need some air."

Ev helped her up, and they walked away from the table. As they were crossing the room, they skirted the edge of the dance floor and Thiyo burst out of the crowd of dancers, flushed with fury. He pointed one imperious finger at Ev—with his good hand, of course. "You!"

Alizhan slipped away from Ev's side. The crowd cleared for her, partly because they wanted to see what Lan would do next, and partly because Alizhan, with sweat at her temples and a hand over her mouth, was doing an extremely credible impression of a person on the verge of vomiting.

Thiyo, on the other hand, was warming up. "I brought you here, *I* did, and you have done nothing but make eyes at other women, you ungrateful bastard!" Then there was a series of words too foreign, too rapid, or too rude—perhaps all three— for Ev to understand. She settled on scowling as an all-purpose response.

Thiyo had managed to conjure tears from somewhere. One had already tracked a wet, black streak through his eye makeup, which was a nice touch. As with Alizhan's nausea, Ev wondered how much of the display was acting, and how much was genuine feeling. Thiyo certainly had reason enough to weep in anger.

Ev had to fill in a lot of blanks in Thiyo's rant. His voice rose in volume and pitch as the tirade intensified.

The facial expressions of the gathering crowd were a good indication of when things got especially shocking or explicit. Ev guessed it went something like this:

"You said you loved me and you left me alone to rot, I know you've been sleeping with other women, you lying sack of shit, I hate you, I wish we'd never met, I wish you were dead, I wish we were both dead, I ought to cut your fucking dick off and stuff it down your throat—"

"Woman," Ev said in Nalitzvan. This form of address had

been Thiyo's idea. Adappyr was, in reality, a far more egalitarian society than Nalitzva. Women were free to work and own property and have a voice in politics. They certainly didn't have to wear ridiculous corsets. But because Nalitzvans thought of themselves as superior, they naturally assumed that Adpri society possessed all the same flaws as their own, only in a more extreme fashion. So they expected all foreign men to be woman-hating brutes. Ev hadn't wanted to confirm their prejudices, but Thiyo had convinced her it would be expedient to give the crowd exactly what they wanted. *People see what they want to see*, she told herself.

And then she said, as nonchalantly as possible, "You don't tell me what to do."

Thiyo shrieked, tossed the contents of his wine glass at Ev, then threw the glass down so it shattered against the stone floor. Blinking wine out of her eyes, Ev had one instant to be grateful Thiyo had aimed the glass away from her feet before he jumped her.

As Ev held off a flurry of surprisingly effective punches and kicks, it occurred to her that they hadn't exactly planned an end to this fight. Alizhan had to be safely out of sight by now.

Then Thiyo, still sobbing and breathing raggedly, hissed, "*Lose.*"

The instruction was in Adpri, meant only for her ears. Ev didn't think it was in character for Lan to win this fight, but while she was trying to think of a way to convey that idea privately, Thiyo finally landed a real hit. He socked her in the stomach. Ev grunted. Then she let him propel her backwards into a table and slam her down. Plates and glasses crunched beneath her or plummeted to the floor and broke. Ev, unwilling to take a ceramic shard in the back for the sake of theater, shoved Thiyo upright.

Then they were surrounded and people were pulling them

apart. Thiyo continued kicking and screaming. Ev spit on the floor and glared at him. That last portion of the fight had been a little too real. Both of them were escorted from the room, the crowd clearing a path but jittering with excitement.

They were marched down a hallway and deposited into a smaller room some distance from the great hall. It wasn't a bedroom, but a salon of some kind, with two couches and several chairs arranged in a loose circle. The furniture was richly upholstered in light blue silk, which matched the rug and the wallpaper. Opposite the door they had entered were two wooden double doors, just barely open. Through the narrow gap, Ev could see an equally richly appointed room with a grand writing desk in polished dark wood. Probably the private quarters of someone royal.

Exactly the sort of place someone might store their papers and their books.

Was Alizhan in there? Had she left already? Ev tried not to stare in that direction.

Someone behind Ev said, "Get out," and the order was immediately obeyed. The person who'd been twisting Ev's arms behind her back dropped her wrists and disappeared. The door shut and the room went silent. Ev turned toward Thiyo for guidance, and realized the person standing behind both of them was Ilyr.

10

LYREBIRD SHIFT, 14TH TRIAD OF SIMOSHA, 761

E VEN IN 745, IT WAS clear to me that I could not accomplish anything alone.

In the lonely, grieving months of my pregnancy, I sought answers from priests of all kinds. None of the answers satisfied me, but the company of one priest of the Balance was a pleasant enough distraction, and I invited him back after our first meeting. I awaited him on a bench in a secluded part of my garden, dressed in a silvery blue tunic and matching trousers. He'd met me a month before, when my belly had been smaller but still noticeable. I'd gazed into his eyes and given his hand a heartfelt squeeze at the end of our visit to remove any thoughts pertaining to my condition. A servant escorted him out of the house in a daze.

For our second meeting, I wanted to see his face when he saw me. There was no hiding my condition by that point, no matter how loose my clothes were. Would this priest be bold enough to remark on how much I'd changed since he last saw me? Would he stare?

I heard him walking down the path before I saw him. The

trailing hem of his grey robe rustled against the stones. He was twice my age, but still younger than the other priests I'd talked to—back then, twice my age was only thirty-six years old. Handsome in a reedy, intellectual fashion. A gaze that appraised the world but gave nothing away. A soothing, thoughtful voice. He should have appealed to me. He didn't. My heart was as dry and empty as the shore before a wave. All I wanted was to talk to someone, and this man had been the only priest to listen to my babbling about waves and agree that the world would be better without them. The others had all told me it was God's Balance and we could never hope to understand it.

He entered the clearing and saw me seated on the bench. He smiled. Then his eyes went wide at the sight of my belly. He blinked in confusion, no doubt wondering why he'd failed to notice it at our last meeting. But he schooled his face into a more neutral expression and admired the garden.

"My lady ha-Varensi," he said. "Your garden is as lovely as you are."

I scoffed. "Do they teach you flattery when you become a priest, Your Reverence?"

"I hope so, since if you're laughing, that means I haven't achieved mastery yet," he said, coming to sit next to me. "And please call me Tsardeya. I'm not old enough to have earned that title yet."

Arav had once had a friend who'd gone by that same nickname, a form of the name Sardas. It seemed a good sign. "You might as well call me Iriyat," I said. I pointed at my belly. "And since we're on such familiar terms, why don't you ask your questions?"

"I only have one. How can I help you?"

I had expected him to ask who the father was, or how I'd kept my condition hidden from him and so many others. I was unprepared to answer.

"This is all in confidence, of course," he continued. "Do you need a hasty marriage?"

"I'd need a groom for that. Are you offering?"

Tsardeya flushed. "No, um, unless—"

"A joke," I said gently. Perhaps you will not believe me, having read the rest of this journal, but I didn't realize until then that he was attracted to me. I was young and not so attuned to these things. I'd thought his flattery was meaningless politeness, since I wasn't feeling lovely so much as fat and tired and cranky. But I tried to tread carefully after that. I never intended to tease him or lead him on. "The baby's father died in the wave and I have no wish to marry anyone else."

"I'm sorry for your loss. Forgive me for bringing up what must be a painful subject. If there's anything I can do for you, please let me know."

"I did call you here for something," I said, smiling. "As you've probably guessed, I'm not going out much lately. I'm bored. I want someone to talk to."

"And you chose... me?"

"You listened to me. You took me seriously. You share my curiosity about the world—you recognized that I was growing blue baliyet and climbing arish when you were last here. And you didn't seem the type to lecture."

"I'm not. And I'm honored, Iriyat."

We talked about my garden for his first few visits—and my intuition about Tsardeya not being the lecturing type was borne out. He had a sharp enough eye to know I was breeding my own plants. Instead of being upset that I was mucking with God's Balance, he was impressed. The fourth or fifth time he came to see me, he noticed the tiny purple flowers I'd been perfecting. He bent down and pinched a stem between his fingers, then offered it to me. "I know it's a sin to think we can improve upon the work of the Maker, but that color belongs in your hair."

"You've been at your flattery lessons again, I see." I tucked the flower behind my ear. "You know we can improve far more than flower breeds."

Tsardeya searched my expression with his eyes, but he didn't tell me not to speak of such things.

"When we first met, I asked you about waves." It was a risk, admitting my true goals to him. But I wanted so badly to share my vision. "You agreed the world would be better without them."

He didn't voice any questions, but they were there in his eyes.

"That's what I want, Tsardeya. I want this child to grow up in a better world. A world where we can predict and control waves—and more."

"Predict, yes, that might be possible. Although no one's discovered a way to do that yet, and people have tried. But control? That's quite a leap."

"There are people who live on tiny islands in the middle of the ocean. They've been there as long as we've been chronicling history. Waves should have flattened their civilizations long ago. They shouldn't exist. How can they live there—unless they know something we don't?"

He nodded. "I see your point. But we know so little of the islands."

"I will change that," I said. "We need to know what they know."

"There'll be more to it than that," he said. "This is a huge undertaking."

"Yes. It's not just waves and the islands we don't understand. It's the whole world. But don't you want to find out what more there is to know? Last time we saw each other, you talked about how much you'd always wanted to travel. To explore. To learn. And what better purpose could there be?"

"I suppose it's not a sin to indulge our curiosity."

I smiled. He wanted to help me. For the first time since Arav had died, the terrible weight of my loneliness eased.

11

BARE HANDS

EV AND THIYO MADE A spectacular scene, but Alizhan's exit from the room didn't go unnoticed. A dozen people remarked on her as she teetered toward the doorway. She had to concentrate hard to feel them. Most of them lost interest when they saw how she swayed and stumbled. Once she was outside the great hall, she doubled over next to a wall and emptied the contents of her stomach onto the floor.

It was a disgusting but effective tactic. The last two people who were watching her turned away.

Alizhan had never done a job drunk, but at least this one didn't involve scaling any cliffs. Just a hallway and a couple of rooms. She was only a little tipsy now. The effects of the *wai* were more troubling. It was as though her ears were ringing, or someone had covered one of her eyes—not a complete loss of the sense, but disorienting. Had Kasrik felt like this when he'd been strapped to that chair? Or had it been nothing but pain?

In the crowded hall, it had been a relief to have her senses dimmed. Here, in the quiet of the hallway, it was daunting. She would have to trust her eyes and ears.

Alizhan staggered away from the wall, in case anyone was

still watching. She'd slur her words and pretend to be lost if anyone caught her out here.

Could she still incapacitate someone with a touch, if she had to?

She'd touched Ev.

Her heart sped up at the thought. No, she couldn't think about that. It was a distraction. She would do what had to be done. If her powers failed her, running away was always an option.

Ilyr's quarters weren't far. The map had been clear in his head. All the servants were occupied at the feast, so there were no obstacles in her path to his door.

The door was so grand that Alizhan would have known it belonged to a member of the royal family even if she hadn't seen it in Ilyr's memory. The wood was carved with some historical scene. Nalitzvans, obsessed with their thousand-year-old kingdom, were always sculpting and painting their past kings and queens. Carved wooden faces meant even less to Alizhan than flesh and blood ones, but she couldn't help reaching out to brush her fingers over the wooden relief. Most Laalvuri would have flinched from the sight of such a flagrant sin against God's Balance, but Alizhan was a sin against God's Balance herself.

The company of her fellow sinners was dull, and she soon turned her attention to the lock. She bent the first hairpin too far in her haste, but her second pin worked perfectly. She slipped the crooked pins back into her hair afterward. If she'd known wearing her hair like this would allow her to keep useful things hidden there, she'd have learned to style it a long time ago.

Alizhan stepped into a room with blue silk wallpaper, couches, and chairs. She knew there were double doors on the opposite wall that led into a study, and that was where she would find the book. It wasn't even locked in a desk, at least in Ilyr's memory. He'd simply left it lying out in the open.

Amazing, that he could treat it so carelessly when it had upended her entire life.

The double doors were locked, too—Ilyr had at least that much caution—but that lock was no harder than the first one. Alizhan stepped into the study, picked up the slim leatherbound volume, and turned.

For the second time in her life, someone had snuck up on her.

This time, instead of a scruffy, skinny teenage boy named Kasrik, it was a pale, petite woman in a stately cream-colored gown. Her hair had once been gold and the years had turned it silver. All silver and cream, she stood out in contrast to the dark wooden doors that she'd nearly closed behind her.

At the sight of Alizhan's face, the woman sucked in a breath.

Alizhan couldn't read her at all. Was it an effect of the venom? Was Alizhan well and truly powerless?

You could stand to use your other senses every now and then, little sister. Relying on Mala's training, Alizhan took a breath and examined the woman again. Perfect posture, beautiful tailoring, elegant jewelry, silk slippers.

Bare hands.

Inappropriate, for a royal gala. It wasn't the *wai* stopping Alizhan from reading her, then. This woman had powers of some kind, maybe memory-altering powers like Iriyat's. She could be the one who had ruined Barold Hyersk's mind and altered Aniyat's memories.

She was blocking the double doors that led back to the salon and the hallway. Even powerless, Alizhan might be able to shove her aside and make a run for it. The woman wasn't stooped or frail-looking, but she was old.

Instead of reaching for Alizhan with one of her threatening

bare hands, the woman spoke. "You're delivering some kind of message for her. What I can't figure out is why you'd be stupid enough to steal it back, or why you broke that godawful abomination out of prison."

"Her who?" Alizhan made a face. She didn't normally have to ask questions like that. Who was this woman? Was she talking about the book? Was she talking about Iriyat? When she said "godawful abomination," did she mean *Thiyo*? As a godawful abomination herself, Alizhan was outraged on his behalf.

"What is she doing with Ilyr?" the woman pressed. "I know it has something to do with the islands. Ilyr came back from Laalvur three years ago with the wild idea to go exploring, and that boy has never had an original thought in his life. It has to be the venom. That boy whore Ilyr brought back is just a distraction, albeit one I was planning to exploit."

God's Balance, people were even more confusing when all you had to go on was their conversation. But this woman did seem to be confessing to kidnapping, imprisoning, and torturing Thiyo, if he was the "boy whore" in question. Whatever this woman was talking about, it would be no great hardship to slam her face into a door.

"Does she know I'm here?" the woman said, even more urgently. "Look at me, you little freak. What's wrong with you, that you can't look me in the eye? Does Iriyat *know*?"

"How do you know about Iriyat?" Alizhan said.

The woman let out a shuddering sigh of frustration and clenched her hands. "You're so stupid, there will hardly be anything in your mind to unravel. Give me the damn book and I'll figure it out myself."

Alizhan tightened her grip on the book, and then she and the woman froze as they heard voices on the other side of the doors.

THIYO CROSSED his arms under his stupid fake breasts, ignoring the pain in his hand, and glared at Ilyr. He could admit to himself that he'd sought this outcome—getting Ilyr alone, or almost alone, in a room—the whole time. He liked Ev and Alizhan well enough, but they were incidental to his real goal. He'd spent his time in the cell dreaming of a dozen different ways the scene could play out.

Was the encounter one last time for the both of them, or was it the start of something new? There was always a fight in Thiyo's fantasies. He would hurl his list of grievances, all expressed with perfect eloquence, at Ilyr. That part never changed. Then sometimes, it was goodbye forever. Finally free of his feelings, Thiyo would turn on his heel while Ilyr sobbed on the floor and clutched at his ankles. Other times, the dream version of Ilyr said everything exactly right, and Thiyo forgave him.

Now that Ilyr was in front of him, bewildered and pale with rage, Thiyo had no idea what to do. As usual, his tongue was a step ahead of his heart.

"Shouldn't you be with your beautiful bride?" he drawled. Thiyo didn't need to switch back to his native language, as they were all equally easy for him. He spoke Hoi anyway, out of pure spite.

"I knew that was a performance out there," Ilyr said, holding fast to his own language. "Your theatrics are always for other people. When you're truly angry, you're as icy as Midnight. Will you tell me what the hell is going on now, or do you need to smash a few more glasses in front of your new friend here to get in the mood?"

Instead of answering, Thiyo peeled the glove off his right hand. It took him a long time. His left hand was shaking, and his right hand was on fire with pain. Let Ilyr wait.

Thiyo raised his arm slowly, and held his hand very still. "You tell me what's going on," he said. "Tell me why I was attacked in my own bed and thrown into prison. Tell me why you didn't even notice I was gone. Tell me why you let your scumbag prison guards starve me and beat me and break my fingers one by one."

"Thiyo," Ilyr whispered.

Eyes wide, mouth hanging open. He looked stupid. Shocked. Sorry. It was everything Thiyo wanted, and he found he couldn't bear it. Instead, he glanced away and saw Ev, behind Ilyr, caught between trying to intervene somehow—she looked like she wanted to say something, even though she couldn't possibly have understood their conversation—and trying to inch out of the room. She pitied him, of course. Thiyo didn't want to look at her, either.

Ilyr took a step forward, obviously wanting to examine Thiyo's hand or offer some kind of comfort. Thiyo whipped his arm behind his back. "Don't fucking touch me."

"I didn't—" Ilyr started.

"I know you didn't," Thiyo snapped, not bothering to let him finish defending himself. Ilyr's face had already confirmed what Thiyo had hoped. Ilyr wasn't a cunning and cruel betrayer who would have his former lover jailed and tortured. He was just a run-of-the-mill asshole who didn't love Thiyo as much as Thiyo loved him. In the moment, the two crimes felt inextricable and equal in magnitude. "But you didn't stop it, either."

"I didn't *know*," Ilyr said. "I searched everywhere. I sent guards to every tavern, every temple, every goddamn brothel— even people's homes! I looked in all the prisons. You were just *gone*. And you disappeared and then those—those poems started showing up in book peddlers' carts, and I thought you—"

Thiyo laughed, and it was an ugly, wet sound. "You thought *I* betrayed *you*."

Ilyr's face was beautiful even in anger. The hard set of his jaw and the line of his brows formed an unspoken challenge. Thiyo shook his head, then wiped his left hand across his eyes, streaking black across the back of his white glove. The few feet of space between them was a chasm.

"I wouldn't do that," Thiyo said quietly. Those poems had been for Ilyr and Ilyr alone. Even at home in Hoi, where no one would have cared about one man writing love poems to another, he wouldn't have shared them. That anyone else had ever seen them was a violation of something sacred and private.

"But you would come to my wedding and scream at a stranger about ripping his dick off," Ilyr said, with an eyeroll and a little smile.

Thiyo responded with the most minimal of shrugs.

Ilyr's words seemed to have sparked his memory, and he turned around to look at Ev, who was hovering by the double doors on the other side of the room. Thiyo was inured to the power of Ilyr's royal presence, having seen him in every imaginable state, but he remembered the awe the prince had inspired in him, those first few times he'd drawn himself up to his full height, squared his shoulders, and stared.

Ilyr was taller than Ev. It must be a rare experience for her, having to look up at someone. Ev withstood his gaze for a moment, but then she bowed her head and spoke Laalvuri. "Ev, sir. Your Highness, I mean."

"Ev," Ilyr said. "Is that a man's name?"

Ev forced a smile. There were rather too many teeth.

"She's a better person than me, Ilyr. Leave her out of this."

Ev shook her head at Thiyo. "I'm in it now. You should both know—there's someone at court who can alter memories—"

From the other side of the door, someone screamed.

THE WOMAN'S TOUCH BURNED. It was only her palm and her fingers making light contact with Alizhan's face—no slap, no grip, no pressure—but the sensation was searing. Paralyzed with pain, Alizhan screamed instead of stepping away.

Alizhan could hardly see or hear, but there was a crashing sound, and then something heavy slammed her to the ground. She was trapped beneath the woman for a moment, but someone wrested the woman's hand from her face. The woman was dragged off of her. Alizhan blinked and when her vision cleared, she turned her head to the side—sitting up was not an option—to see the woman lying next to her, her silver hair spilling across the floor.

The woman was reaching up at something, her clawlike fingers opening. Alizhan refocused her gaze just in time to see the woman's fingers brush Ev's face, and then Ev gave her adversary a cracking punch in the jaw. The woman's arm fell limp.

Satisfied, Alizhan let her eyes close again. How was it possible for her *mind* to hurt?

People were talking. Rude. Couldn't they tell she was suffering?

When it became clear that no one was going to stop talking, Alizhan took a deep breath and started listening. It was a relief to discover she hadn't lost her powers. The woman was as blank as she'd always been, which presumably meant she was unconscious. Ev was dazed. Thiyo was angry. The other person—oh, Ilyr—was confused and angry.

"What is the meaning of this?" Ilyr was yelling. It was a small room. There was no need to yell.

His speech was an echo, an incomprehensible string of syllables representing the perfectly clear question in his mind. After hours at the feast, this phenomenon was familiar. Ilyr was yelling in Nalitzvan.

Thiyo didn't say anything, although Alizhan could feel the answer forming in his mind, a dark swirl of memory and suspicion. Ev was still collecting herself. So it fell to Alizhan. Without opening her eyes, she said in Laalvuri, "That woman is the one who had Thiyo thrown in prison. She wants to undermine you —she's also probably the one who published *Loves*. And if you have any more questions, for the sake of God's Balance, ask them in a language I have half a chance of understanding."

Alizhan could have worked to decipher the conversation in Nalitzvan, but since the use of magic—a funny way to phrase it, as if magic were a hammer or a sword, instead of as much a part of her body as an eye or an arm—was punishable by death here, it was better not to alert the prince. Also, her head hurt.

"'That woman' is a trusted friend and adviser!" Ilyr shouted. He had, at least, complied with her request about languages. "Merat Orzh has been a friend of my family for fifteen years."

"So what was she doing in your study," Alizhan said. She was too tired to give the question its proper intonation. It was work enough to string all those words together.

"Catching a thief, obviously," Ilyr said. She heard someone reach down and pluck the book from the floor beside her.

She sighed.

"Ev said someone at court could alter memories," Thiyo said. "She meant Merat?"

Alizhan nodded, and stars burst behind the darkness of her eyelids. She sucked in a pained breath and then stayed very still. "Merat doesn't like you very much."

"Neither does half my court. That proves nothing," Ilyr said.

"Give me a little credit, it's two-thirds at the very least," Thiyo said. A joke to cover his hurt. Alizhan knew that tactic well. She would've had more sympathy if her brain wasn't sloshing around inside her skull.

"Go ask your wife what she knows about Lan," Alizhan said.

There was a blessed silence.

"What?" Ilyr said quietly.

"You already know," Alizhan said. "Aniyat doesn't remember. At first you thought she was pretending, trying to put the whole affair behind you by acting like it never happened."

Ilyr huffed. Alizhan could feel his resignation warring with his doubts. He was unsettled that she'd characterized him so accurately. He was embarrassed, too, that she'd revealed Aniyat's forgetfulness in front of Thiyo. Aniyat's memory lapse had been convenient, if worrisome. What if Thiyo thought Ilyr felt the same way about his disappearance? It had benefitted him to have the unpredictable, divisive figure of Lady Lan gone from his court these past two weeks.

And yet only two triads after Thiyo had vanished, Ilyr had ridden out into the woods alone and rammed his fist into a tree trunk. Even now, a twinge of remembered pain shot over his knuckles.

He'd been elated to see Thiyo alive this shift. Elated, then heartbroken, then suspicious, then furious. Things were never simple with Thiyo.

Alizhan rubbed her left hand over the knuckles of her right, wishing Ilyr could quiet his emotions. She didn't want to sympathize with him.

Ilyr collected himself, and then said, "But why would Merat do any of that? Why would she alter Aniyat's memory—if such a thing is even possible? Why hurt Thiyo?"

If Alizhan was going to lose him, it would happen now. "I don't know yet," she said. She opened her eyes and tried to make eye contact like a normal person, so he'd know she was sincerely trying to help him. "She thought you were working with Iriyat ha-Varensi in Laalvur. She thought you had some plot about the islands, and venom."

"That's ridiculous. I went to the islands because I wanted to know about the islands. I stayed there for a year for scholarship, diplomacy—"

"Love?" Thiyo interrupted. Then he addressed Alizhan, and the sardonic tone had vanished from his voice, "Merat won't be unconscious for long." Thiyo's thoughts had turned to what Mala had said about *Vines*—Alizhan and Ev had mere hours to get to the harbor.

Alizhan was grateful that Thiyo was a planner. She'd been too focused on the task at hand. She wasn't quite sure what time it was, but the harbor wasn't far. They had plenty of time if they could get out of the palace unseen.

But she didn't want to flee Nalitzva without a translation of the book. What good would it be to return to Laalvur without the one thing they'd crossed the ocean for?

"Merat talked to me at length about the trade in *wai* and raw venom," Thiyo said to Ilyr. "She wanted to import it. I didn't want to work with her. She was upset. I thought it was some trivial offense I had given, so I didn't count her as a real threat. But she's here now, and obviously involved in something. It's possible she perceived me as an obstacle and had me disposed of."

"I don't know what to believe," Ilyr said. "I had every prison in the city searched, Thiyo. You weren't in any of them."

"She makes people *forget!*" Alizhan said. Her frustration was enough to force herself upright to glare at Ilyr. "Are you not *listening?*"

Next to her, Merat stirred. Ev was still staring into space. Alizhan pulled at Ev's sleeve. "We have to go."

"You're not going anywhere. You infiltrated my wedding under false pretenses. You broke into my private quarters to commit burglary. You attacked a citizen and trusted friend of mine. You're obviously not who you say you are. For all I know, you're involved in some plot against the throne."

In response to more tugging on her sleeve, Ev nodded at Alizhan, looking like she'd just woken from sleep. They both stood rather unsteadily. Alizhan almost took a step toward the door, and then she saw the book in Ilyr's hand. Damn it.

He wasn't going to let them go. Ev was too foggy to win a fight. Alizhan's hand twitched. She could touch him and knock him out. She'd done it half a dozen times in the past month. She hadn't been half-drunk, high on venom, or in terrible pain any of those times, let alone all three of those things, but she'd done it. She could do it again. If she had to. Probably.

Thiyo's voice was like silk. "What's your plan, Ilyr?"

When had Thiyo moved so close to Ilyr? Alizhan had kept her eyes closed for too long. They were almost nose to nose. Ilyr was a little taller and a lot broader, but his posture was passive. His hands hung at his sides. Thiyo's closeness startled him, but it was a pleasant surprise. He felt a little unprepared.

Thiyo splayed his good hand over Ilyr's chest and let his fingertips trail down a little.

Alizhan corrected her earlier assumption about Ilyr's feelings: Ilyr wasn't unprepared. He was *disarmed*.

Behind her, Ev came alive with surprise and concern. It was her first clear reaction since Merat had touched her. Of course she was worried. It was Ev's natural state. Reassured, Alizhan returned her attention to the scene in front of them, which kept them both rapt.

"Plan," Ilyr repeated. Then he straightened up and said, more forcefully, "I don't need a plan, I'll just call the guards and let them sort things out. I have to get back to the feast. People will be wondering where I am."

"Call the guards," Thiyo mused. "Let them sort things out. Plenty of empty cells in the city."

"Yes," Ilyr said, and Alizhan wouldn't have heard the hesitation if she didn't already know that Ilyr's guard was back up.

It was too late. He'd said the wrong thing.

"So you didn't throw me in prison the first time, but you'd send me back," Thiyo said.

"I—"

"No," Thiyo said, as calmly as ever. He stroked his hand down Ilyr's chest, and then caressed his cheek. His touch couldn't possibly carry the pain that Merat Orzh's had, and yet Ilyr flinched. "You're going to let Ev and Alizhan walk out with the book. Then you're going to call the guards and have them arrest Merat for breaking into your private quarters."

"And where will you be, while this is happening?"

"What's left for me here, Ilyr?"

Earlier, Alizhan had found conversation with Merat confusing. Faced with Merat's blankness, she'd missed her sense of what was going on underneath. Now, observing Thiyo and Ilyr talking, Alizhan's sense of their feelings only confused her.

She heard Ilyr answer, plaintive but certain: "Me."

A moment later, he added very softly, "You shouldn't have to ask me that."

Even though Thiyo was often hard to read, Alizhan expected to feel a response, a wave of emotion if nothing in words. Whether that emotion would be relief and gratitude or something sharp-edged and bitter, she couldn't say. But there was nothing. He remained tense and watchful. When Thiyo's silence stretched uncomfortably long, it finally occurred to Alizhan that Ilyr hadn't spoken that thought aloud at all. It had been such a clear, isolated thought that she'd mistaken it for speech. Alizhan heard "Me." Thiyo had only heard "You shouldn't have to ask me that."

"You're right," Thiyo said icily. "We both know the answer."

"And why should I follow your orders?" Ilyr said. Thiyo was still leaning in close, and Ilyr was distracted and distressed. *Never could think with him touching me*, he thought ruefully.

Thiyo said nothing, but he must have done something really good with his face because Ilyr snapped right out of it.

"Are you *threatening* me?"

"Do I need to?"

"You said you didn't publish those poems. You said you wouldn't."

"You said you didn't throw me in prison and have me tortured," Thiyo said. "Prove it by arresting the person who did."

"And ignoring these two... thieves?"

"They're only taking back what you took from them," Thiyo said.

Ilyr tore his gaze from Thiyo's face and examined Ev and Alizhan again. With a sigh of disgust, he backed away from Thiyo and stepped toward them, offering them the book. Ev took it from his hand.

"Five minutes," he said to them. "That's all you get." Then Ilyr turned to Thiyo, and switched to a language Alizhan assumed was Hoi. He was obviously hoping for some privacy. Alizhan could offer him no such thing. The words meant nothing to her. But if longing were smoke, all five of them would have suffocated.

Thiyo replied in that same language, a breath of cool, clean air cutting through the clouds.

Thiyo's departure left the room cavernously empty. Ilyr was unhappily familiar with the feeling. The palace had been an echoing mausoleum for two weeks. Now, alone in his study, only the sound of his heart hammered at the walls.

Was he doing the right thing?

Even when they only spoke for a few minutes, Thiyo had the power to make him question himself.

Ilyr took a deep breath and rubbed a hand over his face.

Before Thiyo, Ilyr had long been a dutiful son, a good prince who planned to be a good king. He'd learned all the lessons, followed all the rules, and upheld all the traditions. When his parents had informed him of his betrothal just before he'd left for the islands, he'd sworn to be a good husband despite what was buried in his heart. Ilyr had thought himself motivated by duty, by virtue, by righteousness. He could never, ever have admitted to himself that he was a rule-follower only because he'd never found a reason to break the rules.

And then he'd met Thiyo.

Ilyr had cast aside all his plans and begged to stay in the islands. They'd spent one blissful, secret, stolen year together in Hoi, and then duty had come calling. And instead of promptly returning home alone to wed his betrothed, Ilyr had made what was, until this very moment, the most ill-thought-out and impulsive decision of his life. He'd arrived in Nalitzva with the beautiful and mysterious Lady Lan on his arm.

Ilyr had spent every triad—no, every shift, Thiyo caused trouble even while he slept—of Thiyo's first few months in Nalitzva explaining away some new breach of decency and propriety and etiquette, offering public apologies with a solemn face and then laughing with Thiyo in private.

At some point, the illicit delight of this double life had transformed into a burden—gold into lead, an unwanted alchemy—and it had strained both of them. There was no good solution. Ilyr began to avoid Thiyo. Far from home and bereft of his one confidant, Thiyo had turned to Aniyat.

It still rubbed Ilyr raw to think of that betrayal. Yet here he stood, having broken the rules for Thiyo again. Was this forgiveness, or just habit?

A groan interrupted his thoughts. Ilyr belatedly remembered he wasn't alone. Still prone on the blue rug in front of his desk, Merat put one dainty hand to her face, touching her temples.

Unsure of what to say to arrest someone he'd considered a trusted friend, Ilyr fell back on decades of etiquette education. "My apologies, Lady Orzh, but you are trespassing."

"Oh," she said, and her tone was still colored with pain. "I am very sorry about that. Before we discuss this any further, would you be so kind as to help an old woman get up off the floor?"

"Of course."

He crossed the room and bent down to offer her his hand.

Her grasp startled him with its vicious tightness. Merat Orzh pulled herself up so she could look him in the eyes, and somehow the pain gripping his hand became pain gripping his mind. The past few minutes blurred and faded.

Merat stood, dropped his hand, and patted him on the shoulder in a gentle, grandmotherly way. She had to reach quite a long way to do it, being so small. What was she doing here again? For that matter, how had Ilyr gotten here?

"Are you quite all right, Your Highness? You look a little dazed. You really ought to call the guards before those thieves get away."

12

LYREBIRD SHIFT, 7TH TRIAD OF RIMERSHA, 761

TSARDEYA AND I READ EVERYTHING we could find about the workings of the world. He thought my interest in "superstition," as he called it, was foolish, but he indulged it. He believed the secret to predicting the world's movements would be found in natural histories and observations. I wanted to pursue other avenues as well, in case the secret lay in someone else's senses or someone else's touch. Who could say what kinds of magic existed in the world? There was so little documentation. I could not explain to Tsardeya that I believed so strongly in magic because I myself possessed it, so I allowed him to think of it as my pet interest.

Though I didn't reveal my abilities to Tsardeya, I held him in close confidence on all other matters. He delivered you—with Parneet's grudging assistance. He was a great help to me in that first year, although it crushed me every time I saw him hold you. Arav should have held you. You should have known your father.

And then something happened just before the second anniversary of your birth. Tsardeya tried to pick you up while you were crying and snatched his hands back in pain. He might have dropped you. He might have killed you.

I couldn't let that happen. I took you away from him—physically and mentally. The next time he came to visit, I gave you into the care of a servant who kept you out of sight. He didn't ask after you that time, nor ever again. It was for the best. I trusted Tsardeya with the world, but you meant more to me than that.

That servant also reported that touching you left her in pain, so I dealt with her, too. My fears for you were coming true. Like me, you were a Lacemaker.

My own parents had never told me anything about my earliest childhood, and Lacemakers are so secretive that there was no way to know if this was a normal phase. I could touch you, but no one else could. You walked and talked like other children, but you could never live among them. It hurt me to see you so isolated. I redoubled my efforts into researching magic. What types existed? How could they be controlled? Could I cure you?

Tsardeya, having forgotten you existed, thought I had lost the thread of our research. He tried to persuade me to give up what he thought was a fruitless investigation. We argued. I refused to see him for a few months.

He wrote me letters. Lovely, charming, smart letters. I relented, knowing I'd accomplish more with his help. But I feared keeping him too close to me. At home, you were underfoot all the time. Salacious rumors about what I did in private with my favorite priest were already circulating in pamphlets. Having a man around endangered my reputation. What if it caused someone to discover you?

I persuaded Tsardeya that he should continue his studies of natural history and observations of nature at a distance, and sent him to Estva.

13

LADIES DON'T CARRY SWORDS

IS THIS THE END?

HOW dare Ilyr ask that question, in that tone, as if he hadn't been the one to ruin things? If this was the end, it was Ilyr's fault. Aniyat's fault. Merat Orzh's fault.

Not Thiyo's fault.

Thiyo pulled open the door on the opposite side of the study and stepped into Ilyr's bedroom, unable to look at the massive bed of glossy dark wood with its sheets the color of the Night sky. How often had he slipped out of those sheets while they were still warm? How often had he crept out of this room and stolen down the corridor outside? He'd known the servants' schedules by heart, since he always left Ilyr's room during the servants' shift, when the rest of the court was asleep.

"What did you say to him?" Alizhan asked. She and Ev had followed him into the bedroom.

Thiyo pushed aside the heavy blue curtains and opened the balcony doors. He stepped out. "I congratulated him on his wedding."

"More importantly, who was that woman?" Ev said. She and Alizhan crowded onto the balcony with him. Below them was a private shade garden with high stone walls. Above them, the slope of the slate roof.

"Merat Orzh," Thiyo said. "I told you about her earlier."

"You know what the strangest thing is?" Ev said, ignoring him and addressing Alizhan. "When I first saw her, I thought it was Iriyat. She was too old, of course, but—"

"Iriyat?" Thiyo interrupted. "I was thinking she looked like Alizhan."

"But she was white," Alizhan said.

"Something about the shape of your face, though. Or maybe it was the eyes." A note of apology entered Thiyo's voice as he realized these details would mean nothing to Alizhan.

"She felt like Iriyat," Alizhan said and shivered. Thiyo was about to bring up Iriyat again, to remind them he still had questions, but Alizhan's attention switched to the book. She took it from Ev's hand and shoved it into the bodice of her dress, muttering, "This damn thing is good for something after all."

Thiyo had planned to jump down from the balcony, then somehow get up over the garden wall. The palace was a long rectangular building, with the great hall in the center and two wings extending to either side of it. One long side of the rectangle faced the light, and all the public receiving rooms were on that side, along with a grand, tree-filled courtyard where the palace met the city. The private quarters of the palace were on the shade side, and Ilyr's shade garden seemed an ideally quiet, dim place to make an escape. Once over the wall, it would be a long walk across the grounds, but it would be easy to avoid encountering anyone in the vast expanses of lawns and hedges and gardens. At the edge of the grounds, they'd have to go over or through the external wall, and then out into the city. Thiyo would probably need his right hand to deal with the walls, and the prospect was painful.

If Alizhan could see this plan in his mind, she was ignoring it.

She stepped onto the half-height stone wall of the balcony, grabbed the edge of the roof, found footholds in the palace wall, and boosted herself up. Watching her, an eerie recognition rolled through Thiyo. His body knew those movements—she'd climbed up a wall and shimmied through a window in that memory. Alizhan had been clambering up great heights and sneaking onto roofs her entire life.

At the peak of the roof, Alizhan paused, silhouetted in the low, cool light. Balanced on a narrow line of tiles high above the ground, with her skirts hitched up to her thighs, Alizhan was possessed of all the poise and confidence she'd lacked at the party. Nothing in her posture betrayed fear or uncertainty. She looked like a natural.

It occurred to Thiyo that he had, perhaps, not asked enough questions about Ev and Alizhan's lives before they'd shown up in his cell.

Two silk slippers, one stuffed with Alizhan's remaining white glove, slid down the roof and landed softly at Thiyo's feet, which were still sensibly planted flat on the balcony.

She probably would have dropped her blue silk gown down after her slippers if she could have unfastened it herself. She hadn't been shy about changing clothes in the prison hallway or Erinsk's shop. Thiyo guessed it wouldn't have bothered her one bit to steal over rooftops and through alleys in nothing but her shift. Thiyo spared a moment of silence for her gown, Erinsk's own creation, undoubtedly already ruined by this endeavor.

"Are you coming?" Alizhan called softly.

"How does she intend to get down?" Thiyo asked Ev, aware that their five minutes was running out, and even more painfully aware that clambering up roof tiles wasn't an occupation for a man with only one good hand.

"A tree on the light side, I imagine."

"Ah," he said. "Well, I hope you get to the harbor safely."

"Where are you going?"

Thiyo shrugged. A careless gesture to mask how terrifying he found the question. He wished he could answer *home*, but he didn't know where that was anymore. He held up his injured hand. "Can't stay here. Can't go up there."

Before Ev responded, Thiyo chucked Alizhan's slippers off the balcony and beyond Ilyr's garden wall. It wouldn't be so unusual to find discarded items of clothing on the grounds of the palace after a feast.

"Smoke and fire," Ev said, and Thiyo wasn't sure what he'd done this time, but whatever it was, it was making her sigh. Ev stepped up onto the stone railing, then gestured at the space on the railing between her body and the palace wall. "Come here."

Despite his hesitations, Thiyo did it. Before he fully understood her intentions, Ev put both her hands on his sides. He grunted in surprise at the pressure, and then his feet were dangling several uncomfortable inches above the railing, and two long stories above the ground. She'd picked him up like a child.

"Depths drown you, put me down!"

"Stop squirming. Reach for the roof," Ev huffed.

"And do what? I only have one good hand."

"The other option is," Ev said, and considering that she was still hefting all of Thiyo's weight and he wasn't doing anything to make it easier for her, she hardly sounded out of breath at all, "I throw you."

"What!"

"Sounding better and better all the time," she muttered.

However she got him onto the roof—if she even had the strength—it would still be enormously difficult and dangerous. Astonished, all he could say was, "You don't even like me."

"I'm not leaving you here."

"Can you do this?"

"I carried you before. You're not as big as you think you are."

Before? Oh—he'd woken up in Erinsk's apartment above the shop. He couldn't remember how he'd gotten there, but now he knew. A sudden memory of Ilyr picking him up and carrying him to bed, both of them drunk and laughing, surged forward and Thiyo shoved it aside.

He braced his left hand against the edge of the roof. Then he toed off his slippers and kicked them onto Ilyr's balcony. They were unusually large for women's shoes. Much too big to fit Aniyat. Let Ilyr's servants wonder.

"I'm going to change my grip," Ev warned, and then suddenly her hands were supporting his thighs and she was pushing him higher. Thiyo got both hands on the roof, and then his knees, and he managed to crawl forward on all fours before he had to stop as a spasm of pain shot through his right hand.

As he knelt on the roof catching his breath, supporting himself with his left hand and cradling his right to his chest, he thought, *my dress is ruined*. For some reason it made him laugh.

Ev was not in the mood. "Hurry up," she said. "I'm coming up after you."

"I normally require a lot more romance before I let someone grab my ass like that," he told her.

"I doubt that," she said flatly, and Thiyo laughed again. Then he began to crawl. He made a lurching, unsteady progress up the slope. His breathing became short and fast and labored. The pain in his hand was agony. His skirts were voluminous enough to slow him down, but not nearly thick enough to protect his knees from the hard edges of the tiles. Alizhan had made this look so easy.

Thinking of her, Thiyo glanced up. Alizhan had already picked her way down the center line of the roof. She'd halted, turned toward the light side of the palace, evaluating the trees in the courtyard. Damn. Ev had been right. They were going to have to climb down a tree to get off this depths-drowned roof.

Under his foot, one loose tile scraped against another, a dry screeching sound. Thiyo squeezed his eyes shut and clenched his left hand against the roof. He prepared to fall to his death.

The moment passed. He didn't slide to his death. He breathed. He put his hand forward, then his feet. He continued upward.

Ev, who was less encumbered, reached the peak of the roof before he did. She waited for him, and when he finally dragged himself up beside her, she stood up and offered him her hand. The world wobbled as he got to his feet. He leaned on her for balance. She was so steady, Ev.

He let her go first, and then he followed her at a distance.

Until now, Thiyo had always liked wearing dresses. The sound and feeling of skirts swishing around his legs pleased him. Dresses came in a beautiful variety of shapes and colors. Nalitzvans were always surprised to learn this, since they'd all heard that islanders went naked. This wasn't exactly true, but no one ever listened to Thiyo's explanations about that. It was too exciting for them to imagine a foreign playground, a land of naked lust where nothing was taboo. When they asked him about clothes, they always did so in hushed tones, thrilled by their own boldness. There was always a note of suppressed longing in their questions. Thiyo suspected they were all hoping he'd volunteer to strip naked in the great hall.

Perhaps, if he ever came back here, he would.

Still, he'd answered their nosy questions truly: he really did like all kinds of clothes, especially dresses. Except now that he was tiptoeing across the palace roof, trying not to fall to his death, he wished he wasn't wearing one. It would be nice to be able to see his feet without holding up yards of fabric in one hand.

How sad, that he was standing at the tip-top of the palace, with a view down the hill over the grey slate roofs, white walls, angular stone streets and green hedges of Nalitzva, this city he'd called home for the last year, decorated with square bell towers and narrow temple spires and bordered by the glittering sea, and all Thiyo wanted to look at was his own feet. He could have stood tall and looked across the sea toward the light of Day, or turned his head Nightward to see the horizon darkened with dusky blue. Instead he stared down and put one foot in front of the other.

The walk to where Alizhan was perched was arduous, and sliding down the roof toward the tree she'd chosen was even worse. Thiyo tried not to use his right hand for anything—at this rate, it would never heal—but when faced with a precipitous drop, the instinct to cling with both hands was impossible to overcome.

They waited for a moment when the few scattered people in the courtyard, party guests who slipped outside for some air, were all occupied. There was a cluster of three drunk young men in one corner, stumbling and laughing uproariously over nothing, and a couple on the opposite side of the space, huddled under a tree. It wasn't difficult to guess what they were doing.

Alizhan jumped down from the tree first. She landed in a crouch, without making a sound, her skirts floating to the ground after her. Then she motioned for them to follow. Ev was less practiced but still nimble. Thiyo breathed a sigh of relief when he dropped to the ground without cracking his face against the cobblestones.

The courtyard made him regret leaving his slippers on the balcony. But staggering made him look drunk, and being drunk was a good explanation for being barefoot and filthy, so he made no effort to disguise his gasp every time his foot landed wrong.

It was just a short walk across this courtyard, and then they'd be at the palace gates, and then in the streets, and then back at Erinsk's shop, and then he could get on with the rest of his life.

Whatever that might be.

Easier to think about the cobblestones.

The guards at the palace gate had been too bored, or too distracted by partygoers canoodling in the courtyard, to look up at the roof and notice three people walking along the peak of it. Thiyo assumed they'd be equally uninterested in three disheveled guests making their exit, and they were. The guards waved them on.

The palace gates let out into a grand open square, which Nalitzvans had very sensibly called Royal Square. It was perhaps the only sensibly named thing in this quarter of the city. Thiyo led them out of the square by taking a left down Valor Street, instead of heading right down Justice Street, which had too many aristocratic townhouses with guards outside their doors. The residents of Valor Street, while still quite comfortable, couldn't afford the same security. Only two of the houses had guards.

Thiyo kept a watchful eye on these men, but neither of them took much note of their group. Perhaps they'd make it back to the shop after all. Ev and Alizhan could get their things and change into their old clothes and still have time to get to the harbor to board *Vines*. And Thiyo would go... somewhere.

"Halt!"

The shout came from behind them, with such authority that it could only be a palace guard. Thiyo jerked his head around, saw uniformed guards with swords belted at their sides, and hissed, "Run!"

Ev and Alizhan needed no further instruction. They dashed

down the street. Thiyo ran after them, but lacking practice in running in skirts, with no shoes, it was only a matter of time before he tripped. His face collided with the cobblestones and pain whited out his vision for an instant. Agony radiated from a point on the side of his face.

Alizhan and Ev didn't know the city, but they could figure out that going downhill would get them closer to the harbor. They'd make it without him. The guards were catching up to him, but maybe he could talk his way out—make up something about being tricked by foreigners, bat his eyelashes a little. *Shit.* Was that the sound of a sword being unsheathed?

A glint of metal caught his eye. His heart caught in his throat.

Is this *the end?* Thiyo thought. He choked back a hysterical laugh and cursed himself for believing Ilyr. *Five minutes.* The bastard had probably called the guards right away. Getting through the front gate had been a lucky break. If there was a group of guards here in Justice Street, there must be others searching the palace and all its grounds. Ilyr had never intended to let any of them get away.

Thiyo made the mistake of sitting up.

One of the guards swung his sword toward Thiyo and let the point hover below Thiyo's chin. "Where did they go?" he demanded.

There were only two guards. His first panicked glimpse backwards had made him think there were more. Two wasn't so bad. Perhaps he could get them to fight each other.

"As far as I can recall, last time I saw them, they were running down the street. That way." Thiyo gestured behind himself, very helpfully.

The point of the sword pressed against his neck.

"Such scintillating conversation you make," Thiyo said,

leaning back as far away as he could stretch. "Women probably fall at your feet all the time."

"Pretty face," the guard mused. It wouldn't be pretty a few hours from now, all swollen and discolored with fresh bruises and old makeup. At least it would match the rest of his body. "Shame to ruin it with that smart mouth."

"Hey, I know her," the second guard said, having a moment of epiphany. "She's that savage the prince brought back from the islands and put in dresses."

Put in dresses! If you only knew... Thiyo disliked the direction this conversation had taken. But he also disliked having a sword-point so close to his jugular, and continuing the conversation was his best chance to change that.

He had a small, sheathed knife in the left-side pocket under his gown. Most ladies wore pockets, so he hadn't even needed to ask Erinsk to cut discreet slits in all his petticoats. Thiyo had acquired several knives after his encounter with Barold Hyersk and the venom, just in case he ever dropped his guard and woke up in Hyersk's bed. Ilyr had scoffed at this precaution and Thiyo had nearly stabbed *him* for laughing, thinking Ilyr didn't under-stand how terrifying the experience had been.

"That's not it," Ilyr had said. *"What good is that knife? You can't even get that dress off by yourself. I'll teach you to use a sword instead."*

"Ladies don't carry swords."

"You're not a lady."

Thiyo had accepted a few lessons, but had never gotten around to acquiring a sword of his own. He regretted that now. He'd always thought the knife would do, in a pinch. It would— if only he could worm his hand into his pocket before these two realized what he was up to. "It's true." It was very hard to sound sensual and alluring in his present circumstances, but he did his best. If they wanted to know about savages in dresses, he'd tell them. "I never wore any clothes until I came here."

When Thiyo had first arrived in Nalitzva, he'd had to clamp down on a devilish impulse to add *and everyone agrees my cock is gorgeous, care for a peek?* to sentences like the one he'd just spoken. Although he'd never made that particular joke, a year at court had done nothing to curb his urge to shock these prudish mainlanders.

The sword vanquished that urge entirely.

"Yeah?" the second guard said, with obvious interest. He was standing closer to Thiyo, close enough that Thiyo could see that the straw-colored hair sticking out from under his helmet was damp with sweat. He was still the second guard in Thiyo's estimation, since he wasn't the one with the sword.

The first guard grunted. "Don't get excited," he said. "Let's just take her back to the palace. She probably didn't know no better, running around with thieves."

Back to the palace! Thiyo's only aspiration in life was to get away from the palace. Mah Yee drown these assholes in a wave and let their corpses sink to the bottom!

That was when he saw Ev standing behind the two guards. How had she gotten there? Thiyo wrenched his gaze away from her and smiled at the guards. "We don't have to go back to the palace," he said, in as sultry a tone as possible.

The first guard scowled, but the second guard gave it an instant of consideration. It was just enough time for Ev to yank his sword from its scabbard. The second guard rounded on her, but he was empty-handed. The first guard swung his sword away from Thiyo and toward Ev, and the second guard wisely got out of the way.

The blade would have slashed right across Ev's abdomen if she hadn't turned aside. As it was, it left a long gash across her left flank. Ev gasped in pain, then gritted her teeth and swept her stolen sword in an arc that cut through the air and right into the guard's side. She didn't wound him as badly as he'd wounded her, but it was enough to startle him. Her next swing chopped through his leather jerkin and into his side.

This wasn't the artful dance of Ilyr's lessons. It was fast and brutal and bloody.

Thiyo got to his feet as silently as possible and took a few careful steps away from the fight before breaking into a run. He heard the unarmed guard's boot soles slapping the cobblestones an instant later. Another few strides and Thiyo was tackled from behind, landing painfully hard. The guard came down on top of him and tried to wrestle his arms behind his back, ripping his dress in the process. Thiyo elbowed him in the gut and squirmed as hard as he could.

He twisted his arm hard and managed to free the dagger from its sheathe in his pocket. He stabbed backward blindly. The knife point punctured leather and then something softer, and the guard yowled. Thiyo wrenched the knife out and bucked the guard off his back. He rolled to the side, then levered himself back up and slit the guard's throat before he could think too hard about what he was doing.

The skin parted, blood spurted, and Thiyo gagged.

He looked back at Ev, who was staggering away from her own fight, clutching her side. The other guard was on the ground. Dead, Thiyo assumed.

They were killers.

He tore his gaze from the bodies in the street and turned to where Ev was looking. She was exhaling, barely making a noise but shaping the beginning of the word, "Where... ?"

Alizhan was standing in the street, holding the reins of two horses, a medium-sized chestnut mare and a large black gelding with white patches. The animals were bridled but not saddled.

Neither seemed terribly concerned about their circumstances. Alizhan said, "I saw you get hurt. Can you ride?"

Ev nodded, but she couldn't disguise her wooziness. Thiyo went to her and slipped her coat off her shoulders, then folded it up and pressed it against the wound in her side to staunch the flow of blood. He had to place her hand over the wad of fabric to get her to hold it there, and a moment later, they had to rearrange themselves so he could boost her onto the gelding. *Horses.* Of course depths-drowned horses were their only means of escape. What little he knew about riding would have to suffice. Thiyo put aside his fears and swung himself up behind her, wrapped his bad arm around her waist, and grabbed the reins.

Alizhan got on the other horse and Thiyo took off down the street, praying to Mah Yee that they could hide themselves somewhere before the next guards came after them.

14

ROSEFINCH SHIFT, 10TH TRIAD OF MILSHA, 761

M Y CORRESPONDENCE WITH TSARDEYA BROUGHT me joy, even as I kept things from him. My letters never mentioned you. For years, I did not share my discoveries about the effects of venom on people possessing magic after he expressed concern—as he did not believe in magic, he thought I was harming innocent people, rather than working toward a cure for the suffering they would cause to themselves and to society. And as always, he saw no connection between the two mysteries: the movements of our world and the workings of our bodies.

But from our early correspondence sprang the idea of a network of observers all over the world. Tsardeya wanted everyone in the network to monitor their own surroundings: the tremors in the ground, the smoke and ash in the air around volcanoes, or the level and smoothness of the ocean. It was an excellent idea. I became the hub of all these correspondences. And slowly but surely, I persuaded all my correspondents to report on other things. My mother. The political climate in their city-states. Business opportunities. Local folklore about magic.

I shared only enough to win their sympathies, and no more.

My exchanges with Tsardeya had taught me to keep the truth to myself. I wrote to him once of the awe and beauty of the wave that haunted my dreams—that instant of red and empty shore consumed by a crushing wall of water—and he replied that he was terribly sorry for what had happened to me. *I pray your nightmares will end*, he wrote.

In the long-forgotten folklore of Lacemakers, kept alive through a secret chain of parents promising their children that what we do is good and right, it is said we were born to ease people's pain. To take away memories that tormented and oppressed. To end nightmares.

Without knowing it, Tsardeya had wandered close to the myth of the Lacemakers in his wishes for me. But our legend is a lie and I did not want his prayers. I cherished my memories.

My own visions in sleep were nightmares, and yet they were dreams as well. Witnessing the power of that wave brought me a feeling I have never experienced in any other circumstance. That grandeur, that nearness of death... I wanted to feel it again.

15

DECENT FOLK

THIYO URGED THEIR HORSE AROUND a curve into a narrow, shaded alley. Only the prosperous neighborhoods of Nalitzva had wide, tree-lined streets that intersected at right angles. Here in Shadeside, not far from Dyevyer Erinsk's shop and the prison, the winding streets followed no logic at all. Newcomers to the neighborhood got lost easily. Thiyo was counting on that.

He dismounted, helped Ev down, and gestured for Alizhan to dismount as well. They set their borrowed horses free in the alley with a slap on their rumps. Thiyo took them a little further down, and then they turned another corner into an even narrower alley, one that no horse could fit into. Ev had her right arm slung over his shoulder for support, and the two of them had to maneuver attentively to fit between the buildings on either side.

Thiyo let Ev rest against a wall for a moment. Alizhan stood with her. He pounded his fist against an unmarked wooden door. He'd never patronized Madam Zhenev's establishment himself, but Erinsk was good friends with her. And the tailor had once said, in a particular tone he used for conveying important information, *you might like her*. Thiyo had taken that to mean that he—or Lan—had something in common with Zhenev. He'd kept the location in the back of his mind as a possible refuge in case things went wrong at court. Now that he needed it, he hoped Erinsk's longstanding business relationship with Zhenev would buy him some good will.

Behind him, Ev slumped against the alley wall. Alizhan stayed close to her, hovering, clenching and unclenching her hands. Things had gone far more wrong than his worst imaginings. His contingency plan was starting to look pathetically flimsy.

The door creaked open, just enough to pull tight half a dozen heavy chains keeping it latched, and a woman with iron grey hair appeared in the crack. Above her high, slanted cheekbones, her blue eyes narrowed. Her lips were set in a hard line. Even with that look on her face, she was beautiful. She must have been astounding in her youth. The famous Madam Nataryet Zhenev herself. "What the hell is this?"

Thiyo gave her an uncertain smile. His ruined dress was hanging from his shoulders and he was covered in blood—his own, the guard's, and Ev's. "Help, please."

Zhenev's impassive expression didn't change. "This is a private residence. We don't take kindly to being woken during this shift, when decent folk are asleep."

"Oh, don't worry, we're not decent folk at all," Thiyo joked, and then regretted it immediately. It was too close to the truth, and unlikely to win him any sympathy with the humorless madam. He adopted a more serious tone: "I'm a friend of Dyevyer Erinsk, and I can pay you."

It didn't have the desired effect.

"I don't know you, or anyone by that name, and I don't know what you'd be paying me for."

Alizhan, impatient with this exchange, said, "She's losing blood. Let us in."

Zhenev peered past Thiyo into the shadows, where she saw Alizhan standing next to Ev. She blinked, squinted, and her expression transformed. "Well, I'll be damned."

Thiyo watched in amazement as she undid all the locks and opened the door. "Help or get out of the way," she snapped. Then she bustled into the alley to help Ev up, slinging one of Ev's arms over her own strong shoulders. Thiyo hurried to support Ev from the other side. Alizhan held the door, and then closed it behind them once they were all inside the foyer of the narrow townhouse.

"Get these three a room," the madam shouted. "Number three is empty, right?"

Madam Zhenev's wasn't the high class establishment he'd pictured. Brothels were, of course, illegal in Nalitzva. A low profile was necessary. Thiyo had still imagined this one being spacious and well-appointed, just because Zhenev could afford to dress her employees in Erinsk's tailoring. Apparently she spent all her money on clothes.

Thiyo could easily reach up and touch the wooden beams of the ceiling, which made the windowless foyer feel even smaller. The room was lit with a hearth fire and candles rather than lamps. In another context, the red and orange quality of the light might have made the space feel cozy rather than dingy. As it was, Thiyo was seized by fear that the young woman who ran across the small foyer carrying a bundle of white bedsheets was going to catch them all on fire. It was hard to feel safe with Ev nearly collapsed against him.

The young woman with the sheets ran up the narrow spiral staircase to the left of the entryway, and then Madam Zhenev gestured for the three of them to follow her. It fell to Thiyo to help Ev up the stairs. He cringed every time he jostled her. She didn't comment on how badly he did the job, so she must really be in terrible pain.

Madam Zhenev helped him get Ev into the bed in room number three, while Alizhan hovered near by, twitching with anxiety. The left side of Ev's coat was stained with blood, and red was already seeping into the white sheets beneath her. Thiyo froze at the sight of it. How could a person lose that much blood and not die? He didn't know what to do.

"Get her out of those clothes," Zhenev ordered.

"Why did you let us in?" Thiyo said. The gears of his mind were turning too slowly. It had only just occurred to him to ask. And why ask? Ev was—Ev was—they should be doing something.

It was Alizhan who answered, albeit in a different language. "Some of her workers were in prison. They came home and told her two women—a little Laalvuri one and a big Adpri one—came and let them out. How many pairs like that can there be in the city? She thought it must be us."

Madam Zhenev was giving Alizhan an assessing look, but she didn't say anything. She turned toward the open door and shouted "Henny! Bring your sewing kit and some liquor!" down the stairs. And then, "A *lot* of liquor! And some clean rags for bandages!"

Another young woman appeared in the doorway a few moments later, holding a basket full of everything required. She was yawning. Her sleepy brown eyes opened wide when she got a look at the crowd in room number three. Then, all business, she set her basket on the floor and pushed a long tendril of coppery hair that had slipped free from her bun back behind her ear. She was barefoot and wearing a sleeveless white shift.

"This is Henny," the madam said. "She does neat stitches." Then, noticing that Thiyo and Alizhan hadn't followed her previous order, she glared at them. "Get to it. I didn't invite you in here so that this one could die in one of my beds!"

Thiyo picked up a pair of scissors from Henny's basket and began to cut through Ev's tunic. He cut from the bottom hem all the way up the front, until it parted to reveal the linen wrap that was binding her breasts.

That shouldn't be too surprising to anyone working here, not from what Thiyo knew of Zhenev and her clientele. Henny didn't say anything. Thiyo cut apart Ev's sleeves and Henny helped him remove the fabric. They repeated this process on her other side, until she was clothed only in the linen binding and her trousers. Henny accepted the scissors from Thiyo and began to cut through the binding, careful not to nick Ev with the scissors as she did so.

She kept a bare hand lightly touching Ev's belly.

"Your... touch," Ev murmured.

"Not a word," Henny said, narrowing her eyes at Ev. She spoke Laalvuri with a charming accent that belied her glare. Thiyo liked her. "You say anything, I'll tell everyone you're sick with fever and can't tell Day from Night. You'll have a hard time getting out of prison again in this state."

Ev closed her eyes and did as she was told.

"I am grateful to you, though," Henny said quietly. "I was in that cell."

Thiyo was still focused on Ev's comment. She'd hardly said anything since being wounded. Why remark on Henny's touch? Thiyo purposefully brushed Henny's bare hand when he took the scissors from her. The pain in his left hand dimmed.

Henny narrowed her eyes at him, aware of what he was doing. Thiyo held her gaze. She was just like Mala, then. Henny shifted so her hand was touching his more fully, and the relief he felt was beyond words.

"You're hurt, too," Henny said. Anyone else might have asked what had happened, but Madam Zhenev's employees knew better. Instead, she said, "You'll be no good to me. It'll have to be her who helps." She tilted her head toward Alizhan, who was already vigorously shaking her head.

"It's just blood," Henny said, misinterpreting Alizhan's resistance. "The work has to be done."

"You can do it, Alizhan," Thiyo said. "For Ev. Get a pair of gloves, take a deep breath, and focus on doing what she tells you."

Deprived of Henny's touch, Thiyo sank into an armchair in the corner of the room. It was only fear that kept his eyes open to see Henny cleaning out the gash and instructing Alizhan in how to hold the two sides of the wound together so Henny could stitch them shut. Alizhan's brows were drawn together and her bottom lip was between her teeth, but she was getting through her discomfort.

Exhaustion overtook Thiyo. When his eyes drifted open again, Ev had clean white bandages wrapped around her middle, and Henny and Alizhan were gone from the room. His body protested as he levered himself out of the chair and went to check on Ev.

To his surprise, when he leaned over the bed, she opened her eyes.

"Prison," Ev said, almost inaudibly.

"Yes?" Thiyo said. Had she realized something? Was she giving him a warning? It must be important if she was marshaling her strength to say something to him.

"I was right."

Thiyo stared at her for an instant. She was talking about their escape from prison and her decision to free some of the other prisoners. He'd argued against it. The whole affair felt like ancient history. His mouth hung open for a moment before any words came out. "Did you just step back from death's door to tell me 'I told you so'?"

Ev closed her eyes and gave him a small smile.

"Smug, petty, and unbearably self-righteous," Thiyo told her. "I like you better already."

Alizhan entered the room then, with clean damp hair and new clothes. She looked between the two of them. Was it exhaustion dragging her expression down, or was she hurt? "The guards came," she said, with no emotion. "You were both asleep. I hid and watched. Madam Zhenev let them in, and then one of the prostitutes—a little blond one called Ket—took all the guards by the hand as they left. They all forgot what they'd seen."

"Zhenev has someone like Merat Orzh, then. Someone who makes people forget things." She must be taking in people who'd been cast out by their families, saving them from certain death. Nalitzva was a cruel place for those with magical gifts. Zhenev was sheltering these people, and in exchange, they were using their abilities at her direction. Henny had obviously had training as a healer, and Ket was protecting Zhenev's business from prying authorities.

Alizhan nodded. "Also, *Vines* departed the harbor an hour ago."

"What?" Ev whispered.

Thiyo sat back down heavily.

"There was no way we could have arrived in time," Alizhan said. "And we can't go now, either. You can't go anywhere and the city is crawling with guards. Everyone knows what we look like. Zhenev has offered to hide us until you're well enough to get out of bed."

"How we will get home?"

"I don't know," Alizhan said. "I don't know when *Vines* will dock here again, and it's unlikely that another vessel will take us, unless we can come up with an enormous amount of money."

Thiyo almost offered, but there were only two casks of *wai* remaining in Erinsk's basement. Exchanging *wai* for money would prove tricky if Thiyo was a wanted man—or woman— and Erinsk probably deserved both as payment, besides. Thiyo hoped Zhenev had forgotten his offer to pay her, since those two casks constituted the last of his fortune. There was a wardrobe full of gowns and jewelry in his room back at the palace, all worth a great deal, but all of that was impossibly far out of reach.

"Our clothes," Ev said, and her voice was a rasp. Thiyo wanted to tell her to stop talking and save her breath, since Alizhan certainly didn't need her to speak her thoughts, but that would cut him out of the conversation entirely.

"I know," Alizhan said. "You left some money, including the ring, at Erinsk's shop. I'll see if I can get it back for us. But it won't be enough for passage across the ocean for wanted fugitives, not unless we can find Ifeleh again."

"What, then?"

Alizhan's shoulders lifted as she took a breath. "Zhenev has a wagon. She thinks Henny and Ket could get us through the gates to a village outside the city."

"And then?" Thiyo said, before Ev could.

"We go Nightward," Alizhan said. "To Estva."

"To the Starwatchers?" Thiyo said. Estva was a remote monastic outpost, the farthest Nightward of any human settlement. He'd never been there, but Ilyr had told him about it. Ilyr, who was enthusiastic and romantic about everything, had said things like *the stars, Thiyo, you can't imagine how beautiful they are,* but what Thiyo had understood from their conversation was that Estva was dark all the time and all the buildings were constructed from ice. People had to wear piles of fur before they could stand to go outside. It was sparsely populated and yet still claustrophobic. Newcomers were at risk of something called Night madness—a reaction to the darkness, the cold, and the close quarters. Ilyr, already given to anxiety, had confessed to feeling the creeping beginnings of deep-seated, irrational fear while he was there. It sounded like a desperate place. Poor workers went in hopes of striking gold in the mines, and young initiate priests of various religious orders shuffled in and out, marking the years and studying the movements of the stars. Why would anyone else go?

"It's a sanctuary of sorts. Anyone who's willing to work can stay. They take all comers and ask no questions."

At this point, Ev nodded and then nodded off.

Thiyo wished he could be so complacent about this plan. "Because they're in desperate need of servants!"

"Stay here and get executed for murder, then," Alizhan snapped. "Going back to the palace and wearing silks isn't an option."

"Is that what you think I want?" Thiyo said softly, unaccountably hurt by her outburst. He expected that sort of accusation from Ev, but his rapport with Alizhan had been easier so far. Why was she so angry with him?

He'd almost been getting along with Ev. Was there some rule that only one of them could like him at a time? The thought stopped him short. Ev obviously liked Alizhan. Was the opposite true? Had Alizhan walked in on his little exchange with Ev earlier and felt excluded? Was she *jealous*?

That was absurd. There was nothing to be jealous of. A little camaraderie after surviving a near-death encounter wasn't the same as romance. Thiyo had seen Ev and Alizhan touch hands at the wedding feast. The bond between them ran deep.

But jealousy followed its own logic.

Alizhan scowled and crossed her arms. "Don't be stupid,"

she said. "We almost died and now we're all trapped far from home and wanted for murder—and Ev and I still don't have what we came here for, and who knows if we even *can* go home without getting captured or killed—and we can't get around Nightward country without you and you're being difficult about the only possible solution. You're selfish and mean just like Ev said!"

"Ev said that?"

Alizhan continued scowling, not quite at him, but into the room at large. He supposed he deserved it. He deserved Ev's low opinion, too. She'd already made it clear that she thought he was a slut and a fool besides. She was right. And after this shift, she could add *murderer* to her list of his bad qualities. What were "selfish" and "mean" compared to that?

Why in the watery depths had she run back into danger for him, then? Why take a gash to the side and nearly die, all for the likes of him?

The answer was too easy: Ev would have done that for anyone. She'd spent precious time freeing prisoners she didn't even know.

Thiyo catalogued the wood grain in every plank of the uneven floor while he tried to convince himself that he didn't care at all what Ev thought of him. He didn't care what Alizhan thought, either. He didn't owe either of them anything. He wouldn't be in this mess if not for them.

"Yeah," Alizhan said, reading his thoughts. He hadn't bothered to conceal them. "You'd still be in prison. Or maybe you'd be *dead*."

"You'd like that, would you?"

"No!" she shouted, and he recoiled. "I like you and we need your help and I want you to be stop being mad at me," she added, fiercely.

"You're mad at me, too—you know that, right? And actually," he said, giving in to a childish urge with a smirk, "you started it."

"I'm not mad at you. I'm *right*."

This was obviously a dead end. Thiyo held up his good hand as a request for a cessation of hostilities. "Okay," he said. It was time to address something else Alizhan had just said: *We need your help. We can't get around Nightward country without you.* "So you figured it out, then."

"Figured it out? You mean your gift for languages? Was it ever a secret? Thiyo, I lived one of your memories. That power is in every thought you have. And God knows how you kept your dick a secret for a year, because for someone with a gift, you're terrible at hiding your thoughts."

"People like you are rare here," Thiyo said. "Actually, I'm not sure there *are* any people like you." He didn't acknowledge out loud that she was right. Shielding his thoughts had never come naturally to him. With concentration, he could manage it. He could have developed the skill further, but practice was tedious, so he'd never bothered.

"You weren't even being discreet at the wedding. You were speaking three languages at the table. With fake accents, but still." Fatigue must have sapped her anger. Alizhan sounded very tired. "And you didn't want to drink any *wai*, even though you talked about it like it was delicious."

"I was being purposefully indiscreet," Thiyo agreed. "I want all those people to think about how many languages I speak, and then get suspicious when Ilyr's scholarly career falls apart in my absence."

"I don't care," Alizhan said. Her roving gaze had settled on one of the white walls of the room. "I don't know why you didn't just tell us."

"Habit born of spending a year in a place that slaughters its gifted citizens," Thiyo said. He would have shrugged, but he was too exhausted to move even that much. "Look on the bright side. You came here because you wanted Ilyr to decode that book, right?"

Alizhan nodded.

"You're in luck. Ilyr never could have done that for you, but I can."

"Yes, we're all marvelously lucky, aren't we?" Alizhan said, throwing his words from earlier back at him. Then she sighed. "So you'll come with us, then?"

He was silent for a moment. Nightward was absolutely the wrong direction, if he wanted to go back to Hoi. But what was left there for him? His father was dead and his mother had always known he was a disappointment, and then he'd confirmed all her worst suspicions by abandoning his duties to run off with a foreigner. If he ran back now in disgrace, he'd receive a cold welcome. No one needed or wanted him in Hoi.

"It's just a few weeks of hiding out," Alizhan said. "We'll work and lie low and then we'll book passage on a ship that's leaving the Nightward coast from some other port. Ev and I will go back to Laalvur and stop Iriyat, and you can get yourself home safely."

"Fine," he said. He didn't have any better solutions. He'd slit a man's throat and his hand hurt and Ev had almost died and he just wanted to go back to sleep.

"Don't you dare," Alizhan said. "That chair is mine."

Thiyo glared at her through half-lidded eyes.

"Clean yourself up and take the other half of the bed," she said, pointing to the space next to Ev. "See, I'm not jealous."

He sighed, pushed himself out of the chair, and walked to the door in search of a bath and clean clothes.

"Also, if you come back in and wake Ev or jostle her or put her in any pain at all, you will regret it."

"I regret lots of things," Thiyo told her. As replies went, it was weak, but he wasn't capable of anything sharper, and it had the merit of being true. He shut the door behind him.

Snapping at Alizhan didn't make him feel better. Throwing away his ruined dress and washing the blood off his skin did. He had to ask a stranger for help to unlace his stays, but this request didn't faze the young woman he found in the hall. When he came back, he was ready to apologize, but both Ev and Alizhan were sound asleep. Thiyo blew out all the candles in the room, then crawled into bed next to Ev and joined them.

16

AN UNMARKED LETTER

M Y CHERISHED FRIEND,
PLEASE EXCUSE the tone of this letter, as the urgency of the present situation prevents me from taking the time to craft it with the delicate refinements of style that you deserve, and like a brute, I have simply shoved a few crude sentences into our private cipher.

At the moment I am writing, in your calendar, it is the second triad of Yahad.

First, regarding the revelatory contents of your most recent letter: how mischievous of you to send me after Lady Lan in the way that you did, when you knew exactly what "she" was. Only for you, my dear, will I suffer such humiliations.

That monstrous and unholy combination of man and woman—alias Lady Lan—recently resurfaced at the wedding of His Royal Highness Prince Ilyr, and knowing that the pair of them were (or are?) lovers certainly pushes a few things out of the shadows.

Thanks to this new information that you have so graciously provided to me, it now seems obvious that Lan himself is the author of the obscene *Loves*. I still suspect M in both the publication of this volume—a move calculated to provoke, distract, and undermine Ilyr, whom she views as more your pawn than hers—and in Lan's disappearance from court, but I have not yet determined where Lan was during his absence.

I cannot say how Lan encountered your pet thief and her stray, but I must assume he was responsible for getting them out of prison and into the royal wedding. (I did consider that Lan could have been in prison, but I searched all the prisons in the city after Lan's disappearance, and none of the guards had any memory of a person of Lan's description. You should have told me earlier that Lan was a man, my darling. Your little joke has hurt my work.)

Your thief tried to violate my mind, as you said she would. I was prepared.

Lan and the stray made a scene at the wedding while your pet slipped out to investigate Ilyr's private quarters. Then Ilyr took the other two into his private quarters; conversation inaudible. All three escaped. Ilyr exited quarters later in the company of M. Unsure of M's involvement; will keep you apprised.

Guards were sent out in search of "thieves," stolen goods not specified. Two guards found dead in Valor Street; one slain with sword, one with dagger. There was other blood in the street, but the tracks led nowhere. Two horses were stolen from a house on the street, but they wandered back to their owner only a few hours later.

City guards began searching for murderers matching their descriptions—your girls, that is, not the other one. Ilyr announced the death of Lady Lan that same shift.

The guards have made no progress in the search for these two fugitives, but the guards lack my skills. For me, a few triads of gossip produced a lead: Lan's preferred tailor, an elderly man named Erinsk, scorned for his suspected unnatural tendencies and thus forced to do business in a dingy little shop far from reputable Needle Street. He caters to a few members of the court who share his proclivities, and a few others with adventurous tastes in fashion if not in bed, as well as the high-end whores of his neighborhood. Erinsk's clientele struck me as a good starting point for investigating Lan's connections outside the court, and the fastest way to track down our three troublemakers.

Erinsk has a girl working in his shop, taking orders and doing the books. About fifteen years old, pale skin, black hair, freckles, an unattractive surfeit of intelligence and a total lack of manners. Name of Liyet. She herself wasn't inclined to chat, but when I praised her to Erinsk—the lies required of me in this profession do tax my spirit, that rude creature deserved no praise—he opened up. She'd been sent by his dear friend Madam Zhenev, proprietor of a nearby establishment, who knew all sorts and could always help people in need.

I kept this name in mind as I wandered the neighborhood. I saw no signs marking the establishment. But as I chatted with a book peddler near Erinsk's, it came up again. Of course, the peddler had a copy of a certain volume of filthy unnatural poetry, and he mentioned in passing how popular the volume had been at a whorehouse in a nameless alley two streets away.

Went to investigate the brothel, which was indeed run by a Madam Zhenev. Decided to keep an eye on it. So did city guards. They went away without incident—twice. One of the urchins I employed to lurk in the alley saw a blond boy-whore shaking their hands. Nothing for several triads, and then that same blond boy drove a wagon out of the city. My people followed him and reported that he passed five checkpoints and none of the guards could remember anything about him afterward.

They are headed Nightward, most likely to Estva. I assume you have people there.

. . .

PLEASE ACCEPT, my friend, my most sacred and sincere vows,
MP

17

DRIVEL

"**Y**OU'RE DEAD!" HENNY BURST INTO their room with a small blond in trousers following behind her, breathless. "It's all over the city. They rang bells and everything! They say Prince Ilyr was weeping when he announced it!"

Thiyo pushed himself up from the bed, still groggy. His face ached. He accidentally nudged Ev, and she groaned.

Before everything went to shit, Thiyo used to sleep for as long as he wanted in a gigantic bed in the palace. There were heavy curtains covering all the windows that blanketed his room in blessed, velvety darkness. He missed sleeping in almost as much as he missed having an unbroken hand and an unbroken heart.

"Wouldn't be the worst thing to happen to me lately," he grumbled, and sat back against the headboard. He brushed his hair out of his face, a gesture that was more habit than necessity ever since his stint in the prison and the unwanted haircut that had come with it. He rubbed the sleep out of his good eye. The other one was too swollen to touch.

Henny and her friend were staring at him.

"You're... *Lady* Lan, right?" Henny ventured, and her friend elbowed her in the side.

Oh. Right. He was naked. Nalitzvans always cared so much about whether people had clothes on.

"We're very sorry, your ladyship," Henny's friend said solemnly, cheeks bright red.

"This is Ket," Henny said.

Ket was an attractive young man, slender and compact, with his short hair falling in a thick wave over his blue eyes. Even when sleepy and in considerable pain, Thiyo could be counted on to notice these things. Ket shifted his weight from one foot to another and said, "Are you... like me, then?"

"Badly in need of coffee?" Thiyo joked. He knew that wasn't the answer to Ket's question, but it was the only thing he cared about at the moment. Coffee and medicine.

Thiyo squinted at the rest of the room. Ev was lying in bed next to him, possibly awake but too stubborn to admit it, certainly not moving. Alizhan was curled in the armchair in the corner, definitely awake and looking very cranky. Thiyo remembered he hadn't had a chance to apologize to her last shift. It must be hard on her, being in a house with so many people, and what's more, being forced to touch Ev while Henny stitched her up. And then, of course, there was the problem of her feelings for Ev. No wonder Alizhan had been emotional and unreasonable.

"Not exactly," Ket said, his gaze pointed at the floor. "But we will get you some coffee if that's what you'd like, your ladyship."

"Please stop calling me that. 'Thiyo' will do."

"You're not Lady Lan, then?" Ket looked dismayed by this development.

"I am when the occasion calls for it," Thiyo said. "But right now the occasion calls for coffee." He intended to stand up to follow them to the kitchen, but his body protested. The sheets rumpled over his bare legs presented another problem. "And maybe some clothes," he amended.

"Ket's a man," Alizhan said, when Henny and Ket had left the room.

"Yes," Thiyo said, not sure why this information merited restating.

"Ket asked if you were like him," Alizhan said. She spoke slowly, a sure sign she thought he was being dim. "But Henny and Ket thought you were a woman."

"I'm not dead either, but everyone seems to think so," Thiyo said. "I'll be anything they want if they bring me coffee and food."

His new best friends Henny and Ket came back to the room with clean clothes, coffee, and a tray full of bread, cheese, and cured meat. Henny handed him the mug of coffee while he was still in bed, and set her tray down on his lap. The coffee was hot and bitterly strong. Thiyo beamed at her. Smiling hurt.

His bliss meant nothing to Alizhan, who said, "You're prostitutes."

Henny smiled and shrugged. "Have to earn a living somehow."

"Not me," Ket said, scrunching up his face. "Not anymore. Madam Zhenev keeps me around for other things."

"You make people forget," Alizhan said.

Henny had shushed Ev for trying to talk about her ability, and her eyes went wide with horror at Alizhan's bluntness. Thiyo sympathized, after a year of keeping deadly secrets in Nalitzva.

"Place like this, it comes in handy," Ket said, more placid at being found out. Ket was an impressively even-tempered young man. Thiyo had snapped at people for less. Then again, the power to erase someone's memory would be a source of confidence and calm, and the idea was almost enough to make Thiyo envious. He had no such protection from discovery, and neither did Henny. "I don't mind helping. I'd probably be dead if not for Madam Zhenev. Nalitzva's not kind to people like me."

"People who make other people forget?" Alizhan said. "People with magic?"

"Yes," Ket said. "And people who don't fit into someone else's idea of what it means to be a man."

Thiyo had been cranky and selfish with Ket earlier, and now he felt guilty. Ket had wanted to forge some kind of connection. Maybe Thiyo should say something nice or reassuring. "Not everywhere is as strict as Nalitzva," Thiyo said. "Not everywhere is obsessed with categories. Where I come from, we have all kinds of men and women and people who are both or neither and we just let them live their lives."

"Where you come from, they kill any outsiders who try to enter," Alizhan said dryly.

So much for Thiyo's attempt at being nice. What Alizhan said was true enough. The prohibition against foreigners protected the islanders from disease, corruption, and the deadly greed of mainlanders, who would hunt medusas to extinction, given the chance. The elders had only made one exception to the rule, and that had been Ilyr. He hadn't brought disease or corruption. He'd come and he'd left and he'd taken Thiyo away with him—an indifferent outcome for the nation of Hoi, and a devastating one for Thiyo.

Because Nalitzva was just an endless succession of prisons within prisons, each one lonelier and more hopeless than the last, starting with the glittering palace where you could do anything you wanted except tell the truth.

"Still," Ket said. "I'm glad to know a place like that exists. It makes me think we could make one of our own."

"It's not just Ket. We'd all probably be dead if not for Zhenev," Henny said. "The difference is just which bits of our bodies have been declared a crime against the laws of man and the gods." She held up a hand and wiggled her fingers.

"I feel what other people feel," Alizhan volunteered. "And I know their thoughts. And if I touch them, sometimes they know mine. Or sometimes they pass out."

Henny gaped. "And they don't kill you for that, down in Laalvur?"

"I hide it well," Alizhan said, which Thiyo thought was up for debate. He sipped his coffee. "Shut up, Thiyo. That's not the point. You touch people." This last part was clearly addressed to Henny and Ket, even though Alizhan was staring into space.

Ket nodded. "It took a long time to learn how."

"Ket's good," Henny said. "He's been teaching me better control."

Ket blushed again, and Thiyo didn't miss the way he looked at Henny. Perhaps those lessons in control weren't pure altruism. They were a lovely pair, well-suited in their contradictions. Ket was wiry, his face sharp-featured and angular under the blond wave of his bangs, but his manner was gentle and shy. Although, again, a person with Ket's power could afford to seem gentle. Henny was taller than Ket, but softer in appearance, with big brown eyes and a figure that was evident even under her loose dressing gown. But her softness was only a façade. In conversation, she'd been far pricklier than Ket. Was that an irony, given her healing ability, or a necessity, given where she'd found herself in life?

Would Alizhan be an unwelcome intruder in their private lessons? Thiyo didn't care. He was emphatically for any plan that involved teaching Alizhan better control. If she hadn't been so frayed after helping Henny with Ev's stitches, she might not have been so angry with him afterward. Night madness was enough of a danger in the dark, icy confines of Estva without an *uheko* who couldn't handle close quarters.

"Henny, could you touch Thiyo?" Alizhan said. "He's in pain and it's making him grouchy. He's very *emotional* and *unreasonable*. It's distracting."

"Wh—" *Little eavesdropping wretch.* Thiyo was tired and beaten down and not shielding his thoughts, and Alizhan was abusing her power. And he wasn't being grouchy. He was being a realist. Besides, Thiyo still had questions to ask. They'd hardly had a chance to discuss anything important. Ilyr had announced his death to the city, for Mah Yee's sake. What did that mean? Was there a funeral? How grand would it be? And then there was the book to be deciphered. He couldn't work on that if he was high as a kite. "I'm fine. I'll be fine."

"He's not and he won't," Alizhan said. Thiyo resented being treated like a child, and he wanted to spite her by proving how good he felt. But as soon as he thought about standing up, he realized how right Alizhan was, depths drown her.

Alizhan leapt up from her chair, retrieved the tray from Thiyo's lap and then walked back across the room with her prize. She offered a biscuit to Ket on her way, which he graciously accepted. Thiyo did his best to ignore this little victory march.

"He *is* in worse shape than I thought," Henny said, coming to his bedside and giving him an appraisal. Thiyo normally welcomed attention to his naked body from anyone beautiful, but Henny was less than appreciative. "Couldn't see all those bruises until he was naked. And those fingers need splinting."

Henny brushed her fingers against the back of his hand. As reluctant as Thiyo was to give her his coffee, he found his grip on the mug loosening.

He'd forgotten how good the absence of pain felt.

Thiyo was distantly aware of Alizhan appearing at Henny's side and taking the mug of coffee from her. She drank. She spit her mouthful of coffee back into the mug with a splash. "You *drink* that?"

"I don't, but Zhenev can't live without it, and Henny likes it, too. It's all the rage," Ket said, when it became clear that Thiyo had no intention of answering. "An import from the islands. Expensive, too." This last sentence sounded like a mild rebuke to Thiyo's ears, but Alizhan would neither notice nor care.

Alizhan shoved the mug of coffee—or spit and coffee—toward Ket, and he took it before it spilled. "I thought it would be like tea but instead it tastes like bitter dirt."

Thiyo felt too serene to take offense.

"I can put you to sleep for this, if you'd rather," Henny said to Thiyo, ignoring the exchange at the foot of the bed. "I'll do what I can for your hand. You might need to put that arm in a sling, just to keep yourself from banging it up more than you already have. Not much to be done about the bruises."

Henny's touch was not just the absence of pain, but the presence of something wonderful. Better than coffee. Better than wine. Better than sex. With his eyes closed and his head lolling against the pillows, Thiyo hummed happily in response. "You can do anything you want to me, Henny."

Henny made a sound somewhere between a laugh and a sigh of disgust. In Nalitzvan, she said, "Whatever you're talking, it ain't Nalitzvan. Some time I'll find a man who don't go up in a cloud of steam every time I touch him."

"Ket," Thiyo said, as a friendly suggestion.

That elicited a trill of laughter from Henny and silence from the other side of the room. Henny kept talking after that, but Thiyo didn't understand a word of what she said.

———

EV SPENT two triads in and out of consciousness, waking just long enough to receive bizarre and confusing updates on the world: the city was in mourning for Lan, Alizhan had accidentally knocked out Ket, and Thiyo hated being injured and stuck in bed almost as much as Ev did, but he hated reading *A Natural History of the World* even more.

"So let's read a different book," Ev said. She was awake now, and not feverish, but Henny had ordered her to stay in bed. Henny couldn't be with her all the time, so to ease Ev's pain, Henny brought her a clear, golden tea to drink as a painkiller every shift. It left a half-sweet, half-sharp taste in her mouth, like cut grass, and it made the edges of everything go fuzzy before she drifted to sleep. Ev hated sleeping all the time, and she hated feeling drugged even more, but she still needed the tea. She still hadn't grown accustomed to waking up in the little room, feeling as dim as the light that filtered through their purple drapes. She wanted a distraction.

"Didn't you two sail across the ocean specifically to get me to read *this* book?" Thiyo said.

"Well, we didn't know you were going to whine about it the whole time," Alizhan said. She was curled in her chair in the corner, like a cat that had retreated to its hiding place to lick its wounds after a fight. Alizhan probably hadn't enjoyed knocking out Ket any more than Ket had enjoyed being knocked out. It had been almost half a shift, and Alizhan hadn't moved from that spot.

"I was serious about the book," Ev said, before Thiyo could snap at Alizhan. Lots of time in this very small room was getting to all of them. The injuries and the feeling of being hunted weren't helping anyone calm down, either. She clenched her hands in the thick, red wool blanket that covered the bed. "I don't care what Thiyo does, but *I* want something to read. I'm not good for anything else right now."

Alizhan stretched herself out, stalked from the room, and

returned a few moments later with a book. "This is Ket's," she said, handing it to Ev. No mention of how he was recovering from their last interaction, but if he was lending books, he couldn't be too sick—or too resentful. "He said he has others, if you'd rather read something else."

The text on the front of the little tan book had worn away, but Ev recognized the scrolling design around the edges. It was a volume of *The Sunrise Chronicles*. Ev had read them all dozens of times, but then, Alizhan knew that already. Ev smiled.

Thiyo shot a disdainful look at the book's spine and said, "Ugh, that garbage."

"You shut your mouth," Alizhan said, sitting back down in the chair and pulling her knees under herself. "We love them. I've loved them since I was a kid."

"You have?" Ev knew Alizhan liked the books, but they'd only had one conversation about them.

"Yeah," Alizhan said. "You were always reading them or thinking about them, so I asked Iriyat to get them so I could read them, too. I knew all the endings by then, of course, because of you."

"Sorry."

Alizhan smiled at the floor. Ev wondered, then, if Alizhan had deliberately put distance between them before starting this conversation, before revealing something sweet and yearning and vulnerable about herself. If Alizhan was curled up like a cat in that chair, she was one of those cats who'd never directly approach you or jump into your lap, but would always arrange to be near you, as if by coincidence.

Those cats usually ran away if you tried to touch them.

And with that thought, Ev's little metaphor lost its charm.

"It never mattered about the endings," Alizhan murmured. "I loved them anyway." She looked up for a moment to glare at

Thiyo. "Because they're *great*. I couldn't put them down. Why wouldn't you like them? What's wrong with you?"

"They're sickeningly sentimental," he said. "And so lazy. All the writers ever do is put a man and a woman in the same place, have them look at each other, and we're all supposed to assume immediately that it's love."

"People do that, though," Alizhan insisted. "It happens all the time. Not just with men and women. People look at each other and are overcome with—well, I guess it's usually more like lust than love. But I do think it's possible to fall in love instantly."

"But that's not what happens in *Sunrise*," Ev said. "Have you even read them?"

"Why would I waste my time?" Thiyo said. "A big strong man rescues a dainty woman. The prose is stuffed full of unbearably overwrought descriptions. Members throb. They fall in love. The end."

He was so wrong that Ev laughed out loud. "That's not it at all. How can you judge them without reading them?"

"And what do you have against throbbing members?" Alizhan said.

"I'd love to have something against a throbbing member, but this brothel is in shockingly short supply," Thiyo replied.

"Ket did tell me he had other books," Alizhan said. "Maybe you'd like one of them better. In particular, he mentioned a scandalous book of poems that everyone's been talking about. It had a funny little title. I think it was just called *Loves*."

Thiyo blanched.

"Don't be cruel, Alizhan," Ev said. Thiyo was an elitist asshole, but he'd been beaten for writing those poems, and she wasn't going to kick him while he was down.

"It's in Nalitzvan," Thiyo said coolly. "You couldn't read it anyway."

Ev turned the book in her hands to look at the spine and saw that the title was printed in Nalitzvan. "Oh." She opened it to its first page, foolishly expecting the inside of the book to be easier to read. In theory, she knew how to read the foreign script, but she had to sound it out like a child. With such regular doses of Henny's tea fogging up her head, the novel would be slow going, even if she had read it before. "I guess I could use the practice."

Thiyo sighed. He held out his left hand expectantly.

Ev shut the book and brought it closer to herself as though she were protecting it. "What do you want with it, if you hate it so much?"

"Nothing," Thiyo said. "But you saved my life and almost got killed in the process. I suppose I can read you a chapter of this drivel."

"You just don't want to read any more of *A Natural History of the World* because it makes you feel stupid that you can't figure out what all that blue ink is," Alizhan said.

"I haven't noticed *you* making any progress on that count," Thiyo snapped. "And thank you, Alizhan, for rendering my very small gesture of gratitude hollow and self-serving."

"You did a pretty good job of that yourself," Ev pointed out. Earlier, she'd thought of Alizhan as a cat, and the comparison was tempting in Thiyo's case, too. Ev felt as though the two of them were circling her with their tails whipping. Ludicrous.

"Are you refusing my offer?"

Ev put the book in his hand, moving gingerly so as not to disturb her stitches. "Please," she said, settling back against her pillows. "Go ahead."

"She has it almost memorized, so we'll know if you do a bad job translating," Alizhan said, a little too eagerly.

"I never do," Thiyo said, and opened the book.

DESPITE HIS GRUDGING offer to read a single chapter of "drivel" to Ev, Thiyo was a good reader. The words flowed smoothly. If Ev hadn't known he was looking at a text in Nalitzvan and speaking it aloud in Laalvuri, she never would have guessed. Thiyo never paused to consider his translation, although once or twice he'd paused to groan or make a snide comment.

Commentary aside, Thiyo's reading was a pleasant distraction. Without it, Ev thought about how slowly she was healing, and how trapped they were in their little room at Zhenev's, and how their best option—once she could travel—was to go *farther* from home, even though they'd left Kasrik and Mar and Eliyan and her parents and all those kids without any protection from Iriyat. Ev even felt afraid for Vatik, the head of the guards at Varenx House, who was risking his life by defying Iriyat's orders in secret. All of Laalvur was in peril, and Ev and Alizhan had abandoned the city. It chilled Ev to think of what Iriyat might be doing in their absence. And Ev didn't even know how she and Alizhan would get home from Estva, let alone stop Iriyat.

That was what Ev thought about when she was awake and lucid, which admittedly wasn't very often.

"Thiyo was very disappointed when you fell asleep after chapter one," Alizhan informed her. Ev had no way of knowing if Alizhan was reporting Thiyo's real thoughts or teasing him. "He wanted to keep going."

"Even sentimental garbage is preferable to *A Natural History of the World*," Ev said, smiling.

Thiyo was sitting in bed next to her with a handful of loose pages spread over his lap. His right arm, with his hand now splinted and bandaged, was holding *A Natural History* open while he attempted to compare the strange blue markings with his own transcriptions. The book was desiccated from being stored in salt, its pages crackling and dry, and it rustled whenever Thiyo moved. Somehow the salt had caused the blue ink to become visible. "I will get this," he assured them, chewing his lip and looking from one text to another. The loose pages on the bed were covered in text that was neither the angular, separate script of Nalitzva nor the looping, connected writing of Laalvur. "Do you see this string of characters? And this one? They're the same. It must be a repeated word. There are other repetitions, too."

"It's long," Ev remarked.

"This isn't even all of it," Thiyo said. "Pages and pages of text written on top of another text, in invisible ink *and* a language that no one can read. At that point, why even bother to write anything down?"

"It has to be Iriyat's, right?" Ev said. "She must really have wanted to preserve something. She must have wanted to communicate something with—someone. Whoever could read that language."

"No one," Thiyo said. "No one can read this. It looks like no other script in the world."

"How do you know that?" Ev said, and when he looked at her, Thiyo's smile was slow and sure and smug. "Really? You know *all* of them?"

"Except the one we need him to know," Alizhan said.

"*How* do you know all of them?" Ev said, still stuck on this point. "And if you know all the others by magic, why can't you read this one?"

"It doesn't work like that," he said. "I was born with a gift, but I still had to be trained. Everyone needs to be trained." His gaze flicked toward Alizhan, but then he continued quickly: "I spent my whole childhood with an old *ohokutho*—that's a person who remembers everything—reciting the epics of different cultures at me, until I knew them all."

"Is that what you are? *Ohokutho*?"

Thiyo shook his head. "I remember words, and sounds, and

structures, but that's it. Not experiences or images or conversations or what I ate for a particular meal a decade ago. I don't have perfect recall of everything that's ever happened to me. But the words stick with me. Although I don't need to have encountered a word before to understand it. I can't explain it. I need a little exposure to the language, but after that I just... develop a sense of what things mean."

"Like looking into water," Alizhan said. Ev had no idea what she meant. No longer concerned with Thiyo's failure to decode the book, Alizhan was smiling. "A current of sounds with their meanings shimmering underneath."

Thiyo stared at her. "You remembered that. I've never said that—not in those words—to anyone. But yes, that's how it is." He shook his head and composed himself. "And in a sense, all magic is like that. A sensing of what lies beneath. It's what you do, too."

"Sense what lies beneath people's outsides, you mean."

"Yes. Some people can transform what they sense. Mala and Henny sense pain and transform it into pleasure. Ket's like you, in a way—he can read minds if he's touching people. And he can transform what he finds."

"I can't do that."

Thiyo arched an eyebrow. "You've done it to me *and* Ev. And every person you've ever knocked unconscious."

"That's not what Ket does."

"I suspect you could do what Ket does if you practiced."

Alizhan shuddered.

A good opportunity to redirect the conversation. "So how long will it take you to... sense this?" Ev asked.

"I don't know. But it will come," he insisted. He rubbed at his eyes, smearing a trail of ink across his face. For an instant, Ev imagined herself licking the pad of her thumb and brushing it over his temples and the bridge of his nose, the way her mother had always tried to clear the smudges from her face when she was a child. But Thiyo wasn't her family—he was hardly even her friend—and she couldn't reach out and touch his face like that. It would be intrusive, and in her current state, extremely painful.

The ink streak wasn't a terrible addition to his face, besides. It would soften whatever arrogant thing he planned to say next.

"I'm a genius, after all."

"Yes," Ev agreed. If she looked at Alizhan, Ev would giggle, so she held Thiyo's dark gaze as solemnly as she could. "But I bet even geniuses need to take breaks."

"Really," Thiyo said flatly. "This whole time, you've just been angling for chapter two."

But he was reaching for *The Sunrise Chronicles* without another word of encouragement, so Ev lay back and listened. She didn't intend to mention how much less reluctantly Thiyo had offered to read the second chapter, and she hoped Alizhan would leave him alone, too. There were so few pleasant things in her life at the moment.

The next triad, it was Thiyo who brought up the possibility of reading chapter three, and when Ev eagerly accepted, he did the whole thing without any mockery. By chapter four, Thiyo had crafted different speaking styles to distinguish the characters. Vesper, the hero, had a steady, deep voice. Privately, Ev thought Thiyo was making him sound like Ilyr. And Aurora, the smart, prideful princess, bore more than a passing resemblance to Lan. Their banter ricocheted back and forth, making Ev forget where she was stuck, and why.

But she did heal, and every time she woke up, her head was clearer and she was in less pain. She could sit up now, and get out of bed, and walk short distances. Ev wasn't ready to fight anyone, but she would just have to hope their escape from Nalitzva wouldn't require that of her. It was time to go.

18

IRIYAT TO ILYR, LYREBIRD SHIFT, THE 17TH TRIAD OF YAHAD, 764

LYREBIRD SHIFT, 17TH TRIAD OF Yahad, 764

I lyr,

An urgent matter spurs my hand.

More urgent and tragic even than the loss of your Lady Lan. I know she was dear to you, and I was grieved to hear of her death. I know she was a treasured friend and colleague, and that she helped you with your writings.

How strange, that the deepest grief is so often hand in hand with the highest joy. I hope your new marriage is bringing you much of the latter. Your life is in tumult, my friend, and soon we shall write each other true letters to discuss it.

But for now I have no time to dwell on that.

I have received terrible news from Adappyr. Two different sections of the city have caved in over the last week. Whole neighborhoods are blocked off and impassable due to the collapses. People are starving behind the collapsed walls, or buried under the rubble. It guts me to learn of such random loss of life. I have hired the Lampgreen Company to trade their swords for shovels and commanded them to go to Adappyr to dig out anyone they can.

I am sure you are wondering what this has to do with you.

I am plagued by the notion that this tragedy might have been prevented, if only we knew more about the workings of our world. For it must have been a quake that caused the formerly solid walls and columns of Adappyr to crumble and cave in—what else could ruin these structures that have stood for centuries?

Could these collapses herald an eruption? A wave? Are they a sign of more to come?

I beg you, for the sake of our Adpri friends, and for our own sakes, to save us all. We are in danger. I am but a messenger. You will be the hero.

I know you remember well our conversation about the islands three years ago. I know, from your tender letters of recent years, that you traveled there and found a fullness of the heart worth more than any treasure. I know you care for those lands and those people as you do your own, and as I do my own, and we must now extend that feeling to the people of Adappyr, and the people of all the world.

I must ask you to travel to the islands again. Lives depend on it.

It pains me to capitalize on the death of your dear friend Lady Lan, but her passing provides you with the perfect cover to return to the islands. Say you are bringing home her remains, and go at once. To have survived so long in their home amid the towering ferocity of the ocean, the islanders must possess knowledge of the events that shake our world—quakes, waves, eruptions—and you must bring it back to us.

Further instruction is enclosed. Destroy this letter.

. . .

IRIYAT

19

NIGHTWARD

Z HENEV'S WAGON JOLTED OVER THE cobblestones and Ev bit her lip. Henny was holding her hand, and Ket was driving as slowly as possible, but movement was still painful.

The week had its good moments, but it had mostly been dull, when Ev was foggy from the medicine, or tense, when the whole brothel went silent because another guard was at the door. As grateful as Ev was to Madam Zhenev and everyone who lived in her house, leaving was a relief.

Or it would have been, if she weren't rattling around in the back of a cramped, dark wagon. But once this wagon ride was over, they'd find some village inn, and that would be a relief. No matter how grungy the rooms were, they would be immobile. It would be a long journey to Estva, but Henny and Ket had offered to accompany them all the way there. Ev wouldn't have to ride a horse or walk long distances.

Alizhan and Thiyo were sitting in the back of the wagon in unnatural silence. Alizhan had somehow convinced Thiyo to accompany them Nightward, early in the week when Ev had been unconscious, and whatever they'd said to each other, their rapport had hardened from something easy and fluid to something brittle. They were still wary of each other.

In some ways, they had all recovered.

Ev's wound wasn't infected. It was healing clean.

Alizhan had suffered a nearly lethal fit from being in a crowded street in Laalvur only last month, but their stay in Zhenev's very full house had hardly affected her. She'd practiced controlling her touch with Henny, Ket, and Thiyo throughout the week. And here she was in a wagon with three other very tense people, breathing as easily as it was possible to under the circumstances. The prospect of living in extremely close quarters in Estva—and perhaps her brief touch with Ev at the wedding—had lent new urgency to her practice.

Thiyo's broken fingers were splinted, his hand was bandaged, and Henny had even convinced him to wear a sling. She thought that if he exercised his fingers properly once the splints came off, he might regain most of the use of his hand. Ev wished she'd been unconscious for that conversation. Thiyo had delighted in asking questions about what exactly constituted a "proper" exercise of his fingers. Henny, a professional, was amused, not abashed. Ev had wanted to die.

In other ways, Ev thought they might never recover.

She had killed a man. Perhaps it was only fair his blade had scarred her side for the rest of her life.

The wagon halted. Had they already arrived at the city walls? Ev heard a brief, indistinct conversation outside: Ket and the guards. Ev held her breath, but only a moment later, they began to move again.

"They forgot to check, just like that," Alizhan said, keeping her voice down.

"That was an extra stop," Henny said. "We can't be at the walls yet."

They made slow progress. There were two more stops before

they reached the city walls, one at the walls, and one outside the city. All the stops followed the same pattern: Ket had a conversation with the guards while the four of them held their breath in hiding, and after a few tense moments, the wagon began to move again. The guards never looked inside the wagon.

"A useful man to have around, Ket," Thiyo said. "Nice when they're on our side."

"Thank you," Ev said to Henny. "We'll have to make sure Ket knows how grateful we are, too."

"Anyone suspected of 'unnatural tendencies' is put to death," Henny said. Ev thought Henny meant this as a reminder of the risks Ket was taking, but she continued, "We might've died in that prison, if not for you. We owe you."

"Is that why you were in prison? They caught you?"

There was just enough light through the wooden slats for Ev to see the coppery glint of Henny's hair as she shook her head. "Not using magic. Ket and I went out dancing. There was a raid. Ket could have got away, but instead he got himself arrested along with me like a damn fool. He thought he could get me away from the guards. But there were too many for him."

"Couldn't you get yourself away from the guards?" Alizhan asked.

"With my touch?"

"You put Thiyo to sleep," Alizhan pointed out.

"I can't do that with a flick of my fingers!" Henny said. She must have witnessed Alizhan knocking Ket unconscious, the one bad moment in their week of lessons. "It takes concentration. And I'd've needed four more arms for that many guards, and a lot more strength, besides. And once Ket got himself caught, I just wanted to make sure we stayed together. We thought we'd be able to slip out of the cell, but we had to wait for the right moment. We were in there six triads before you opened the door. The guards almost never came in, and besides, there were those other women in the cell, and we were worried they'd turn on us if they figured out what we were."

"Even if you were helping them escape?" Alizhan said.

Henny nodded.

"This place never ceases to amaze," Thiyo murmured.

"People are afraid of us," Henny said. "Usually it's because they don't know anything about us. Other times, it's because they do."

This last sentence was uttered with a look in Alizhan's direction. Alizhan didn't react visibly, but she did say, "It was an accident."

"I know," Henny said. They must be talking about Alizhan knocking out Ket. "But it was one hell of an accident."

The conversation lapsed into silence. Ev closed her eyes, but even with Henny's help, sleep was impossible in the rattling wagon. They paused occasionally along the way to rest the horses and stretch their legs. Ev stayed in the wagon. Getting up was too much trouble unless she absolutely had to, and every time Henny left her, even lying still and breathing made her side ache. It was a long time before they rolled to a stop at the village.

"This'll be Ernyetzva," Henny said. "Would you believe it's the farthest from home I've ever been?"

Alizhan leapt out of the back of the wagon, eager to be away from them, and Ev heard her gasp. It was several long, uncomfortable moments before Ev could join her, since both Henny and Thiyo had to support her as she sat up and climbed down from the wagon.

Ev gasped, too.

She'd never seen the sky so dark. It was as if God has spilled ink over the dome of the heavens, and it had washed down to stain the walls of the sky Night blue.

Night blue. She'd never understood that phrase before.

"Look," Thiyo breathed, pointing at something just over the

horizon. Little white gems of light twinkling against the blue. "Stars."

THE NIGHT SKY lost its charm for Alizhan about five minutes after she first saw it in Ernyetzva. Night was *cold*. Her body started trembling uncontrollably, and every time she sucked in a breath, it shocked the back of her throat. She hated it.

Meanwhile, five triads and five sleepy villages later, everyone else was still thrilled. Henny and Ket thought this whole affair was a grand adventure, instead of a terrifying slide into uncertainty that was taking Alizhan and Ev farther and farther from home. And Thiyo and Ev wouldn't shut up about how beautiful the sky was, and they talked about the stupid *poetry* of it every time they went outside.

So much for Thiyo being worldly and cynical. So much for Ev being practical and stoic. They were unbearable romantics, both of them. They kept talking about how clean the air was, how pure the snow, how stunning the stars.

Alizhan's snot was frozen inside her nose. Where was the poetry in that?

And weren't they cold? Alizhan was shivering even inside the stupid smelly fur coat that Thiyo and Ev had bought for her, and she had her hands shoved down into her pockets, her equally furry hat pulled down as low as possible, and her chin tucked into the thick collar of her coat. The fur of her collar was tickling her nose.

"And to think *you* had to convince *me* to come here," Thiyo said. Somehow he and Ev both looked heroic and dashing in their furs. If Thiyo could sense her thoughts, he'd say *of course I do, darling*, which was exactly why Alizhan didn't say anything.

"You're so small and yet so full of rage," he continued, amused. "Why is that combination so endearing?"

"Next time you have an inappropriate thought, I'm telling everyone."

"Please. I'll tell them myself."

"You'd talk yourself to death, Alizhan," Ket pointed out. "And he wouldn't even be embarrassed. You need a better plan."

"And some of us don't want to hear Thiyo's inappropriate thoughts, so we'd all suffer," Ev said. She took a step closer to Alizhan. "Here, you poor thing, you look miserable."

There was one nice thing and one nice thing only about the cold: Ev could wrap her arms around Alizhan and hug her tight with no worries. With so many layers between them, there was no danger of accidental touch. Ev was the warmest, safest, most solid and reliable thing in the world, and if she hadn't recently been wounded, Alizhan would squeeze her as hard as she could. Happily, Ev was generous with her hugs, so Alizhan could make up for all the lonely years where only Iriyat had touched her, and never as much or as affectionately as she wanted.

Ev yearned for this—and more—just as much as Alizhan did. Alizhan could feel it like a second embrace.

Somehow, Alizhan would learn to do this without protection, as casually and carelessly as anyone else. She'd thought of touching Ev's hand at the wedding so often it was a miracle the memory wasn't faded and cracked like an old, well-loved book. Next time, she wouldn't need *wai*.

"I'll listen to your inappropriate thoughts, Thiyo," Henny was saying, "but men usually pay me for that sort of thing."

"You'll have to educate me," he said. "As of right now, all of Nalitzva has read mine and I haven't seen one single tyek of profit."

He pulled his bag out of the wagon and headed for the door of the village inn.

"He made a joke about it," Ev marveled. "He must be feeling better."

The words had tasted frosty and bitter, and it hadn't been the Night air. But Ev couldn't sense what Alizhan could. Thiyo might joke and tease, but he was hurting, and she didn't know how to help him.

———

HOURS LATER, lying awake, Alizhan regretted mentioning Thiyo's inappropriate thoughts. It had been difficult to sleep for the whole journey, surrounded by people, but now her mind had seized on the moment and wouldn't let go.

Ev had *lied*.

She did want to know Thiyo's most intimate thoughts, no matter what she said.

She wanted Alizhan, too, of course. No doubts about that. But it was possible to desire more than one person at a time. Alizhan had sensed from the beginning that there was an attraction simmering between Ev and Thiyo. Ev was deep in denial about it and would be incredulous, embarrassed, and upset if Alizhan brought it up. "I don't even like him," she'd say, and Thiyo would laugh and agree that she didn't. But he'd be pleased, because he was always pleased when people were attracted to him, and because he liked it when Ev was flustered, and because he was attracted to her, too. And they were starting to enjoy each other's company.

If Alizhan didn't mention it, neither of them was likely to act on the feeling—Ev being in denial and Thiyo being heartbroken —but it was there all the same.

That was the question that kept her awake: *should* she mention it? So far, she hadn't wanted to explain it to them. Let Ev think her feelings for Thiyo were pure irritation. Let Thiyo sit with his sadness. Let the two of them be oblivious and stubborn together. But was she being selfish? Was she jealous, like Thiyo had said at Madam Zhenev's?

Alizhan wanted Ev, but she also wanted Ev to be happy. It would be a long time—if ever—before Alizhan could touch Ev the way she wanted to be touched. And Alizhan wanted Thiyo to be happy, too. What if they'd be happier if she told them? After the initial embarrassment and resistance, they might be.

Thiyo and Ev could touch each other, here and now, with no effort and no trouble. Maybe she should encourage them to.

She'd know if they did, of course. She'd know every last stroke and moan.

And there was the real problem. Did she want that? Was it wrong to want that? It felt wrong, the way that Merat Orzh publishing Thiyo's poetry without his knowledge was wrong, even if Thiyo was shameless the rest of the time.

It had taken Alizhan weeks to admit to Ev that she could feel attraction and desire, that no matter how impossible it felt, she wanted to learn to act on them. She wanted to touch Ev, to kiss her, to do the things she saw in Ev's dreams—even if it took years. But confessing that to Ev had made her feel like she was standing on the edge of a cliff. The view made her heart soar, but one wrong step and she'd plummet to her death.

And now she wanted to make things *more* complicated? The whole situation was absurd. A hysterical laugh bubbled up and she suppressed it.

There was no way she could tell them. Alizhan rolled over, pressed her face into the pillow, and prayed for sleep.

ALIZHAN KEPT her thoughts confined to the artificial darkness of the bedroom. She was so quiet, riding in their wagon the next triad, that Ev gave her a reassuring one-armed squeeze without being asked. Alizhan was grateful, but not surprised.

Then, at their first stop, Thiyo drew her aside to ask what was wrong.

Out here, the road cut through snowy plains and the darkness permeated everything. The silence was only interrupted by their wagon wheels rolling. It terrified Alizhan to contemplate how much of the world was plunged into darkness. The natural state of things here was lightless and soundless. The pinprick stars above were an interruption, just like the sound of their wagon and their voices on the road.

None of that was really what was wrong. Thiyo was standing close to her, waiting for an answer, the air around him tinged with concern. "Nothing. The cold."

"I deserve a better lie than that."

"Do you want to talk about what's making *you* unhappy?" Alizhan asked, because she knew the answer.

"Nothing. The cold."

"Exactly. Except it's an even worse lie in your case, because you love it here." Would they talk about their feelings if they were friends? Were they friends? Alizhan could read Thiyo some of the time, and she still didn't know. He was helping them, but his motivations were mixed. Occasionally, he thought of himself as repaying a debt, but he wasn't like Ev. He didn't have a strong sense of duty. If there was somewhere he wanted to be more, he'd already be gone. But there wasn't. The only thing keeping him from feeling totally lost and aimless was his sense of curiosity. He'd never met anyone like Alizhan or Ev, and he'd never seen the script that was in their mysterious book. Alizhan had brought him a puzzle he couldn't solve, something no one else had ever been able to do.

"Well... no," Thiyo said. "I don't love the cold. Or the

constant dark. But I've never been so far Nightward. I'm interested in it. It's new."

And that was it. Like the snow and the stars, Alizhan and Ev
and all their problems were a novelty. They'd have Thiyo's attention until a better distraction appeared.

That was the key to making Thiyo hurt less. A simpler
method than trying to play matchmaker. He liked riddles. "Have
you made any progress with the book?"

"You know I haven't," he said. "It's impossible to work when
we're on the road. Maybe you can help me. Tell me about the
book. No, actually––tell me everything. How you got here. What
you're caught up in. And Iriyat."

Parts of the story had come out during their stay at Madam
Zhenev's, but Alizhan and Ev had never told him the whole
thing in order. They'd glossed over a lot. If she were being
honest, Alizhan could acknowledge that she was afraid to talk or
think about Iriyat—afraid of what she might have to do to stop
her—but it was always easier to be honest with other people
than with herself.

The others had finished their business, and Henny was
helping Ev settle back into the wagon. Alizhan and Thiyo went
to climb in behind them. Thiyo sat down next to Alizhan so they
could continue their conversation. He'd come alert at her
mention of the book and now it was all he wanted to think
about. There'd be no wriggling out of his questions.

"Why Iriyat?" Alizhan asked, but she already knew. The
book was a locked box and he was feeling his way around the
edges. Weighing it and tapping it and shaking it, pressing his ear
to the outside to listen for what might be inside. But Alizhan
didn't want him examining her insides as well as the book's.

"The book belongs to her, doesn't it? I've heard enough to
gather that she's the one you're running from. And you think she
looks like that shriveled-up old bitch Merat Orzh."

Ev spoke up. She was lying on a pallet they'd made in the bottom of the wagon. She could sit up now, but still found it easier to rest if she was flat on her back. On the other side of the wagon, Henny was sitting on a bench, but she had one hand on Ev's. "She was actually quite beautiful for a woman of her age."

Thiyo huffed in disagreement.

Alizhan had no opinion on Merat Orzh's face, but she knew what Ev was thinking. "Rich people," she said with a smile. "They don't break themselves with labor, and they can afford whatever creams and powders and treatments are in style to keep themselves looking young."

"Who are we talking about?" Henny asked. "And can I rob her powder room?"

"A woman at court. Lady Merat Orzh," Ev said. "She's the one who had Thiyo thrown in prison."

"Well, let's rob her bank vault, too, in that case."

Alizhan liked Henny.

"But I think Thiyo wanted to talk about Iriyat," Ev said, because she was far too perceptive. "It's like when you told us about your childhood training—you needed a teacher to learn those other languages. To give you something to work with. That's what you're asking Alizhan to help you with."

He was genuinely grateful, and Ev was pleased to have remembered something useful. Alizhan's stomach twisted.

"We can't be sure that Iriyat wrote this," Alizhan said.

"No," Thiyo said. "But she's our best lead. Unless you have a better idea."

"No."

"So tell me about her."

"I don't know how to explain it," Alizhan said. She exhaled roughly. "I don't have a family. I'm an orphan. Or I was, until Iriyat took me in. I lived in her house—"

"Varenx House," Ev offered. "One of the Great Houses of Laalvur. Not just any house."

"Tell me about that."

"There's a Council of Nine that rules the city," Ev said. "Four Great Houses and five Lesser. They're the richest and most powerful merchants and bankers in Laalvur."

"They all hate each other," Alizhan said. "At least a little. Or they fear each other. They spend a lot of time at parties pretending to be nice to each other."

"And you know that because Iriyat took you in," Thiyo said.

Alizhan nodded. "I spied for her."

"So she knew about your gifts."

"I never thought of them that way, and neither did she, I think," Alizhan said. "Being the way I am has always been more of a burden than anything else. But Iriyat took me in when no one else would, and I tried to make myself useful to her."

"But no one else knew," Thiyo said.

"Not until recently."

"That's our first secret," he said. "Good. What other secrets can you tell me?"

"I don't follow," Ev admitted.

"This text was written in invisible ink *and* in a script no one else can read. It's a safe bet that it contains secrets. If I have an idea about the nature of those secrets, it'll help me crack the code. Tell me what happened that made you two flee Laalvur with this stolen book."

"I found out that Iriyat can alter memories," Alizhan said. "Just like Ket and Merat Orzh. She touches people and they forget things."

"She's *uheko* like you," Thiyo said.

Ev had never heard that word. "What?"

"*Uheko* is what we call people whose gifts can pass through their hands," Thiyo said, holding up one of his in an unnecessary demonstration. "I'm not one, but Alizhan, Henny, and Mala are all *uheko*. So are Ket, Merat, and Iriyat. They're one of the more dangerous kinds."

Henny waved her right hand and lifted Ev's with her left.

Thiyo paused. "It's a power that's most effective when kept secret."

"Very few people know about Iriyat," Alizhan said. "I couldn't ever read her. I only discovered it recently. Although looking back, it's possible that I found out in the past and then she forced me to forget. Who knows how many times that might have happened?"

She made all those words come out of her mouth in the usual order, at the usual volume, even though it felt like a bottomless pit had opened up inside her and everything she knew was pouring into it. Iriyat was doing bad things. Vile, cruel, brutal, unforgivable things. She understood that. But she still wanted to keep a few of those golden, sun-soaked childhood memories—Iriyat stroking her hair, Iriyat kissing her cheek—untouched by all this ugliness.

But nothing in her life was untouched by Iriyat.

"Well," Thiyo said. "That gives me something to think about. I think we can stop there for now."

And then, instead of asking what was wrong, he pulled her to his side and gave her a squeeze. Alizhan lay her head on his shoulder and neither of them moved for a long time.

As MUCH AS Alizhan hated traveling Nightward, now that they'd finally made it to Estva, even she could admit that the sight before them was impressive. The city's walls of ice towered above them, rising out of the snowy ground and glimmering white in the darkness.

"How can it possibly be warm in there?" she muttered.

"The city's not made of ice," Ket said. He was still seated on the driver's bench of the wagon. He and Henny, well suited to the cold, had spent the last few hours there together. "Just some of the walls. But I heard there are outposts farther Nightward, little huts dug into the snow and built out of ice, with a firepit in the middle. Supposed to be quite warm. The tribes use them when they go on long hunts."

There were very few animals on the frozen plains, but on their journey, they'd passed a few oases—thermal pools with strange plants growing in their hot, sulfurous water. Grey caribou gathered to graze there.

"Will they really let us in?" Ev said, peering at the walls from her position inside the wagon.

"Only one way to find out," Thiyo said.

He and Alizhan walked along the wall until they reached the gate, and Ket drove the wagon slowly behind them. Ket got down from his bench, and Henny helped Ev get out of the wagon, so the five of them could stand together in front of the gate.

There were two guards. It was hard to see their faces through the slot in the gate, even though it was lit with torches on either side. Alizhan couldn't distinguish their thoughts. Perhaps it was the distance, or the gate, that prevented her from learning more. The guards had a moment of conversation with Thiyo, and from their voices, Alizhan determined they were women. They were as pale as Nalitzvans, but both short, which Alizhan had heard was a characteristic of the Nightward tribes who roamed outside Estva.

"Anyone who agrees to work and follow the rules is welcome for as long as they choose to stay," Thiyo translated.

"So what do they need walls for?" Ev said.

One of the women said something to Thiyo in Estvan, and her companion laughed and added something else.

"Bears, wolves, Nalitzvans," Thiyo translated. Ket and Henny both shifted nervously. Alizhan had no idea why the King of Nalitzva would bother to march his army through the snow to capture this remote outpost, but apparently the inhabitants had been motivated to build strong walls.

"And the second woman, what did she say?" Ev said.

"People who don't follow the rules."

"How hard can it be to follow the rules?" Alizhan said. "Let's be good so they'll let us inside where it's warm."

Thiyo conveyed their consent to this agreement, and the huge wooden door swung open to let them in.

20

LYREBIRD SHIFT, 4TH TRIAD OF
BARSHA, 761

A FTER YEARS OF OBSERVING—WAITING—it came to me that I would die before I found real answers. Our world's eruptions, quakes, and waves are separated by years. True understanding would never be possible within my lifetime.

Unless I could create my own.

A wave was out of the question, as was an eruption. But a quake seemed possible. I would simply need a way to move a huge quantity of earth all at once.

I knew I could not share this revelation with Tsardeya. He would not have the stomach for it. But the pursuit of knowledge has always required sacrifices. Our greatest scholars of medicine have been grave-diggers and torturers, flaying and dissecting and stringing bodies back together so we might save others in the future. The success of my own experiments would save even more lives.

As a matter of coincidence, at the moment I was considering this question, my contact in Adappyr had provided me with a primer on local politics. The murder of a charismatic leader in 740 splintered the city into factions for years. There was fighting in the streets. Neighborhoods belonged to one faction or another.

By the time my correspondent described this to me, in 750, peace had been achieved. Adappyr was then a prosperous place, and if people have enough to be comfortable, it is harder to goad them into a fight. But for some, the old tensions were still there, he wrote, simmering beneath the surface.

Beneath the surface of an underground city. Here was my quake. Political instability could be transformed into physical instability. Enough violence could endanger the structural integrity of the city—moving a huge quantity of earth all at once. Would it cause a quake? Perhaps even an eruption of Adap? I went in search of business opportunities in Adappyr as cover for a trip there. I began to plan.

21

FAR FROM HOME

INSIDE ITS INTIMIDATING EXTERIOR WALLS, Estva wasn't impressive. Squat stone buildings, their roofs white with snow, clustered together inside the walls. Estva's original building was a meeting hall that had once housed all the residents together. Several dormitories and a few other buildings had been haphazardly added over the years. Some above-ground corridors connected the buildings, and Thiyo assumed there must be tunnels below. Going outside, even for only a moment, required preparation.

"There are a lot more women here than I thought," Thiyo said to their guide as they walked through the main hall. Thiyo could reach up and touch the exposed beams of the ceiling, but at least the massive hearth fire was keeping the room warm. The room was furnished with long wooden tables and benches, and would be full at mealtimes.

Their guide, Pirkko, one of the guards who had let them in, nodded. Her heavy blond braid didn't budge. "Women who come here tend to stay here, as opposed to the young men who pass through hoping to strike gold. And women are better at following the rules."

"What exactly are these rules?" Thiyo asked, not pausing to translate Pirkko's answer for his companions. He could feel the four of them gathered behind him. They were all listening with interest despite the language barrier. He could summarize this conversation for them later, in private. Henny and Ket might be able to pick out a few words here and there, since Estvan, through structurally very different, did share some words with Nalitzvan. Thiyo remembered that from his childhood training.

Although his mother had been crushed that he'd inherited her gift rather than his father's, once she'd identified his potential, she'd forced him to spend shifts and shifts listening to an *ohokutho* recite texts in every world language from memory. Even for a child who loved languages, it had been a perishingly lonely way to pass the years. His early dreams of learning all the mainland languages had soured as he'd grown, and Thiyo remembered arguing with his teacher at length. *It makes sense to learn Shade-side Hoi, and all the varieties of Li and Kae. But why bother with Nalitzvan, or Laalvuri, or Estvan, of all the depths-drowned useless things to learn. They don't come here and only a handful of wai traders ever go there!*

And who do you think we send out into the world to trade? Halelitha, his implacable *ohokutho* teacher had said. And then, without waiting for Thiyo's undoubtedly indignant and impertinent answer—why would he ever go to some desolate Nightward encampment full of unwashed mainlanders?—she'd gone right back to reciting the Estvan epic he'd interrupted. Something about a warrior with a sword forged in the belly of the earth. The phrase *stars as white as snow*, which had never meant anything to him as a child, had been repeated endlessly. The warrior had probably had a monster to slay, or an invading army to defeat. Thiyo wasn't *ohokutho*, so his imperfect memory never retained the stories. But the words—their sounds, their systems —stayed.

Thiyo had never appreciated the old memory-keeper and her endless mental library. Perhaps her own gift had seemed more like a curse, since it had saddled her with the thankless job of educating him. Halelitha hadn't always understood the words she was teaching him, and Thiyo had been an unruly and ungrateful student. He'd been a perennial disappointment to both Halelitha and his parents, first being born with the wrong gift, and then being born without the dedication and ambition to put the gift he did have to honorable use.

If Halelitha was still alive, and if he ever got home, he would thank her. He'd ended up needing depths-drowned Estvan after all.

He'd asked Pirkko what the rules were, and she was answering.

"If you came here to work in the mines and you strike gold, the city takes one third in return for housing and feeding you while you work," she said. "The other two thirds of what you mined are yours to keep. If you came here to work in the ice trade, the city will take a cut of your profits once you sell the ice. The cut will be determined by how long you enjoyed our hospitality. Two other Estvans will accompany you to Nalitzva—or anywhere else you choose to sell—to ensure that your payment makes it back to the city."

Pirkko recited all this as if she'd said it many times before. *Women who come here tend to stay here*, she'd said, and Thiyo suspected she'd been here a long time, perhaps her whole life. Attuning his ear to the nuances of Estvan accents would require a few more conversations, but Pirkko sounded at ease in the language, as if she'd grown up speaking it.

Of course, so did he.

"Is that why people come here? To mine gold and sell ice?" Thiyo asked.

She was leading the five of them across the main hall. She

stopped by a table near the opposite wall, next to a set of wooden doors that led into the rest of the building. The table had a gigantic book lying open on top of it. The left page was about half full of handwritten text. Estvan used the same script as Nalitzvan. Thiyo's gift for listening and speaking other languages did extend to reading and writing, but if he encountered a new script, he still needed time to understand it. Comprehension wasn't instant. He'd once made the mistake of complaining about this to Ilyr, who was completely devoid of sympathy. *Some of us have to learn* everything '*the hard way*', he'd said.

"Some people seek their fortune," Pirkko answered. Her gaze roamed the room as if she was looking for examples, but the long tables were empty save for two or three people speaking in low voices near the hearth. "You will also find many priests and scholars of different nations who have come to study the stars. People who do not mine gold or ice are hosted in exchange for the work they do to maintain the city, whether it is keeping our accounts or peeling potatoes. In addition to the scholarly community, Estva also houses a certain population of people who... left their former homes."

"Voluntarily?" Thiyo pressed. Estva was legendary for providing sanctuary to criminals on the run from Nalitzvan authorities. Now that he was one of those criminals, he needed to make absolutely sure the legends were true.

"Everyone is welcome in Estva as long as they do their part," Pirkko said. "No one is to be made to feel unwelcome because of their nation, their religion, or their personal history—whatever it may entail. We ask no questions. The only rules we care about are our own. Making someone else feel unwelcome is a violation of the rules, and there is only one punishment."

"Being thrown out," Thiyo said.

Pirkko nodded again. Shorter and thicker than Thiyo,

decked out in furs and leathers, with no trace of a smile on her round face, she didn't look like a woman who would hesitate to throw rule-breakers into the icy Night.

"Is that it, then? Pay your dues and make everyone feel welcome?"

"No killing, no raping, no fighting, no stealing," she said, counting the fingers of one leather-gloved hand with the other. "No shirking work. No unnatural behavior."

"What exactly constitutes... unnatural behavior?"

Pirkko pinned him with an unimpressed gaze of pale blue, then continued to list the rules as if Thiyo's question had been a joke. "Babies born in Estva stay in Estva until they reach the age of twenty, as do their parents."

Were you one of those babies? Thiyo wondered. Or had Pirkko come here to escape something? He wasn't supposed to ask. He didn't have a good idea of how old she was, either. Her serious expression and air of authority made her seem older, but her skin was smooth and her hair had no grey in it. She might be twenty-five or thirty-five. All Thiyo said was, "Unless they break the rules."

"Unless they break the rules," she agreed. "I see you think this rule is unjust. It isn't. Babies require resources, and resources are scarce. Many young women run away from home and come here. Sometimes they're already pregnant. Sometimes they get pregnant here. It doesn't matter. We help them, in exchange for the promise of their help in the future. We need people here. We need people who will stay."

"So there aren't any rules against sex, then?" Thiyo said, taking a different angle on the question of unnatural behavior. "Or drinking," he added, as the thought occurred to him.

To his surprise, Pirkko broke out in laughter. "It's dark and cold here all the time. What do you think we do for fun?"

Thiyo smiled tightly. *Unnatural behavior* meant magic, then.

He was already breaking the rules, and Alizhan was, too. Henny and Ket weren't planning to stay long, but he would have to warn them. He hoped no one asked him any questions about how or where an islander had learned the language of the world's most remote Nightward settlement. Nalitzvans had been eager to believe that their genius prince could take credit for Lady Lan's language skills, but they weren't in Nalitzva anymore. And Lady Lan was dead.

Here he was contemplating serious matters when Pirkko had just made a joke, so Thiyo came back to himself and forced a smile. "Good point."

Pirkko's mood seemed to have lightened considerably. She gestured to the book and said, "Please write your name and the names of your companions in the ledger."

Thiyo's right hand was stiff and still discolored with bruises, but he'd been doing Henny's exercises, and he was able to tug his left glove off before he picked up the quill. He dipped it in ink and glanced back at his companions. He knew none of their surnames. He also wasn't sure he wanted a written record of their presence in Estva.

"We use this ledger to keep track of who is staying in Estva so we can distribute food and work," Pirkko reassured him. "Whatever name you choose for yourself will be your name while you're here. If anyone outside Estva is looking for anyone inside Estva, they can only enter if they also agree to follow the rules. We extend the same protection to everyone who enters the city. We don't ask questions, and we don't answer the questions of outsiders."

That was the second time she'd said *we don't ask questions*. She hadn't even asked how he'd learned her language, or commented on his foreign looks or his unusual fellow travelers. Thiyo nodded decisively, and under the date, he wrote *Thiyo, Alizhan, Ev, Henny, Ket.*

"You and your friend will sleep in the men's dormitory," Pirkko said, indicating Ket with a tilt of her head. "The other three can follow me to the women's dormitory."

"Not much privacy, is there?" Thiyo said.

"Who needs privacy, if there is nothing to be ashamed of?" Pirkko said. She had a nice smile. Her hand brushed his as she took the quill from him. "Outsiders are sometimes surprised, but they shed their old ways quickly. A visit to the hot springs will do you good."

"Hot springs?" Thiyo said. Hoi was dotted with thermal pools. He'd taken Ilyr to all his favorites, ones that required long hikes through the steamy, fern-dappled forest, with brilliant, pure turquoise water and no other visitors. Ilyr had been so shy about swimming naked the first time. He'd blushed all the way down to his navel. Adorable.

Ilyr had flushed pink the second time, too, but for different reasons.

That didn't bear thinking about. Still, hot springs were a bit of good news. Thiyo had missed them. Perhaps they'd be good for Ev, since her newly healed wound had left her stiff and sore. Thiyo looked at Ev to see if she was considering this, but then he remembered she couldn't understand the conversation.

"Of course," Pirkko was saying. He needed to pay attention. "Estva was built to take advantage of the springs. They also provide us with *rysuotavkasvi*."

"A plant you eat?" Thiyo guessed, after disassembling the word in his head.

Pirkko had promised not to *ask* questions, but Thiyo thought he saw one in the brief quirk of her eyebrow before she answered: "A plant that grows in the thermal vents, without sunlight, and the only food we don't have to import from more Dayward climates. The Nalitzvan word for it is *nightvine*."

Thiyo nodded his understanding, and then began to summarize the conversation in Laalvuri, which had been their common tongue throughout the journey. Pirkko didn't move away from him or pretend not to listen, so Thiyo took care with his translation.

"They don't care what we've done in the past. As long as we do our part and don't cause any trouble, we can stay here and they'll feed and shelter us," he explained. With a pointed look at Alizhan, Henny, and Ket, he added, "On the other *hand*, it is very important to follow the rules. They won't tolerate *unnatural behavior*."

"Really? Because—" Alizhan stopped talking abruptly. She must have felt Thiyo's surge of panic—Pirkko was standing right there listening, for Mah Yee's sake. "Well, we don't tolerate it either, of course. I mean, why even mention it to us, since we all behave *naturally* all the time anyway—" Alizhan broke off again, and not an instant too soon. Thiyo had been thinking *stop stop stop* as hard as he could.

"I'm very tired," Ev said. Bless her. "Perhaps we could sleep a shift? Or eat something? Henny and Ket would like to rest before going home, too, I'm sure."

"We'll stay a few triads," Henny said. "I'd like to see what life is like here, and I don't mind working."

From Pirkko's expression, she'd understood the whole conversation, but she didn't offer a response until Thiyo dutifully translated it into Estvan for her. Directing her answer to Henny, Ev, and Alizhan, she began to speak. Thiyo translated, "The women's dormitories are down this corridor. Take the second right, and then another right. Choose your room based on sleep shift—you should be able to tell which rooms are getting ready to go to bed, even if you can't read the signs outside the doors. Any unmarked bed is yours to claim."

Pirkko turned back to Thiyo and Ket. She reached for Thiyo's left hand. He blinked, but didn't pull away. "I'll show you to the men's dormitory."

His friends were a study in facial expressions: Ket went wide-eyed, Henny wore a close-lipped smile, Ev frowned, and Alizhan's brow furrowed. No one said a word.

They split up with an agreement to meet back in the dining hall in a couple of hours when the bell rang for the next meal. He and Ket followed Pirkko down a long hall, through several turns, before arriving at the dormitory.

They'd left Nalitzva with very little, but Thiyo had managed to acquire a small pack of clothing on their journey Nightward, which he set down on one of the empty bunks when they reached the dormitory. There were many identical rooms in the building, all long and narrow and bare, distinguished only by the sign on the outer door marking which shift the inhabitants typically slept. From the number of rooms, Thiyo estimated the dormitory housed about five hundred men. He hadn't counted the buildings outside, but there were ten at most. Even if the dormitories were all full—and they weren't—Estva hardly deserved to be called a city.

He didn't plan to share that opinion with Pirkko.

"Are you going to meet her in the hot springs?" Ket asked quietly, once they were alone in the dormitory.

"What?"

"I catch a word in Estvan every now and then. She said something about hot springs. And she grabbed your hand. That was an invitation if I ever saw one," Ket said.

Thiyo had been too distracted by his memories. As soon as Ket mentioned Pirkko's behavior, it was obvious.

"You do... like women, right?" Ket said. "Henny says a man who's as good at doing hair as you are has got to be queer. But from the way you looked at Henny, I thought you must like women, too, but I guess it could have been her—"

"I do," Thiyo confirmed before Ket could get any more specific. "Like women, that is. But we probably shouldn't talk about Henny's *qualities*. And we should all keep our *hands* to ourselves."

"The rules," Ket surmised.

"Yes." Thiyo was glad not to have to explain any further.

"Are they going to care about," Ket started, and then glanced to either side as if someone might be listening.

"You being in the men's dormitory?" Thiyo said quietly. He'd intuited the rest of the question even before Ket glanced pointedly downward. "As far as I can tell, that's not against any of the rules. They seem pretty relaxed about everything except their particular definition of 'unnatural behavior.' But I'll keep an eye out and make sure no one comes in while you change, if you want."

"Just in case," Ket said, agreeing. Then he added, "You never answered my question. About Pirkko. And whether you're going to meet her in the hot springs."

"Oh," Thiyo said. He'd already forgotten the question. "No."

Ket raised his eyebrows. He obviously considered the invitation tempting.

Thiyo's own reaction took him by surprise. Pirkko was charming, in her own serious, dry, Nightward way. And under all those furs she was wearing, probably beautiful. And she just wanted to pass the time in an amusing way—an attitude much more in line with those of Thiyo's homeland than Nalitzva. Her invitation to the hot springs should have appealed to him.

"There's a rule about babies," Thiyo said. "I don't know if you caught that one. They need people to stay here, and both parents of any babies born here are required to stay for twenty years."

Even as he said it, Thiyo knew that wasn't the real reason he didn't have any interest in the invitation. He knew how to entertain a partner in a way that couldn't result in a child. But Pirkko had said "hot springs," and his first thought had been Ilyr. Remembering happier times with Ilyr was like biting into a sweet fruit and having his mouth flooded with sour, rotten fluid.

Thiyo should want to wash it away. He should want to replace it with something else—a new taste, a different taste, any other taste—but instead, the rot had contaminated the very idea of eating. His stomach turned.

It was as though Thiyo hadn't really had time to think about Ilyr, between the prison and the wedding and the fights. Absurd. He'd done nothing *but* think about Ilyr. But before he'd been righteous, enraged, betrayed. He'd been full of fury and purpose. And now Thiyo was here, and Ilyr was there, and they'd never see each other again, and there was nothing to distract Thiyo from how very hollow and far from home that made him feel.

Thiyo sat down and was silent for such a long time that at some point, Ket simply patted him on the shoulder and left the room.

———

THIYO WASN'T the only one in a daze when the five of them reconvened in the main hall for a meal two hours later. His companions stood together in a little cluster and gave the massive room bleary glances, enough to figure out that they didn't need to do anything more than seat themselves at one of the long wooden tables in order to be served. They all sat down on two empty benches. Thiyo sat with Ev and Alizhan, and across the table from them, Henny slouched down next to Ket until her head was on his shoulder.

"Whatever they eat here, I hope they bring me a lot of it," she said. When all five of them were together, they spoke Laalvuri, and while Henny and Ket hardly ever made mistakes in the language, they both had soft accents that Thiyo loved—a tendency to roll their *r*, to linger over vowels, and to take extra care in crisply pronouncing the last consonant of every word. They also both called him *Diyo*, as opposed to Ev and Alizhan, who could get his name almost right. It was a pleasure to listen to.

"You aren't worried you might not like it?" Ev asked.

"Henny eats everything," Ket said.

"You make me sound like an animal foraging in garbage," Henny said.

Ket's cheeks went pink. But he smiled, put an arm around Henny's shoulders, and then said to Ev very solemnly, "Henny is enthusiastic about many different cuisines."

The hall was bustling, which caused Thiyo to question his earlier estimate of Estva's population. There must be more to the city than he'd seen. That was good news, because it meant there might be more quiet, out-of-the-way spaces to find. Unlike Pirkko and her Estvan compatriots, Thiyo did feel the need for privacy. His affair with the encoded text of *A Natural History* would be almost as exciting as whatever people got up to in the hot springs, he was sure. And the prospect of reading and deciphering something was considerably more appealing than intimacy, in that it didn't make his insides twist and shrivel.

His parents had always wanted him to take his studies more seriously. Maybe someone should have broken his heart sooner.

Pirkko arrived, interrupting his morose thoughts. She sat down on the bench next to Alizhan and said "Hello," in Estvan. "Don't worry, the food will be here soon."

"Thank you," Thiyo said, and then translated for the others. Any further conversation among their group would have to pass through him.

"What kind of work would you like to do here?" Pirkko said.

"We need people everywhere, but if you have special skills, we will try to put them to use." She leaned toward the table, looking past Alizhan and Ev to meet Thiyo's gaze. "You speak Estvan and Laalvuri. Can you read?"

"Yes," he said, trying not to bristle with offense. She wasn't calling him a savage. She was trying to offer him work he'd be suited to.

"There's a press and a bookbindery," Pirkko said. "I'll put you there and they'll train you. What about the others?"

"She's asking where you want to work," Thiyo explained.

"Medicine," Henny said immediately. "It's what I'm best at."

It was also the domain where she'd be most tempted to break the rules and use her gift to soothe people's pain, but Thiyo couldn't say that out loud. He nodded.

"I'll go with Henny," Ket said. "I'm good at following instructions."

"Is there an infirmary?" Thiyo asked Pirkko, who looked at Henny and Ket and nodded. "They'd like to work there. They can't speak much Estvan, but they understand some." Then he turned to Ev and Alizhan.

"Anywhere is fine with me," Ev said. "Wherever it won't matter that we can't speak their language, and wherever they need the most help."

Thiyo translated this to Pirkko, while Alizhan said, "I want to go with Ev."

Pirkko didn't wait for a translation. "The kitchens," she said. "We always need the most help in the kitchens."

Thiyo explained this. Ev nodded. Alizhan did nothing. She'd been withdrawn since they'd arrived. "Well, that's settled," he said to Pirkko, secretly hoping she might perceive it as the end of their conversation and leave them in peace. But she made herself comfortable, putting an elbow on the table and leaning in.

"I hope you like it here so far," she said. "I'll introduce you to the people you'll be working with, if I see them. Oh, look, here's our food!"

Two servers brought out plates stacked with thick slices of brown bread, hard yellow cheese, some little silvery smoked fish, and a pile of very dark cooked greens. It didn't resemble the food Thiyo had become accustomed to at the palace, where the courses arrived in an excruciatingly complex and rigid order, or the simple, fresh food of his distant, sunny homeland. But he was too hungry to be particular, and when a fork and a knife were dropped on the table next to his plate, he picked them up and dug in.

A few minutes passed in silence while everyone ate.

Well, almost everyone.

"Alizhan," Ev said in Laalvuri, turning toward her. "Are you alright?"

Alizhan hadn't touched the food. She didn't look as grey or as clammy as she normally did in crowds, though the racket of conversation and the clatter of plates and glasses hemmed them in on all sides. She scanned the room with narrowed eyes. Had she heard something? Was she worried?

"It's so quiet," Alizhan said.

"What?" Ev said, and Thiyo couldn't blame her. It was hard to hear in the mess hall.

"It's quiet," Alizhan repeated, and Ev and Thiyo shared a look. *That* kind of quiet. A kind only Alizhan could perceive. "I hear them sometimes, when they're loud," she said, looking at Thiyo, Henny, and Ket, "but I can really only hear you, Ev."

"Perhaps we should go somewhere else," Thiyo suggested, aware of Pirkko sitting so close to them while they discussed how Alizhan was breaking one of Estva's few rules. Pirkko still hadn't revealed how much Laalvuri she understood. If she knew they were talking about magic, Thiyo didn't want to find out the hard way.

But if Alizhan couldn't sense anyone in the room but Ev... Thiyo chewed his lip in thought. Anyone with a gift would protect their mind by instinct, although his own instincts weren't worth much, as Alizhan already knew. And that instinctive protection wasn't impenetrable for anyone. Training could strengthen it. Training could also help people without gifts, but since magic was forbidden in Estva, how would they have managed to train this many people? Why would anyone be motivated to protect themselves if there was nothing to protect themselves from?

Ev would have to train herself at some point, and Thiyo sympathized with her. He'd never had the patience and dedication necessary to maintain control at all times—it was so much less glamorous and dazzling than what he could do with words —and besides, his thoughts were usually delightful. Anyone who could read his mind was welcome to admire whatever they found.

"God," Alizhan muttered.

Thiyo ignored her. She'd given him a riddle to work out and he was still sorting through it. Presumably, Henny and Ket possessed the same instinct Thiyo did for keeping "quiet," as Alizhan called it. So it made sense that she rarely heard them. Earlier, when Pirkko had told them the rule against "unnatural behavior," Alizhan had said "Really? Because—" and then stopped herself. Now Thiyo could guess the end of that sentence. Pirkko could shield her thoughts from Alizhan. Alizhan suspected Pirkko might be engaging in some "unnatural behavior" of her own.

But Pirkko was just one person. There must be five hundred people in the room. They couldn't all be gifted. Could they?

"I thought you liked quiet," Ev said lightly. "I thought you wished everywhere was quiet."

"I've never been anywhere quiet, not really," Alizhan said. And then she hugged herself, rubbing her upper arms. She was obviously unsettled.

Pirkko misinterpreted her gesture as simple shivering, and she laughed and reached over to slap Alizhan on the back and sling an arm over her shoulders. "Cold, little one? It's nothing some meat on your bones won't fix!"

Pirkko indicated Alizhan's untouched plate with her free hand.

Alizhan sat wide-eyed, stick-straight, and stock-still, as if Pirkko had just draped a deadly snake over her shoulders instead of an arm. Thiyo translated what Pirkko had just said, but he doubted that Alizhan heard a word of it.

Breathe, he thought, because he couldn't say it out loud. Alizhan was wearing layers and layers of clothing, and Pirkko was blank, besides. Unlike Henny and Ket, Pirkko didn't know what Alizhan could do, and thus she had no reason to be afraid. Unlike Ev, Pirkko wasn't simmering with powerful longing. She was neutral. Harmless. Nothing was happening, and nothing was going to happen. It was just a touch.

"She's a vegetarian," Thiyo explained to Pirkko, hoping to allay some of the awkwardness of Alizhan's frozen reaction.

"Ah, yes," Pirkko said. "I forgot. Laalvuri don't eat meat. Not even fish. Well, there's plenty of other things to eat. You won't go hungry here!"

Slowly, Alizhan nodded and began to breathe again. "Yes," she said. But Thiyo didn't miss the look of relief on Alizhan's face when Pirkko stopped touching her.

22

RULES ARE RULES

ALIZHAN CHOPPED VICIOUSLY AT THE pile of greens on her cutting board. They'd been limp and bitter at the meal last shift, and she didn't think her novice cooking skills would improve them for the next meal. This strange new green whose Estvan name she couldn't remember or pronounce, Thiyo had called it *nightvine*. It was Alizhan's job to wash it, stem it, chop it, and boil it into submission.

She didn't plan to eat it.

The kitchens were underground, and the series of long, windowless rooms was lit with candles. No sense wasting expensive lamp fluid on a room that already had fires in it. Sweat trickled down her sides. She hadn't felt warm since coming Nightward, and suddenly she was trapped in this stifling room with twenty people all furiously slicing and roasting food.

Beside her, Ev was faring better, kneading bread dough with practiced ease. Ev had grown up with a family, on a farm, doing chores. She knew so much more about living a normal life. Alizhan was good for reading minds, picking locks, and scaling walls. She didn't know how to cook a goddamn thing.

Alizhan hadn't realized all the steps that went into making

food until she caught Ev thinking about washing the greens, and taking the stems off, and so on. Without surreptitiously scanning Ev's thoughts for guidance about what to do next, Alizhan would've been lost. She certainly couldn't understand any of what the other workers were saying—or thinking.

"I wish you believed me," Alizhan said. Ev thought she was being ridiculous. Obsessed. Irrational. Alizhan wasn't. This place gave her the creeps. She'd never been anywhere so silent. And there was a *rule* against her *existence*. And if nobody else here was using magic, then how were they all hiding from her?

"I do believe you," Ev said. "I just don't know what you want me to do about it."

"You believe me, but you think I'm overreacting," Alizhan clarified. "You think I'm being *paranoid*." She emphasized the word, which had been in Ev's thoughts only an instant before. "But it's not being paranoid, it's being sensible. Something is *weird* here. We can't trust these people. What if they're keeping secrets? What if they're in league with Ir—I mean, spying on us?"

"Alizhan," Ev said softly. "Consider, for a moment, how I felt when you told me to trust the stranger we met in a prison cell."

"You weren't sure about him."

"Yes. Because I couldn't see into him like you could."

"Right! And here, I can't see into *anybody*, so we can't be sure about a single person!"

"Yes," Ev said. She spoke so calmly, and she kept kneading the bread dough beneath her fists. "Before I started spending all my time with you, that was how I lived. That is, in fact, how almost everyone lives."

"You think I'm *whining*?" Alizhan said.

"That's not what I said," Ev replied, but Alizhan could still read Ev, even if she was quieter this shift than usual. Ev would never tell Alizhan that she was whining, but she wasn't exactly overflowing with sympathy.

Alizhan took a deep breath. It wasn't Ev's fault if she didn't understand Alizhan's feelings. Ev couldn't read her. That meant Alizhan had to explain it. "Ev. Please. I can't even tell people apart if I can't read them. You know that. You understand how disorienting that is for me, right? And we're in a place full of strangers and I can't speak their language or understand their facial expressions."

Ev was nodding, and Alizhan could feel the flow of sympathy begin.

"Next time, start with 'Ev, I feel powerless and scared' instead of 'Ev, the people who have taken us in from the cold must be plotting against us.'"

Alizhan hadn't wanted to admit that first part. "They could both be true."

"I suppose," Ev said. "But one thing at a time. Normally, you tell me if you think strangers are trustworthy. Here, I'll tell you."

"But how will you know?" Alizhan's major experience with trusting someone unreadable—Iriyat—had gone catastrophically wrong. They wouldn't be trapped in this cauldron of a kitchen otherwise.

"I won't," Ev said. "But I'll listen to people, and watch their faces, and I'll be cautious."

"People keep secrets," Alizhan reminded her. "They lie constantly."

"I know," Ev said, with just a hint of fatigue. "But I'll keep an eye out. That's all we can really do for now."

Someone walked into the kitchen. Alizhan turned and saw a woman—probably a woman, based on the height and the long blond braid—dressed in brown suede and grey fur, far too warmly for the kitchen. From Ev's thoughts, Alizhan recognized Pirkko.

"Hello," she said in Laalvuri.

Alizhan stiffened. Was Pirkko going to touch her again? It hadn't been painful the first time. But Alizhan had an entrenched, lifelong association between human contact and pain, and she didn't want strangers to touch her.

"Hello," Ev said.

"I go work," Pirkko said. "But first I come here. See you. Work good? You happy?"

"Yes," Ev said, which was an exaggeration in Alizhan's case, but Pirkko didn't need to know that.

Pirkko didn't need to know anything about them. Why was she here? What was the purpose of this surveillance? It made Alizhan's skin prickle, not knowing.

"Good," Pirkko said. "Later we eat, yes?"

"Together?" Ev said, with some surprise, and Pirkko nodded enthusiastically, which made Ev warm up with happiness and amusement. Alizhan scrutinized their faces. They were both smiling. What reason could they have for that? Ev's thoughts lingered on Pirkko's face, and an ugly suspicion uncurled in Alizhan's gut. She tried to ignore it. Jealousy was a foolish waste of time.

"Hello," Pirkko said again, bowed her head, and left.

"That's cute," Ev said. "They must use the same word for 'hello' and 'goodbye.' We'll have to ask Thiyo what it is."

Cute. So much for Ev being cautious. "You think she's trustworthy," Alizhan said.

"She hasn't done anything alarming yet," Ev said. "She's just being friendly. I'll be friendly in return, until I have a good reason not to."

"Or we could be *unfriendly*, until they give us a good reason to stop."

"We'd never have met if I'd treated you like that," Ev said, and Alizhan didn't have a response.

THE PRESS and bookbindery were in a different building from the main hall and the dormitory where Thiyo had slept, and it was a long, winding walk through half-lit tunnels to get there. The room he emerged into did have windows, which was a welcome relief from the closed-in tightness of Estva's other buildings, but of course, there was no light.

The blue-black expanse of the sky, brushed with a glittering sweep of stars, drew him. Thiyo couldn't stop himself from walking across the room to stare out the window. The glass was cold underneath his fingertips. The dim white landscape of the ground below was an afterthought. Night was another ocean. A vaster, deeper one.

All islanders grew up with a healthy fear of the ocean, and the thought of something even grander and more powerful made Thiyo shiver. But he kept looking.

There was a low chuckle from across the room. "I was the same, when I first arrived."

Thiyo turned. The speaker was a man with the same warm bronze skin and shiny black hair as Alizhan, but his hair was cut short and there were silver strands around his temples and faint lines around his eyes. Dressed in a grey robe, he was standing in front of a plate of movable type, looking down at his work through a pair of spectacles.

"Sardas," he offered, without glancing at Thiyo.

"My name is Thiyo."

"Can you read?"

The question didn't make him bristle this time. "Yes."

Sardas turned around to look at him at last, and if he was surprised to see an islander in his workshop, it didn't show on his face. "Estvan?" he specified.

"Yes," Thiyo said. They were speaking Estvan, after all. "And

Nalitzvan." The languages shared a writing system. Then, in Laalvuri, he added, "And Laalvuri, too."

Sardas laughed again. It was a nice sound. "We don't get enough people here who can say that," he said in Laalvuri, pleased. "It feels good to hear it. You could be a great help to us. We print books—calendars and star charts and scholarly treatises, mostly—in all of those languages. I don't suppose you read Adpri, too?"

"I do."

Sardas grinned. He was a little unkempt, with two triads' worth of stubble on his cheeks and cowlicks in his hair. It was rare to see anyone at the Nalitzvan court with even such minor lapses in attention to grooming. It was even rarer to see someone who would smile so warmly and openly. Thiyo was a long way from the palace.

"I hope Night agrees with you, Thiyo. We can do good work together if you stay."

Thiyo nodded, and Sardas gestured for him to come closer. He showed Thiyo the sets of movable type and demonstrated how to work the press. His long, ink-smudged fingers moved the tiny letters deftly, and Thiyo found himself watching and listening with interest. He hadn't expected to like the work he had to do, or anyone he had to work with, so Sardas and his workshop were a pleasant surprise. The press was in the middle of the room, but the walls were covered in cabinets and open shelves, every one full to the brim with books and unbound stacks of paper. The light in the room came from green lamp fluid, which wasn't flammable, and every white sheet seemed to glow with it.

"I came Nightward about fifteen years ago," Sardas said. "I wasn't terribly young then—not as young as you—but I was still searching for my purpose. I was already a priest, but I felt lost. I told them I'd do any work when I got here. They had me working in the laundry at first, in a windowless cave. By the time I finally got up here and saw those windows, I thought God was welcoming me to paradise. I fell in love with the stars, and then with the work, and when the time came to return home to Laalvur permanently, I just couldn't do it. But I don't think I realized how much I missed the sound of home until you spoke just now. Estva, for all its wonders, can be a lonely place. But we should return to speaking Estvan, so I can introduce you to the others."

Sardas picked up a wooden cane that was leaning against one of the cabinets. "I took a bad fall on the ice a few years ago and never quite recovered," he said, holding up the cane. "Be careful out there, or you'll end up as old and stooped as me."

Sardas was only a little bit shorter than Thiyo, so he could hardly be called stooped, and his hair was still mostly black. He was perhaps fifty. Thiyo just nodded.

Sardas strolled across the room with his cane and led Thiyo through a door on the opposite side. The next room was the bookbindery, and it smelled of glue and paper. There was a pale young woman with a shaved head sewing stacks of pages together. She was sitting in a chair with wheels. A thick line of black makeup barred her face from temple to temple, and when she closed her eyes, Thiyo could see her eyelids were also painted black. Where the collar of her brown coat lay open, a black robe was visible. Thiyo glanced at the end of her coat sleeve and saw black feathers poking out.

"You're a priest of Doubt," he said. He'd never met anyone from the Laalvuri sect but he'd heard enough to recognize their distinctive style.

She flicked a glance up at him, the whites of her eyes like snow against the Night sky.

Her irises were blue, her skin was the same faint melon color as Ilyr's, and her shaved head had blond stubble. And Sardas said he hadn't heard anyone speak Laalvuri in a long time. "And you're Nalitzvan." Thiyo was aware of Sardas watching him, as well as the other two men in the room. He'd made them uncomfortable. His curiosity had gotten the better of him.

"Doubt knows no nation," said the woman. Her focus had returned to her needle and stack of pages, and she continued sewing.

Doubt apparently didn't have any manners, either.

"This is Ayat," Sardas said, gesturing at the woman with a note of apology. "We accept all sorts in Estva. Most of us are priests of some kind. We need literate workers to make books, and there are lots of priests who come here to study. Next to Ayat is Fama, and standing by the desk over there is Rin."

Fama, a dark-skinned young man whose tight black braids fell to his shoulders, was seated next to Ayat, gluing stiff boards to the fronts and backs of uncovered books. He offered Thiyo a cautiously friendly nod, as did Rin, a Nalitzvan man of middle height, his short hair fully grey, who was sorting through pages.

Sardas clearly wanted to ask Thiyo if he was a disciple of some religion—and which one, and which island, and which other languages—but questions like that skirted the bounds of Estvan propriety. Thiyo was grateful for it. He wasn't sure how he would explain his presence here, if asked.

Besides, Thiyo had questions of his own to answer. As soon as Sardas left him alone, he slipped the folded pages where he'd transcribed the mystery language out of his pocket. He shuffled them into the stack of manuscript pages that Sardas had given him to print. Whenever he had a few unobserved moments, he returned to them, tracing the unfamiliar characters with his gaze until he imagined he could feel their curves and angles under his fingers like cast metal pieces of movable type.

AT DINNER, Thiyo was quiet and distracted and Alizhan was practically mute, picking miserably at the food she and Ev had cooked. Henny and Ket eventually gave up on trying to engage either of them and talked to each other in Nalitzvan, leaving Ev stranded. Ev didn't mind the food, although it wasn't impressive. There was satisfaction in having worked hard. But dinner was always better with company.

The dining hall was loud, and she had ample time to look around and examine her fellow Estvans. The tables seemed to be divided between laborers, people who had come to mine gold or ice, and scholars, people who had come to study the stars. There was a third group, much warier than the first two, of people who hadn't come *to* Estva for any reason other than coming *from* somewhere else. Ev supposed she and her friends were part of this group, although that didn't make her any more eager to get to know the others.

She might have guessed that the laborers would be more raucous than the scholars, but it was the opposite. Having worked hard all shift, they were content to eat in companionable silence. The scholars, on the other hand, argued fiercely and at great volume. The arguments were in Estvan, so Ev had no chance of understanding them, but she understood their gestures and expressions well enough. She was watching a pair of men argue, their hands slashing and jabbing through the air like birds of prey, when one man stood up and yanked the other closer by the collar of his robe.

He ground out a few words directly into his struggling, squirming victim's face, and then spit.

His victim shoved at him, breaking his grip, and then came back swinging his arm toward the robe-grabber. His clenched fist connected with the man's nose, and then the man grabbed a plate of food off the table and tried to smash it into his opponent's face.

No one had intervened. The other scholars were watching in awe, and the rest of the dining hall was studiously ignoring the whole scene. The food had slopped onto both men and the floor, and the men were grappling with each other, one still holding the plate in his hand. The plate was still intact for the moment, but if it shattered, one of them could easily use a shard to kill the other.

Ev was up and striding across the room before she could even consider her decision. She was taller than both of them, and probably better at fighting, besides. It was just a matter of stepping in and pushing them apart.

She yanked the plate out of the man's hand before he'd realized what she was doing, and then she set it on the table. She pulled their arms apart and forced herself between them. They were still snarling at each other over her shoulder, and a fleck of spit hit her cheek. She shook her head to get rid of it—an impulse, not a calculated move—and lost her grip on one of the men. He immediately stepped around her to continue haranguing his opponent.

Ev's best hope now was simply to drag the man still in her grip away from the fight. She tried to position herself between the two men, but they scrabbled to get at each other, paying no attention her.

Then suddenly, someone grabbed the free man from behind and pulled him away. When he'd been carted unwillingly backward a few steps, Ev saw a short, thick blond woman behind him. Pirkko.

The hall went silent.

The man in Ev's grip stilled, and so did the man in Pirkko's. Pirkko let go, then stepped into the space where they'd been fighting. She said something to both of them in a loud, lecturing tone. Then she used a tone that Ev recognized from childhood, despite the language barrier, as *I'm not mad, just disappointed.*

The men couldn't look at her, or each other, and for a long moment, they cast dejected glances at the floor. Then both of them stood straighter and marched for the exit, one at a time. They kept a safe distance between them.

"What happened?" Ev asked Pirkko.

"They break rules," Pirkko said shortly. "They leave now."

"Now?" Ev said. "They can't even go get their things?"

"Rules are simple," Pirkko said.

"What were they fighting about?"

Pirkko shrugged, uninterested. "Priest nonsense. What stars. Which God."

"Oh." Ev's father suspected that religion was a scheme to control people and keep them apart. Her mother said it probably didn't hurt to pray anyway. Owing to their intercultural marriage, her parents were considerably more relaxed about the question of religion than anyone else in her village. Fighting over which gods were real, and what the stars meant, struck Ev as unnecessary. And Pirkko apparently felt the same.

Still. "It's not right to just kick them out in the cold like that," Ev said. "They'll die out there, even if they don't kill each other."

"Maybe. Maybe not. But rules are rules," Pirkko said. "They make choice."

Ev wanted to protest this vicious, draconian policy, but Pirkko seemed to have some kind of authority as an enforcer of the rules—both men had stopped struggling as soon as she'd shown up—and Ev didn't want to be on the wrong side of it.

Around them, the clinking of forks and knives against ceramic slowly resumed, and conversation along with it. Ev wanted to go back to the table—or to leave the room entirely—but Pirkko was still standing in front of her, and she didn't have the impression she'd been dismissed.

Ev must not have angered Pirkko with her questions, since Pirkko beamed at her and said, "You, next shift, with me."

23

LACEMAKERS

"WHAT WAS THAT?" THIYO AND Alizhan hissed simultaneously from either side of Ev as they left the dining hall. Henny and Ket were close behind, eager to hear the answer.

"I thought you were going to get thrown out with them," Alizhan said. She sounded terrified. Not being able to read anyone's mind, she'd assumed the worst. "I thought Pirkko was coming to kick you out for fighting."

"No," Ev said. "She wants me to work with her."

"What?"

"She asked me to work with her," Ev repeated. "Our next working shift."

"So you won't be in the kitchens with me."

Ev had promised to stay with Alizhan and help her navigate while she was temporarily powerless. Guilt twisted her gut. "I'm sorry," she said. "I don't think I can really say no to Pirkko, though. I get the impression she gives the orders."

"She's young to be giving the orders," Thiyo observed.

"I don't claim to understand it," Ev said. "But you saw what happened when she walked over toward the fight."

"Yes," Thiyo said. "Which raises the question of why she didn't do it far sooner."

There was a pause. "Don't look at me," Alizhan said, although nobody was looking at her. "I can't answer any questions about anybody's secret motivations here. Except if they're about Ev. And Ev doesn't like that."

Was that a statement of fact from Alizhan or some kind of resentful little dig at Ev? Or was it a remarkable display of restraint, since Alizhan could have chosen to air all of Ev's dirty laundry in public if she'd wanted to? Whatever it was, Ev decided to ignore it. Alizhan had a right to feel hurt. Ev had made a promise she couldn't keep.

"Pirkko was watching you," Ket said to Ev, inserting himself into the conversation from behind the three of them. "I think she wanted to know what you were going to do."

"Well, she knows now," Henny said, joining in. "I suppose you can find about more about her when you go to work together."

Ket stopped walking. "This is us," he said to Thiyo. "We turn here to go back to the men's dormitory."

"I know," Thiyo said. "I have something I need to talk about with Alizhan. I'll be back in a little while."

Had he figured out part of the text? No, he'd be acting cockier if he had. Ket nodded at Thiyo, then waved goodbye and went off to his own dormitory.

"More questions," Alizhan complained. She'd come to the same conclusions as Ev. "We came all the way across the ocean to find a genius, and instead we got you."

"Rude," Thiyo said, as though he were passing down a judgment. He didn't sound terribly broken up about it. "Take the book to someone else, then. See what they can do."

Alizhan laughed. So they were only teasing and bickering—batting their paws at each other's noses, not about to have a real fight. Ev let the two of them walk a step ahead as they made their way to the dormitory, so they could talk in low voices. Henny stepped forward to keep pace with Ev.

"Ket was right about Pirkko watching you," she said in a low voice. "But I wouldn't make it sound so sinister."

"What do you mean?"

Henny shrugged one shoulder. "I work in a whorehouse. I know that look."

Ev blinked.

"She cozied up to Thiyo, too, when we arrived," Henny said. "I'd wager she's lonely."

"I guess it's a small place," Ev said. She didn't know what to do with this unexpected thread of conversation. Was Alizhan listening? Would she find this topic upsetting? Would she find it extra upsetting if she knew—as she certainly would—that Ev's face was hot? From pleasure or embarrassment or both. Pirkko *had* given her quite a smile at the end.

Ev had no idea what any of it meant. What were she and Alizhan to each other? They'd never named the thing between them. Was there a name for it? For two people who loved each other but could barely touch? The only word Ev knew for that was *suffering*.

And Ev only knew her own experience. Unlike Alizhan, she couldn't say what anyone else was feeling. And Alizhan rarely voiced her thoughts. They'd promised to try. But there'd been little time for practice, since life lurched from one crisis to another. And Ev had promised to wait. But did waiting mean never even thinking about anyone else? It wasn't a crime to enjoy a beautiful smile.

Was it a betrayal for Ev to feel flattered that Pirkko might be interested in her? That Pirkko might want to offer her what Alizhan could not?

Ev realized she'd been staring down the hall in silence for a long time. "Sorry," she said to Henny. "Got distracted."

"Just thought you should know," Henny said lightly, as they entered their dormitory room. "I'll let you three get up to whatever it is you're doing. Talking about that book, most likely. Speaking of books, I guess you haven't finished reading *The Sunrise Chronicles* yet."

Ev shook her head. That had been such a nice little interlude. She wished they could go back to it. "We haven't had time. Does Ket want it back?"

"Oh, keep it," Henny said. "I'll buy him another one. And it's given you so much happiness."

The bare room around them had only a few other people in it, all of them women getting ready to go to bed. The far end of the room was dark because some of them had already put out their candles. The sight of Thiyo caused them to murmur among themselves. When he sat down on Alizhan's bed and pulled out a sheaf of papers, one of the women protested.

Thiyo said something back to her in Estvan. He sounded a lot more polite than he ever had with Ev.

"What are they saying?" Ev asked Henny, who had a better chance of guessing.

"She says it's quiet hours in this room. She doesn't want him in here making noise. He says he'll be very quiet," Henny said. "It's a reasonable complaint."

"We may have to find another space," Thiyo said. "The print shop is nice, but I assume there's another shift of workers in there right now. I haven't had time to find anywhere else. There's light in here, at least."

"You just want to talk, right?" Alizhan said. "We'll talk quietly and if anyone gets upset, we'll move."

Thiyo nodded. Alizhan sat down on her bed with him—very

close to him, Ev couldn't help noticing, and the sight wrenched her foolish heart out of shape—and they bent their heads over the pages until they were almost touching.

Henny went to her bed, on the other side of Ev's, and started unbraiding her hair to comb it as if nothing else was happening. Ev sat down and watched Thiyo and Alizhan. "After our last conversation," Thiyo was saying, "I thought about what you told me about Iriyat and her ability. If that's one of her big secrets, it makes sense that it would be mentioned here—*if* she's the author of this encoded text."

That last addition had obviously been meant to placate Alizhan, who'd flattened her mouth into a stubborn line. It hadn't worked.

"Based on her name, I'm assuming that Iriyat Varenx is Nalitzvan?"

Alizhan nodded. "We call her Ha-Varensi now that she's the head of Varenx House. But yes, Varenx House was founded by Nalitzvans. Iriyat speaks the language."

"And she's educated," Thiyo said. "Speaks two languages, at least. Owns the whole series of *A Natural History of the World* in her library."

Alizhan nodded again. Her shoulders were tight and she was still frowning.

"This portrait of Iriyat is where I started. She's wealthy, educated, powerful, beautiful. And she really wanted to share this secret with someone—otherwise why write it down? So I thought she might be a little bit of a showoff. She'd write in a refined way. And maybe she'd throw in unusual words. It wasn't until I started thinking of Old Nalitzvan words that I found something," Thiyo said. "I told you our word *uheko*, for people like you and Henny and Iriyat and Ket. People whose gifts flow through their touch."

At the sound of her name, Henny gave a lazy wave from where she was lying on her side in bed with a book, and then went back to ignoring their murmured Laalvuri conversation. She wasn't as riveted as Ev. She had no reason to be, since she barely knew who Iriyat was or what she'd done.

"Our words for different types of *uheko* aren't creative," Thiyo continued. In his excitement, he struggled to keep his voice quiet. "We just called people like Iriyat and Ket 'memory changers.' But because there's such a longstanding hatred and fear of magic in Nalitzva, there are many more words for people with gifts. Most of them are slurs—not words that people would use to talk about themselves. But in Old Nalitzvan, there was another name for memory changers—*smaroi*. It means 'lacemakers.'"

"You found it," Alizhan said. There was no triumph in her voice.

"Yes," Thiyo said, still delighted, but that one word was like the last breath of passion rushing out of him. Alizhan's early, numb reaction left him deflated. His shoulders slumped. He'd wanted them to be excited, too. He continued, far more soberly, "Iriyat's invented script contains all the characters necessary to write Laalvuri words, but the diphthong *oi* doesn't occur in Laalvuri, so this word contained a combination of characters that stuck out. I started thinking about it and—well, anyway, I found many instances of words that are likely to be forms of 'Lacemaking' or 'Lacemaker,' and we have no reason to believe the text is about the creation of actual lace. I haven't made my way through the whole thing yet. But this is the key."

"Good," Alizhan said, and it couldn't have sounded further from the truth. "This doesn't mean anything for certain, though. Someone else could still have written the text."

Thiyo stared at her, unsure what to make of that. The book

belonged to Iriyat. His discovery had been predicated on knowledge of Iriyat's personality. The simplest answer was that Iriyat had written the encoded text. But Ev understood, although she didn't want to. Every time she thought about Alizhan's long history with Iriyat, her stomach threatened to turn over. It was hard to grasp just how poisonous it was. Iriyat had isolated Alizhan from the world and exploited her. Worse, Iriyat had centered herself in Alizhan's world as the only source of love and comfort, so that even now, after everything they'd learned, Alizhan still occasionally defended her.

Ev regretted killing the guard who had attacked Thiyo in Nalitzva. She didn't think she'd regret killing Iriyat, if she ever got the chance.

If Alizhan overheard that thought, it didn't show.

"Maybe we should tell Thiyo the rest of the story," Ev said. She didn't think he really needed it, now that he had a pathway into the text, but it might help him understand Alizhan. "Just in case it makes his job easier."

"Please," Thiyo said. "We only got as far as you discovering that Iriyat is a Lacemaker. What is she after? Altering memories alone isn't enough to make you run. You didn't run from Ket."

"We're not sure," Alizhan said. And then she told the whole story, starting with Kasrik's theft of the book from Iriyat's study. It took some time to retell all the events, and Ev was amused, though not surprised, to find herself portrayed in Alizhan's account as some kind of idealized, righteous figure of legend—a little bit like Vesper in *The Sunrise Chronicles*. Ev hadn't felt, at the time, like she was making heroic choices. More often than not, she'd felt lost and overwhelmed. She just hadn't wanted Alizhan to get killed. And then once she'd found out that Iriyat was hurting and killing other people, she'd wanted that to stop, too. What other choices were there?

Alizhan, in her own version of events, veered between clever and hapless. She broke into Mar ha-Solora's mansion with ease, but couldn't figure out how to stop upsetting Ev in conversation. That last bit didn't really belong in the story, and Ev looked to Thiyo, expecting to see his false patience wearing thin. But instead, he was wide-eyed. And he was stuck on one particular detail of their story.

"People just... leave their children?"

"In orphanages, yes," Alizhan said.

"*Orphan* means a child with dead parents," Thiyo said. "That's not what you're describing."

"Well, no."

"You're describing people voluntarily abandoning their children. And your religion *encourages* it."

"Only certain kinds of children." Alizhan shifted her weight on the bed. She never seemed to mind mentioning this topic in her rapid, light way—*oh by the way, either my parents are dead or they abandoned me*—as if the horror of it would be diminished by speaking as briefly as possible. Thiyo's reaction, honest and unwilling to brush aside the ugliness of it, disturbed her. "And if you're worried about me, don't. Ev and I figured out who my father was, we think, and he died in the wave when I was a baby. And for all we know, maybe my mother died in the wave, too. I probably *am* an orphan. Nobody willingly abandoned me. So it's the others you should be sad for, and not me."

"I don't see how *any* of that makes anything better."

In the twenty-two triads they'd spent together, Ev had rarely seen Thiyo get emotional about anything that didn't directly affect him. The wider world didn't concern him. He had time only for his own happiness, his own hurt. But now, with his good hand, he reached for Alizhan's, stroking his thumb over the back of her hand. "I'm sorry," he said. "I wish things had been different for you."

Alizhan turned her face so neither of them could see it, but she didn't pull her hand away. "Don't," she said, her voice thick. "Don't be nice to me. I don't know what to do when you're nice. Just go back to being funny and arrogant and mean."

"How dare you," Thiyo said, pretending offense. "Maybe *you're* the arrogant, mean one, did you ever consider that?"

And they were play-fighting like cats again. But for a moment, the curtain had been pulled back, and something else had been exposed. None of the three of them seemed to know what.

But before they could say anything else, one of the women across the room hissed a warning at them. Thiyo apologized to her in Estvan, then began to gather the pages. "I'll let you know what I find," he said. He touched Alizhan on the hand again, and left.

WORKING with Pirkko wasn't what Ev expected. The first thing they did was pass half a shift walking the length of the ramparts together. The ramparts weren't all ice, as Ev had thought when she first arrived. They were stone in most places, and it was easy to walk along the broad path at the top of the walls.

Pirkko stopped to show Ev each guard station, introducing her to the people who were working there. A few of them were able to speak to her in Laalvuri, but most weren't, and Ev was embarrassed. She was so useless. She could hardly do good work here, unable to speak to anyone.

Maybe Thiyo could teach her. No, that was foolish. He had his own work, and the book to decipher.

"Can you teach me Estvan?" Ev said to Pirkko, as they continued their walk. They might not stay long, but she wanted to do good while she was here.

Pirkko replied with a word Ev didn't understand, and when Ev looked confused, she burst out laughing. "*Ol*," she said again. "*Ol* is mean yes."

"Ol," Ev repeated, but apparently not to Pirkko's satisfaction.

"Ol-luh," Pirkko said, dragging out the last consonant.

Ev tried again, and although she felt ridiculous, Pirkko beamed. They went back and forth with a few more words and phrases—*hello* and *goodbye*, which were the same, and *no*, and *my name is*—and Ev stumbled over all the new sounds. Pirkko laughed a few times, but never maliciously. Mostly she smiled. She was so much less serious out here. It was hard to reconcile this young woman, her laughter lighting up the darkness, with the enforcer who'd exiled two men into the cold last triad. Maybe learning the language would give Ev some insight.

When they'd finished walking around the city, they stopped at the main gate where Ev had first entered. In addition to the guard post, where there were always at least two people, there was a stock room full of spears, bows, staves, swords, and other weaponry that Ev had never used.

"What you know?" Pirkko said, gesturing around the room.

Ev picked up a staff, and Pirkko smiled, nodded, and picked up a second one, then pointed out the door. She went into the courtyard, and Ev followed. They faced off without another word. Pirkko came at Ev, spinning her staff, with a wild grin on her face. Despite the smile, her first attack was no joke, and Ev had to move fast to block it. She began to swing her staff to gain momentum for an attack of her own, but worry distracted her. She thought of Pirkko forcing those men into exile. How serious was this sparring? A few bruises meant nothing to Ev, but would Pirkko feel the same? Should Ev let her win to avoid any trouble?

Pirkko's staff slammed into her side. *Smoke*. No more distractions. Ev sucked in a breath and retaliated hard. Pirkko stepped to the side, just out of range, but Ev almost caught her. Ev's reach was longer—an advantage. She began to force Pirkko back, gaining ground one swipe at a time, keeping Pirkko on the defensive. In an instant between warding off Ev's attacks, Pirkko raised her staff to swing it at Ev, and Ev brought her own weapon lower. She hit Pirkko's legs, knocking her to her knees. Pirkko dropped her staff and raised her hands in surrender, laughing.

"You good with stick," she said. "Good with sword too?"

Relief swept through Ev. Pirkko wasn't angry. She smiled shyly and shrugged one shoulder. "Want to find out?"

Even knowing that they were sparring, play-fighting, not actually trying to hurt each other, Ev was happy to see Pirkko pull out two wooden practice swords. Pirkko proved to be better with a sword, and she disarmed Ev in a matter of minutes. Ev insisted they try again, and the second match lasted longer. But just when Ev had found her footing, Pirkko sent her sword flying out of her hand, dropped her own sword, and barreled into Ev. Ev fell backwards with Pirkko on top of her, and they rolled twice on the hard-packed snow. Ev ended up with Pirkko pinning her to the ground, and Pirkko locked eyes with her and leaned down so their noses almost touched. Ev didn't breathe. What was she doing?

Pirkko pulled at Ev's coat collar with one hand and shoved a handful of snow against her bare skin.

"Smoke, that's cold," Ev shouted. She threw Pirkko off and fought back with a snowball of her own. It exploded on impact and snow caught in Pirkko's blond hair and the fur lining her hood, glittering white against her flushed cheeks. Pirkko blinked it out of her eyes with a grim expression on her face, and then when Ev opened her mouth to apologize, a snowball hit her in the face.

ALIZHAN HAD NEVER THOUGHT she'd miss that little room at
Zhenev's, but Estva made everywhere else feel like paradise.
Alizhan's life was divided into her time in the kitchen—miserable—and her time in the mess hall, which was also miserable,
and her time lying awake in bed—the most miserable of all.

"I'm sorry you don't like it," Ev said. "But you have to eat
something."

Alizhan pushed a lumpy bite of overcooked greens across
her plate. "Nightvine smells awful," she said. "It tastes worse.
And I spent all shift cooking it. Breathing it. I just can't, Ev."

"There's bread, then. Don't stop eating, too. I already know
you're not sleeping."

Alizhan should have been able to sleep. It was true there
were twenty people in their dormitory, but Ev was the only one
Alizhan could sense, and even she was quieter and quieter.
The dormitory should have been a constant carnival of flash-
ing, squirming dreams. Instead it was a graveyard. Once,
Alizhan might have said the former scenario was torture and
the latter was luxury—but the tomblike silence was fraying her
confidence. She'd always assumed she was a bad sleeper
because of her secret. Her power. The thing that was wrong
with her. But if that thing was gone—and if it was gone, was it
gone for now or forever?—then Alizhan was just a person. A
person who still wasn't good at sleeping. A person who still
couldn't see faces or get along with strangers or enjoy touching
other people.

When there was nobody else in Alizhan's head, instead of
blessed, peaceful emptiness, her own feelings crowded the space
until they were leaking out of her—in a bewildering and
horrible way. Her eyes had filled with tears when she'd arrived
in the kitchen at the start of her third shift and the hours of dull

work had spread out before her like the icy Nightward plains. And Ev had left her there alone.

Rationally, Alizhan knew Ev didn't have much choice, but that didn't change her stupid, awful feelings. She let her fork clatter down on her plate. Next to her, Ev sighed. That was the only indication Ev had any thoughts on the matter. A sigh. Alizhan couldn't sense her. She missed Ev's constant stream of repressed irritation and judgment. Her amusement, her affection, her desire, her embarrassment, her worrying. All gone. Ev was right there, and Alizhan was lonely.

"When can we get out of here?" she asked, almost under her breath.

"Thiyo's making progress. It won't be long."

Alizhan said nothing. Ev was trying to make her feel better. She'd even noticed that Alizhan spent her sleep shift lying still and awake on her bed, which was unexpected. It wasn't like *Ev* could see inside *her*, after all. But Ev was observant. She took care of Alizhan.

Or she tried, at least.

"I think Pirkko might have a room to herself," Ev said. "There are houses outside the dormitories, too. Not everybody here lives the way we're living. If it would help you to move into different living arrangements, maybe we could ask."

Fucking Pirkko. Alizhan hated her dumb face. She didn't even know what it looked like, but she knew she didn't like it. "And say what? My *unnatural* friend here requires privacy to sleep?"

"Give me a little credit. I could come up with something better than that."

"I don't think talking to Pirkko is a good idea."

"Give her a little credit, too," Ev said. "She's nicer than you think."

Ev was trying to tell Alizhan what people were like on the

inside, since Alizhan was useless now. She didn't like being useless, but she hated being told what to think even more. Alizhan knew exactly what Ev would say if she mentioned it—some slyly smiling version of *oh really? and how does that make* you *feel?*—and the answer was *guilty*. It made Alizhan feel like she should apologize to Ev. They were not going down that path. Not when Alizhan hadn't slept or eaten.

Alizhan picked up her fork again and drew the tines through the mess on her plate. The metal screeched against the ceramic and the noise pierced the room for an instant. It was a clamor of voices and utensils and furniture creaking or being shoved across the floor, a meaningless mishmash of sound with no feelings simmering beneath it and no thoughts rising above it. What good were her ears, if this was all they could perceive? How did anyone live like this?

Ev was just guessing about people's insides. And she was wrong about Pirkko, who ran some kind of police force for this evil place that left people to die in the cold for being different, and was definitely *not* trustworthy. Pirkko had taken away Ev—Alizhan's only source of comfort and happiness in this icy hell-hole—and Alizhan wasn't planning to forgive her for it now or ever. And she had a dumb face.

Alizhan was being childish, she knew. But it was terrifying, being cut off from her senses and isolated from her friends. And something was rotten in Estva and everyone was ignoring it but her. Where had all these people's feelings gone? Could *all* of these people have magic, even though it was against the rules? That didn't make sense. Why would it be against the rules if everyone had it? Were these people even real? Were they alive? Had they done some kind of experiment on themselves to remove all their emotions? Was that why it was so easy for them to exile people into the Night to die? Was that why they could eat gross food all the time and not care?

One of those things was a much bigger problem than the other, and Alizhan ought to feel bad for equating them. Maybe she was the problem. Iriyat had always wanted to "cure" Alizhan, and now she *was* cured—maybe—but she still wasn't normal. Estva was making it clear that there were things wrong with Alizhan that had nothing to do with mind-reading. Would she always be this way? Was there no way to fix her? And how long could a person go without sleeping before they died?

Alizhan hated this place and what it was doing to her. Before, she'd been fucked up, but she'd been special. Now she wasn't special.

She shoved her plate away and stood up. "I'm going to bed."

"DON'T FOLLOW HER," Thiyo said when Ev stood up to go after Alizhan. "Give her some space."

"Really? Is that what you'd want?"

To Ev's surprise, Thiyo gave her question some thought. "Sometimes. Ideally, I'd sulk alone for a little while and then when I was ready, Ily—someone would come fawn over me in a way that made me feel better. But she's not me. Why don't you go somewhere else for little while and let me talk to her?"

It made Ev's heart squeeze painfully tight to let Alizhan go off alone when she was so clearly upset about something. But maybe it was Ev's fault. Was Alizhan still mad at her for switching jobs? Ev hadn't had any control over that, which Alizhan knew perfectly well. It was unfair of her to hold a grudge for it. Still, maybe Thiyo was right and he should be the one to speak with her.

"You said she hasn't been sleeping," Thiyo said. "She's probably just tired. And hungry. I'll sneak her some better food and she'll cheer up."

"Why don't you come down to the hot springs with me?" Henny said. "I want to see them, but I'd rather go with friends. Ket, do you want to come, too?"

He nodded. "Sorry to go without you, Thiyo. Maybe you can persuade Alizhan to come with you and both of you can join us."

"Oh, I... no, thank you. I have work to do."

It was rare to see Thiyo stumble like that. Maybe he wanted space as much as Alizhan did—if that was what she wanted. Ev couldn't figure either of them out. It was a relief to follow Henny and Ket. For an instant, she didn't have to wonder what the hell she was supposed to do next.

Estva was deceptive. It felt claustrophobic, only a few large buildings and little clusters of houses beyond them, but there was a whole system of underground levels that connected all the buildings. The hallway sloped and they were funneled into a spiral staircase that led down into a warm, misty cavern. There was green lamplight ringing the edge of the room. The pool in the middle glinted with reflections. The ceiling rose up above them, a smooth dome over their heads.

"Wow," Henny said. "I thought it was going to be small and bare and dingy like everywhere else around here."

"I had no idea," Ev said.

"They take their hot springs seriously. I guess we're lucky to have it to ourselves."

Ev walked to the edge of the pool. The surrounding stone was dry, so she sat down and removed her boots so she could dip a toe in. The heat of the water wavered between welcome and overwhelming and the striking change in temperature sent a tremor through her body. Behind her, she could hear the soft sounds of Henny and Ket murmuring their amazement in Nalitzvan and shedding their clothes. Ev wished Alizhan were with her, so they could marvel at this place together. Would

Alizhan even like this? Or was she so unhappy here that nothing would give her a moment's relief?

Ket kept some of his white linen underclothes on, covering his chest and his thighs, but Henny had no hesitations about stripping naked and sliding into the water. She sighed and laughed as the hot water enveloped her. An instant later, she was floating in the pool with her red hair fanning out in the water. Ket followed more cautiously.

"This is worth all that time we spent in the wagon," Henny said. Her eyes were closed and she was smiling. "And of course we believe in whatever your mission is."

"Right," Ev said. She stood up, turned away from Henny and Ket, and began to shed her clothes. It was silly to face away from them, but something about removing her clothes seemed so much more vulnerable and intimate than simply being naked.

"We do, though," Ket said, far more sincerely. "At least, I do. I don't know all the details of what you're doing, but we'd heard so much about Lady Lan... did Thiyo really do all those things?"

"I don't know what you heard," Ev said. She slid into the pool as quickly as possible, covering her nakedness with water. The heat shocked her skin. She'd gone too fast. "But knowing Thiyo, my guess is yes."

"There were rumors that Lan had an affair with Ilyr," Henny said, dropping out of her float and putting her feet on the floor of the pool. "If that were true, we'd have learned something very interesting about our prince."

"Yes, ah," Ev said, uncomfortable with the heat and the topic of conversation. Thiyo should tell his own secrets. She settled on a stone ledge at the edge of the pool, letting the water lap at her shoulders. "That part is true."

Ket smiled and Henny frowned. It was a funny image, the two of them standing together with opposite facial expressions. Then Henny noticed Ket smiling and her frown deepened.

"You're such an idealist," she said. "This isn't going to change anything."

"It might," Ket said. "He'll be king eventually. And he's like us. And if he knew Thiyo, he knew someone... even more like us. And he didn't have Thiyo executed."

Henny was shaking her head. "The rules have always been different for royals. You think we've never had a king who loved men before? Or someone in the royal family with gifts? We have. Zhenev's had royal clients with every kind of request—she told me. They do what they want, and hang the rest of us."

Was there anywhere without such cruelties? Was there any place where all people treated each other with kindness? It angered and exhausted her. Wrongs were everywhere, and every right thing in the world, no matter how trivial, had come from a hard-fought victory. Justice didn't spring up naturally. It didn't grow wild. It had to be tended.

"Laalvur is no better," Ev said. "Different, but no better. We're trying to change things, too."

But Ev couldn't do it alone.

ON HIS WAY to the dormitory where Alizhan was staying, Thiyo ran into Ayat. More accurately, she ran into him. Rolled her chair right over his foot. What could he possibly have done to deserve that? They'd barely spoken. She didn't apologize. Her glare was so fierce that for an instant, he almost felt as though he was the one who should—no, that was absurd. Even when Thiyo knew he was in the wrong, he rarely apologized. Why should one little streak of black eye makeup and some uncreative rudeness unsettle him so?

"Don't trust anyone here," Ayat said.

"Including you? Not that you were on my list."

"You're new here," she said. "I'm trying to help."

"Are you allowed to trust anyone?" Thiyo asked with genuine curiosity. "Aren't you supposed to doubt everything?"

"You think you're smart," she said, and went on her way without another word.

Would it be pathetic to say "I don't think I'm smart, I *am* smart" to her back as she rolled away? It was hardly a good enough retort to shout down the hall, but Thiyo didn't like to let anyone else have the last word. And why didn't she like him? Or was she like this with everyone? Maybe doubting everything made people unfriendly.

Alizhan was leaning against the doorframe when he arrived at her room. Her arms were crossed over her chest, squashing the thick rope of her braid against the brown leather of her coat. Poor thing, she must still be cold. It was stifling in the dormitory, but Alizhan was small and easily chilled.

Then Thiyo glanced down and saw she was wearing boots, too.

"Going somewhere?"

"Who were you talking to in the corridor?" she asked.

"Ayat," Thiyo said. "She works in the bindery. I don't think she likes me."

"Probably a safe bet."

"Don't be mean," Thiyo said. Alizhan had actually sounded a little sad, even as she'd been so brutally honest. She didn't usually have to make bets, no matter how probable, about other people's inner lives. "That's my thing."

"So why did you come to check on me?" Alizhan asked. "I was expecting Ev. She's the nice one."

"How do you know I wasn't just out for a stroll?"

"I don't," Alizhan said, and she pushed off the wall and walked down the corridor, forcing Thiyo to follow her. She led them out of the building and into the biting Night air, making

Thiyo glad he'd worn his coat to dinner. Their feet crunched in the frost on the ground. Alizhan headed straight for a staircase set into the ramparts and she didn't stop until they were both at the top of the wall, staring out into the endless shades of blue and black.

"People weren't meant to live like this," Alizhan said, and Thiyo wasn't sure if she meant the darkness, the cold, the isolation, or something else.

"What's got you so upset?" Thiyo said. "You barely even flinched when we talked about your tragic past. But you've been on edge since we arrived."

"Do you ever feel like there's nowhere in the world for you?" Alizhan said, more or less ignoring him. Her eyes were trained on some distant point where snow and sky faded into the same shade. There was just enough light from the city below that he could trace the proud outline of her profile against the darkness —the line of her brow, the sharp angle of her nose, and the inky richness of her hair, blacker than Night. He'd rarely seen her still and contemplative.

But her thoughts weren't vague or dreamy. Even without being able to read him, she'd posed precisely the question that was bothering him. Maybe it was bothering her, too.

"If there's nowhere in the world for me, that's a problem with the world, not me."

"That's how you talk, not how you feel," Alizhan said with unerring accuracy.

"Maybe I talk that way to convince myself," Thiyo said. "And as lovely as it is out here, I thought you hated the cold."

"I hate the silence more."

"As for the world, you'll make somewhere for yourself," he said. "Isn't that what you're trying to do, in a way? I know it's about getting justice for those kids and stopping Iriyat from hurting anyone else, but if it works, you'll have carved out a space for yourself."

"Maybe," Alizhan said after a long moment, her breath clouding the air. Thiyo had come out here to reassure her, and he left feeling even less sure of himself.

24

AN UNMARKED LETTER

MY CHERISHED FRIEND,

OUR PRINCE has left us to deliver Lan's ashes to Hoi—though perhaps he simply couldn't stand the thought of his new wife. I don't suppose you'd have anything to do with his wild impulse to visit the islands, would you? I recall that you inspired his first trip, although your goals remain mysterious to me. What is there to be gained from contact with those savages? They are undoubtedly experts in violence and depravity, but you have no interest in such things. What knowledge could they have, isolated as they are by an ocean so ferocious and unforgiving that you still do not dare set foot aboard a ship?

More importantly—M has not been seen at court since shortly after our dear Prince's wedding and Lady Lan's absurdly extravagant funeral. I regret to report that her whereabouts are unknown even to myself. Given that M was in Ilyr's private quarters with your pet thief and her entourage just before they escaped the city, I'd wager she's followed them Nightward.

Have your people in Estva keep an eye out.

It's been a long time since she's left Nalitzva. She may be coming your way at last. Prepare yourself.

. . .

PLEASE ACCEPT, my friend, my most sacred and sincere vows,

MP

25

TROUBLE

TEN TRIADS—A FULL WEEK—passed in relative peace, and then Thiyo and Ket were preparing to go to sleep in their side-by-side cots when Ket reached out and put a hand on Thiyo's arm. Ket's candle was the last one flickering in their dormitory and his hair was brilliant gold in the warmth of its light. The shadows deepened around his eyes. He kept his voice as low as the light. "Have you been having any... trouble?"

"All kinds," Thiyo said dryly, thinking of the book he'd barely had time to look at, and Alizhan's increasing alienation, and his bizarre encounters with Ayat.

"No. I mean, with... talking. Listening. Understanding. Whatever it is you do."

Magic. Suddenly, their soft conversation felt too loud. "No. Have you?"

Ket shook his head. "No. Well, I haven't tried. But Henny—"

"Shouldn't be trying anything, either."

"If you saw the people who come to the infirmary—people with their bones crushed in mining accidents—you'd want to help them, too," Ket said. "And I haven't noticed you using any self-restraint in the matter, so spare her your judgment."

"That's different," Thiyo said. He couldn't stop using his ability—not without copious quantities of venom. Or Henny's touch. But Thiyo's gift wasn't instantly identifiable as magic. Plenty of people spoke more than one language. "I can pass."

"I can pass," Ket said, and Thiyo had never heard that dark edge in his voice. Because Ket was shy and sweet, and so relaxed and reasonable all the time, it was easy to forget how dangerous he was. But in the same way that bears and big cats could curl up and nap anywhere they pleased, Ket never had to worry. He was a deadly predator, too. "And so can Henny, most of the time. She makes hurt people feel better, and that's what healers do. No one complains."

"The danger isn't the people she's healing. It's other witnesses," Thiyo said, even though Ket had just made it clear that witnesses were never a problem for him. Better not to go down that path. "And I understand you both want to help people, but she shouldn't do it at the expense of her own life."

"That's just it. She isn't."

That was unexpected. It piqued his curiosity enough that he forgot his warning tone. "But she's been trying?"

Ket nodded. "It's not working."

"So we need to identify the problem. Is it her or is it here?"

"How do we figure that out?"

"She needs to test it on you," Thiyo said. "Discreetly, of course. I assume that will be more pleasant than the other way around."

"Right," Ket said. "And one more thing."

Thiyo waited.

"Do you, um... do you think the women here are a little... forward?"

Thiyo raised an eyebrow. "Compared to the brothel where you live?"

"No, I'm being serious, I—women don't usually—" Even by the light of a single candle, it was obvious Ket was blushing.

They couldn't be more than five years apart in age, but somehow Ket managed to make Thiyo feel old. He'd started this conversation by warning Ket about keeping their secrets and now he was feeling even more protective. It was a novel experience. Until now, he'd never wanted to protect anyone other than himself. "Are you being harassed?"

"No, no, none of them have done anything wrong. I'm just... surprised."

"Well, in that case, enjoy the attention."

Ket let out a single, short laugh, loud enough that someone else in the room grunted a reprimand. Ket dropped his head, covering his face with his free hand. "You have no idea what it feels like to be shy, do you?"

"No," Thiyo said. "The whole concept is baffling. Ket, are you uncomfortable with women flirting with you because you're waiting for Henny?"

Ket looked up, letting his hand fall back into his lap. "Me and Henny, we're complicated. We like each other, but we have... different opinions."

"I hope it's not about what's between your legs," Thiyo said. He knew some people were just born liking one thing or the other, with no choice in the matter, but the idea was as foreign and perplexing as the thought of someone not enjoying attention.

"No, no, Gods, no," Ket said quickly. If possible, his cheeks were redder than before. How had this poor man survived life in a brothel? "She, uh... she's... satisfied." A tiny cough. Thiyo would have announced that fact with far more enthusiasm. "But I asked her to quit working and she won't."

"Ah."

"I want us to move out, get a place together," Ket said. "I'll keep working for Zhenev, but we don't have to live there."

"And what is Henny going to do, in this imagined future?"

"Anything she likes."

"Except work."

"She could work! She could do other work, different work. I just..." Ket sighed.

"I don't think we're going to solve this one," Thiyo said. "At least, you're not going to solve it by talking to me."

Ket sighed again and blew out the candle. "Sleep well."

"Sleep well." The reply was automatic and meaningless. Instead of calming down for sleep, Thiyo's mind was already sorting through everything Ket had said. Was Henny really losing her power? When they'd arrived, Alizhan had said the mess hall was quiet. Was she losing her power, too? Were they all in danger? Was it something about this place? If Ket lost his ability, he'd lose his job at Zhenev's, and his imagined life with Henny would be gone with it.

If Thiyo lost his gift, what would become of him?

IT WAS a relief to get back to work next shift, even if Ayat was there, eyeing him every time he glanced into the other room. What had he done to her? Did she watch every new arrival so balefully?

Sardas was better company, humming to himself as he assembled movable type. At one point, he said cautiously, "You know, I've never met anyone like you."

"No one has." The quip was out before Thiyo could consider it. He gave Sardas a smile to make sure he knew it was meant in good humor.

Sardas nodded and smiled back. "I suppose that's true for all of us."

A beat of silence passed before Thiyo recognized the priest's opening statement for what it was—a question. A very Estvan question. Sardas thought Thiyo was declining to answer—which, in a way, he was. Saying nothing was the wisest course of action.

And yet.

He wanted to talk to someone. Someone who hadn't been trapped in a wagon with him for a week. Someone who wasn't consumed with paranoia. Someone who loved books and words as much as he did.

Ayat had told him not to trust anyone. And she didn't seem to like Sardas—but she didn't seem to like anyone. And as a priest of Doubt, she'd be naturally inclined to dislike priests of the Balance. Thiyo had even heard that the two sects had brawls in the streets of Laalvur sometimes. He'd have to ask Ev and Alizhan if that was true. Priests of different traditions certainly didn't hesitate to trade blows in the Estvan mess hall.

And besides, Thiyo had never done what he was told.

"I'm from Hoi," he told Sardas, and it was worth it just to see the older man's face light up with a smile.

"I wondered," he admitted. "But I know so little of the islands. There was no way for me to guess which one you were from. You know, there's a text in one of these cupboards that no one's ever been able to read... Perhaps you could take a look?"

"Of course," Thiyo said. Sardas went to one of the cabinets along the wall. He rested his cane against it then bent down slowly to open it. He pulled out a towering stack of books and papers. The top half slid off and books fluttered and thumped to the floor. A cloud of dust rose into the air. Thiyo knelt to help him collect the mess, handing things back to Sardas, who shuffled through them. As he sorted the books and papers, putting some back into the cabinet, Thiyo noticed a tiny spot of faded color on the floor. It was a circle smaller than his fingertip. At first he thought it was a scrap of some expensive paper, but when he touched it, his index finger came away with a miniature star-shaped bloom resting on top. A pressed flower. It must have fallen out of the stack. Some of the fanciest paper did have leaves and flowers pressed into it. Thiyo smiled and stuck the little thing in his pocket.

Sardas finished sorting and restacking the books. "Damn," he said. "I can't find it. Maybe I put it in storage. I'll look a few other places later."

"Perhaps in the meantime you'd tell me more about yourself —if that isn't terribly rude of me to ask. Or even if it is. I've always been more concerned with other peoples' manners than my own."

Sardas laughed. "Most people are, but few would admit it so frankly. As for me, there's very little to tell that I haven't mentioned already. I'm from Laalvur, but I've spent most of my adult life here. As you saw, I've been here long enough to adopt the Estvan custom of not asking questions. But I don't mind if you ask me things."

"Did you learn other languages because you wanted to see the world?"

"Oh, it was nothing so purposeful as that," Sardas said, laughing again. "I've loved them since I was a child. You'll think me a dull, dried-up old man for saying this—and that's true enough, since I haven't left Estva in years and I rarely even leave this room—but new words are a thrill."

It was Thiyo who laughed then. "Not at all. I understand completely."

"There's a kind of animal pleasure in sound, I think," Sardas mused.

"Yes, absolutely. Forming the sounds with your tongue and

teeth, it's so physical, and it's delicious. My mother always said that if I could eat words, I'd never come home for dinner again."

"Is that a saying among your people, or was it specific to her?"

"Oh, it was all hers," Thiyo said. He rarely smiled when he thought of his mother. No doubt she would still be seething if Thiyo ever made it back to Hoi. But Sardas had an easy way about him, and he was asking Thiyo more questions about language, so Thiyo pushed aside his other thoughts. They made pleasant conversation and the rest of the shift passed so easily that Thiyo forgot all about decoding the book or avoiding Ayat's suspicious eyes.

ALIZHAN'S COMPANIONS tried hard to cheer her up every time they shared a meal. Each of them always had some mundane detail of their shift to retell. Henny and Ket talked about their grateful patients. Ev talked about people she'd met on her rounds. Thiyo talked about the books he was preparing to print. Alizhan wanted to be grateful, but she felt as dead as the Estvan air. There were no feelings outside her or inside her.

"Oh, look at this. I found it on the floor at work," Thiyo said. He retrieved something from his pocket and stretched his hand across the table. At the tip of his finger was a tiny pressed flower.

Ev, Henny, and Ket all leaned toward his hand and smiled, but Alizhan froze. A dreamlike memory filtered into her vision like sunlight through a gap in the curtains. *Iriyat, seated on her bed, twirling a tiny purple flower between her thumb and her index. The star-shaped blooms were one of Iriyat's own breeds.* "Where the fuck did you get that?" she hissed. Heedless of the danger of touching Thiyo's hand, she grabbed the flower and brought it closer to her face, pinching it like it might escape. Five pointed petals in Varenx House lavender.

"I just said—" Thiyo started, still holding his hand out in the open, too surprised to withdraw.

"This is Iriyat's," Alizhan said. Her pulse beat in her ears. There was no escape from Iriyat, not even in this furthest Nightward corner of the world. Alizhan should have known. "It can't be here. Not unless she's here."

"It's just a flower," Thiyo said. "I'm sure it fell off some fancy paper in one of our cabinets."

"This is a flower that Iriyat bred," Alizhan said.

"That's a sin against God's Balance," Ev said. "She's so religious. Are you sure she breeds—"

"It's a sin to murder and torture people, too," Alizhan snapped. "She's not likely to balk at breeding new plants."

"Alizhan, breathe. Iriyat can't be here. You've said yourself she's afraid to sail. Maybe it's a coincidence. You know there are plants here that can't grow in Laalvur. Like nightvine. Things that grow in the springs. Maybe that flower just looks similar to one you saw at Varenx House."

"You don't believe me," Alizhan said. Incredulity echoed through her voice. Why couldn't they see? Why didn't Ev trust her anymore? That hurt, but it hurt in the distant way that used to mean someone else was experiencing pain close to Alizhan. But this time, it had to be her own pain, since there was no one else she could read.

She rubbed her fingertips together, crumbling the flower, and walked away.

EV THOUGHT her new job would keep her outdoors, on or around the ramparts, all the time. But Pirkko explained that one of their duties was to find people who hadn't shown up for their work shift.

"The rules," Ev said. She couldn't keep the edge of suspicion out of her voice.

"Good rules," Pirkko said. "Make sure people not fall down mine shaft."

"That is important," Ev allowed, although when they were called down to the kitchens, she had a sinking feeling. They weren't going to pull anyone out of a mine shaft in there, and Ev knew exactly who was missing.

The heat in the long, narrow underground room weighed on her. She shouldn't have left Alizhan alone down here. Ev stood by, sweating, while a large, dour woman in an apron explained to Pirkko what Ev had already guessed. Alizhan hadn't come to work.

"Your friend," Pirkko said, and Ev nodded with resignation. "You find."

"I'll find her," Ev said. Alizhan wouldn't react well if she showed up with Pirkko in tow. She might not react well even if Ev was alone. Why was she drawing attention to herself like this? Couldn't she just lie low for a few triads? They were so close to getting out. But that tiny little flower had really set her off. "Maybe you should go look for the next person on your list."

Ev was grateful that Pirkko accepted this proposal without asking any questions. Now all she had to do was find Alizhan and drag her back to the place she least wanted to be. Where would she go? Ev hadn't spent much time with her since their arrival. But she'd been alone with Thiyo while Ev had been in the hot springs with Henny and Ket. Maybe he'd know.

The long walk to the rooms that held the press and bindery did nothing to calm Ev's nerves. Thiyo didn't even look up when she appeared in the doorway, absorbed as he was in arranging tiny metal characters on a plate. He was laughing at something the handsome older priest with the cane had just said. Through the door on the other side of the room, Ev could see a white-skinned, black-robed priest of Doubt with her kohl-dark eyes narrowed.

At least Thiyo seemed to like his work better than Alizhan.

"Thiyo."

He lifted his head from his work and turned to her. "Switching jobs?"

"No. Looking for Alizhan. She didn't show up for work. Do you have any idea where she might be?"

"We went up on the ramparts for our little chat," Thiyo said. "I assume she was looking for a suitably dramatic spot to feel melancholy. I'd check the ramparts and any roof she might be able to get to."

"In her case, that's all of them."

"Sure you don't want to switch jobs?"

Ev couldn't laugh. She shook her head instead. "I don't know why she'd do this."

"That was a serious offer," Thiyo said. "I'll look for her, if you want. She's upset in general, but I think she might be especially upset with you."

"But I didn't do anything!"

"Exactly," Thiyo said, whatever that meant. "Sardas, will you excuse me for a moment? We need to go check on a friend. She didn't show up for her work assignment and we think she's not well."

The older man nodded. "Of course."

When they were in the corridor, farther away from anyone who might overhear, Ev whispered, "What do you mean, 'exactly'?"

"Let's find out if I'm right first," Thiyo said. Then he turned to go up the stairs at the end of the corridor and led her up three flights. It was still a shock to exit into the darkness every single time. The light never changed in Laalvur or Nalitzva, but at least there was light.

Thiyo was certainly right about Alizhan's chosen sulking spot, although it took them four tries to find her. Even then, they almost missed her, huddled at the corner of the roof like the world's most pitiful gargoyle. She was crouched on a narrow stone railing and she didn't move when they approached.

Of course not. Her senses were dull here.

"Alizhan," Ev said.

Alizhan whipped around and jumped down from her perch. She put her back to the railing and clutched it with both hands, like she might have to leap over it at any second. Then she said, "Thiyo. And Ev."

"Are you alright?" Ev asked. "You didn't show up for work and Pirkko—"

"Perhaps the better question is how much longer you can stand to be here," Thiyo interrupted smoothly. "One triad? Two? I'm almost finished, and then hopefully Henny and Ket will be willing to take us to the coast and then the two of you can get back to Laalvur."

Alizhan's expression twisted in misery at the idea of staying two more triads in Estva. Ev supposed if she'd been deprived of food and sleep, she'd feel the same. Although it was hard not to feel that Alizhan was depriving *herself* of food and sleep. They could find a solution if Alizhan would only let them help. Was this the Night madness Thiyo had mentioned? Ev didn't want to believe that. "That's not long," she said, trying to sound encouraging. "You can make it another two triads."

Alizhan hugged herself and shook her head. "They *know*, Ev."

It took a moment to understand. Alizhan must mean that the people of Estva were aware of her abilities. But how could she know that? "I thought you couldn't read them."

"I can't! But why would they hide from me if they had nothing to hide? They're Iriyat's spies! Maybe not all of them but —someone here is spying for Iriyat. She keeps up with people all over the world. She's always writing letters. Some of them came from Estva. I know there's someone here. We can't trust anyone. And this place is evil! They force people out into the cold!"

"Alizhan…"

"Stop. I know. I haven't been eating. I haven't been sleeping. You think I'm crazy. You don't believe me about that flower. You. Both of you. The only people—the only—" she tried to breathe and her body was wracked with a sob. No one was more surprised than Alizhan.

Thiyo moved first. Ev watched as he wrapped Alizhan in a hug and held her until she stopped crying. His long arms fit so easily around her small frame. "Hey," he said, and it was jarring to hear his voice so gentle. "Why don't you come work with me this shift? I don't think Sardas will mind. The kitchen will be short one pair of hands but I'm sure they'll manage. We have to go back to work or we'll draw unwanted attention to ourselves. And Ev has to be able to say that she found you and that you're earning your keep. She'll make up something very convincing, I'm sure."

Alizhan sniffled and nodded, then strode ahead without another word.

———

ALIZHAN ENTERED the room with the press with tentative steps and wary eyes. Sardas gave her a welcoming smile, but her gaze didn't stay on him for more than an instant. Thiyo showed her around the bindery and introduced her to Fama, Rin, and Ayat. Alizhan hardly looked at any of them, but Fama and Rin shared an unsettled glance from across the wooden frame where they were clamping manuscripts. Rin, being Nalitzvan, might be fearful and alert to any signs of witchcraft, as he'd call it. Thiyo hoped he wasn't the type to report the rules being broken. Fama was Adpri, so there was a chance he'd recognize Alizhan's gifts, but less of a chance he'd inform the authorities. At least Thiyo hoped so. Alizhan didn't come close to them, and they made no move to greet her with anything other than a nod.

Maybe they were just wary. They'd treated him the same way.

Ayat said nothing. She threaded her stack of pages as though nothing unusual was happening, but she wasn't as good at hiding her curiosity as she thought she was. Spitefully, Thiyo hoped Alizhan's total lack of interest hurt her feelings—if she had feelings to hurt.

When Thiyo brought Alizhan back to show her how the press worked, she whispered, "It's like an empty room."

"You have eyes and ears," he said. "Use them." Sardas was loading new paper into the press, close enough to hear them if he wanted to listen. And Thiyo was well aware of how silently Rin, Fama, and Ayat were working. With good hearing, they might catch a few words. This was why the damn book was taking him so long—he never got a moment's privacy to work on it. Everywhere he turned, people were watching and listening. Mad or not, Alizhan wasn't wrong about that.

Alizhan sighed despondently.

Thiyo busied himself with arranging the tiny metal letters on the plate. When he showed it to Alizhan and asked her to proofread it, the first few paragraphs were an exact copy of the manuscript they intended to print, but the last sentence said *you can't read Ev anymore.*

"That's right," Alizhan said after a slow appraisal. So she'd been feeling a general sense of isolation, compounded by being cut off from the person she loved and relied on most in the world. And Ev hadn't believed her about the flower, which must have stung. That explained some of her erratic behavior around Ev. And it must hurt to see Ev develop such easy camaraderie with Pirkko. Thiyo had seen them together, and their relationship was everything that Alizhan and Ev's wasn't—fresh, uncomplicated, and full of casual physical affection. Alizhan passed the plate back to him.

"Oh, look, we missed something." He disassembled the last sentence. In its place, he wrote *you're upset*.

"Some genius," Alizhan muttered. There was a little twitch in her eyelids that suggested she might start crying again.

Thiyo took that as a yes. He wanted to ask some questions, to start a real discussion—Alizhan was depressed and hadn't seen the potential advantage of her position—but it required more space or characters than he had available. With limited resources, he opted to share news instead of feelings.

not alone HK also having trouble

"You're taking your time," Alizhan said lightly. "We'll never get this book printed. What's next?"

That would end their conversation, since they'd have to fix the plates into the press and Sardas would see what they were doing. Wasn't Alizhan interested in his discovery? Was she relieved to learn she wasn't the only one having difficulty? And why hadn't her mind wandered in the same direction as his? She'd sounded so lonely on the ramparts when they'd been alone, asking if there was space in the world for someone like her. But when people said *space*, they meant something else: acceptance, respect, love. As usual, Thiyo had to provide all the answers around here.

"Alizhan. Let me show you something." Was there a discreet way to tell her that he wasn't going to shield his thoughts? "I'm going to be very open with you."

She fixed her eyes on the metal plate and didn't move. Luckily, she was on Thiyo's left, so he was able to use his good hand without much trouble. He lifted his hand and placed it right next to hers. She'd taken her gloves off to work in the press, so all he had to do was slide his hand over hers. There was nothing but the feel of skin on skin. No pain. No headache. No new memories. Hard to imagine that delicate little hand had ever posed a threat to anyone.

Harder still to imagine that touching hadn't been her first thought when she'd realized she couldn't read Ev. Night madness indeed.

"You see what I mean?" he said. He squeezed her hand lightly. Then he trailed his fingers back over her wrist. He'd have gone further, but the heavy brown sleeve of her coat blocked his progress. "It's easy. You can do it, too."

Alizhan met his eyes. He'd never seen such a mixture of awe and bewilderment. She turned her hand over so she could grip his. She gave it a few experimental squeezes, then slipped her hand out from under his and raised her arm until she could touch his face. Her fingers trailed over his cheek, and then suddenly both her hands were on his face, cupping his cheeks and tracing under his jaw. He bit his lip trying not to laugh. He hoped whatever Sardas was reading across the room was *really* engrossing.

Alizhan removed her hands from his face, lowered them, then turned them this way and that, staring.

"You didn't think of this, did you?" Thiyo said.

"No. I've been so consumed with—" Alizhan stopped herself. The ruse that Thiyo was teaching her to work the press had been stretched beyond belief. She shook herself, then jumped up and kissed his cheek. She laughed. "I've never done that to anyone before. You're a genius."

"I know," Thiyo said. "Although that's not really why I'm a—"

"Show me what happens next," she repeated, gesturing at the press. She couldn't seem to keep her hands still. Her fingers wiggled and she curled and uncurled them. She shoved them into her coat pockets and bounced on the balls of her feet.

She wanted to talk about the press now? Thiyo needed to explain himself further. "Just a second." He reached for the plate again and rearranged the final line of text until it said *kiss her*.

KET AND HENNY were waiting outside the men's dormitory when Thiyo finished work. They were both smiling, which was a nice change from working in close quarters with Alizhan and Ayat. What had they found to smile about?

"Let's take a walk," Ket said. He spoke Laalvuri, despite the fact that all three of them could speak Nalitzvan, and for Ket and Henny, that would be the far easier option. But Nalitzvan was a more common language among the residents. Laalvuri would make it harder for anyone to overhear them. Ket led them outside to one of the staircases that climbed the ramparts and didn't speak again until they'd all reached the top. "We did a test, like you said. And we can still affect each other, but it's much harder now than it used to be."

"So it's not us," Henny said, her breath a white puff in the darkness as they walked. "It's them."

"Well, it's us, too, now," Ket said.

"At first we thought we'd both lost our abilities—or were gradually losing them. Seems like it's happening to Alizhan, too. But I got someone new in the infirmary this shift, someone who'd just started working in the mines, and *he* was very grateful to me. It was just one little touch and—boom. Pupils dilated. Dopey smile. He felt better. That hasn't happened since we arrived. I couldn't even get a smile out of Ket when we tried a couple triads ago."

"Something about this place makes people resistant to us," Ket said. "Our abilities don't work as well—or maybe sometimes they don't work at all—on people here. And now that we've been here long enough, that includes us."

"Did anyone see you?" Thiyo asked Henny.

"No one but my patient, and he wasn't gonna say nothin'."

"Good. Don't do it again. Now we have to find out what it is about Estva that's causing this. My guess is the food. It's one thing everyone has in common. And the one food in Estva that's different from everywhere else is nightvine. We should quit eating it and then repeat the tests." Thiyo stopped walking. "Alizhan hasn't been eating it. She tried it once when we first arrived and hasn't touched it since."

"We should do the test on her, then," Henny said.

"We'll have to wait—we can't do it now," Thiyo said. "I just told her to go find Ev."

THE REST of Ev's shift passed minute by gut-churning minute. Was Thiyo right? Was Alizhan—for whatever reason—especially upset with her? What had Ev done to deserve that? She and Pirkko found several other absent workers over the next few hours, but Ev didn't find any answers to her questions. Instead of confronting Alizhan, Ev went straight down to the hot springs when she finished work.

The cavern was empty and the water was still. There were greenish reflections on the surface from some scattered lamps. Ev left her boots and clothes in a neat pile and slipped into the heat of the water. It eased some of her tension. Grateful, she sat down on the stone ledge at the edge of the pool and let the water come all the way up to her shoulders. She rested her head against the wall and tried not to think of anything.

It was only a few minutes before footsteps disturbed the silence. Ev had closed her eyes and didn't want to open them, but when a cheerful voice said "Hello, Ev," she did.

Pirkko was grinning at her, brighter than any lamp. All the light in the room seemed to stick to her, illuminating her face and glinting off her hair. She was bent over, balancing on one foot, pulling off her boot. Her long blond braid was swinging while she accomplished this. One boot thunked down, then the other. She dropped all her clothes on top of them, left the pile in the middle of the floor, then strode toward the water. She picked up her braid and tried to wrap it in a coil above her head and pin it in place. It took two tries to get it to stay. Each time Pirkko raised her arms, the movement lifted her breasts.

She had a softer, rounder figure than Ev expected, having sparred with her. She caught Ev staring and paused at the water's edge. Smiling broadly, she cupped her breasts and then patted her belly. "For keep warm."

Ev intended to say a word—which one, she wasn't sure—but changed her mind halfway through and let out a strangled cough instead. She averted her eyes toward the surface of the water, which transformed from stillness into ripples.

Pirkko slid in right next to her. "You want look, you look," she said, her tone warm and amused.

Ev did want to look. But Alizhan would know if she gave in to the urge. She'd know about the urge itself, too—maybe that was why she was already so cold and angry. Ev hadn't even done anything.

God, but it was hard to have all her thoughts scrutinized constantly. She was tired. And if Alizhan was going to be angry no matter what Ev did...

"I want look," Pirkko said, as shameless and carefree as ever. "You very beautiful."

Pirkko put a hand on her arm, the lightest of touches, under the water where no one could see. And then she trailed her fingers up the back of Ev's arm until they broke the surface of the water and curved over Ev's shoulder. Water ran down everywhere she'd touched, warm rivulets retracing her steps. Ev couldn't help it—she glanced up. And Pirkko was smiling, gazing at her like there was nothing in the world she wanted more, and what was there to do but smile back? Her lips lifted before she'd had a chance to think.

That was all the invitation Pirkko needed. She leaned in and touched her mouth to Ev's, an instant of light contact posed like a question, just like her touch to Ev's arm a moment ago. When Ev didn't flinch or recoil, Pirkko kissed her. She angled her head to fit their lips together, interlaced her fingers behind Ev's head, then slid her tongue into Ev's mouth. Ev tilted her head back to receive the kiss and lifted one hand to lay it on Pirkko's shoulder. What did she intend? Impossible to say. There was nothing beyond the next instant, nothing beyond the pulse of *want* thrumming through her body. At Ev's touch, Pirkko moved, cutting smoothly through the water, swinging one leg over and straddling Ev's lap. They were skin to skin, still kissing. The heavy press of her breasts against Ev's was as hot as the water.

Pirkko unlaced her hands, letting one cradle Ev's head and the other drift down into the water, following the curve of her waist and her hip. She paused there, letting her fingers splay over Ev's thigh, and just as her hand began to slide down in between Ev's legs, a sound echoed in the cavern. Footsteps.

Ev broke the kiss. "I'm sorry," she said, and wished it hadn't come out so breathless. "I can't. I don't—" Ev couldn't say *I don't want to*. It was an obvious lie. "I shouldn't."

Pirkko sighed and slid off her lap. "Sure?"

"Yes."

"In love with little funny one?"

"Yes. Maybe. I don't know. She's mad at me. I might be mad at her, too. I don't even know why. It's stupid."

"Only say yes. Say little funny one your forever love. Better for me that way. Heart less broken." Pirkko touched her heart in mock solemnity. "Still broken, but less broken."

"I'm so sorry. I shouldn't have let this happen—it was wrong to treat you like this. If you're angry with me, I understand."

Pirkko shrugged. "Felt good. More would feel better." Then she put her hands on her hips and gave Ev a half-cocked smile. "She make you mad again, find me." She got out of the water, toweled off, and dressed.

Ev twisted around in the pool, trying to look back toward the entrance. For an unbearable instant, she'd imagined it was Alizhan hovering in the doorway, watching. That reverberating sound might have been her shoes slapping the ground as she ran away, mortified and betrayed. But there was no one there.

26

UNNATURAL BEHAVIOR

E V WASHED HER FACE IN the dormitory before her next work shift, glancing into the mirror to see behind her the whole time. Did Alizhan know what had happened? Could she sense it? Or had she witnessed it? She hadn't said anything. When Djal had kissed Ev back in Laalvur, Alizhan had blurted that out right away. She'd asked if Ev was in love with Djal and Ev had laughed and said no. That had been good. Alizhan had believed her, of course, because back then she'd known exactly what Ev was feeling. The whole thing had taken five minutes and then they'd sorted things out and gone back to being friends. Or more than friends. Whatever they were.

Whereas right now, Alizhan was uncharacteristically silent and slow. She was changing clothes perfunctorily, with no expression on her face. Ev patted her own face dry with a towel, and when she looked into the mirror again, Alizhan was gone from sight. Ev glanced toward the door just in time to see Alizhan leaving the room. Dropping her washcloth, she hurried out, assuming Alizhan had gone to the mess hall to eat before her shift. But she'd walked in the opposite direction. Toward the print shop?

"Alizhan!"

No response.

It took only a few long strides to catch up to her. "Are you alright?" Ev said. "Are you upset with me?"

Alizhan continued walking through the corridor and into a tunnel that connected their building to the one that housed the press. She didn't look at Ev or say anything.

"Please tell me you're okay. I just want to know you're not going to disappear again, or—" Ev didn't want to finish the sentence, so instead she walked Alizhan to the door of the print shop, which Alizhan entered without saying goodbye. "See you later," Ev said weakly.

She still had a few minutes to walk back to the mess hall and eat something, but between Alizhan's silence and the thought of spending a shift with Pirkko, her stomach turned.

ALIZHAN CLEARLY HADN'T TAKEN his advice. She ghosted through the print shop at their next shift, wordless and unfocused. The absence of her usual chatter and jitters unnerved Thiyo. He caught her standing in front of the same finished plate of text for several minutes. She didn't move when he said her name. He let her be.

Sardas normally moved at a stately pace, but he was a whirlwind of activity next to Alizhan, and Thiyo went to help him remove a set of pages from the press. Alizhan was a complex problem, one he couldn't solve in a single step. For now, he'd pull on a different thread. "I was just wondering if you could tell me about nightvine, Sardas. I've never encountered it before."

"I hadn't either, before I arrived here," Sardas said. "Only Estvans eat it. There's something particular about the thermal vents that allows it to grow. It doesn't seem to need light."

Thiyo didn't need that information. But he also didn't want to get any closer to his real suspicion. He stepped around the question. "And they've never thought of exporting it?"

"Who would want it?" Sardas asked. "Surely you agree it's an acquired taste."

"I'm sure Alizhan would agree," Thiyo said. He wanted to nudge her into reacting, but he refrained. "Myself, I rather like it. It's not so different from some of the greens I grew up eating. There must be nostalgic former residents out in the rest of the world who'd like to rediscover their past with a taste of nightvine."

"Perhaps," Sardas said. "But it's not easy to grow food here. We need it more than anyone else does."

"True," Thiyo said. "Still, I can't help feeling that there might be a market for such a rare and exotic delicacy."

Sardas laughed. "You have an enterprising spirit."

"It would be best for sales if we could develop a reputation—if we could tell people that it had some special property," Thiyo mused. For the first time during the conversation, Alizhan lifted her head as though she might be listening. "Like dreamweed or those calming teas."

"Unfortunately, you'll have to stick with your first approach and appeal to people's nostalgia for their time here," Sardas said, still laughing. "There's nothing special about nightvine."

Thiyo laughed to show that everything was in good fun, but he wasn't convinced. Maybe Sardas genuinely didn't know. Maybe no one in Estva knew, since "unnatural behavior" was against the rules. Or maybe the rules prevented anyone from discussing nightvine's effects. If Thiyo could get Henny and Alizhan together, he could test his theory. And if he was right, that opened up a world of possibilities. If they needed to protect themselves from a memory-changer, nightvine was the answer.

THEIR SILENT MEAL was interrupted by shouting in Estvan. People all over the mess hall got up from their tables and ran to the huge double doors to hold them open, blasting the room with cold air. A crowd gathered around the doors and then half a dozen men dragged a sled into the room.

Ev had to stand up to see what it was. There was a man in the sled, pale and groaning, his clothes dark with blood and his left leg twisted at a wrong angle.

"They're new arrivals. He'd just gotten down from driving the carriage and was unhitching the horses, but one horse got spooked, slipped on the ice, and fell on top of him," Thiyo translated from what he was hearing in the crowd so Ev and Ket could understand. Alizhan had declined to come to dinner. "His leg is broken."

Henny hadn't even waited to hear that. She was gone from their table already, pushing her way through the crowd, shouting a Nalitzvan word that Ev had learned meant "healer." She was wearing her brown suede coat, but her hood was off, and the brilliant copper of her hair made it easy to follow her progress.

She went to her knees next to the man and began to examine his leg, already barking orders at the people standing around her. Some of them backed away and others ran to grab supplies. The man let out an agonized sound as she touched his leg, and Henny reached up and touched his cheek with her bare hand. A simple gesture of comfort—except that the man relaxed so fully and so instantly that it could only be magic.

The hall went silent.

And then Pirkko was standing over Henny and the man with the broken leg, her expression grim. Ev bolted from her place at the table and shoved her way there, knowing what Pirkko would say. Henny was practicing unnatural behavior and would be sent into exile. "Please," Ev was saying, before she even finished pushing people aside. When the crowd finally thinned, she nearly stumbled into the empty space around the wounded man. "Please don't do this, Pirkko. She was only trying to help him."

"So you agree she broke rules," Pirkko said. She didn't look at Ev, but instead let the crowd surrounding them see her stony expression. She addressed them in Estvan. Ev didn't need to know the language to know what was being said. When Pirkko turned back to Henny, she said in Nalitzvan, "Go now."

"This man needs my help," Henny said.

"We have other healers," Pirkko said. "*Natural* healers. You go now."

Henny's brown eyes flashed and she reached up and touched the wounded man's face one more time. When she withdrew her hand, his face went grey in the absence of her touch. She stood, stared at Pirkko one last time, then turned on her heel and marched out into the Night.

"This isn't right," Ev said to Pirkko. "It's not right and you know it."

There was nothing more to say and the crowd was closing in, people returning with surgical supplies and other healers in tow, so Ev made her way back to the table. Ket was in the middle of a passionate monologue in Nalitzvan, addressed to Thiyo, of which Ev caught the words "Henny," "Night," and "die."

"Go after her," Ev said in Laalvuri. "Don't worry about us. Henny needs you."

"They're our ride," Thiyo said.

"They can go back to Nalitzva," Ev said. "Zhenev will keep them safe. No one is looking for them to throw them in prison or execute them. Henny and Ket brought us here out of the kindness of their hearts, but they never signed up for more. We can't go back to Nalitzva—and we need to head for the coast to book a ship, anyway. We'll figure it out. Ket needs to pack up and go now."

Ket nodded sharply and then strode out of the room.

"I'll inform the city that he's leaving," Ev said. "But it's forbidden to go to the aid of the exiled, and there's no way I can convince anyone that he's not going out there to help her survive, so that means both Henny and Ket have to forfeit their earnings from their stay."

"By 'the city,' you mean Pirkko?" Thiyo said. "What happened there? I thought she liked you."

Ev shook her head. "We don't have time for that. Can you find Alizhan? We can't go back to Nalitzva with Ket, but we need a plan to get out of here."

"Of course," Thiyo said. Then he grabbed Ev's wrist. His stare focused on someone in the crowd. "Tell me that's not who I think it is."

Framed by the huge dark square of the open double doors and the crowd of Estvans in brown coats stood a small woman dressed in spotless white. The fur of her hat and her cuffs and collar was like new, unblemished snow, and underneath her white hat, her hair shone silver. Her slate-grey eyes bored into Ev and Thiyo, and her bow-shaped lips curled into a smile.

"Merat Orzh," Ev whispered.

Thiyo's grip on her wrist clamped even tighter. "What in the watery hell is she doing here?"

"Nothing good. And she's already seen us. We need to get away from here."

Merat made her way to Pirkko to introduce herself as Ev watched. There was no question of approaching Pirkko on Ket's behalf now. Ev didn't want to go near Merat. What would bring a Nalitzvan noblewoman to Estva? She had to be following them. But why? It was a long, arduous journey to a destination far less luxurious than her court apartments. Was the book worth that much to her?

"She won't be as dangerous here," Thiyo said, as though he were trying to reassure himself. "Not when everyone's been eating so much nightvine."

"What?"

"I haven't had time to tell you," he said. He moved even closer and kept his voice low. Mindful of what had just happened to Henny, Ev leaned in and listened. Thiyo took a step to get them out of the room, and Ev moved with him. They didn't rush, just ambled away from the crowd and the main door and Merat and Pirkko. "Henny and Ket and I figured out that nightvine is affecting all of us. It makes people resistant to— well, you saw what Henny just did. She could only do that to someone who'd just arrived here. Someone who hadn't been eating nightvine."

"So it's not that Alizhan changed, but that everyone else did," Ev said. Her heart sped up. Alizhan couldn't read her. Alizhan didn't know what she'd done. But then why was she acting so angry? "So as long as I eat nightvine, she can't—"

"Exactly," Thiyo said. They exited the mess hall into a corridor, and the din receded, but they continued to talk softly. "You could kiss. I told her to kiss you already, but she's in a snit about it. I don't know what happened last triad, but it obviously wasn't good."

"Oh no," Ev said. "Oh, smoke. You told her to kiss me last triad—"

"—and she went looking for you after we finished our shift," Thiyo said. "What happened?"

"I, um—Pirkko—" Ev's throat was going to close up. Her face burned and her insides knotted. God, why had she done that? Had those footsteps she'd heard really been Alizhan's? How much had she seen? If she could just talk to Alizhan, maybe she could apologize. "We were in the hot springs."

"*Evreyet*," Thiyo said. He was far too amused. They were shoulder to shoulder. His hand was still on her wrist, no longer such a viselike grip, just a warm touch. The contact was simple and pleasant—nothing could have felt more like an accusation. Ev snatched her arm away. "My, my. I didn't know you had it in you."

"I hate you."

"Oh, I know. Refresh my memory. Didn't you once tell me how stupid I was for sleeping with Aniyat?"

"We didn't have sex!" Ev said. It came out too forcefully, far above a whisper. She and Thiyo were still walking close together, and he turned to smirk at her. He was one of very few people in her life tall enough to look her in the eye. "And you *were* stupid, and so am I, and we both have bigger problems to solve right now."

"Yes. I'm well aware that the woman who had me thrown in prison and fairly well ruined my life has just arrived in this icy pit of a city, presumably to ruin what's left of us. We should leave with Ket. It's the only sensible choice."

"But what if knowing what Merat wants helps us understand what Iriyat's after?" Ev asked. "And leaving with Ket isn't an option. If all five of us go, it'll be obvious that we're leaving together—Pirkko won't turn a blind eye for me now—and we'll all have to forfeit our earnings. We need that money to book passage on a ship. Because, as previously mentioned, going back to Nalitzva means ending up in prison or dead."

"Ugh," Thiyo said. "I suppose you're right."

"Where's the book?

"Alizhan has the original. I don't know what she did with it. My transcription—and my almost-finished translation—are hidden inside the copy of that drivel you borrowed from Ket."

"*The Sunrise Chronicles*? You know I almost gave that back to him a few triads ago."

"Well, it's a damn good thing you didn't," Thiyo said. "After all the work I've done! I even took it apart in the bindery when no one was looking and sewed the new pages in. And to think, now everyone in the men's dormitory thinks I read that sentimental bunk to myself before sleeping. The sacrifices I've made..."

Ev rolled her eyes. "Your courage is astounding."

"Here, we're almost to my room. I'll get the book and then we'll find Alizhan."

27

BARSHA OR KIRISHA

A LIZHAN WAS LYING MOTIONLESS ON her cot, her unfocused gaze directed at the ceiling. "Alizhan," Thiyo said. "Henny got kicked out."

She sat up. "Are we leaving?"

"Henny and Ket are going back to Nalitzva, and the three of us are going to figure out a way to get somewhere else on the coast," Ev said. "We'll walk to the nearest village in that direction if we have to. We have to leave soon because Merat Orzh just arrived."

Apparently they were speaking again, because Alizhan said, "What the hell is *she* doing here?"

"That's what I said," Thiyo said.

"She must be looking for the book," Ev said. "Thiyo says you hid the original. He brought his copies."

"Is Ket gone?" Alizhan said. "I'd like to say goodbye if he's still here."

"He's probably in the stables getting the wagon ready," Ev said. "We can go look."

Thiyo muttered something that sounded like "how do you even know where the stables are," but Ev ignored him and he followed her without further protest, as did Alizhan. Ev had been to the stables on her rounds with Pirkko. Out of habit, she tried to chase thoughts of Pirkko from her mind, since Alizhan was right next to her and it would be rude to expose her to that. Then she remembered Alizhan couldn't sense what she was thinking.

They walked out into the Night with Estva's white and grey buildings looming around them, lit by a scattering of lamps and torches. Ev thought about how huge the world was, how desolate and uninhabited, so much of its surface frozen or scorched. The air was cold and quiet and she missed Alizhan talking aimlessly in response to her thoughts. When she'd shared everything with Alizhan, all she'd wanted was a little privacy, and now that she had it, Ev couldn't remember what to do with it. Instead of relief, loneliness spread through her, crystallizing on the surface of every thought like a frost.

The stables were enclosed but the wide aisle down the center of the building and the high ceiling of the barn made them feel gigantic compared to the rest of Estva. Ket was hitching his horses to the wagon and he smiled sadly when he saw them.

"I'm sorry it ends this way."

"As long as you and Henny make it back, we won't be sorry for anything," Ev said. She hugged Ket. "Thank you again."

"You're welcome. It was more exciting than anything that happened at Zhenev's while we were gone, I'm sure."

"Maybe not," Thiyo said. "There are probably still people watching Zhenev's. Erinsk's, too. Be careful."

Ket pulled a glove off one hand, raised it and waggled his fingers, his blue eyes bright. "I'm always careful."

"Maybe you can teach Henny," Thiyo said. Ket didn't laugh, but Thiyo continued, "She's a strong-willed woman, Ket. She's not going to do what anyone tells her—not even you. You should think about that."

To Ev's surprise, Ket nodded. "I will." Then he hugged Thiyo, going up on tiptoes to whisper something in Thiyo's ear. When he broke their embrace, he said, "I know you probably won't ever come back to Nalitzva, but if you do, you know where to find us."

"And if you come to—well, who knows where I'll be," Thiyo said. "I'll write."

Even in the light of the barn's hanging lanterns, Ket's blush was radiant. Ev remembered then that there was a copy of *Loves* in Ket's bedroom at Madam Zhenev's. Henny had offered to lend it to her during their stay.

Thiyo was grinning. "Not that kind of writing. Not unless you're very lucky."

"I, um—"

"Let this poor man breathe, Thiyo," Ev said.

Alizhan had been hovering behind them, but she stepped forward. "Thank you for everything."

She didn't raise her arms to hug him, but Ket pulled her into an embrace. Ev thought of him as a small person, but he was still tall enough to rest his chin on Alizhan's head. He touched her fearlessly, given that she'd once knocked him unconscious. "I'm glad to have met you," he said. "I hope you change the world."

Alizhan had no response to that except to blink with her wide, grey eyes, and Ket smiled and patted her on the shoulder. "Well, I can't leave Henny to wait in the cold any longer. I feel I should say something final, like 'sincere vows' at the end of a letter, but our acquaintance started in a brothel and it's ending in a barn, so that doesn't feel quite right. Goodbye and all the fucking luck in the world to you."

"You too," Thiyo said. Ket pulled his hood up, mounted the

front of the wagon, and drove the horses out the barn door. When he was gone, Thiyo looked around the stables. "You know, I don't *want* to stay here, but there aren't many people around..."

"That's because we might as well be outside," Alizhan said, crossing her arms over her chest and rubbing herself to keep warm.

Ev ducked into the stall that Ket had left open. "This is more privacy than the dormitory provides."

Thiyo pulled the stall door closed behind them, although it was only half-height. Then he removed a book from inside his coat.

"You want to read to us here?" Alizhan said.

Thiyo glanced around the stall and toed a pile of straw with his boot. "No." He sniffed. "I'd never have come with you in the first place if I'd known things were going to be so *dirty*." Ev scooped up a handful of straw and threw it at him. Some of it caught in his hair and he picked it out meticulously before continuing. "We need to talk about what you want to do next, but you shouldn't make any decisions until you know what's in here."

"It's the translation," Ev explained to Alizhan. "Not that I'd mind if Thiyo finished reading *The Sunrise Chronicles*, but we could do that inside, where it's warm."

"Finally," Alizhan said. She sat down in the straw without any hesitation, and Ev sat down next to her, drawing her knees up and letting her back rest against the wall. Thiyo remained standing, with another doubtful glance at their surroundings.

"The first key to deciphering this was the word 'lacemakers,'" Thiyo said. He leaned one shoulder against the wall. "But after that, I started thinking about keeping records of secrets, and I noticed a few more repeated words—always at the tops of paragraphs, after line breaks—and I wondered if they might be dates. And they were. This text is a personal journal. The first entry is dated 'Lyrebird shift, 30th triad of Orsha, 761.'" And with that, Thiyo opened the book and began to read. "I do not want to tell this story, but I must..."

The journal entry was from the point of view of a woman— Ev needed no convincing that the wealthy young Laalvuri woman described was a young Iriyat ha-Varensi, but Alizhan would resist—and it wasn't what Ev expected. It was intimate, if a little pompous, and it was a portrait of a bored teenage girl getting shipped off to meet her betrothed and developing a crush on a sailor instead.

Although Ev had to admit, the sailor was dashing. Surviving the fight with the medusa was a hell of a story.

"What does this have to do with *anything*? What effect could this possibly have on our decision of how and when to leave Estva?" Alizhan said. "How many entries are there? How long do we have to stay out here in the cold?"

Ev wanted to scoot closer to Alizhan and put an arm around her to keep her warm, but would Alizhan accept it? They were speaking again, and Alizhan hadn't brought up what she might have witnessed at the hot springs, but Ev didn't want to presume. She'd done something wrong, and Alizhan had a right to feel hurt. She let the space between them hang open.

Thiyo sighed a very put-upon sigh, made eye contact with Ev, and said, "Sacrifices." Then he sat down in the straw between them. He fussed for a moment, smoothing his clothes and picking invisible straws off himself. After that, he drew Alizhan toward him and she willingly huddled up next to him.

The next journal entry was not so different from the first, although it contained no sea monsters, to Ev's disappointment. The narrator recounted her first few encounters with the sailor, as well as her efforts to avoid her parents' surveillance, and her passion for gardening. She mentioned a Laalvuri saying that Ev had heard often but never thought much about: *the gardener's hand should not be seen.* Laalvuri preferred gardens that appeared natural and wild, as though there were no gardener and the plants had all sprung up in that arrangement, just so. Ev had to agree, having seen the sad, stark gardens surrounding the Nalitzvan palace. The gardener's hand was all too visible there. But given Iriyat's unseen political maneuvering in Laalvur— aided by her power to alter memories—the phrase took on a sinister cast.

Ev's thoughts were interrupted by a slight change in the rhythm of Thiyo's reading. "But all that matters is that when we broke apart," he was saying, more slowly and clearly than he'd read the rest of the passage, a description of a kiss. "He looked right at me with those clear brown eyes, tucked a stray lock of hair behind my ear, grinned, and said, 'Iriyat.'"

Alizhan groaned. "Fine. This is Iriyat's journal. She wrote it. Is that why we're out here?"

"No," Thiyo said. "We haven't gotten to that part yet."

In the next entry, young Iriyat and the sailor—Arav— discussed having sex and possibly having a baby, and Ev guessed where Thiyo was going with his reading. Then Arav revealed that he'd always been able to sense people's thoughts and feelings, until his encounter with the medusa that had left him scarred, and Ev knew. Arav had to be Alizhan's father. Eliyan Matrishal, a priest of the Balance in Laalvur who'd helped them smuggle orphans out of the city—Ev suspected she was Alizhan's aunt—had told them her brother, a sailor, had those distinctive black scars from a giant medusa, and that he'd died in the last wave to hit Laalvur. This was further evidence. Thiyo was trying to show Alizhan her parents.

He read smoothly through the description of Iriyat and Arav's youthful romance and only faltered when he reached a scene where Iriyat's parents discovered her as she re-entered the garden at Varenx House. They were waiting for her. Thiyo took a breath and read, "'Merat,' my father said, addressing my mother."

Iriyat's parents attacked her, trying to wipe her memory, and then they locked her in her room and the entry ended. Thiyo closed the book, keeping one finger between the pages. "That's what I wanted you to know right now."

"Merat is a common enough Nalitzvan name," Alizhan said. "And the woman here is named Merat Orzh."

"Well, she couldn't very well go around calling herself Merat Varenx, could she?" Thiyo said. "And we know she's a Lace-maker. And Ev said she looks like Iriyat. It's too many coincidences."

"Iriyat's parents died in the wave," Alizhan said.

"And you believe that because everything else Iriyat told you about herself has been true," Thiyo said.

"We have to consider it, Alizhan," Ev said, less pointedly. "Merat came all the way here because she found out about the book—and she saw you with it back in the palace. She's probably involved with Iriyat somehow. We should find out how."

"We'll just have to ask her," Alizhan said sourly. "I couldn't read her even before I came to this tomb."

Ev choose not to respond to that. Instead she asked, as gently as possible, "What do you think of the rest of the journal?"

Alizhan shrugged. "It's sweet, I guess. I don't see why she went to such lengths to encrypt it."

"It's addressed to someone," Thiyo said. "The first entry says 'you are the one thing in this world for which I care.' It was only meant for one person."

"Maybe it's for the guy," Alizhan said, and Ev knew then that she was being willfully obtuse. *The guy*. There was no way she'd failed to learn that his name was Arav.

"Before she described their lovemaking, she wrote 'you might rather not know the details of what we did,'" Thiyo said.

"Presumably, having been present for the act, Arav would already know the details. That's not how you talk to your lover. It's how you talk to your child. A daughter, I'd say, if I had to guess."

Alizhan pushed away from Thiyo and stood up to face both of them. The light from outside the stall illuminated her from the side and she loomed over them. "You think *Iriyat* is my *mother*."

Ev and Thiyo exchanged glances. "Well..."

"That doesn't make sense! I can't believe you both fell for it. It's stupid. It can't be true. I'm an *orphan*. My father died in the wave—my mother probably did, too. Everyone else abandoned me because I never stopped crying. I cried every time another human being touched me. You *know* that's true. It makes *sense*.

"Iriyat found me and took me in, sure, but that's because she saw how awful my life was at the orphanage and took pity on me. She knew she had the resources to keep me safe. She knew no one else could do it. That's what happened. And eventually, she saw that I could help her, and she taught me how, and I did. It makes sense.

"And then we find this stupid book and finally decode it, and it's nonsense! It's *bullshit*! Iriyat's not my mother. We don't look anything alike, first of all."

"Alizhan," Ev said softly.

"Stop. Stop it. You're going to tell me that I don't know what anyone looks like. But I know enough! Iriyat is white and blond and buxom and I'm," Alizhan gestured at herself, demonstrating that she was none of those things. "People would have thought about it. They would have noticed! And you," Alizhan glared at Thiyo before he could speak, "you're going to ask how I know all that about the orphanage, and I know you think that it was all Iriyat who told me, and yes, it was, but—it still doesn't make sense!

"If Iriyat was my mother, she would have *told* me. She might have lied to everyone *else*, and obviously she has that power, but she would have told *me*. And if she was my mother, she wouldn't have treated me like a servant my whole life. Like a thing to be *used*. Would my *mother* be ordering the murder of innocent people? Would she send armed guards after me? Iriyat's not my mother. She can't be. She wouldn't have *lied* to me. Not about that. Not for my whole life. Everyone else, maybe, but not me. Why would she—why would she—"

Alizhan abruptly stopped talking and walked out of the stall. The half-door slammed.

Ev moved to go after her, but Thiyo stuck his arm out. "Give her a moment."

"Do you think she really doesn't believe it?" Ev said. "That journal can't possibly belong to anyone but Iriyat. And if she had a baby with a dark-skinned Laalvuri man..."

"That baby might grow up to look a lot like Alizhan," Thiyo agreed. "She knows it's true. She might even have suspected it before this. It's still a hard thing to hear."

It had been hard for Ev to hear from her aunt Ifeleh that her father had, in fact, killed someone. Even if the act was justified, it was still a difficult thing to accept. It had made Ev question her own character—of course, at the time, she hadn't killed anyone herself. Now she understood better. Sometimes the world left you no choice. But her father had killed his own father to save the rest of their family, whereas Iriyat had abused and killed children. It was unconscionable. Ev shook her head as if she could free herself of the memory of the burning orphanage in Gold Street.

"I wouldn't want it to be true, either."

THE BARN HAD FELT COLD, but it was nothing compared to the open air. Alizhan drew in stinging lungfuls of air as she walked outside, let it hit the back of her throat and freeze her skin. There was a tightness in her cheeks and behind her eyes, as though something heavy were pressing against the back of her face, ready to burst forth. God, but it would be miserable to cry out here in the cold. Maybe she'd scream instead.

Estva never slept, but it always had the air of a dead place, since no one stayed outside if they had the option to be indoors. There were people patrolling the ramparts and guarding the gates, but any work that could be done inside was. With tunnels and protected passages connecting so many of the buildings, hardly anyone crossed the open spaces in between.

The woman in white glowed from the sparse light of lamps and torches. When she called, "There you are," Alizhan thought at first that she'd imagined it. That she'd finally lost it and now there was an apparition haunting her.

But Alizhan knew that voice. She'd heard it in Ilyr's private quarters. Merat Orzh was coming toward her. Alizhan's skin burned with the memory of Merat's fingers touching her face. Alizhan remembered her hands as scraping claws, but that was a flight of fancy. They'd been well-manicured, clean, soft, aristocratic hands. That image—and the memory of her light, inconsequential touch—contrasted with the spike of pain Merat had driven through Alizhan's mind. She clenched her hands in the pockets of her coat. Was she strong enough to withstand an attack?

If Ev and Thiyo are right, she's my grandmother. The thought had no effect on the chaos that had already consumed her insides. What did it matter who else was in her family, if Iriyat was her mother? She'd dreamed of meeting her mother her whole life—and if Ev and Thiyo were right, she'd always known her. How many times would Iriyat dupe her?

Merat's extravagant white coat and fur hat were immaculate. "I've been looking for you."

"Did you come here to kill me?" Alizhan's own voice emerged from her throat as if she were a machine operated by someone else. Emotionless. Mechanical. She hadn't known she was going to say those words. But their last encounter had been violent. She had no reason to expect anything else.

And if Merat answered yes, Alizhan had no reason to expect she'd survive.

"How much space do we have to give her?" Ev asked Thiyo. Neither of them had moved since Alizhan stormed out, so they were still sitting in the straw. "Do you really think she should be alone right now? She's spent so much time by herself lately, and I think she feels alone now even when we're with her—"

"A few minutes. Then you can run after her and talk all about your feelings. Spare me that conversation."

Thiyo hadn't been so short with her in weeks. Not since he'd been in pain. Once the suspicion took hold, Ev couldn't shake it. Thiyo had both his hands in his lap, resting atop the closed book. His right hand was no longer discolored with bruises, but he still treated it gingerly. His crooked fingers curled toward his palm like a half-closed flower. Ev hadn't noticed until now.

She took his hand in both of hers, examining it with her touch. His skin was warm and unblemished, but his fingers were stiff. "Henny told you to do exercises."

"She also told me it wouldn't heal if I didn't rest. I can't rest. I need both hands to work. It's not just using the press here—it's everything. Eating. Getting dressed. Climbing up the occasional roof to save my own life. And sometimes I don't realize how

much it hurts until the pain becomes impossible to ignore."
Thiyo sighed. "As for the exercises, I did some."

"Some?" Ev asked. She didn't look up from his hand. Henny
had poked and prodded at it regularly while they'd been on the
road, and she'd always stared like she could see right down to
his bones. Ev's stare didn't reveal any such wisdom. There were
no more bruises to mark where the pain was. Thiyo's tan skin
was smooth and blank. "But not others?"

"Couldn't find anyone to do them with."

"What do you m—" Ev stopped. When she met Thiyo's eyes,
they were sparkling with some joke. The conversation with
Henny about what Thiyo ought to do with his fingers came back
in all its mortifying, sexual detail. She averted her gaze.

"Are you volunteering?"

"No!"

"Pity," Thiyo said. He slouched against the wall. "That feels
nice."

Ev wasn't doing anything but holding his hand. And if he
was going to be sharp-tongued and shocking, she'd stop.

But maybe he wasn't going to tease her. When he stayed
silent, Ev thought about how sad and frustrated he'd sounded
about his hand. And when he'd said *that feels nice*, it had been
quietly content, not taunting or smirking or trying to goad her
into something uncomfortable. She didn't always understand
him, and she wished he'd speak with less innuendo, but he
wasn't a bad person. Like her, he'd stumbled into intrigue he
knew nothing about, and he'd suffered for it. And right now, all
he wanted was for her to touch his hand. A small comfort. It
would be easy to give. A few minutes where they wouldn't have
to think about how either of them would ever get home, and
what would be waiting for them if they did—a future as
encroaching and impenetrable as Night.

It was for Thiyo, of course—his health, his happiness, his

reassurance, not hers. And since Alizhan wasn't around, no one could probe any further into Ev's motives than that.

She'd seen Henny do this often enough. She stretched out his fingers, one by one, slowly and gently. She massaged little circles into his palm, then turned his hand over and did the same. He let slip a little sound of pleasure. When Ev risked a glance at his face, worried that his lips might be curled with amusement over some joke she didn't want to understand, his eyes were closed.

He opened them. There was more warmth in his dark gaze than she expected, and she wanted to look away, but couldn't. Somehow he managed to make Ev feel he'd caught her doing something indecent—and that he was pleased with her for it.

There was nothing to do but change the subject. "She would have come back by now if she were coming back. What if she fled? She's wanted to leave for so long and we finally crossed some line—"

"She brought us all the way out here to the stables to say goodbye to Ket," Thiyo said. There was none of the earlier scorn and exasperation in his voice. "She's very sentimental and attached, even if she doesn't always know how to show it. She won't leave without you."

Ev wished she felt that kind of certainty.

"OF COURSE NOT, DARLING," Merat said, her tone cloyingly sweet. She reached through the darkness for Alizhan, and even though her hands were gloved, Alizhan took a sharp step backward. "I finally figured out who you are. I put it all together. We're *family*."

"I'm not your family or your darling," Alizhan said. She kept her hands in her pockets. They were bare. She hadn't been able to overpower Merat last time, but this time she'd be prepared. "You tried to hurt me. You tried to hurt Ev, too. And you had Thiyo thrown in prison."

"Fine," Merat said, returning her own hands to her pockets. The change in her speaking voice transformed her into a different person. "We don't have to like each other. Let's stick to business. You're out to get Iriyat, and that gives us something in common. Let me help you."

It was a relief that Merat was no longer reaching for her and no longer playing the role of some long-lost, loving family member. But Alizhan didn't relax. "This isn't what you wanted when we met in Nalitzva. What changed?"

"I thought you were working *for* her, not against her. I assume you're going back to Laalvur," Merat said. "I can get you there."

"How did you figure it out?"

"I thought the book was a message you were delivering. But why steal it back, in that case? And in my brief brush with it, I saw Iriyat's name stamped inside. She's not stupid enough to send an encoded message that has her name on the outside. That means the book was stolen from her. You must have brought it to Nalitzva in the hope that our famous scholar prince would help you understand it somehow." Merat laughed, a dainty little sound. "No wonder you had to run off with the boy whore."

"Don't call him that." Alizhan didn't want to speak to this woman anymore, so she turned to walk away.

"Wait," Merat said. "I'm sorry. I overstepped. You befriended him and that's very sweet. You obviously didn't get that sweetness from me. But think of what I can do for you. I was serious about that."

"We're not family."

"My darling, if we weren't family, you wouldn't remember

your own name right now. But because you're my blood, I'm treating you with respect—unless or until you prove yourself unworthy, like your mother did."

"She's not my mother."

Merat laughed again. Alizhan hated the sound. She'd wanted to know her family her whole life and instead, she'd gotten this cruel joke.

"That fierce stubbornness is hers through and through. It's a shame you didn't come out looking more like her. She's flawed inside, not outside. But let's leave that subject alone, since I see it's making you unhappy. I'm sure you want to leave this horrible place even more than I do. I can get us to the coast in a triad. There's a ship waiting."

"What'll it cost?"

"Nothing."

"Liar."

"I've wanted to see my disgrace of a daughter ruined since she ran me out of my own home and told the world I was dead. I can't do it alone. But if you intend to take her down, I will pour all of my considerable resources into helping you."

Merat was dangerous, both petty and ruthless, and she'd already hurt Thiyo. She and Iriyat really were like mother and daughter, though neither of them would want to hear it. Two beautiful, polished women with something vile and vicious slithering underneath. Merat couldn't be trusted. But the offer made Alizhan hesitate. They had to get out of Estva and back to Laalvur somehow. Their next-best option was working until they had the money to book passage on a ship, which might take another week—they'd still have to travel to the coast, and the ship would undoubtedly be slower than what Merat could provide.

"How do you know we're family?" Alizhan asked instead of accepting the offer.

"It's all over your face."

"You said yourself I don't look like her."

"I met him once," Merat said. "Your father. A great brute of a man. Iriyat likes them big and dumb. I'm sure she's found hundreds of replacements to fuck since the moment your shell-collecting fool of a father sailed right into that wave."

"But you didn't know when we met in Ilyr's quarters."

"As I said, it took me some time to place the resemblance and work it all out. I only met him once, after all. But you're involved in her life somehow, and you're the right age, and you look just like him—no, that's not it, it's not your face itself, but something about your expressions. Even now, your mouth is working like you want to say something but can't remember how. Your eyes are blinking and your eyebrows want to leap off your forehead. He could never keep still, either. It's enough for me." Merat tsked. "She kept you a secret from the world, as though she was ashamed of you. No wonder you crossed the ocean to expose her secret correspondence."

Alizhan didn't care about being kept secret from the world. She cared about being kept secret from herself. Merat's insults were missing the mark, at least. Looks meant nothing to Alizhan —and given the choice, she'd rather look like "a great brute" than Iriyat, no matter how beautiful. And if Thiyo's translation was really Iriyat's journal, then her father hadn't been a brute at all.

Bile rose in her throat. Was that acceptance? Did she believe Iriyat was her mother? Was she just going to stand here and let this woman talk as if it were true? How could it be true?

How could it not be true?

"How old am I?" Alizhan said. She wished her voice still sounded flat and mechanical, instead of small and choked and uncertain. Why was she even asking? She didn't want any of it to be true, and she certainly didn't want to learn any more details from Merat.

Merat hummed a note of mild surprise. A hesitation. But she'd mentioned Alizhan's age, so she must have done some calculation. "I'd guess you were born in Barsha or Kirisha of 745."

"Nineteen," Alizhan said. The precision was new. Iriyat had always given her age as an estimate: "you're eight *or* nine." But she'd known.

"She never told you," Merat marveled. "She does love her secrets. That's what's in the book, I assume. Some secret that will ruin her. I look forward to it."

It was a stupid piece of trivia, her age. The month she was born. But she'd wondered her whole life. The one person who could have told her had kept it from her on purpose. And for what? One last final stitch in the tapestry of lies that made up Alizhan's life?

Merat might be cruel, but at least so far she was honest. She'd stated her intentions plainly.

"*I* am the secret that will ruin her," Alizhan said. "When does your ship leave?"

"Excellent," Merat said. "We can leave Estva by the end of the shift. I don't want to stay in this hovel any longer than I have to. By the way—what's your name?"

28

NOT FRIENDS

E V AND THIYO WALKED OUT of the barn. Two small figures stood in the snow in front of them. Even in the darkness, that woman in white could only be Merat, and the diminutive bundle of furry coats facing her had to be Alizhan. Ev dashed for them, not waiting to see what Thiyo would do. Merat couldn't be that close to Alizhan. One touch of her hand could ruin everything.

She could hurt Ev, too, but what did that matter? Ev shoved herself in between them. "Get the fuck away from her," she said to Merat, pushing her back with both hands flat on her chest.

"Ev, don't!" Alizhan's hand shot out and snapped around Ev's bare wrist.

The world froze. It was nothing like the other times Alizhan had touched her. There was no pain. No magic exchange of feelings or memories. It was just a small, hot grip around Ev's arm. Skin to skin.

Ev wasn't holding Merat in any way, and the older woman took advantage of her shock and stepped out of reach. "We'll continue this conversation," she said to Alizhan, and slipped away into the darkness. And when she was gone, there was nothing but the two of them, standing side by side in the snow. Touching.

There was nothing to feel but Alizhan's hand. But Ev was still awake and aware enough to feel it, and that was new.

She dropped her arm down, hoping that Alizhan wouldn't let go—she didn't—and turned to face her. She positioned herself closer than she'd ever dared. Lifting her arm, she brought Alizhan's grip closer to her face. She examined it, just as she had with Thiyo's, but there was nothing out of the ordinary about her hand. Ev had never had the chance to look with leisure. To stand so close without fear.

Ev ought to ask what the hell Merat had been talking about, and if Alizhan was okay, and she ought to apologize for so many things, but all her attention was on their hands. Every point of contact between them was alive. Time was suspended and dreamlike. She would have had to measure in breaths or heart-beats, but each one felt a thousand years apart. Was this real?

And then Alizhan pulled Ev's right hand toward her face. She kissed the tips of her fingers. Her palm. The inside of her wrist. Everything around them was so still, interrupted only by the boom of Ev's pulse. The press of Alizhan's lips against her skin was slight, but it carried the weight of some ancient ritual. An invocation. A prayer.

Ev wanted to answer it. She cupped Alizhan's cheek and Alizhan let go of her wrist and let herself be pulled toward Ev. Even with Alizhan standing on tiptoes, Ev still had to dip her head down to kiss her.

Everything between them was so fraught and fragile. Ev kissed Alizhan with slow caution. The tip of Alizhan's nose was cold against her face. But as soon as Ev parted her lips, Alizhan kissed her fiercely and practically climbed her body. It made Ev laugh, how much themselves they were, a little breathless hitch in their kissing. Alizhan clamped her thighs around Ev's waist and Ev obliged, putting her hands underneath her ass to hold her up. Once Alizhan was at the same height as her, she deepened the kiss, sweeping her tongue into Ev's mouth. Alizhan's bare hands touched her cheeks, her jaw, her neck, eager and reverent. Her fingertips traced the shape of Ev's earlobes and the edge of her hairline. Ev shivered at the intimacy, at the hot shock of desire that ran through her, and she pushed back against Alizhan's tongue with her own.

Unlike with Pirkko—something she had let happen, an instant of directionless desire that had overwhelmed her—with Alizhan, Ev knew exactly what she wanted. She wanted this to go on forever. The present blossomed into ten thousand vivid futures—combing her fingers through the loose silk of Alizhan's hair, sucking a bite into the tender skin of her neck, smoothing her hands over her naked skin, laying her down and opening her up with kisses—and Ev wanted every single one of them.

There was the sound of a throat being cleared.

"For the record, I did not watch that, because I am given to understand it would offend your delicate mainlander sensibilities if I had," Thiyo said. "Although I will point out that it was in public and I could hardly be blamed for being in the vicinity, since I was trying to make sure Merat Orzh didn't liquefy your brains. But since I—for some terrible, unknown reason—seem to care what you two strange creatures think of me, I promise I looked pointedly away as soon as it became clear that you were not in danger. I am, of course, very sorry to interrupt, and I offer you both congratulations on being slightly less hopeless than I assumed, but for now, I think we ought to discuss what the watery hell Merat Orzh is doing in Estva, and if there's any way we can arrange for her to end up in prison. Or dead. That would also be fine with me."

"What were you planning to do if we were in danger?" Ev

asked. She'd set Alizhan back on her feet during Thiyo's speech, but they hadn't moved far apart. "If the two of us couldn't defend ourselves against her, what hope did you have?"

"I resent that question," Thiyo said. "What did you want me to do, abandon you to your fate?"

Not so long ago, Thiyo would have been raring to do exactly that. But Ev didn't say so, and Alizhan couldn't hear her thinking it, so there was a moment of silence.

Then Alizhan said, "Merat offered us a ship to Laalvur."

"And you told her to fuck right off to the drowned depths she crawled out of, I assume."

Ev stared at Alizhan. She hadn't heard any of what had been said before she'd arrived, but apparently Alizhan and Merat had talked at length. Guilt seeped in. Ev had been in the barn with Thiyo doing—whatever they'd been doing. That had been foolish. If Merat had wanted to hurt Alizhan, Ev wouldn't have been there to stop it.

"I didn't," Alizhan said, and Thiyo's jaw dropped.

"You didn't?" Ev asked.

"I'm not *stupid*. I don't *trust* her. But she hates Iriyat, and she wants us to destroy her, so until that happens, we're on the same side. And she can get us to Laalvur fast. And quietly. It solves all the problems we've been worrying about. Every other method we've come up with to get home takes way longer. And we'll be together. We can handle her."

"She threw me in prison," Thiyo said, biting off every word.

"I know," Alizhan said. "And once we're in Laalvur, you can kill her for all I care."

"Alizhan," Ev said.

"What?" Alizhan shrugged. "I know both of you had to have long internal debates about whether you're bad people now that you've taken lives, but I'm not like that. Sometimes killing a person is the answer. We can try to get her thrown in prison if you'd rather, though."

"Who is this 'we' that's going to Laalvur?" Thiyo said.

"The three of us, of course," Alizhan said.

"Thiyo never agreed to that," Ev said. "We should help him get home if that's what he wants."

"It's not," Alizhan said. "My senses might be dead now, but I still know a thing or two. Thiyo doesn't want to go back to Hoi. But he can't go back to Nalitzva, either. And he's always wanted to see Laalvur. I think he'll go with us."

"Not if you're traveling with Merat Orzh," Thiyo said. "I'll go anywhere in the world except wherever she's going."

Ev glanced between them, torn. She understood the urgency that Alizhan felt to get home and solve things. But if they left Thiyo here, she knew in her heart that they'd never see him again. And even though she'd wanted that when they'd first met, somehow over the course of their travels, something had changed.

But Alizhan was set on this and nothing Ev said would dissuade her. And Ev couldn't let her go alone. "We'll miss you," she said, and it came out sadder and softer than she'd expected. She stepped forward to hug him and he hardly moved.

"You shouldn't do this," Thiyo said. "Don't get on that ship."

"Let's go inside," Alizhan said. "You can tell me how foolish I'm being where it's warm."

No one laughed. As they walked back toward the dormitories, none of them said a word.

"You look like you could use a drink," Sardas said when Thiyo showed up for his shift.

Alizhan and Ev had left. With the woman who'd had him beaten and starved. How could they have been so stupid? He'd pleaded and argued for hours, said a few things he'd regret if he ever saw them again—which he wouldn't, because Merat Orzh would kill them both. Or worse, she'd use them up and toss them aside and they'd never be the wiser. And still they'd left.

Ev had tried to hug him. "I'm not giving you a last embrace before sending you to your death," he'd hissed, and she'd dropped her arms fast. After that, Alizhan hadn't tried.

"We won't forget you," Ev had said.

"You don't know that," Thiyo had said. Then he'd stalked off to the men's dormitory to lie awake for hours, because there was something jagged and angry scraping against his insides and it wouldn't let him rest, and now he was here. He gave Sardas a grim, red-eyed look in response to his comment. "The shift just started."

"Your friends left," Sardas said. "I don't know what happened between you, but I've been in Estva for years. People leave. It never gets any easier. Let's take the shift off. No one here will report us." He craned his neck to look into the bindery. Fama and Rin had overheard him and they were nodding. They liked Sardas and had almost warmed to Thiyo. They wouldn't say a thing.

Ayat made a brief instant of eye contact with Sardas and Thiyo. "Their authority only has meaning if we give it meaning," she said in her usual monotone. Thiyo understood that as an offer not to report their absence, but he couldn't be quite sure. Perhaps that was Ayat's goal. She sowed doubt with everything she said.

"Meet me in the library," Sardas said.

"There's a library? Why is this the first I'm hearing of it?"

"I'll explain," Ayat said. Was she volunteering to talk to Thiyo? What a strange shift this was. "You go," she said to

Sardas. "He'll join you in a moment."

Sardas nodded at each of them, then picked up his cane and strolled out of the room. Once he was gone, Ayat rolled her chair closer to Thiyo, forcing him to move into the corridor. Sardas was already out of sight.

"'The library' is what we call the storage room where we keep the books before they get shipped out," Ayat said. Disappointment crept in. Thiyo had been hoping for a real library, not some closet. "No one else ever goes into it, so sometimes we use it for other things."

"The occasional mid-shift drink?"

She tilted her shaved head to the side, causing her black feather earrings to flutter. "Among other things. Privacy is hard to come by in Estva." Ayat paused. "We don't tell people about the library very often."

"I see," Thiyo said, a little hurt that Sardas hadn't seen fit to tell him until now. He could have used a private room to talk to Alizhan and Ev. Not that he would have shared that with Sardas. Or Ayat. He wanted to know what she meant by "other things," but questions never worked on Ayat, so he didn't bother asking.

"The door is marked 'storage.' Take the second right, go all the way to the end, and go right again. You have to push hard on the door to get in. Keep your voice down once you're inside." Ayat was unbuttoning her coat and digging through the voluminous folds of her black robe. "But that's not what I came out here to tell you."

It wasn't? Thiyo was suddenly conscious of how alone they were in the hallway and how low she'd kept her voice. Ayat pulled out a small, unmarked burlap sack. She handed it up to him and it was far lighter than he'd expected—not that he'd expected any kind of gift from Ayat. He squeezed it lightly and the bag rustled. "What is this?"

"Dried nightvine," she said. "I heard you asking Sardas

about it. And I have a friend who does the kitchen accounts, so this won't be missed."

"I'm not sure what's more surprising, the fact that you're giving me a gift or the fact that you have a friend."

"Funny," Ayat said, her voice dead flat. "No wonder everyone loves you. And it's not a gift. I want you to find out what it does. Keep asking questions."

"That's why you're giving me this? Because I was curious?"

"They were good questions. You were asking them wrong."

"That makes no sense. You *have* to know that. You just like to be cryptic because it goes well with the robes and the makeup." What could Ayat possibly mean? What was the right way to ask a question? And why was she helping him now? She offered him no response. "You hated me, then overheard me indulging an idle curiosity, and now you're giving me a sack of pilfered land seaweed and we're friends. I've had stranger friendships."

Ayat glanced sidelong around the hallway, her black eyelids nearly closed and the whites of her eyes a sharp, mobile interruption in the black streak across her face. "I've seen the company you keep," she murmured, and if she was passing judgment on Ev and Alizhan, or Henny and Ket, Thiyo would spit on her. But she had nothing more to say on the topic, and instead continued with, "For the Temple of Doubt, there's no such thing as idle curiosity. But don't get ahead of yourself. We're not friends." She lifted her chin, indicating the bag in his hands. "Hide that. This never happened."

Thiyo tucked the bag into his coat. If he'd been at court, wearing a fashionable dress, he wouldn't have been able to hide it. But it had been a long time since he'd selected clothes for any quality other than warmth, so it was easy to make the nightvine disappear into an inside pocket of his bulky, shapeless coat. He was even momentarily grateful for the practicality, which was a truly sad comment on the state of his life. But there was hardly any point to looking good in Estva, since he'd lost the pleasure he took in it, and there was no one to impress.

Ayat took her leave of him with a nod, rolling her chair back into the press, and Thiyo followed her directions to the storage room.

It was neither a library nor a cramped closet. Sardas sat in the center of a small room lined with bookshelves and filled with wooden crates of books. Half the wall opposite Thiyo was spotless glass windows—this room must originally have been for some nobler purpose—and the glittering blue-black sky sprawled before him. The window didn't look out onto the city but out onto the plains, an awe-inspiring expanse of emptiness that underlined the grandeur of the sky. Sardas was so focused on the view that he didn't turn when Thiyo pushed the door open. There was a wooden chair next to him. On the stack of crates in front of him stood a bottle of some amber liquid and two empty glasses. Thiyo sat down.

Sardas poured him a glass. "Sometimes my friends' departures have made me think of leaving, too."

They clinked glasses and Sardas swallowed the contents of his in one gulp. Thiyo took a more cautious sip. He didn't want to talk about friends departing. Instead, he said, "Back to Laalvur."

"I suppose."

"I'd like to see it," Thiyo said. A dangerous admission. Sardas might have guessed Alizhan and Ev were returning there, and if so, he'd wonder why Thiyo hadn't gone with them. People in Estva didn't ask questions, but they still seemed to know lots of answers.

"You might yet," Sardas said. "You're young."

Thiyo didn't feel young. It was hard to feel anything other than angry and tired and lost. *I don't know what you should do, but it shouldn't be this*, he'd told Alizhan and Ev. He swallowed down some of what Sardas had poured. A whiskey of some kind. If Thiyo were more sophisticated and less pissed off, he might appreciate its flavor. Right now, he appreciated its fire. What else could burn up the hard, sharp, scraping thing in his chest?

"You never left, though," Thiyo said. Maybe he'd never leave either. Maybe he'd die without seeing the sun again.

"I might yet," Sardas said as if he were giving himself advice. He smiled. "I've been thinking of going back. Waiting for the right moment, I suppose. I'd like to see the Temple of Doubt. Having met Ayat, I want to know if they're all like her."

Thiyo laughed. The tightness he'd been carrying in his body began to ease. "Can you imagine?"

"Truly, I can't." Sardas kept smiling as he shook his head to himself. Then he placed a hand—lined, but not weathered—on Thiyo's. "I know we haven't known each other very long, but I like you, Thiyo. I always enjoy talking to you."

Their two hands sat there on the table and Thiyo didn't know what to make of it. In Hoi, people touched each other all the time, far more than on the mainland. It was friendship and familiarity. In Nalitzva, touching had always carried a sensual suggestion with it, so Thiyo had come to interpret all touch that way. But this didn't feel sexual.

"You make me wish I'd taken on an initiate," Sardas continued. "I'd like to have had a student like you. But I think we're too late for that, and you already know more than I ever could have taught you."

Was Sardas being... fatherly? Thiyo's own father had never behaved like this, so it was hard to tell. But it was a kindness at a time when Thiyo desperately wanted it, so he smiled and nodded, too. And when he moved his hand away to pick up his drink, he found himself regretting the loss of contact. Could he put his hand back? No, that was too much. He took a drink instead. His glass was empty.

Sardas poured him another. Then he got up from the table and went searching through the room. "I found that book I was telling you about," he said. He pulled down a small, tan volume from a shelf and handed it to Thiyo, who put his glass—already empty—down on the table to examine it.

He opened the left flap as if it were a mainland book, and was confronted with the final pages of a text in Hoi script. He blinked. Until a little over a year ago when he'd left Hoi with Ilyr, the council of elders had forbidden the export of books, even seemingly harmless ones like this. He flipped it over and started from the beginning. It was a short treatise on medicinal and recreational uses of *wai*. Where had Sardas acquired such a thing?

And why did it seem so familiar? Thiyo had never handled this book before.

"That's been here for years," Sardas said, gesturing at the book. "I don't even really know what language it's in. But a wild guess led me to believe you might."

Thiyo'd already had too much to drink, if this little book was bothering him so much. Should he translate it for Sardas? The council had been bitterly divided on whether Thiyo should be allowed to leave Hoi, and if so, what he should be allowed to share. Thiyo's own mother had led the isolationists.

"They will learn our secrets and destroy us with them," she'd said, her eyes on Thiyo. Her party members murmured agreement behind her, and a few others in the room looked sick with uncertainty. Thiyo had raised his chin and stared back at his mother. Ultimately, his lofty speech on opening up to the world —for love and freedom and knowledge—had narrowly defeated what he'd thought were her outmoded views on preserving their way of life. The council members had agreed to let him leave with Ilyr, under the condition that he exercise thoughtful judgment about what it was safe to share with outsiders. His mother, staunch to the end, had been silent as the council announced their decision. In all his years of disappointing her, she'd never looked so furious and betrayed. Luckily, the vote allowed him to put an ocean between them. Thiyo had won.

The memory of his victory in the council felt hollow and sad. What did Thiyo know of good judgment?

He shut the book and changed the subject. "So the Temple of Doubt didn't exist when you left Laalvur?" He stopped. He shouldn't have said that, but for a moment, he couldn't remember why. "Oh. Questions. Not supposed to ask."

"It's fine, Thiyo. We don't have to treat each other with distant politeness. Neither of us is Estvan by birth, anyway. And in answer, no, the Doubters were just a collection of grumbling priests of the Balance back then. They'd only just begun to murmur about calling themselves something else. It seemed wiser, as a young initiate, not to associate with them."

"Wiser not to associate," Thiyo repeated. He could have used a little of that wisdom. He was always associating with the wrong people. People who left. He took a drink.

"One of my few smart choices at that age," Sardas said. "I made more than my share of mistakes."

"Me too."

"Mostly women," Sardas admitted. "One in particular."

"You loved her," Thiyo said. He tried to intone it just right so it wouldn't be a question, even though it was. It was difficult. Was he drunk already? He'd only had two drinks, hadn't he? Sardas was pouring him another, and he couldn't remember what number it was, but he was lifting the glass to take a drink. What did it matter? He wasn't going anywhere.

"I would have done anything for her," Sardas said. "But she didn't love me."

"Stupid," Thiyo said fiercely. Sardas was still handsome, and he would have been glorious in his youth. And he was brilliant.

And he cared about Thiyo after knowing him for only a few weeks, so he must have cared deeply for this woman. "I would have loved you back."

Sardas raised his brows. Thiyo shouldn't have said that.

"I'm sorry, I didn't mean—"

"Oh, don't apologize. I'm flattered. And I appreciate your candor. I've never... had those inclinations, myself, but I understand them to be just as worthy as feelings between men and women," Sardas said. "But don't blame her. It wasn't her fault. We met in a tragic moment. A terrible wave had just hit the city. I'd only just joined the Temple, and suddenly I was presented with the enormously challenging, but vital work of offering comfort to grief-stricken survivors. That's how we met. I was young and clueless and not very good at my job, but with her... everything felt easy. And she was so beautiful. I can hardly describe... but I suppose it wouldn't mean anything to you, if you don't like women."

"Why does everyone always assume that I don't?" Thiyo muttered. "Have you *seen* women?"

Sardas laughed. "I didn't want to assume, but—point taken."

The liquor was making him say things he shouldn't. He looked down at the table. "Sorry. Please continue."

"So yes, we had a connection. But she'd lost someone and taken it hard. I don't think she's ever really loved anyone since. She couldn't help not loving me, just as I couldn't help loving her."

All the good people in the world suffered far too much. That deserved another drink. And he might as well take advantage of the moment to ask a few more improper questions. There was something intriguing about this story—a beautiful young Laalvuri woman surviving a disaster and losing everything—or something familiar. His thoughts swam. He needed to know more. "What happened?"

Sardas shrugged. "Nothing. She didn't love me and I couldn't make her. I came here."

"You never saw her again."

"We write to each other sometimes," Sardas said. "I enjoy our correspondence very much. It's so rare to meet someone with a mind like hers. She's remained a dear friend."

Sardas was still in love with someone who'd never love him back. He'd spent half his life in this icy, sunless hole, waiting for letters from her, knowing she wasn't waiting for his. "That's sad," Thiyo said, and his tongue stuck to the words. When he shook his head for emphasis, the room spun. It had been a long time since he'd felt so intoxicated.

"I told her about you. She said she'd like to meet you." Sardas tapped the book that was lying closed on the table. "She's the one who sent me this, you know. She was hoping you could read it."

Everyone always wanted Thiyo to read some book. This one wasn't even in some special, unbreakable code. It was just a bunch of normal words. And it wasn't unique. Thiyo had seen it before. He remembered looking for it once, for some reason—pulling all the books off a shelf, flipping each one open until he landed on this one. Then he'd crawled out the window.

Thiyo laughed to himself. A window. Why had he done that?

"Thiyo?"

"I'm drunk," Thiyo explained. He wasn't going to read any books. And Sardas's friend was all the way across the ocean in Laalvur, where Thiyo wasn't going. "And I'm here and they're— she's there. And I'm drunk." It was the best way he could think of to express the problem.

Sardas laughed. "I can see that. That is what we came here to do, isn't it? To take your mind off your friends who left for Laalvur. Alizhan and... what was her name? Ev?"

"I need to lie down."

"Yes, I think you're a bit too tall for me to carry you," Sardas said, amused. "Let's walk."

Sardas put the liquor on a shelf and helped him up. With Sardas supporting him, they walked out the door. Sardas was being so nice to him. Thiyo thanked him profusely, in between explaining that he didn't get drunk very often since the time that Barold Hyersk had tried to rape him, and that normally he carried a knife, but he hadn't lately, not since he'd had to use it, which had disturbed him viscerally and emotionally and he hoped never to do again, and for a while he'd thought that even if life was dangerous, maybe he could rely on Ev, or even Alizhan, to watch out for him, but he couldn't now because they'd left him—how *could* they, why didn't they *listen* —but it was what he ought to have expected from the beginning, because everyone left, because he wasn't worth staying with…

Sardas hugged him around the shoulders, which jolted the whole world and made Thiyo want to throw up, but was kind of nice anyway.

"I'll be embarrassed about this when I'm sober," Thiyo slurred, because even though everyone thought he was shameless, it wasn't quite true.

"With any luck, you won't remember," Sardas said. Their progress toward Thiyo's bed was slow and dizzying, but they did eventually arrive. Sardas had to guide him toward the cot, which kept moving and was never where he thought it was. When Thiyo finally got settled, Sardas pulled a small vial from the pocket of his grey robes. "You're likely to be miserable when you wake, but this might help. Drink it."

Thiyo did as he was told and then let his head fall to the pillow. Sardas gave his shoulder a paternal squeeze. But before Thiyo could let go of his consciousness entirely, there was one more thing. Something Sardas had said a while ago was still bothering him. "They're not my friends. I'll never see them again."

"Oh," Sardas said. "I wouldn't be so sure of that."

Thiyo passed out.

29

AN UNMARKED LETTER

4TH TRIAD OF SIMOSHA, YEAR 764 of the Balance

My dear Iriyat,

M arrived in Estva in extremely dramatic fashion, accompanied by a man with a broken leg. If she intended a diversion, it didn't work. I noticed her, and so did your ragtag band of adventurers. But Estva's strict exile laws worked in her favor, and she dispensed with two of them without lifting a finger. Only your girl, her friend, and the islander remained, and M persuaded the first two to go with her. The islander evinced some stubbornness—M had previously mistreated him, which may work to our advantage, and misjudged his value.

Speaking of poor judgment, I want to apologize for all these years of willful ignorance on my part. You were right about magic. It's absolutely a worthy object of study. I've finally begun to take Estvan folklore seriously and have made some exciting discoveries about the effects of the local plants. I will bring you a sample, along with the islander.

That means I'll be sailing on M's ship to Laalvur. I'm an old man now, and nostalgia does overtake me on occasion. It's been so long. I would like to see Laalvur—beautiful, brilliant, blond Laalvur—once more.

This puts me in an excellent position to report on M's designs to you. I'll do everything in my power to make sure you're ready. I know you've been waiting a long time for this homecoming.

Yours,
  Tsardeya

30

CASUAL INTIMACIES

H IS INSIDES SLOSHED. IT STAYED dark even when he tried to open his eyes. There was a wad of cloth stuffed into his mouth and something tied around his wrists. Something rocked him back and forth. Was that the sound of hooves? Thiyo didn't know where he was.

He ought to be terrified and struggling, but his heart beat sluggishly in his chest. *Drugs.* He'd been drinking with Sardas. Then he'd gone to bed. Had there been something else in the liquor?

Was Sardas alright?

Or was that the wrong question?

His thoughts were all out of order. How much time had passed? Which direction were they going—and who were *they* in the first place? Was Thiyo condemned to be drugged and dragged from bed and imprisoned every few months? He couldn't remember how he'd gotten to prison the first time —*Merat*—but it must have been something like this. Even more reason for alarm.

Ah. His stomach was alert to the threat—and the movement

—even if his pulse and his mind remained slow. Bile rose in his throat.

Thiyo made a sound of protest and horror and then a rag was placed over his face and the world fell away.

―――

THEY'D LEFT Estva in a matter of hours. Pirkko's goodbye had been chilly and Thiyo's had been as icy as death. Pirkko's mood couldn't be helped, but it was a stab in the gut, making Thiyo so angry and having no way to fix things. Ev had known, in a distant way, that he'd leave eventually—that one of their conversations would be the last—but she'd never imagined it would hurt so much. And she didn't want to miss him, vain and irritating as he was, but she did. She'd spent the first few hours of their ride expecting some clever barb about what dismal company Merat's guards were, how the unrelenting darkness really brought out their best features or their highly refined sense of style or something. But Thiyo was gone. No one had said anything witty at all.

Leaving felt like the wrong decision, even if physically walking out of the gates of Estva had been easier than she'd ever imagined. They'd spent so much time feeling trapped there. If only they'd had more money, they could have left long ago.

Merat had traveled in a finely appointed carriage, so Alizhan and Ev had opted to ride alongside. Merat's entourage was three men, down from four, since they'd left the man with the broken leg in Estva to recover. Two men drove her carriage and the third rode with Ev and Alizhan. They were frugal with their conversation, speaking short sentences of Nalitzvan-accented Laalvuri when they had directions to give, but they were obviously listening every time Ev and Alizhan said anything to each other. Ev spent long, silent stretches of their journey assessing the men, wondering if she could take two at once. Three was out of the question, and she had a feeling they all knew it.

They were headed for the small coastal city of Koritz, where Merat's ship awaited them. Koritz was governed by Nalitzva, but was small and sleepy enough that it was unlikely to be crawling with guards. Ev and Alizhan would keep out of sight once they arrived, just in case. And if there was trouble, Merat had coolly promised to make it go away—whatever that meant.

It would take two triads to ride there. They broke up their ride in the tiny village of Din Yaritz, where they found lodging at Night's End Inn, a hopeful and farfetched name, given that the sky of Din Yaritz was still very dark. But the blackness had ebbed into deep blue, and the Night was not so absolute as in Estva. Even though it was no warmer outside and they were both exhausted, Ev had talked Alizhan into taking a walk. It was easier to talk when they were far from Merat and her men.

Din Yaritz was surrounded by a stone wall and they circled the inside of it, ambling past cozy little houses and piles of snow that felt as ancient as the stones. Eventually, Alizhan sat down in an alcove built into the wall, and Ev sat with her, shoulder to shoulder. They'd hardly stopped touching since the kiss. Soon enough, now that Ev had stopped eating nightvine, that would have to change.

"I didn't want it to end like that with Thiyo," Alizhan said. The bench in the alcove hadn't been cleared of snow, and she picked up a handful next to where she was sitting. "I wish he hadn't been so stubborn."

"I'm sure he wishes the same of you," Ev said. The way they'd ended things with Thiyo weighed on her like a stone crushing her heart. It was hard to shake the feeling that they'd made a mistake. "He was right, you know. This is a bad idea and there's a strong chance we'll get hurt or killed."

Alizhan traded the snow from one hand to another, packing

it into a sphere. "You're always so cheerful and optimistic. That's what I love about you, that you always expect the best of every situation."

Even in that joking tone, the word *love* fell on Ev like another weight. She was carrying too much guilt. "There's something I have to tell you," she said. Alizhan still couldn't read her. Ev wanted to confess of her own volition before the effects of the nightvine faded and Alizhan found out the truth.

"I'm really sorry," Ev said. "For everything. For Iriyat and how she treated you. For—"

"You know what's extra awful about the thing with Iriyat?" Alizhan interrupted. "I keep having this fantasy, a dream of this other life, one where she told me. Nothing else is different. She's still killing people, still making people forget, and I don't care. I'm her daughter and she loves me and none of this," Alizhan hurled her snowball out of the alcove and it powdered the drifts outside, "ever happened."

"We wouldn't be friends, in that life," Ev said, the words falling as quietly as Alizhan's thrown snow.

Alizhan kept staring into the dim blue light of Din Yaritz. After a long time, she said, "It's a bad thing to want. But I want it anyway."

Was that an opening? An invitation to apologize? An indication that Alizhan might forgive Ev? "You've always known a lot about what people want."

"The funny thing is, I want that, but at the same time, I want none of it to be true. I wish Thiyo had kept translating and discovered that it was all some terrible mistake." Alizhan huffed. "I'm still hoping that when we read the rest of his translation, that will be the case. I don't make a lot of sense."

"You'd know better than anyone that people want conflicting things all the time. We don't necessarily make sense."

"No," Alizhan said, drawing out the word. "We don't."

"I didn't finish my apology earlier," Ev said. "I'm sorry for how I treated you in Estva. I did something really stupid, Alizhan, and I regret it, and I understand if you don't want to forgive me."

Alizhan folded her knees up and rested her chin on them. She dragged her index finger through the pile of snow. "It was Pirkko, wasn't it?"

Hadn't she seen? *Oh.* Of course. She'd witnessed what had happened in the hot springs, but without her abilities, she couldn't recognize anyone—except Ev. There'd been other dark-skinned people in Estva, but none of them had been women of her height.

"You don't have to answer. I already guessed. I'm useless now, but even I could figure that out." Alizhan sounded resigned.

"I shouldn't have—"

"Why her, though? You could have kissed dozens of other people."

Ev shook her head at Alizhan's inflated opinion of the number of people who wanted to kiss her, but it was hard to see in the alcove, and Alizhan never paid attention to that kind of gesture, anyway. "I'm really sorry, Alizhan. I don't have a good answer."

"You do. You just don't want to say it."

Ev sighed. "She's beautiful and she wanted me and she was right there. Is that enough?"

"And it was simple," Alizhan said. "Simpler than it would have been with me."

The truth was piercing. It was so silent that Ev could hear her own heartbeat, and for an instant, it surprised her. The sound should have been the crystalline shattering of glass, the crunch of shards. Ev closed her eyes, pushing tears through her lashes and onto her cheeks.

"Are you crying?" Alizhan said with curiosity and sympathy.

"I'm sorry. I can't feel it at all. The whole world feels dead since Estva. It makes me feel dead, too. I didn't mean to make you cry. I just wanted us to tell the truth. And as long as you're kissing me, I don't really care if you're kissing anyone else."

Ev had never had Alizhan's senses, but sometimes she didn't need them. "Bullshit."

"Well, fine," Alizhan said. "I did care. I was angry. But I'm trying not to be angry anymore. Because I understand about wanting things to be simple. And I wouldn't have been angry at all if you'd picked someone better to kiss."

"Someone better?"

"You knew I didn't like her! She was awful and she threw Henny out in the cold and I still think she might have been a spy for Iriyat and even if she wasn't, we shouldn't have trusted her. If you really had to kiss someone, I'm sure Henny or Ket would've said yes if you'd asked nicely, and you wouldn't even have needed to ask Thiyo."

They had swerved from seriousness into absurdity.

"Henny and Ket are in love with each other, and Thiyo's accustomed to royalty—he thinks I'm a dull, plain country bumpkin. And more importantly, I don't want to kiss any of them! Not even Pirkko," Ev said, then she amended it. "Or at least, I don't want to kiss anyone nearly as much as I want to kiss you."

"That's good to hear," Alizhan said. She laid her head on Ev's shoulder. "But I'm trying to tell you something and you're not listening."

"Tell me, then."

"I'm aware that I'm... difficult," Alizhan said. "Even more than usual in Estva. And I'm sorry for it. I want to be a person that you can love all the time."

"You are," Ev said. "Even when you're difficult. Sometimes because you're difficult."

"Good," Alizhan said. "I'm not finished. Things are good between us now, and I love kissing you, but we both know it might not last. And I don't know where we'll get more nightvine. Or *wai*. So we should enjoy touching each other, but we have to keep in mind that it's temporary. And there will be times when I can't give you what you need. And I want you to be happy, Ev, even if it's not with me." Alizhan paused to take a deep breath. "If you want to kiss someone—even if that person is Pirkko— you should. Life is short and ours might be shorter than normal."

"I can't believe *you* teased *me* about being a pessimist not half an hour ago," Ev said.

"I'm being practical."

"In that case, I think you should kiss me while you're still alive to do it."

Alizhan's lips were warm against Ev's and Ev could feel her smiling. "You know," she murmured, breaking the kiss. "If we're not going to *talk*, I don't care if anyone overhears us. We could go back to Night's End."

"We could," Ev agreed, grinning, and an instant later she was tugging Alizhan back toward their room. Pragmatism or pessimism, Alizhan's argument had rendered every touch that much more urgent. They raced up the stairs and slammed the door, dropping gloves and scarves and coats on the floor of their room. After so many weeks of thick layers, it was a surprise how much smaller Alizhan was without her coat on, and how bright her printed tunic was compared to all that mottled brown fur and leather and wool. She looked as beautiful and as wildly out of place as if a warmth-loving Day flower—yellow lady's lace or red sawleaf or climbing arish—had burst through the frozen ground and bloomed in spite of the dim, cool sky and the blankets of snow.

Alizhan propelled her toward the bed. Ev fell back willingly when her calves ran into the mattress, and Alizhan toppled with her. The bed was hardly big enough for Ev alone, but the two of them tangled their limbs together and managed to pull their remaining clothes off, laughing between breathless kisses. Ev threaded her fingers into Alizhan's hair, and then Alizhan pulled the tail of her braid over her shoulder and began to undo it.

"You know, I thought when this finally happened that I'd know exactly what you wanted," Alizhan said.

Was she *nervous*? Ev ought to have expected that, even with Alizhan's ferocious kisses. Mind-reader or not, Alizhan had never done this before. The nightvine made it impossible for her touch to hurt Ev, but it also took away the one advantage she'd been counting on. Ev took her half-undone braid from her hands and finished the work herself, loosing Alizhan's hair until it curtained their faces, its ends tickling Ev's collarbone and breasts. "And how did you expect me to know what *you* wanted, mm?"

"I don't," Alizhan paused, her breath catching as Ev palmed one of her breasts and stroked a thumb over the nipple. She closed her eyes. "I didn't think about that."

"I did," Ev said, smiling. She let her hand glide down the smooth skin of Alizhan's belly and the tangle of dark hair between her hips, then lower until her fingers skimmed slickness. Alizhan shivered above her, clenching her thighs around Ev's. "And I'm sure we can figure it out."

Ev slid a finger in and had to stop to catch her own breath, overwhelmed. She couldn't feel what Alizhan was feeling, not really, but the sensation of being inside someone else—the silky, wet warmth of it, but more than that, the intimacy of being invited to this most secret place—was almost as powerful. Alizhan leaned down and kissed her, then rocked her hips, encouraging Ev to move. It was easy enough to find a rhythm

that made Alizhan sigh and gasp, and when she came, shuddering, it was almost too soon.

Alizhan let her head drop to the pillow. Next to Ev's ear, she
murmured, low and throaty, "God, that was good."

Ev expected her to relax into languor for at least a moment,
but instead she sat up, beaming. "I want to do that to you. And
then you can do it to me again. Actually, let's just stay right here
and keep doing that forever."

Then they were kissing again, and Ev absolutely would have
signed on to Alizhan's plan to stay in bed if someone hadn't
banged on their door. They both froze.

"Let them knock. They'll go away if we ignore them,"
Alizhan whispered.

The banging happened a second time.

"Open up," Merat said. "A friend of yours just arrived."

"We don't have any friends," Alizhan said. "Henny and Ket
are far away by now, and Thiyo's too angry to come after us."

As Alizhan had just proved, they did have friends, and Ev
couldn't risk leaving any of them alone with Merat. She extricated herself from Alizhan, dressed, and padded to the door,
cracking it open to hide the haphazard piles of clothing on the
floor.

Outside, Merat stood next to one of her hulking guards, who
had one arm braced around a limp, unconscious Thiyo. His feet
were on the ground, but not supporting his weight. His head
tipped forward. A dusting of snow melted in his hair, which had
grown longer since they'd been in Estva and now hung down
into his closed eyes. Ev let the door swing wide and held out her
arms, hoping desperately that Alizhan had dressed by now.
Merat could draw her own conclusions about the messy state of
their room. Ev didn't care. The guard dumped Thiyo on her. She
caught him, which was awkward since he was almost as tall as
her, a long and ungainly burden.

"What happened? How did he get here? Why is he unconscious?"

"He was overcome with regret after you left, and drank himself into a stupor talking about how much he wished he'd come with you," Merat said. "I'd rather not have a drunk degenerate on my ship but if you take responsibility for him, I'll allow it. Sardas speaks well of him, but that priest is a soft-hearted fool."

"Sardas?" Alizhan had come to the door—fully clothed, thank God—and was peering around Ev and Thiyo.

Ev vaguely remembered the name. Hadn't that been the priest who'd worked in the press with Thiyo and Alizhan?

"Yes," Merat said. "A priest of the Balance and a long-time correspondent of mine—I believe he mentioned that he knew you. I'd offered him a berth on the ship, in case he wanted to return home again. He declined, but he must have changed his mind out of pity for your friend here. I suppose they'll be joining us. Now, if you'll excuse me, I was resting."

Merat spun on her heel and went down the hallway to her room. The guard followed her.

Ev maneuvered Thiyo toward the bed and Alizhan shut the door.

"What the fuck," Alizhan said, latching the door, and Ev couldn't think of anything else to add.

Thiyo was breathing but still solidly unconscious as Ev laid him down. "How did Sardas even get him here? We rode for hours before arriving. Was he drunk the whole time?" She sniffed. Thiyo did smell like liquor, but he didn't reek in the way she'd expect if he'd been guzzling the stuff while on horseback all shift. "Thiyo's not even that good at riding when he's sober."

"Is he okay?"

"I think so," Ev said. She couldn't stop staring. Considering how troubling the context was, Thiyo looked eerily serene in sleep. "I just can't fathom what made him change his mind, or why he'd arrive in this state."

"We won't know until he wakes up," Alizhan said. She moved to cover the single green lamp in the room with a cloth and then she sat down on the opposite edge of the bed. Thiyo lay between them. "I guess it would be inappropriate to keep having sex now that there's an unconscious man in our bed."

"Yeah," Ev said. It wasn't so much Thiyo's arrival as the sight of Merat's face that had ruined her mood.

"Even though it might be our only chance. Even though, out of all the people we know, he's the least likely to be offended. We could just push him to the side a little and be really careful, and look how out he is, we probably wouldn't even need to be quiet—"

"Still not gonna happen." Ev wasn't sure if she wanted to laugh or cry. This wasn't a conversation she'd ever expected to have.

"Although now that I think of it, I said Thiyo wouldn't be offended, but realistically, if we did and if he ever found out, it'd be sort of like we had a party and didn't invi—"

"Alizhan." Ev grabbed her hand and gave it a squeeze. "It's not our only chance. We will have more time. We will *make* more time."

Alizhan sighed. "I know, I know. Something is terribly wrong and we have to be watchful and you'd feel guilty forever if Thiyo died in our bed while we were having sex. You're always so moral and responsible."

"It's a curse," Ev agreed.

"No, it's what I love about you," Alizhan said, suddenly serious. "You're so good at right and wrong. If I were better at right and wrong, I might have seen through Iriyat long ago and saved us a lot of trouble. I spent so many years working for her. I made it possible for her to do evil things. You wouldn't have done that."

"I'm not a saint, Alizhan. I make mistakes. Wasn't I just apologizing to you for one?"

"Kissing Pirkko hardly compares to the torture and murder of innocent people."

"You didn't torture or murder anyone yourself. And the context is important. She lied to you and abused you. She isolated you from everyone else and made you believe she was the only person who could love you. Of course you worked for her. Anyone would have."

"I'm not sure that's true," Alizhan said. "But my point still stands. You care about doing the right thing more than me."

Did that mean *you care about doing the right thing more than I care about doing the right thing* or *you care about doing the right thing more than you care about me*? Ev didn't agree with either option, but the thought of parsing them made her very sad and tired. "We have to ride out in a few hours. We should sleep."

"You sleep," Alizhan said, settling back against the headboard and drawing her knees up. "You were right about keeping watch and making sure Thiyo doesn't die."

As Ev recalled, it had been Alizhan who'd said those things. But closing her eyes was more enticing than arguing.

EVERY TIME THIYO STIRRED, Ev and Alizhan tried to ask him what had happened. But he could barely stay conscious. Ev had to carry him out of their room. "He has to travel to Koritz in the carriage," she said. "It's the only way."

"He won't like that," Alizhan had said.

"He won't like sliding off his horse and snapping his neck,

either," Ev said. "There's no way he can ride in this state. This is no normal hangover."

"We can't leave him in that carriage alone with Merat. One of us has to stay with him."

A silence.

"This was your idea," Ev said, quiet and firm.

Alizhan sighed. When she was riding outside the carriage, she could pretend that they hadn't made a bargain with a monster. But for the next four hours, she'd be staring Merat in the face.

Thiyo's eyelids flicked open once or twice while Ev hauled him into the carriage. For an instant, Alizhan thought he'd see Merat and wake up from his daze kicking and screaming. But nothing happened, at least as far as she could tell. Thiyo and Ev were still unreadable to her.

Merat said nothing as Alizhan sat down with Thiyo.

"You want me to come with you, this is how it goes," Alizhan said. "Don't touch either of us."

"I can't imagine why I'd want to."

Sardas climbed into the carriage and seated himself next to Merat, on the bench opposite Alizhan and Thiyo. He shut the door behind him and pulled a cloth off one of the lamps to illuminate the leather-upholstered interior. He glanced around and said, in a voice tinged with sympathy, "Oh, Thiyo."

Alizhan couldn't read any of them, but she didn't fall for that tone of voice. What was Sardas doing here? Merat said he'd come with Thiyo. Had Thiyo been unconscious the whole time? Had Sardas drugged him?

If Thiyo were awake, he could talk to her. If he hadn't been eating nightvine for weeks, she wouldn't even need him to talk. She could answer her own questions.

Alizhan put her arm around Thiyo's shoulders and drew him down until his head was lying in her lap, a movement she managed with surprising grace, considering how much bigger Thiyo was, and how heavy and unconscious and uncooperative. Once she'd settled him there, she laid a hand on his head and turned the full force of her stare on Merat. She felt like an animal staking a claim.

"What a funny little group we are," Merat observed, all false courtly lightness.

Alizhan didn't want to make small talk to lift the tension. *Touch me and die*, she didn't say. Could she actually kill someone with her touch? And if so, could she kill someone like Merat, someone powerful and experienced with their own gifts? If Merat reached for her, Alizhan would find out.

"I can tell the two of you are close," Sardas said to Alizhan, nodding at Thiyo asleep in her lap. "He was upset when you left. He told me he'd made a big mistake, letting you leave without him."

Fucking nightvine. Alizhan knew he was lying but couldn't sense what the truth was. He sounded so friendly. "A change of heart," she said dryly. "Followed by a sudden illness."

"Sometimes those happen when the people we love disappear from our lives," Sardas said. "And as for his sickness, I'm sure it will pass. I had no idea islanders were so ill-affected by liquor."

Thiyo had avoided *wai* at Ilyr's wedding, but he'd sucked down glass after glass of wine. Alizhan couldn't say how many he'd had because she'd had far too many herself. Unlike her, he hadn't been affected. "I've never seen a hangover like this."

Merat made a little noise of protest at the vulgar word *hangover*, as if she weren't the type of woman who had her enemies dragged from their beds and thrown in secret prisons.

"Have you met many islanders?" Sardas asked.

"Somehow I don't think that's the problem," Alizhan shot back.

"Now, now," Merat said. "We're stuck in this carriage for half a shift, and then we'll be aboard *Honesty* together for a long time, so let's be civil."

"An excellent point," Sardas said. "Perhaps we could pass the time in conversation. Would you like to tell me about yourself?"

"No," Alizhan said and resumed staring balefully and silently at Merat.

Merat laughed, as though apologizing for this outlandish behavior, and said, "Sardas, I'm sorry, but stubbornness is a family trait."

So Sardas knew they were family? How much else did he know?

If Thiyo were awake, he could navigate this conversation for her. He'd be better at saying elegant, mean things to Merat. He could walk the line between socially acceptable and vicious. It had only been a little while, and Alizhan already wanted to resort to baring her teeth and growling.

Alizhan peeled off Thiyo's hat and stroked his flattened hair. The wild, dark waves of it fell over his eyes. It was shiny and soft, but Alizhan knew Thiyo missed having long hair. She ran one of the short locks through her fingers. To Merat and Sardas, the gesture might look sweet and absentminded. A useful illusion. There were no casual intimacies in Alizhan's life. Every touch was deliberate and considered.

Wake up, Thiyo. Wake up and remember.

Nothing happened. Alizhan continued to touch him, just in case.

"That's often the way," Sardas was saying. "So many things run in families."

"My little girl used to refuse to wear anything but purple," Merat said. "You could offer her dozens of tunics and dresses and skirts, in all the finest fabrics, with the most delicate embroidery—you've never seen such beautiful clothes—and she would throw them on the ground and stomp on them unless they were purple. In the end, it was easier to bend to her will. It was our house color, after all."

My little girl meant Iriyat. It was jarring to think of her as a child. Iriyat never spoke about her family. Alizhan had always assumed it was because the loss of her parents was too painful.

Merat sighed. "I wish she hadn't gone mad."

Alizhan didn't want to talk to either of them, didn't want to ask any questions, didn't want to be drawn into Merat's ploy, but she wanted very badly to know more. Merat thought Iriyat was mad?

"I'm sure you'll do your best to set things right," Sardas said.

Alizhan blinked. *Set things right* wasn't how she'd describe committing a murder. Sardas must not know. If Merat was lying during this conversation, the lies weren't meant for Alizhan.

Merat put a hand on his knee. Shockingly familiar, for a Nalitzvan aristocrat. "You've been a good friend to me, all these years. When I felt most abandoned by the world, there you were. I am both sorry you have to witness this low moment in my life and relieved that you are here, all at once. You do like to give shelter to the lost."

This last sentence was spoken with a look at Thiyo that even Alizhan perceived. Merat was doing that thing—Thiyo's thing—where you said something in which none of the individual words was mean, but somehow the impact of the whole was insulting.

"He's fascinating," Sardas said. "You should give him a chance."

And Sardas was doing something else—the words all sounded nice, and yet somehow they didn't add up to treating Thiyo like a person. Sardas had been warm and friendly to Alizhan when they'd first met. He'd been harboring secret plans the whole time—what secrets exactly, she still didn't know. But he'd lured Thiyo into a trap. The carriage felt too small and enclosed, and they had so many hours to go.

The least these two awful people could do for Alizhan was to give her some useful information about her family. But to get that, she'd have to speak. Alizhan took a breath. "When did she go mad?"

"She was always troubled, but she could be managed until your father died," Merat said. "I didn't approve of him, I'm sorry to say."

She didn't sound sorry. Besides, Alizhan was glad to hear it. Her father was the only person in her newly discovered family, besides Eliyan, that she liked. She would never meet him—except through Thiyo's translation. If Alizhan had let Thiyo continue reading his translation of the journal instead of storming out, she'd know Iriyat's version of the story.

"He was a sailor and he died in the last wave. Iriyat always blamed me for that. Grief makes people irrational. It's not as if anyone controls the ocean."

Sardas laughed. "Truly a mad aspiration." He paused to consider it. "But a rather wonderful one, don't you think? Wouldn't the world be a better place if we could control the waves?"

"You've always had a taste for whimsy, Sardas. Anyway, mad with grief, Iriyat attacked us—her father and myself—shortly after discovering that the sailor had died. I'm afraid she killed Orosk—her father and your grandfather. But she told the world we were both dead and wrested Varenx House from my hands, playing the part of the victim the whole time."

"And now you're going to... set things right," Alizhan said.

"With your help," Merat said. The satisfaction in her voice turned Alizhan's stomach.

31

MISTAKES

THIYO'S BRAIN WAS WRUNG OUT like a wet rag. He'd woken up a few times over the mess of the last few hours —shifts? triads?—to relieve himself. And to throw up. Mah Yee, there'd been far too much of that. He'd barely eaten anything, but his body was purging itself of something. He'd accepted water from Alizhan and Ev and stared dully while they'd asked things like "How did you get here? What happened that made you leave Estva?"

Thiyo didn't know. Alizhan and Ev had treated the subject so gingerly. At first, they'd asked him over and over again if he was sure he wanted to come with them. Whatever the plan was, he must have objected at some point, but his objections, whatever they'd been, had vanished. And now, since they'd stopped asking, and since the rolling motion and wooden creaking of his surroundings must mean he was on a ship, Thiyo assumed they'd decided for him.

Awake, he probed the gap in his memory the way he'd use his tongue to poke at a space between his teeth: absentmindedly, incessantly, to the point of madness. It was dim in this cabin, and dimmer still in his narrow berth, and he didn't bother to examine anything else around him. He was too busy sifting through his own mind. It was sickening to be so aware of the gap —and he was already sick to begin with. His head throbbed. It felt like he'd been poisoned. But who would have done that?

It was too warm. He was still dressed in the coat he'd been wearing in Estva, which meant the clothes underneath were likely rank, but there was nothing to be done about it. He unbuttoned his coat, pausing when his hand brushed a strange lump in one of his inside pockets. He pulled out a brown cloth bag. How had that gotten there? It was light for its size and it rustled when he shook it. Thiyo picked apart the seam at the top.

Dried nightvine. He should know how this had come into his possession, but his aching head supplied no answers. He poked a finger into the loose contents of the bag and discovered a tiny, folded piece of paper. He shook it free of the leaves and unfolded it.

Don't trust S.

The message was in Nalitzvan, in handwriting so neat it might as well have been printed. There was a black smudge at the end of the sentence, made of a substance that didn't look like ink. Thiyo touched it—*eyeliner*. A woman with black eyeliner and no hair. Ayat. A priest of Doubt at the press in Estva. She'd given him this bag of nightvine and she must have written the note, too.

S must be Sardas, then. What did Ayat mean? Thiyo's memory was full of holes. Some things remained: he remembered living and working in Estva for weeks. He'd translated the journal in secret and discovered that eating nightvine protected people from magic. Henny had broken the rules to heal a man with a broken leg and been kicked out. Ket had left to save her. And there was a gap, except for the foggy memories of Alizhan and Ev looming over him, their eyes huge with concern.

Someone had altered his memory. Sloppy work, if he could notice it.

He'd been eating nightvine for weeks. Was that why someone had poisoned him? To make it easier to alter his memory? That would make sense. It didn't do anything to calm the swell of nausea in his stomach.

Outside his cabin, there was the murmur of conversation. He identified Alizhan and Ev and someone else—a soft, feminine voice. Thiyo knew that accent—Nalitzvan so hard and delicate it might as well have been carved with a chisel, scraping away any hint of soft Laalvuri consonants. But why would he recognize that voice? Who was speaking?

The conversation ended and Ev and Alizhan came in.

"Oh, good, you're awake," Ev said.

"I found this," Thiyo said, sitting up and handing her the bag of nightvine and the note. "And this. And someone altered my memory."

Alizhan promptly sat down on the edge of his berth and Thiyo regarded her with apprehension. "We thought so. And I just," she started, reaching a hand toward his head. "Nothing's come of it yet, but I have a stupid, inexplicable urge to touch you like this, so will you let me?"

"Your urge to touch me is neither stupid nor inexplicable," Thiyo said. Then he sniffed. "Although I admit I've smelled better in my life."

Alizhan put her hand in his hair, and a memory rose out of the fog of the last two triads. She'd done this before. He remembered her fingertips on his scalp. Without a word, he repositioned himself so he was lying with his head in her lap. She put her other hand in his hair and began to massage little circles into his skin. It felt lovely—so gentle—a balm to the ache of loneliness he'd grown accustomed to, a kind of sweetness he'd almost forgotten existed in the world.

"Who wrote this?" Ev said, peering at the note. "What's this Nalitzvan word here?"

"Ayat wrote it. It says 'don't trust S.' You should take that nightvine and keep eating it so you and Alizhan can touch each other."

"So she's talking about Sardas," Ev said, ignoring his advice. She didn't hand the bag back.

"Yes, although I don't know—ow! You can't do that if you're going to pluck out my hair, you little fiend."

"I didn't," Alizhan said. "I wouldn't do that."

"I was watching and she didn't do anything differently," Ev said. She pushed Thiyo's bent legs aside and sat at the end of the berth. As though finally accepting that they were going to be here a long time, she set the bag of nightvine aside.

Alizhan continued massaging his scalp, a pleasant, firm pressure that contrasted with the ache behind his eyes. He wasn't at his best. Maybe he'd imagined the pain. "Well, I won't make you stop, in that case."

"Anyway, Sardas seems to be friends with Merat," Ev said.

"Who?" Thiyo had no idea what Ev was talking about. And then the ship lurched. Alizhan's hand splayed over his temple to hold him in place. Thiyo yelped at the spike of pain. *Merat.* That was the woman with the distinctive accent. Merat Orzh Varenx. A Lacemaker. Alizhan's grandmother and a figure in the journal he'd translated. The woman responsible for his stint in a Nalitzvan prison. She must have touched him and made him forget. But if so, then how had he remembered?

The ship groaned beneath them and Alizhan stroked her hand through his hair. That spike of pain he'd felt—that had been Alizhan, restoring a memory. She wasn't just touching him for show, or for comfort. She was working.

A chill of disappointment settled over him—she hadn't simply wanted to touch him. But that was absurd. She was doing something important and he was being pathetic. And he'd just learned something crucial. "That's why you two have been so ridiculously apologetic." Thiyo swatted at Alizhan's hands and sat up. "We're on this ship with Merat. I told you this was a bad idea and I didn't want to come. So why the depths-drowned *fuck* am I here?"

"You remember her!" Alizhan was delighted, grinning despite the dark circles under her eyes. "It worked! What else do you remember?"

"I remember asking a question one second ago and not getting an answer."

"We left Estva and rode for Din Yaritz without you," Ev said. "And then a shift later, while we were at an inn, Sardas showed up with you in tow. You were unconscious. We think he abducted you. We tried to get the story out of you every time you blinked, but we couldn't. And we couldn't leave you behind in that state. So you're on this ship now. We're really sorry."

"Sardas?" Thiyo said in disbelief. The kindly old priest had abducted him? Had Sardas poisoned him?

"Ayat tried to warn you," Ev said, holding up the note. "We didn't get the message until it was too late."

"I'm still not sure why Sardas did it, though," Alizhan said, yawning. "Merat doesn't like you."

"I don't care much for her, either."

"You must have some value to her," Ev said. "Or to Sardas."

Thiyo looked at Alizhan. "Do it again. Touch me."

She reached for him, putting a hand on either side of his face. They faced each other for a long time with nothing happening. Alizhan's eyelids fluttered closed and she swayed with fatigue. Thiyo steadied her with his hands on her shoulders. Now that he'd had a moment to observe her, he could see there were long strands of black hair slipping out of her braid.

Her tunic was wrinkled and grimy. Ev hardly looked any better. It had been a difficult few triads.

Alizhan didn't move her hands from his face, but she said, "It's not working."

"What did we do right last time?" Thiyo said. "It felt like the ship moved, and then this lance of pain went right through my head, and suddenly I knew who Merat was. Before that, when Ev mentioned her, the name meant nothing to me."

"You think the ship moved?" Ev asked. "I didn't feel anything like that. It must have been something between you two."

Alizhan nodded. Her eyes were open now, but shadowed with sleepiness. "You mentioned Merat, and I suddenly knew what it was Thiyo had forgotten. And he was thinking about it, too."

"So you worked together," Ev said. "That means Thiyo should think about Sardas."

Thiyo visualized the priest's face, with its long, angular nose and its laugh lines, and the grey robes he always wore. A bolt of pain shot from left to right behind his eyes, as though it had come from one of Alizhan's hands and gone through his head. An image swam through his mind: Sardas leaning over him and offering him a small vial of something to drink.

Sardas had gotten him drunk and then given him something to drink, and fool that he was, he'd accepted it. That was how Sardas had poisoned and abducted him. But why?

Mah Yee, Thiyo regretted every swallow of liquor and every friendly word. What a mistake he'd made, trusting Sardas.

At the thought of mistakes, pain sparked. Thiyo didn't want to think about anything else that would bring him pain—he'd had quite enough—but that twinge of discomfort was a road sign for some important memory that Merat had locked away. He had to find it. *Mistakes, regrets... oh.* They'd been drinking in the library, that little room with giant windows dominated by the Night sky. Sardas hadn't been as drunk as Thiyo, but he hadn't been sober, and the liquor had made him reminisce.

Thiyo's head pounded. His breath came fast and shallow.

Sardas talked about a woman he loved. She didn't love him back because she'd lost the love of her life in the last wave to hit Laalvur—just like Iriyat had written in the journal. Sardas hadn't been able to stop himself from loving her, and they'd kept up a correspondence for years, even after he'd moved to Estva. Now he wanted to return to Laalvur.

Sardas had shown him a book in Hoi. A treatise on *wai*. Thiyo hadn't been able to place it at the time, but now he knew he'd seen it before—in Alizhan's memory. She'd stolen that book at Iriyat's request. *She said she'd like to meet you. She wants you to read it.*

That came with such a head-splitting blast of pain that it took Thiyo a moment to understand that he wasn't the only one howling. Alizhan had wailed and snatched her hands back. Thiyo made an instant of eye contact with her before her eyes rolled backward and she collapsed forward into his lap.

"Sardas didn't bring me here for Merat," he told Ev. "He's working for Iriyat."

ALIZHAN WOKE up in Thiyo's berth feeling like someone had drilled into her skull. Thiyo and Ev weren't there, but the bag of nightvine and Thiyo's translation were both in the bed with her. She pushed herself upright. How long had she been out? Half an hour? Four hours? Impossible to say.

She'd passed out just as Thiyo remembered that Sardas was working for Iriyat. And Sardas had abducted him. That made more sense than her previous theories. Merat didn't value Thiyo and had been content to abandon him, whether that was in prison in Nalitzva or in a dorm in Estva. But Iriyat had always been interested in the islands—and in people with gifts.

And she'd built that room with the chair and the restraints and the jars full of medusa venom and had someone keep Kasrik there and hurt him. There was no good reason for Iriyat to meet Thiyo.

Wherever Thiyo and Ev had gone, Alizhan hoped they'd come back soon. It was a small ship. They couldn't go far. Her head felt tender and full to bursting with Thiyo's memories stirred into her own. The thought of going out and running into Sardas or Merat exhausted her.

She picked up the journal instead.

The writer was almost an endearing character. A little pompous, but she was honest about her shortcomings and made no secret of what she wanted. It was hard to think of her as Iriyat, and harder still to think *my mother*. But it was easy to read about Arav and think *my father*, to skim those passages with a strange, new feeling. Iriyat had loved him so much. She made it seem easy. He must have been lovable. What would it have been like to know him? If Arav had lived, what kind of life would they have had? How different would Iriyat have been?

Were other people like that—one tragedy away from committing evil acts? Was Alizhan like that?

Still, when Merat and Orosk Varenx locked Iriyat in her room and Iriyat wrote in her journal "I will not treat my child the way they treat me," Alizhan hurled the book across the cabin. Iriyat hadn't repeated her parents' mistakes, but she'd made her own. In this case, different wasn't better.

And it was one thing for Iriyat to have had that thought twenty years ago, but she'd written this particular entry in the Year 761 of the Balance. Three years ago. Alizhan had been sixteen, living in Varenx House, desperate for the barest hint of Iriyat's affection, still harboring a secret hope that her family was out there. Iriyat could have told her at any time. Instead she'd written this journal in secret code, in invisible ink, like Alizhan was something to be ashamed of.

Why tell the story at all?

There'd been one entry that stood out, an "incursion of the present," as Iriyat called it, describing her meeting with Ilyr. Alizhan appeared as a minor character in the long story addressed to her: "You declined to tell me Ilyr's secret on the first triad of his visit." Alizhan had thought she was protecting the prince. She'd felt a kinship with him, a man who loved men. And she hadn't wanted to tell Iriyat out of a perverse fear that sharing Ilyr's secret might reveal her own. But these were details and not the principle goal of the entry. With some help from Mar, Iriyat had persuaded Ilyr to go to the islands. She'd been convinced it would benefit her somehow. In the conversation she'd recorded, she'd spoken of the trade in venom—Alizhan thought of that room again, and her stomach lurched—but the journal entry had suggested there was more.

Alizhan hated Iriyat for all the lies she'd told and for all the hurt she'd put into the world. She didn't want to know that woman any better. But she wanted to know what had happened to young Iriyat, the one who'd been so in love. And she wanted to know why this journal existed. She picked the book up.

Mere pages later, Merat and Orosk—her grandparents—tried to force Iriyat to have an abortion. "Fuck," Alizhan said out loud.

Things were obviously going to get worse.

"WHERE ARE YOU GOING?" Ev called. Thiyo had laid Alizhan down gently in his berth, then stood up and marched toward the door. Ev recognized something of Alizhan in those movements

—that decisive walk disguising his unsteadiness, that determination to do something absolutely scorching reckless.

"We know something Merat doesn't," Thiyo said. "That puts us in a position of power."

"An extremely tenuous position." Ev crossed the cabin in a stride and closed the door behind her. Thiyo had just exited, but she caught up, got in front of him, and blocked his path. She used her size to back him into the door. "Maybe we should talk about it."

He stepped to the side, forcing her to move to block his path again. Merat's cabin was right next to theirs, but Thiyo had been unconscious since they'd boarded. Ev refrained from looking in its direction. When it became clear that Ev wasn't going to let him pass, he threw up his hands. "There's no time for this. We have a choice between Merat and Iriyat, and while I'm not eager to befriend either of them, Merat is just a cunning, amoral courtier who sometimes has inconvenient people thrown in prison. And she's been transparent about what she wants—Iriyat dead and herself restored to power in Varenx House. Iriyat, on the other hand, is possessed by some kind of deranged ambition to control the world, and she will torture and kill any number of innocent people to achieve that goal."

With that, he stepped past her and got two paces down the deck before Ev said, "Wait, what?" and stopped him. Iriyat wanted to run Laalvur, certainly, and she had no compunctions about torture and killing. But the world?

"Ah," Thiyo said. He kept his voice low. "You haven't read that far in the journal. Trust me. It's a miserable choice—especially given that Merat has a particular hatred for me—but there's only one sane option. We betray Sardas to Merat and maybe, just maybe, we can disembark in Laalvur and not get dragged right into a cell in the basement of Varenx House." He paused to breathe. "That's also in the journal."

Cells in the basement of Varenx House. Ev wished the detail surprised her. "So we tell Merat. Then what?"

"I don't know. She has Sardas restrained and we question him? All I care about is not sailing right into Iriyat's clutches. We'll figure the rest out—"

"Thiyo." As quiet as they'd kept their voices in the midst of the noisy deck, they'd still attracted the attention of at least three sailors and a man Ev recognized as one of Merat's guards. The men were approaching slowly, affecting indifference, as though they just happened to be walking by. But one of them was holding a spear. Ev knew what it felt like to be purposefully surrounded. When Thiyo locked eyes with her, she said, "Run."

There was no time to see if he took her advice. *Hope you listen to me for once in your fiery life.* She spun on her heel and punched the man behind her in the nose with a crunch before he could move on her. Her fist came away bloody. He was gripping a knife and his arm jerked up when she attacked, slashing at her. He was using one hand to staunch the flow of blood from his nose. He swung the knife at her middle, but she backed out of range. At the end of his swing, she grabbed his wrist and bent it backward. She yanked the knife from his hand, and still holding his arm, she forced him down and brought her knee up into his already-broken nose.

When the second man came for her, she stabbed him in the gut.

The other two men should have come to their comrades' aid by now, but since they hadn't, Thiyo must still be here. Ev whirled. There he was, backed all the way up against the railing, leaning backward toward the water, a spear at his throat. The last man was also armed with a knife, brandishing it to prevent Thiyo from escaping, but when he saw that Ev was free, he charged her. She dodged his first strike and they circled each other. Undistracted by a bloody nose, this man was more precise with his movements, and his second swing sliced at her middle, leaving a shallow cut. But Ev surprised him by dropping her own knife and disarming him as she had the first man. When she bent his wrist, his knife clattered to the deck and she kicked it over the edge. She brought her elbow down hard on the back of his arm and shoved him down. Should she pick up her knife and stab him? Was everyone on the ship hostile to her? She was weighing the consequences versus her chances of survival when she heard shouting.

Thiyo was gone.

Her pulse exploded in her ears and she barreled into the man with the spear, crushing him to the railing and wrenching the spear from his grip. A glance over the edge revealed Thiyo bobbing in the dark water far below. Had he been stabbed? Was he still alive?

The moment of distraction cost her, and the former owner of the spear twisted them around so Ev had her back to the railing. Unable to fend him off with one hand clutching the spear, she let it fall into the water below. She shoved at her attacker with both hands, but he was as heavy as her, and his grip on her arms was unshakeable. Then there was a knifepoint pricking her neck —the other man, holding the knife she should have stabbed him with—and a searing pain as she jerked away. Blood ran down her torso. And then there were two men lifting her up and over the railing, pitching her into the air.

She plummeted down into the water.

32

BLINK

E V AND THIYO SHOULD HAVE come back by now. Alizhan had read the whole journal, even the parts that had made her want to set the damn thing on fire. Her headache had subsided. There was nowhere to go and nothing to do on this ship. Worry sparked in her mind. She threw open the cabin door and searched the deck with her gaze. No sign of them— just sailors. She stepped out and called their names, caught between hoping they'd pop out from some hatch and dreading that she'd run into their bloody corpses.

Neither happened. Alizhan strode to Merat's cabin and banged on the door. "Where are Ev and Thiyo?"

Merat sighed. "This is what I get for not having dealt with you sooner."

What did that mean? Alizhan forced her way in, making Merat take a step backward. Their eyes were level, and Merat's grey gaze was cold. They were alone. Merat's cabin was tasteful and luxurious in a way that made Alizhan want to rip the stuffing out of all the pillows and shred all the sheets. "Answer my fucking question. Where are Ev and Thiyo?"

Merat held up her hands with her palms facing Alizhan.

From anyone else, it would have been surrender. From Merat, it was a threat. "Such language. Of course I had to take care of them. You shouldn't be surprised. I've told you all along that it's my goal to restore the glory of Varenx House, and how can I do that when you keep company with peasants and deviants?"

Where were they? Were they really dead? Alizhan felt something rising up around her, overtaking her, filling up all the air and leaving her no room to breathe. She struggled to keep her head up and draw breath. Anger and despair would drown her. She wanted to scream, or run for the rail and throw herself over it, or throttle Merat. She wanted all that and she couldn't move. Rationally, she knew her heart must be racing, but she felt each pounding beat distinctly, as though time had slowed. She forced a breath in and a question out. "Then why let them come in the first place? Why lie?"

"Well, I had to get you on the ship, didn't I?" Her voice was all wrong. Bored. Casual. Too soft. It should have been all hard edges and shouting, or low and hissing, or quavering with terror. If she was really confessing to murder, how could she do it so calmly? Merat ought to suffer through what Alizhan was feeling. Instead, she wiggled the fingers of one of her still-raised hands. "I had them disposed of. Don't worry. It won't mean anything to you in a moment."

Alizhan's throat tasted of acid. "You killed them."

"Are you slow, in addition to everything else? That's what I'm trying to tell you. But you don't have to take it so hard. Come here. Let me help you," Merat said. "It'll be much more pleasant. You'll skip all these unfortunate feelings. All that anger twists your face up. It'll give you wrinkles. You don't want that."

"You killed them," Alizhan repeated. Merat had murdered them and now she was going to wipe them from Alizhan's memory. It wasn't enough for her to kill them once.

"To be clear, I didn't intend to kill your tall black friend,"

Merat said with exaggerated patience. "I would have let you keep her in some suitable role. But the other one had been nothing but trouble to me since Ilyr dragged it home from that godsforsaken island, and I simply couldn't have that on my ship. And the Adpri tried to stop me."

How could this be real? Was Merat lying? If there'd been a fight, why hadn't Alizhan woken up? Why hadn't she been there to help them? She couldn't breathe.

"Oh, I thought your fidgeting and twitching was awful, but it's even worse when you go so still. You're such a funny little creature. Hard to believe we're related. We'll have to train that out of you, or at least keep you docile until you whelp. Here, I'll fix this."

Merat's hand landed on her temple, the pain like a knife, and Alizhan snarled and grabbed her wrist, digging her nails in. Merat grunted, but kept her hand in place. Her fingers weren't moving, but inside Alizhan's head, claws dug through her mind, scraping at memories. Twenty years ago, Merat had wanted to erase her from existence and now she was trying to erase Alizhan in pieces. Would Alizhan even remember Thiyo and Ev? Would she know their names, their voices?

Then she remembered a passage of the journal.

My mother could not take anything from me. My practice had paid off. I had grown strong enough to withstand her. But the pain was real, and it was easy to pretend she had succeeded. I knew exactly the reaction to imitate: the blinking, wobbling daze that marks victims of our craft. It is exhausting, having one's memory altered. My fatigue was genuine.

Alizhan pushed the memory from her mind. Instead, she thought of all the snow blanketing Estva, and how deadly quiet that city had been. All those cavernous rooms full of people with no thoughts or feelings at all. That was what she needed to do right now. She had to be blank. Iriyat's victims had seamless memories, the gaps sewn over and undetectable. Merat's victims were the guests at Ilyr's wedding—their minds ransacked and empty. Thiyo had been aware of the missing time in his memory. Merat didn't have Iriyat's fine control. Alizhan would have to be strong enough to withstand her.

She let her hand fall from Merat's arm and hang limp at her side. Iriyat had left such precise instructions. Blink. Wobble. Alizhan even managed a little smile.

"There," Merat said. "In time, we might even fix you up as halfway presentable. You're my blood, after all. We'll get you married to someone respectable to purify the line. It's best to get you pregnant as soon as possible. I want an heir who can rule Varenx House when I'm gone."

Alizhan nodded despite her horror. She kept her expression and her muscles slack.

Merat turned away, waving a hand. "Run along. I have things to do."

Alizhan snatched her hand out of the air and did everything she'd learned not to do. She forced everything she was thinking and feeling toward Merat, squeezing her hand as she tried to pull away. Merat choked out half a word, then her eyes welled up with tears. Her breathing turned irregular. She stopped resisting Alizhan's touch. Alizhan took a step forward and put her other hand on Merat's temple. She tore open Merat's mind with her own, pushing aside everything in it. There was nothing but fury. That torrent charged through her and she let it flood Merat, blotting out every thought, every memory, every feeling, every sensation, channeling the airless, drowning force of her grief and rage.

Merat jerked under her hands, her eyelids fluttering. Her mouth hung open. She fell to the floor and Alizhan followed her down, still touching her. Merat's limbs spasmed. Her eyes rolled back and reddened. Her tongue lolled. She pissed herself, a puddle of yellow spreading through her white skirts. And then she stilled.

Alizhan held on until her pulse stopped. Then she dropped Merat's hand, turned, walked two steps, and vomited.

Her vision swam with black spots. She held herself upright, opened the door and braced herself. "This is my ship now," she called. Her voice rang in her ears. Fuck, she needed to lie down. Maybe forever. Her whole body remembered Merat's death—the shaking, the pain, the violent loss of control—as if it had happened to her. Of all the terrible ironies, she wished someone could make her forget that.

There were two sailors on the deck, but they only glanced at her and went back to work. Sardas strolled into view a moment later.

"About that," he said. He nodded at the sailors, and they returned the gesture respectfully. "Your mother says hello."

33

DEPTHS

EV FELL WITH HER LIMBS all spread out like she'd never dived in her life. She plunged into the churning water. He swam toward her as fast as he could, encumbered by his clothes and the spear he'd caught when it had fallen over the side. Ev shot back up, spluttering and flailing. He held the weapon away from her and reached out with his good hand, calling her name. She grabbed his arm, then shifted her grip to his shoulders, clutching any part of him she could reach. He floundered under her weight and lost his hold on the spear. The whites of her eyes were visible and she was gasping. He'd never seen her look so panicked. *She can't swim.*

Thiyo opened his mouth to talk to her and got splashed with saltwater instead. Before he could spit it out, she pushed him under. Submerged, he wrestled himself away from her. A long-ago swimming lesson from his father bubbled up in his memory and Thiyo circled around behind her. He thrust his arms under hers and brought his hands back toward himself. She was still flailing and he had to kick powerfully to keep them both afloat. But he had control now and he could speak right into her ear.

"Calm down, Ev. Calm down right now. Don't breathe in any

water." He paused to gulp down a breath. His legs ached from keeping their heads above the water.

Could she hear him or was she in shock? Was it already too late? She stopped struggling against him.

"Good. Kick your feet," he told her. "Little kicks. That's how you stay afloat. Can you do that for me, Ev?" She could. He felt her take his advice. Breathing got easier. She wasn't going to drown right here in his arms. Later—he couldn't think about later. "Yes, yes, okay, that's it. Breathe. Just like that. See, you're swimming. Just keep kicking and breathing. That's all you have to do. Okay—oh, fuck, you're bleeding, that's not good."

There was a wound in her neck. The blood wasn't spurting, so the knife had missed everything important, but there was a nasty, jagged cut at the base of her neck, down the left side of her collarbone and over her chest. A thin trail of blood colored the water.

"Ev, do you see that spear over there? We're going to swim toward it, and you're going to grab it."

They swam until the spear came within reach. One lousy piece of wood wasn't enough to keep them afloat, but Thiyo had grabbed it on impulse when he'd seen it fall from the ship, before he'd fully understood his circumstances. Maybe it would make Ev feel better to hold something buoyant. It would make Thiyo feel better, too, even though he already knew how this ended.

"Okay, good. Can I let go of you? Will you keep kicking?"

He felt her nod before he heard her say, "Yes."

He let go and swam around so they were facing each other. Ev was breathing steadily, but she still looked shaken. She was holding the spear out to the side to keep it away from them. He put a hand on her other shoulder. Like him, she was still dressed for cold weather, and her waterlogged coat squelched under his fingers. "You okay?"

An absurd question. How could either of them be okay? Ev saw him examining her cut. Seawater was washing over it. *That must sting.* She grinned. "Yeah. They missed."

"Oh yes, I'd say we won that fight unequivocally. A real triumph." They'd tried to slit Thiyo's throat, too. He'd thought it was his last moment alive, so he'd chosen to die by the ocean instead of by someone else's knife. He'd flung himself over the railing. There'd barely been time to straighten his legs and enter the water feet-first. Now, looking around at the vast expanse of water and the swiftly departing ship, he didn't know why he'd bothered. He should have conked his head on the way down to speed along the inevitable. He let go of Ev's shoulder and she put her hand on his instead, unwilling to be parted from him.

"How do we get back on the ship?"

"The ship full of people trying to murder us?" Thiyo said. *Honesty* was sailing away from them, cutting through the water at a steady pace. The Dayward wind was with them. Not even the strongest swimmer could keep up. He tried to keep his voice soft and serious for what he had to say next. "Even if we could catch them, which we can't, they wouldn't help us get back on board. I'm sorry to say it, but this is it for us. We have a few hours at most. And that's if nothing but the water gets us."

Ev blinked seawater out of her lashes. She'd caught on quickly and was paddling her feet in the water to bob along with him, but her hands were still clenched—one around the spear, and one around his shoulder. "So why did you save me?"

The question didn't make any sense. "What?"

"I would have drowned. You swam over here and stopped me. If we're going to die anyway, then why?"

She was questioning his decision to save her. Incredible. "You'd rather I have let you drown? Did you want me to watch while it happened?"

Here they were, stranded in the middle of the ocean, likely in the last hours of their lives, and Ev was rolling her eyes at him. Maybe they'd kill each other before the ocean did. "It was a genuine question. I suppose a genuine answer was too much to hope for."

Thiyo had never been out this far—how could he have?— and the water wasn't clear and warm like it was at Hoi's shores. It wasn't icy, merely cool. But all islanders learned to fear and respect the ocean. It was no accident that they swore by the watery hell. Even warm water could kill. If you were stranded long enough, you'd get colder and colder until your arms and legs stopped working and then you'd drown. Thiyo was still kicking, and he could feel all his toes, but he knew it was coming. He thought about how much was below their feet, that unknowable darkness, and felt faint. Water was every horizon.

"I don't know, Ev. I didn't even think about it," he said. He hadn't thought about flinging himself into the water to get away from that knife, either. He'd had an instant to choose and he'd chosen. "But in all sincerity, I meant what I said earlier. I couldn't watch that happen to you."

Ev nodded as if he'd satisfied her. She would have done the same. She *approved*. Mah Yee, why did that mean so much to him? And why did he feel such a pressing need to ruin it with the truth? She thought he'd been brave when really he'd been spineless. She was the only thing to look at for miles around and suddenly he could hardly face her. Ridiculous. A coward to the end. "And I suppose... I didn't want to die alone."

"I don't want to die at all."

Thiyo couldn't say how he'd wanted her to react, but now that she'd said that, he couldn't help the little laugh that slipped out. He'd tried to drag them into murky emotional and moral territory and she'd refused. She didn't forgive him because she didn't think there was anything to forgive. It was so simple and straightforward and *Ev*. He smiled at her. Ev was the one thing out here he didn't have to fear. And they were both going to die. Might as well gaze at someone beautiful in the time he had left. "Ah. Well. Now that you mention it, there is that."

"I'm so sorry, Thiyo. You knew this would happen. You shouldn't even be here."

"Don't bring that up now," he said. He couldn't bear to think about that, and he didn't want to spend the end of his life blaming the only company he had. It wasn't Ev's fault, anyway, except in the oblique sense that he wouldn't be here if he'd never met her and Alizhan. He'd be dead in a Nalitzvan prison instead.

"At least you've probably come up with some devastatingly witty last words." Her teeth were chattering just a little. It had already started.

"Oh, dozens. But none of them seem to apply here," he said. "But I will, of course, dutifully accept any final confessions you wish to make."

She laughed. "You make me wish I had something good to confess."

"Did you sleep with Alizhan, at least?"

He expected a protest that he was prying, but she just sighed. "We were interrupted."

"Damn. I was rooting for both of you. But you told her you loved her, right?"

"I—yes. Sort of. I could have said it more. I hope she knows." Ev closed her eyes and her throat worked. "God. I can't believe we're talking about this. It doesn't feel real." Ev glanced around, searching the horizon for some sign that this wasn't the end. "Thiyo."

She was staring behind him, so he turned. And turned again. There was nothing in the wide swath of his view. *Honesty* was far enough away now that the water had stopped churning in its wake. The sea was calm. "I don't see anything." They were still closer to the Nightward side of the world, and the cool light made it futile to peer into the water. The darkness here differed from the plains in Estva, which gave a sense of the infinite. The impenetrable ocean, as huge as it was, shrank the world. It surrounded them. There was nowhere to go. They were as trapped as if they were in a prison cell.

"No, I saw—"

A glow gliding under the surface. A massive, ghostly shape drifted toward them.

"We're going to die a lot sooner than predicted," Thiyo said. The same kind of monster that had killed his father would end him, too. At least his mother wasn't waiting on the beach for his return. It was almost funny—he'd spent his whole life digging his heels in and refusing to become a hunter, crushing his parents' dreams. Yet here he was, about to get eaten by a medusa.

"Thiyo. It floats."

"I'm not sure what that has to do with anything. It's also a gigantic carnivorous monster surrounded by deadly tentacles."

"We have a spear."

"You just said those words in absolutely the wrong tone. We have a *spear*. A stick with a pointy end. That thing is a giant medusa. It's coming toward us to murder us, dissolve our bodies, and absorb them. It will be extremely painful. Come to think of it, perhaps we should go ahead and drown ourselves."

"Arav killed one with a spear," Ev said. "You know that. It was in the journal."

"And he was almost the sole survivor!" Medusas could kill a team of trained hunters protected with sharkskin and armed with specially crafted harpoons, the barbed tips designed to pierce the bell and impale the transparent nerve cluster at the center. Thiyo should know. It was a miracle that Arav had survived his encounter, ignorant and ill-equipped as he'd been.

"We're definitely going to die if we don't," Ev said. "In Arav's account, he said they could sense movement."

"Yes, of course they can sense movement. Everyone knows that." It was one of the first things Thiyo had ever learned. All the island cultures held them in such importance because medusas predicted waves. People who were born with the ability to sense and track medusas in the water were the heroes of the islands. At every test, that was what they'd told him before they'd dunked him in the water.

"What—never mind. It can't sense anything else, right? No sight or sound?"

"Just currents. Movements. Maybe the blood from your cut. I don't know, I never wanted to learn anything about these things because I never wanted to meet one!" Thiyo's voice rose in pitch. He'd failed the test so many times, and every time, secret relief had bloomed. He didn't want to hunt monsters. He wanted to stay on land and read. Could he die from how fast his heart was beating?

"Calm down. A minute ago, we had both just about accepted death. We're definitely going to die if we do nothing. So why not try doing something, instead?" And then Ev described a very simple, very stupid plan to him, and Thiyo gaped at her.

"The worst, most insane part of this plan is how much of its success rests on me."

"You're a stronger swimmer than me."

"You know I had almost accepted my useless, accidental, anonymous death? And now I have to die in a foolish burst of glory like one of your book heroes, except no one will ever know about it. What a waste."

"So live," she said and handed him the spear. She met his eyes. "And his name is Vesper, and you love *The Sunrise Chronicles*, and the only reason you're not confessing right now is that you know we're not about to die—because this is going to work."

Her voice was brimming with such confidence that he almost believed her.

As Thiyo swam away from Ev, she began to kick and flail her arms, moving as much as possible. His limbs felt heavy and stiff with cold, but he forced himself to swim. He had to slip through the water as stealthily and carefully as possible. When the seas were calm, medusas sensed prey that moved. Ev had offered herself up as bait.

The medusa's tentacles flowed behind it. It pulsed through the water, the shape of its bell inflating with each thrust. Thiyo had to come in from the side to avoid the venomous tentacles. He remembered his first sight of one of these, his father holding his hand while the rest of the crew pulled the carcass they'd netted ashore. *It can sting even after it's dead, see? That's why they wear those suits with the gloves. And you see where the harpoon went in? They only die if you lance the nerve cluster.*

Thiyo had been small enough then that his parents had still assumed he'd work with his father when he got older. Instead, Thiyo had grown up to read Iriyat's journal, and now he couldn't stop thinking of the descriptions of Arav's fellow sailors being dismembered by the venom. *One good strike*, his father had said. All he had to do was hit those nerves. If only the damn thing had shown up sooner, he'd be able to control his arms a little better. He aimed his spear.

Ev had given him some advice, too: *Don't strike until you have the perfect shot. But do try to kill it before it kills me.* She was still splashing around. Thiyo had no idea where she'd found the energy. Swimming this short distance had almost made him give up on everything.

Mah Yee, the medusa was so close. It loomed in front of him, huge and silent. Was he one spear-length away?

Ev screamed.

Shit. Not all of the thing's tentacles were flowing straight behind it. Some of them fanned out around it. Ev had been stung through her clothes. Thiyo gripped the spear, lifting it out of the water. It felt like it was made of stone. One good strike. Maybe the last thing he'd ever do.

He brought his arm down and rammed the point of the spear into the medusa's gelatinous body. Its flesh split, spurting transparent green fluid into the water. The bell quivered from the force of the strike. But the point of his spear was still a handspan from the nerve cluster, and now he'd lost his stealth advantage. The wounded monster would move toward him next. He had to act.

Watery fucking hell. Thiyo ripped the spear back out, kicked forward, and slammed it back into the wound. He thrust so deep that the monster's wobbly body enveloped his hand. Its slimy fluid coursed over his skin and flowed into the ocean. The point of his spear had impaled the nerve cluster. It was dead.

"Ev! Ev, I killed it!" Thiyo had never felt anything like this in his life. Triumph. Relief. Disgust. And still a healthy amount of fear. Those tentacles were venomous, even attached to a corpse. He let go of the spear and pulled his hand out of the tunnel he'd left in the thing's corpse, trying not to think too hard, but still shuddering with revulsion.

Ev said something so faint he couldn't hear her.

"Can you swim to it?" Her eyes were half-closed. Her head was bobbing just above the surface of the water. Was one sting enough to kill a person? Fuck. Thiyo left the spear embedded in the monster and kicked his way over to Ev. "Ev. Ev. Say something, depths fucking dr—" Thiyo stopped himself. He'd never felt the true terror of his people's traditional curse until now. *Depths fucking drown you* was a singularly inauspicious thing to say to someone stranded in the middle of an incomprehensible amount of water.

She was awake enough to look at him.

"You're alive. You're alive. Mah Yee's scaly ass, I will fucking drag you onto that thing and you will *not* die. I killed a monster for you and we're going to live, you understand?" Something shocked the bottom of his foot and he shrieked. The fucking venom had eaten through the sole of his shoe. The pain was searing. But it didn't knock him unconscious—not yet. Ev must have been stung more than the one time she'd screamed. "Fuck, you're tough. Now come on. Let's swim together. You can do this."

He held her from behind, hooking his arms under hers, just as he'd done when she'd been drowning. Kicking through the water closer to the medusa was like swimming through glass shards. Every stroke blazed with agony. But it was a short distance, and he'd killed a monster, and Ev wasn't going to die for that. He grabbed hold of the spear, yanked himself up onto the bell, and then dragged Ev up behind him. He was pulling her through its tentacles. She'd stopped reacting.

Thiyo flopped onto his belly, not letting go of Ev. They were both partly out of the water. Their clothes were shredded. His body was somehow both freezing and on fire with pain. He was panting. Every beat of his heart felt like lifting a huge weight. "I told you," he said to Ev, breathless. Was she listening? Was she conscious? "I said I didn't want to die alone, but I don't want to die at all. So don't you fucking die."

There, floating on a medusa's corpse with its tentacles radiating out into an ocean as huge and cold as the sky, Thiyo closed his eyes and kept breathing.

READ ON FOR AN EXCERPT...

Shadebloom, **book three of** *The Gardener's Hand* **and the sequel to** *Nightvine*, **is available now.**

SHADEBLOOM

I riyat plucked a thornfruit from the bowl and pinched the brown rind between two manicured nails until it popped and split. She lifted the fruit, its newly revealed pulp as red as her lips, and ate it in one bite. She dropped the rind into an empty bowl on the table between them, then gestured at the overflowing bowl next to it. "Don't you want some? You used to love these."

Alizhan stared at her white hand hovering over the little mound of fruit. When Sardas had commandeered *Honesty* and sailed back to Laalvur under Iriyat's orders, she'd envisioned herself in a cell in the basement of Varenx House. Instead, she'd been directed back to her childhood bedroom to sleep and then invited to a meal on the terrace. Iriyat had even lit a fire in the terrace's fire pit—a decorative touch, since Laalvur was never cold. The comforts were a small difference. Cell or no cell, Alizhan was a prisoner.

And what did it matter? She'd had some foolish, grand plan to return home, to accuse Iriyat of her crimes and force her to stand trial. To bring the journal to light. To see justice for the people she'd already hurt and to protect the ones she might hurt in the future. To save the city. To change the world.

But what was the point of the world? Ev and Thiyo were dead.

"I'm not hungry," Alizhan said. They'd force-fed her on the ship. She wasn't sure how much time had passed between that terrible shift when she'd killed Merat and their arrival in Laalvur. Seven or eight triads, probably, since she'd woken up with a smear of blood between her thighs this shift. Enough time to die of starvation, if only someone would let her.

"Are you sure?" Iriyat said, the picture of concern. "You look thin. Sardas told me you weren't eating. You've always been skinny, but I don't want you to waste away. And you love thornfruit!"

"I'm not hungry," Alizhan repeated.

"I want to apologize," Iriyat said. "I know you've had a difficult time. And I'm to blame for some of it." Iriyat pulled two books out of her lap. One was a Nalitzvan copy of *The Sunrise Chronicles* into which Thiyo had sewn his own translation of Iriyat's journal. The other was volume eleven of *A Natural History of the World*—Iriyat's original, encoded journal. Sardas had taken both from Alizhan when he'd put her under guard. Those two texts represented Alizhan's best chance at persuading the rest of the world that Iriyat was a criminal, so she ought to feel panic, seeing them in Iriyat's hands. Instead, she felt hollow.

"I was going to provide you with the cipher," Iriyat continued. "When you were ready."

"When I was ready." Alizhan couldn't muster the energy to do more than repeat what Iriyat had said in a dead tone. When could a person be *ready* to find out her mother had been lying to her and exploiting her all her life?

"There was so much I wanted to tell you, and I thought I could do it more clearly in writing, but instead I've caused you a great deal of suffering. So I want to apologize and make things right. And I think that starts with this."

With a single, elegant movement of her arm, Iriyat dropped both books into the fire. Alizhan jumped up, meaning to plunge her hands into the blaze. Flames were already licking at the pages, which were curling, crackling, and crumbling into the fire pit. She hesitated. Then Iriyat was upon her, moving faster than Alizhan had guessed, pulling her arms behind her.

"Don't, darling. I hate to see you hurt yourself."

Those two books together represented months of struggle. She and Ev had sailed across the ocean to find someone who could read the encoded text. Thiyo had labored for weeks on that translation. Ev and Thiyo had *died*.

With that thought, all the fight went out of Alizhan. Iriyat had a tight grip on her wrists, but it wasn't necessary. There was nothing worth fighting for.

Alizhan didn't resist when Iriyat spun her around. She didn't even startle when Iriyat pulled her into a hug.

"I was very sorry to hear of your loss," Iriyat said.

"Don't."

"If you ever want to talk about it, I'll be here. You know now that I also lost someone I loved, so I understand."

Not even the allusion to her father made Alizhan soften. There was nothing left in her but ashes. She turned her head to watch the smoke rise from the fire. At last, Iriyat drew back. "Will you sit?"

What choice was there? Would her legs even hold her up? Every time she thought about Ev and Thiyo, she wanted to crumple. The chair was the only thing that kept her from puddling on the terrace.

"Please eat. I went all the way out of the city to get these, you know. One of those dusty little villages on the outskirts. Orzatvur, I think? It was the funniest little farm. A big, hulking, surly Adpri exile sold me these. From the way he treated me, you'd have thought I was holding his family hostage."

Orzatvur. Iriyat had found Ev's family somehow. Panic spiked. "Or threatening him," Alizhan muttered.

Iriyat's laugh was as delicate and manicured as her fingertips. She picked another fruit out of the bowl and squeezed it till it split. A drop of red juice plopped onto the tabletop, ruining the geometric pattern of the tiles. "Indeed. I can't imagine why."

Were Obin and Neiran—and even Ajee, God help him—in danger? Ev wasn't here to protect them. *They don't even know she's dead.* Alizhan's voice went so low it cracked when she said, "You'd never hurt them, of course."

"Of course," Iriyat said smoothly. "But I wanted to meet them, since they raised the young woman who stole you away from me."

At least they were giving up on the pretense that the Umarsad family were random strangers. "That's not what happened."

"Ah well," Iriyat said, contemplative and nostalgic. "I suppose all parents feel that way about the people their children fall in love with."

Alizhan went still for a moment. She'd become accustomed to her grandmother's bigotry and disgust. Merat had loathed Ev and Thiyo. Alizhan had conflated her hatred of them with her ruthlessness, and she'd expected Iriyat to be just like Merat. But she wasn't. What Iriyat had said about Ev stealing Alizhan away was a casual figure of speech. It was jarring to realize Iriyat didn't hate Ev. She'd even said she was sorry.

Alizhan still didn't want to hear it.

"My parents felt significantly less charitable toward Arav," Iriyat said. "My mother was a monster, as you know. It's grisly, but I am grateful to you for killing her. Sardas told me."

It was hard to think through the fog of grief and panic. But there was something important: Iriyat had slid almost imperceptibly from *my parents* to *my mother.*

Because her father was still alive. Alizhan had been the little ghost in Varenx House, and he'd been the other ghost. The one in the room upstairs who never came out. Alizhan's pulse picked up just thinking about it. But what good would it do her?

"But let's put that aside. I wrote it down because it was the only way I knew to share it with you, but I want things to be different between us now."

"I don't want anything from you." Alizhan didn't even want justice anymore. She just wanted to be done.

"I know this is a difficult moment for us, but I believe we'll get through. We just need some time to talk. I have to leave for Adappyr in a triad, but I was hoping you'd come with me. I won't force you, of course. It's your choice. Although I worry about leaving you alone in this state, so if you want to stay here, I'll have to have someone—Sardas, perhaps—watch over you."

"A choice," Alizhan said flatly. "Go to Adappyr with you or stay here under Sardas's constant surveillance."

"I just want you to be safe."

"Fuck off," Alizhan said, standing up. "I'm going back to bed."

ALIZHAN DIDN'T EVEN HAVE the energy to pull the curtains closed. She collapsed onto her bed and lay there, staring at the ceiling. She preferred to sleep in total darkness, when she had preferences at all. But her room was never bright, since there were no Dayward windows, only a perforated stone wall on the Nightward side meant to let cool air pass through. As it had always been, the room was full of potted plants bursting with blooms of all colors and leaves reaching in all directions. Iriyat's hybridized creations.

Something scratched at the stone screen. Alizhan ignored it, but it continued for many long minutes, developing a steady rhythm. Not an animal, then.

Her bedroom was on the second story. There were no trees or vines on the Nightward side. Anyone who'd climbed up the stone screen had gone to a great deal of effort to contact her. Alizhan didn't get up. There was a short list of people who might have taken the trouble, and she didn't want to see any of them. She didn't want to see anyone who wasn't Ev or Thiyo.

The scratching stopped. "Fuck you," came as a low hiss through the screen. "I know you're in there. Get up and come talk to me."

The voice was that of an angry teenage boy. *Kasrik*. Alizhan pushed herself upright and went to crouch next to the screen. The holes were too small to get a good visual, but from the sound of his voice, she could tell where Kasrik was. "What?"

"What do you mean, what? I came to give you the news. Fair warning, all of it's bad. We'll work on getting you out of there, too."

"Ev and Thiyo are dead," Alizhan said. There was no way to soften the blow—or maybe there was, and she didn't want to.

"Who the hell is Thiyo?" Kasrik said. "Never mind. I'm sorry about Ev. I liked her better than you."

Alizhan said nothing.

"Sorry. I shouldn't have said that. Shit, Alizhan, I don't know what to say. I'm really, really sorry. But let's talk about the rest of it. Did you get that book translated?"

"It doesn't matter."

"Of course it fucking matters! Do you even know what's going on here? God. I'm sorry about Ev, I am, but while you were gone, Iriyat got her hands around this city's throat and if we don't stop her, no one will." There was a pause, and then a tightly rolled tube of paper was pushed through one of the holes in the stone. It dropped to the floor and uncurled. Another one followed. "These are some pamphlets. I don't have time to stay here and tell you everything. Me and Eliyan have work to do. But try to be in here during Rosefinch shift, and I'll come back. I worked it out with Vatik so he's the one patrolling the grounds while I'm here. You can still trust him."

Alizhan had let most of his words pass over her, and she hadn't bothered to pick up the pamphlets, but that gave her pause. He shouldn't know about Vatik. Kasrik had lost his powers when he'd been tortured. "How do you know?"

"I'm getting better," he said, a touch of pride in his voice. "Ev told me to pay attention to faces, and that was all I could do for a while. But once I started to learn that, little by little, the other stuff—thoughts, feelings, you know, all that came back. Sometimes I see Mala when *Vines* is in port, and she thinks it's getting better because I'm young and still growing. I'm not the same as I was, but maybe I could be, eventually."

"Good," she said softly. That was one less burden to bear. "I'm glad."

"Does that mean you'll stop sulking? Ev wouldn't want you to sulk."

Alizhan huffed. *Presumptuous little shit.* It helped that he was right. "Fuck off."

"Alizhan." He said her name like a warning. "She got Mar."

"What do you mean, got Mar?" There was no point in asking who *she* was.

"Read the pamphlet," Kasrik said. She heard the sound of his shoes scraping the stone as he climbed down.

ACKNOWLEDGMENTS

Thank you, as always, to my live-in science consultant, who never gets to read these novels without spoilers, but who is nevertheless willing to entertain discussions about hypothetical ecosystems, cryptography, and the motivations of fictional characters. The live-in science consultant also keeps me alive, in both a figurative emotional sense and a literal one, since without him I would subsist on peanut butter eaten out of the jar, our house would fall down around me, and I'd be too miserable to do anything about either problem. That counts as helping to write the book, I think.

I am also grateful to Lis and Kristin, fellow writers and trusted beta readers, for all their encouragements and commiseration, and to my brother, who once described to me a course that he took on how to save people from drowning, and who probably doesn't realize how instrumental he was to this book.

And thank you to you, for making it this far. Book 3 is finished, I promise.

ABOUT THE AUTHOR

Felicia Davin is the author of *Thornfruit*, *Nightvine*, *Shadebloom* and *Edge of Nowhere*. Her short fiction has been featured in *Lightspeed*, *Nature*, and *Heiresses of Russ 2016: The Year's Best Lesbian Speculative Fiction*.

She lives in Massachusetts with her partner and their cat. When not writing and reading fiction, she teaches and translates French. She loves linguistics, singing, and baking. She is bisexual, but not ambidextrous.

You can find her at feliciadavin.com or on Twitter @FeliciaDavin.

CPSIA information can be obtained
at www.ICGtesting.com
Printed in the USA
LVHW091357190621
690661LV00003B/647